NOTH
PERS(
David Rollins

Special Agent Vin Cooper, #8

This is a work of fiction. Similarities to real people, places, or events are entirely coincidental.

NOTHING PERSONAL

First edition. May 29, 2024.

Written by David Rollins.

For Sam.

Foreword

Not many people read the foreword, so I think I can say that this book is based on true events safe in the knowledge it will remain a secret between us.

It's because I write books like this that I hear things, and quite a few years ago, I heard told that we civilians didn't really know what went on in Operation Iraqi Freedom. Not so surprising, right? That's what governments do: keep information to themselves and the people at the coal face doing the actual heavy lifting are sworn to secrecy. I don't wish to be melodramatic about this, but maybe an amount of WMD was, in fact, recovered. That was my reading of the conversations I had. Vin questions several characters in this book, and their exchanges closely mirror talks I had with participants in the war. I'm not going to say which characters or conversations because I don't want to get anyone into trouble. As I said at the outset, some things are meant to remain a mystery.

Moving on...

To spare me embarrassment, several willing guinea pigs read this book prior to publication. Thank you, Michael, Shane, Trisha, Nin, and Steve. Reading a manuscript takes time and concentration, and I very much appreciate your efforts on my account. Indeed, I would've been reluctant to release this book into the wild without you.

And, to the super-patient fans who love this character, I wouldn't have even put pen to paper in the first place if it weren't for you. I really do hope it was worth the wait.

— David

1

"Everyone has a plan until they get punched in the mouth."

— Mike Tyson

NORTHERN IRAQ, APRIL 9th, 2003

The Iraqi sun beat down on SAS Warrant Officer Tom Wilkes and his unit, the temps pushing 90. Wilkes wondered what the actual temperature was inside their Mission Oriented Protective Posture gear or MOPP suit, the American term for the full chem-bio warfighting suit currently mandated for forward-deployed troops. It had to be in sauna territory. He was tempted to disobey the order to wear the full kit and tell his men to ditch at least the hood and respirator. But Objective Weber, otherwise known as Qadisiyah Airbase, the Iraqi air force HQ, was in plain view, and intelligence reports indicated that it would be a likely reservoir for Iraqi nerve agents — sarin and mustard gas.

Wilkes listened to his breathing, pushing through the filters in his gas mask, before speaking in low tones over the comms. The unit responded, dispersing, moving forward, and picking up cover behind scrub. Three of the men slid into a dry wadi, its jagged fingers heading in the direction of the base's outer wire.

The Iraqis were leaving, and they were in a hurry, departing the front gate at speed in all kinds of vehicles, from Toyota pickups and beat-up Peugeots and Mercedes to Russian BTRs.

"Gentlemen, start your engines," came a voice in Wilkes' headset.

"Wacky Races," said another.

Wilkes smiled. Broiled alive, the boys could still find room for a laugh.

High above, Coalition warplanes on bombing runs were carving wide contrails against the blue. A distant sonic boom rolled across the sand and rock landscape. Wilkes glanced up. The option was available to call hell down on this fleeing convoy, but he decided against it. The Iraqis were leaving behind a perfectly serviceable airbase. Might as well let 'em go quietly.

3

Nevertheless, the Australian SAS warrant officer was wary. From the first day of the invasion, the Iraqis had proved to be tricky sons of bitches. You might think you had them on the run, but you could suddenly find yourself in the middle of an ambush if you gave chase. "Sit tight," Wilkes told his unit.

Two Soviet-era T-72 main battle tanks joined the rush. They left the sealed road and took to the dirt, throwing up clouds of fine dust behind them that hung in the air, creating a thick orange and tan fog. With the sky full of tank-buster Warthogs and M1 Abrams tanks running around, Wilkes thought, the last place you wanted to be was in one of those tin cans.

"Might as well take out a TV advert on your whereabouts," observed Sergeant Gary Ellis over the comms, Wilkes' number two, thinking along similar lines.

A yellow Rolls limo took to the escape road. "Get a load of Penelope Pitstop," someone observed. "Where do you think they're all going?"

"Acapulco is nice this time of year," Wilkes quipped.

More vehicles streamed out, many of them leaving the sealed road, causing a cloud that obscured the exodus. It was then that the rattle of machine guns sounded. A blocking force of Australian Commandos was taking fire somewhere on the other side of the base.

"Boss," Ellis warned. "Nine o'clock."

Three pickups, each with a .50 caliber machine gun mounted in the bed, suddenly coalesced out of the dust cloud heading for the SAS positions.

Do they know we're here? Wilkes wondered. Maybe not. The Iraqis hadn't fired on them but were coming on regardless, so confrontation was inevitable.

One of the troopers in the wadi fired two single shots at a Toyota as it approached, picking off the Iraqi in the bed behind the .50 cal.

The man slumped as the vehicle hit a rise, catapulting him skyward as if plucked by an invisible hand from above.

Wilkes was relieved to see the flying Iraqi wasn't wearing a chem suit. If the enemy wasn't mopped up, it followed there weren't any nerve or bioagents deployed.

"You can ditch the goofy hat, boys, but keep it nearby just in case," Wilkes advised the men, unfastening his own hood and peeling off the respirator. Exposed to clean air, even the direct desert sun felt almost refreshing.

"Thank fuck," said someone.

"Halle-fucking-luiah," another muttered.

More pickups joined the attack, their guns spraying the wadi with lead. A TOW missile answered the volley, jumping out of the wadi and rocketing on its way, zeroing in on one of the pickups. An instant later, a massive blast turned the Toyota into burning metal, which was subsequently hit by the vehicle trailing immediately behind and turning it into a second fireball. The impact spat the Iraqi operating its bed-mounted machine gun over the roof and into the flaming wreckage of the vehicle ahead.

Wilkes shot a driver through his open window, and the pickup carved a sudden turn, which became a rollover, the vehicle tumbling into a vacant arm of the wadi and exploding, its ammo then cooking off.

One of the remaining three pickups braked to a halt, a dirty white singlet waving surrender from the passenger window. The other two pickups took the same option and pulled over, the drivers and passengers showing their hands out the windows. The shooters manning Brownings had no choice but to do likewise.

"Move in," said Wilkes, standing, the M4's crosshairs on one of the drivers. The sound of machine-gun fire on the far side of the wire had also ceased.

An unexpected pickup arrived, erupting from a thicker part of the dust cloud, barreling straight for Wilkes' back. "Hey!" warned a voice in his ear. The warrant officer turned and fired off a burst into the windshield. The pickup kept coming but changed course and seemed to accelerate as it slammed into a pair of desert palms beside a sign in both Serbo-Croatian and Arabic that loosely translated said, "Welcome to Qadisiyah Airbase. Have a nice day."

A pair of F/A18s screamed past overhead. The SAS sigs op, Corporal Stu Beck, piped up in Wilkes' ear. "Boss, those Hornets are ours - RAAF. Asked if we needed their help."

"Tell 'em we're okay."

"Roger that. They passed on some good news — we won."

"The War? Already?"

"Nah, the World Cup final. Fuckin' Ponting scored a hundred and forty off a hundred and twenty-one!"

The Australian Commandos' senior officer beamed, "It's all yours," shook hands with Wilkes, and then climbed into one of several Bushmasters and departed with the Iraqi prisoners. Mission accomplished. One captured airbase, the headquarters of Iraq's air force, and not a single casualty in either the SAS or Commandos unit.

Wilkes and his team now had this real estate to themselves. A cursory inspection of the facility in partnership with the commandos revealed warehouses, hangars, and hardened aircraft shelters abandoned in a hurry. The expected booby traps were, at least so far, found to be non-existent. Cups of the sweet tea favored by the Iraqis were still warm to the touch, so maybe they didn't have time to rig anything, was the conclusion. Evidence suggested the order to abandon ship had come suddenly, the allied invasion sweeping across the desert at break-neck speed. The race to hit the road had the Iraqis climbing over each other to get the hell out, departing without a backward glance. And what they left behind was a treasure trove of fighter aircraft, helicopters, weapons, spares, manuals, serviceable runways, and taxiways — everything a new post-invasion Iraqi air force would need to get operational.

Wilkes glanced at the loosely assembled men in his unit. They were relaxed but wary, heads turning, eyes scanning for possible threats. Professionals. This was a new unit. After all this time, Ellis and Beck were still with him, but three of the troopers were operations virgins — Warren Oates, who claimed Torres Strait Islander heritage; Jagvir Singh, whose parents emigrated from India when he was twelve; and Chris Park, a naturalized Australian from South Korea — a United Nations of Arse Kickers.

"What's next?" said Park, taking in the scenery.

"Stu, you sent the report to CENTCOM?" Wilkes inquired. Command HQ needed to know the base had been secured. Wilkes had no desire to be bombed by the Coalition air force.

"Done. Just been informed this patch of real estate has a new name — Al Asad. It means the lion. Also, they've asked for a rough inventory of the equipment left behind. There's a team arriving the day after tomorrow to inspect for WMD."

Wilkes readjusted his webbing. His unit already knew the place was vast and had seen where most of the obvious equipment was. "We'll revisit the hangars, shelters, and warehouses first. Stu, Wozz, with me. We'll take the east end of the main runway and head north." Turning attention to Ellis, Wilkes continued, "Take the west end of the runway and go north to the valley that splits this place in half. Meet back here in four hours. We'll reassess once we have more intelligence. Time permitting, we'll all reconnoiter south of the second runway. Keep your comms live, take pictures and notes, and assume there are still hostiles. Avoid picking up girlie magazines or cute teddy bears."

Wilkes knew he didn't have to issue a warning about IEDs but said it anyway. He marked the time on his watch and moved off. Four hours later, standing in the forecourt of a vast ammunition dump, he extended the rendezvous time another three hours to sunset. The ammo complex was a storehouse of millions of kilos of explosive ordnance: all manner of bombs and missiles, hundreds of thousands of rounds of small arms ammunition, and mines, both anti-personnel and anti-tank. There were also tens of thousands of grenades, plastics, detonators, fuses, and other items. No indication so far of WMD. A team of engineers would take a good week to survey the structure, let alone complete an inventory of its stores.

Park's voice sounded in Wilkes' earpiece. "Boss, so far, we've counted around 30 Migs, old Soviet-era types. Many of those Yugo-built hardened shelters and the planes under 'em have been destroyed. Looks like bunker busters got 'em. Thought that was it, but right now, I'm standing in a palm grove in the valley next to three Foxbats buried up to their wings."

"Mark the position," Wilkes told him.

Park continued, "Also seen some aircraft hidden under the trees beneath camo netting. Gary's heading there now to see what they are."

"WMD?" Wilkes asked.

"Not so far, boss," came the reply.

Wilkes was mildly baffled. At the mission briefing, intelligence suggested that Qadisiya would be a primary location for chemical and biological weapons, given that missiles would be one of the leading delivery platforms. Made sense that there'd be WMD here somewhere.

Later, as a burnt orange sun touched the shimmering horizon, the team rendezvoused as planned. "What have we got?" Wilkes asked.

"All manner of shit," said Ellis to general agreement. "And no serious attempt to trash any of it."

"We cleared a barracks not far from here," said Wilkes. "We'll camp there for the night and collate the data for upload."

"Wozz and I will take the first watch, boss," Singh offered.

Wilkes nodded. "Three-hour shifts."

As night descended on the desert, Wilkes killed the main power circuit breakers, cutting all base lighting to maximize the effectiveness of their night vision goggles. A lit candle would now appear like a beacon in the NVG's lime-green landscape.

Lying in a comfortable Iraqi cot, Wilkes' sleep was light, as if he expected to be woken at any moment. He was not disappointed.

"Tom." Ellis, speaking in low tones, was crouched beside the cot. "Boss..."

"What?" replied Wilkes, reaching automatically for the security of his M4.

"You need to come and see this."

Wilkes put on his helmet, powered up the NVGs, lowered the device over his eyes, and followed Ellis to the front door. "What is it?" he asked once they were outside.

"An Iraqi convoy, a big one. Heading northwest."

"They on the road?"

"No. Off-piste. Stopped for some reason."

Wilkes and Ellis checked in with Beck, who was maintaining watch at the main entrance. They then headed west across the desert in a patrol vehicle, the darkened convoy soon visible against the night sky in the NVGs.

Parking behind a low rise on the desert floor, Wilkes and Ellis set up a high-powered night scope around 600 meters east of the stationary line of B-doubles.

Wilkes pressed an eye to the lens and adjusted the scope. "Low loaders. I count ten, eleven, twelve of them... Several other heavy lorries and at least a company of soldiers riding shotgun. Make a juicy target from the air."

"Stu called up CENTCOM already and informed them. The response was, 'no available assets at this time.'"

Why is it they only seem to be standing by when you don't need 'em? Wilkes wondered.

"We don't have the resources to take on that convoy," Ellis observed.

Five against how many? With no intelligence or air support? And hitting the convoy would mean abandoning their objective. Wilkes took his eyes off the viewfinder and then repositioned himself. "Hard to make out, but I think one of the low loaders at the rear of the convoy is in trouble. Maybe they picked up a flat tire..." He then added, "Maybe not. A lot of panic for a puncture." Wilkes made further minor adjustments to the scope, moving it left and right. "Bingo."

"What?"

Wilkes backed away from the scope. "Tell me I'm not dreaming."

Ellis leaned forward and squinted into the lens. "Shit, eh? Noddy suits all 'round."

"Get some snaps for the album."

Ellis activated the scope's inbuilt camera and captured a range of images. "Where do you think they're going?"

"It ain't Acapulco."

"Wow, check out this freakshow riding up front on the lead truck. If he's an Iraqi, I'm Mr. Wonderful."

"Where?" Wilkes took back the scope.

WARSAW, THE PRESENT

"*Doktor*! He is back with us!" I heard the woman say as she swam into focus, looking down at me, hovering overhead, brow furrowed.

I croaked, "Where am I?" Hardly original, but the best I could manage at the time.

"*Warszawski Szpital Dla Dzierci,*" the doctor informed me, a guy in a blue plastic apron with an accent I couldn't place. "How do you feel?" His turn to lean over me, his hair quivering, shiny, black, and gelled. A hard light beam flicked into one eye and then the other.

Various machines, winking and beeping, were connected to my arms and fingers with tubes.

"You're in hospital — *Warszawski Szpital Dla Dzierci.*"

"Hospital?" Why? How?

"They say you have automobile accident, but..."

He seemed disbelieving. I moved a little, triggering a sharp pain like a hot nail driven into my ribcage. I groaned.

The doctor did his thing with the pencil torch again. "You speak Polish?"

"No. He is American," the woman advised over his shoulder.

The doctor held my face and rotated my head from side to side. "You know you are in Poland?"

Poland? I had no idea what that was, even that it was a place. And "American." What's that?

"Where does it hurt?" the doctor asked.

I moved a little and quickly decided that was a bad idea. "Ask me where it *doesn't* hurt?"

He played along. "Where does it not hurt?"

I moved a pinkie.

"Hmm, you have many injuries. The nurse will give you something. Allergies? You have allergies?"

12

I couldn't answer. I recognized the word "allergy," but there was no meaning attached.

"What day is it?" he asked.

Again, no idea. I couldn't bring to mind anything even vaguely relevant. That was puzzling and alarming. Why couldn't I remember? What else had I forgotten?

A large white folder lay over my legs. The doc grabbed it and took out a bundle of X-rays — a human skull and neck. Mine, I guessed.

"Who is American President?" he asked me, holding the images to the overhead lighting.

Sounded official. "Same as always," I said. "Some rich guy."

"No, it is a woman."

A woman president? "Maybe shit might get done for once," I said.

"Your fiancé has mild amnesia," Doctor Gel concluded. "But not total. Selective."

Fiancé? Weird. I knew exactly what that meant.

Another check of those X-rays. "He has concussion, perhaps a little bruising of the brain. No indication of swelling or bleed. It will pass."

"When?" the woman asked.

"Ten minutes, an hour or two... A day at the most. He is not Jason Bourne."

"Who?" I asked.

The doctor grinned, pushed back from the bed, and muttered a few words of complete gibberish — what they spoke in Poland, I figured — to the woman. Then, turning to me before leaving, he said, "If you need anything, the nurses will give it."

My inner voice told me I should have been able to follow that with something amusing but couldn't, which, along with the searing pain in my ribs, told me I was in some kind of trouble.

He walked out.

The woman leaned in, dropped her voice. "Your name is Vincent Cooper. You work for U.S. Department of Agriculture — expert on bees." She checked that the coast was clear. "Which is not true because everyone, they know this is CIA, and you know nothing of bees."

Vincent? Bees? "Who are you?"

"Agent Kazia Strahovski of the *Agencja Bezpieczeństwa Wewnętrznego.*"

"What?"

"ABW. Polish Internal Security Agency."

Good, I'd have trouble pronouncing the rest of it.

"Call me Kazia."

"And the CIA? What's that?"

"The CIA — Central Intelligence Agency. You know what spy is? CIA is spies."

It was all a blank.

A nurse entered the room, brandishing a small cup, which she placed on a tray beside the bed, and gave Kazia instructions before walking out.

The agent poured water into a plastic cup. "For pain."

I hoped she meant for ending it.

She handed me both cups. "The pill. Drink."

I took the pill, drank the water, and asked, "You know what happened to me, right? Car accident?"

Kazia removed the chart from the end of the bed and scanned it. "You have head injury, concussion, contusions, two cracked ribs, one fractured, severe bruising, some stitches, and abrasions.

A car accident seemed reasonable.

"The doctor does not believe it was car accident because the nurse found this in your pocket." From her shoulder bag, she pulled out a pair of brass knuckledusters slicked with what appeared to be dried blood. "They found this when they cut off your pants."

"What?"

"You must listen and do as I say." She moved a parcel from a cupboard to the bed. "New clothes. Get dressed. They will look for you. Wagner. They did this to you."

"Who's Wagner?"

"Not a person; Russian mercenaries. You don't remember?"

"Russian?"

Kazia looked at me for a few long seconds, then dismantled the parcel, releasing a pair of white undershorts, runners and blue socks, blue suit pants, and a dark brown long-sleeve shirt with a pattern of black vertical stripes and diamonds. It was stylish. I hoped I could pull it off. In the meantime, I had trouble moving anything, so an appreciation of the clothes admittedly came later.

Kazia whipped out the cannula from the back of my hand while I was distracted.

"Oww!"

After a lot of grunting and some of it from me, the woman managed to lever me up into the seated position on the side of the bed. I breathed shallow because going deeper hurt. I sat, aware that my body was held together by a girdle of surgical tape and bandages. And then my memory suddenly came back. One moment, I had no idea about anything, and the next moment — I *knew*.

Jason Bourne... Funny.

The who, what, where, when, and why awakening didn't come as a jolt or a shock but more like a slide, like turning the page on an empty photo album and seeing a double-page spread of random images, some of them disturbing. And one of the things I knew from those pictures was something important Kazia hadn't mentioned — that I'd recently killed a man. I recalled strobe-like flashes: brass knuckles smeared with bright blood, the crunch of bone, the dead weight of the man in my arms that I dropped onto the sidewalk who then rolled into the gutter beneath a "No Parking" sign. These knucks... I'd levered them out of the man's dead fingers.

There were two assailants. The other guy had a tattoo, some kind of animal skull on his hand. I recalled a severed foot in a boot, blood spatter everywhere, and a strange mechanical rattling sound. The next thing I recalled was waking up engaged to Claudia Schiffer here, and that pretty much brought me up to the present. "My memory," I informed her. "It just came back. Some of it. In pieces."

"Good."

"So...we're engaged? You're my fiancé?"

"No."

I took in the blonde bob hairdo fashionably brushed forward, the flawless skin, the crystal blue eyes, the cute button nose, and the vaguely swollen lips like she'd maybe slept on them, and I'll admit to being just a little disappointed.

Kazia's attention switched to a woman power walking down the hallway toward us. Tall, longish chocolate brown hair in a high ponytail, olive-skinned, and a light spray of sun freckles across the bridge of her nose. I knew this woman, and the reason I knew her was prompted by memory flashes of the both of us in the sack. At least I hoped I knew her, and those flashes weren't pure projection. Her name was...it came to me just in time. "Anna..."

"Jesus, Vin..." She stopped in front of me, rested a hand lightly on my shoulder, and searched my face with electric blue-green eyes. "You're a mess, and if you tell me I should see the other guy, I'll hit you myself."

"I don't do cliches."

"Since when?" Anna turned to Kazia. "What's the worst of his injuries?"

The Polish agent ran through the list of contusions and finished with, "We go now to morgue. He killed a man."

WASHINGTON DC
THE PRESENT MINUS ONE MONTH

"Mr. Sands will see you now," said the tightly wound executive assistant. This was the sixth interview she'd led the way to with various senior execs at the defense company, but not the slightest hint of familiarity came my way. An on/off smile and carefully coordinated androgynous clothing informed me that her other half was a PowerPoint presentation.

I followed her down a carpeted hallway lined with posters of various Sands Aerospace & Defense products – satellites, drones, missiles, radars, guided artillery rounds, and rockets — into an expansive, well-lit corner office. Or maybe it was a showroom. In the center of the ample space was a half-size scale model of an advanced SAM missile battery that the company had developed and sold to various air forces, including the USAF. Beside it sat a full-size hypersonic scram engine with cutaways. Other more analog products were displayed in a far corner adjacent to a casual lounging area — raised on a plinth a single Browning .50 caliber machinegun, the 100,000th unit manufactured in 1942 according to a plaque, by Sands Industrial, the company's name prior to various mergers. And beside it, an "M45 Quadmount," a towed anti-aircraft defense system from 1944 featuring four Browning machine guns, also manufactured by Sands Industrial. Belts fed the guns with polished rounds from full boxes.

"My great uncle's creation," Ely Sands called out from the far end of the room, teeing off at Augusta, according to the floor-to-ceiling video screen he was firing the ball into. "We used to make washing machines and refrigerators. Dubya-Dubya Two changed all that. More money in defending American values than there is in cleaning

American clothes. Don't tell anyone, but that ol' Quadmount still works, and the ammunition is live. Fires 2,300 copper-jacketed steel rounds per minute with a magnesium tracer every fourth round. I like to keep it real. Why don't you climb into it?"

I thought he'd never ask. I stepped up onto the checker plate platform and lowered myself into the seat, a steel shell crudely shaped to the human body — one size fits all. The air-cooled machine-gun barrels stuck out like lances in front of me, a basic sight centered between them — a crude series of circles with a cross bisecting them. This beast only needed to find the target's general area to be effective.

"Start her up," Sands insisted. "It's the green button on the control panel located on the base beside your knee. It's powered by a couple of car batteries. That lever on your left cocks all four barrels. The trigger is on the handle."

I found the button, pressed it, and a hum rose from mechanicals in the base. The entire structure pivoted a few degrees to the left and then to the right as if resetting itself. I pulled on the levers under my hands and spun sharply to the left. Sands was now square in the gunsight.

"Don't tell me," he said with an easy smile, "you wanna renegotiate your salary package."

I reached down and slapped the red kill button. The whine ceased, and the entire machine seemed to sag a little. I wondered what pulling the trigger and letting those four barrels rip would be like.

Sands handed the driver to the EA, who was standing more or less at attention.

"You play golf, Vince?"

"Not so much these days."

"What's your handicap?"

"When I called it quits, twelve."

"That's pretty handy," Sands considered with a nod. "Shoulda kept at it."

"That's twelve balls," I confessed.

"Ha! Right. Well, when you join us, we can work on that. You look like you could send a ball down range a hell of a way. You are joining us, aren't you?"

Was it up to me? "That's the plan, sir."

"Good, good. And call me Ely." He led the way to a low table serviced by a couple of tan leather chairs and a gray wool sofa. "Can we get you something? Coffee, hot tea, water, a finger of Glen Keith?" He winked at me. Sands had done its homework, but what did I expect?

"I'm fine, thanks," I said.

From seemingly out of nowhere, the EA produced a pitcher of water flavored with slices of lemon and poured two glasses. I was going to drink whether I wanted to or not. She wasn't a robot, but she moved with the precision of one. I pictured her masked, wearing a leather catsuit, snapping her leg with a riding crop and demanding subservience. People wound that tight tend to wear it as a disguise. Loosen the bindings and try not to get hit by what flies out.

Sands reclined on the couch, arms spread wide, legs crossed, relaxed success personified. This was our first face-to-face, though, of course, I'd also done some digging of my own. Ely Sands was a smooth, no-sharp-edges character with a Ph.D. in computer science and electrical engineering. He was in his late 50s, hair still mostly black, fit, tall, good-looking with clear gray eyes, and stinking rich. He liked to wear two-tone business shirts, so no one's perfect. Today, it was blue with white collars and cuffs.

Sands inherited the company as a young man from the son of a great uncle, a Canadian who'd flown Spitfires in North Africa against the Luftwaffe. Ely tracked down the aircraft his father had flown and had it restored to flying condition. Today, the Spitfire sat in the company's foyer and was let loose at the occasional air show.

Marriage — he'd done that three times, the first to his childhood sweetheart and the second to the daughter of an English aristocrat. Third time around, he'd hit the jackpot, getting hitched to a former Victoria's Secret angel more than 20 years his junior, the blonde one from South Africa who reminded me of vanilla ice cream.

Another man walked in and made himself comfortable in the leather chair opposite. "Vince," he said by way of greeting.

Chase Overton, company CFO. I'd spent twenty minutes with Overton previously, interview number four. In a lineup of Dr Phils that included Dr Phil, Overton would be picked as Dr. Phil. He did not, however, possess Dr. Phil's ease.

Looking at these two businessmen, if Ely Sands was a Ferrari, Willy Overton was a '77 Buick Malaise.

"Gotta say, Vince, hell of a service record," Ely continued. "I'm looking forward to getting you drunk and finding out what's behind all the redaction. I have a high-security clearance, and whole pages are just black."

"I don't think they'll even let me look at my record, sir."

Sands chuckled. "Well, I am — we are — thrilled to have you join our senior management team."

"Thank you, sir." And I'm looking forward to putting my feet up on a desk just like yours.

"So, you've spent several hours with us examining our operation; what's your take?"

"You make a lot of stuff that either kills people or saves people's lives, depending on whether you're the giver or the receiver."

Sands smiled easily. "That's the bigger picture."

I continued, "You have a lot of leading-edge intellectual property at the heart of all your systems. Numerous bad actors out there would love to get their hands on it." Does it hurt to tell someone what they want to hear?

"You're damn right," Sands said. "Which is why we want to offer you the position of chief gatekeeper in our family. What's the official title, Will?"

"CSO — Chief Security Officer," said Overton.

"And the sooner, the better." Sands took the water jug and poured a double into my glass.

I was aware that I would be replacing the previous CSO who had died from a heart attack, aged 45. Pressure of the job?

"When do you want to start, Vince?"

Vince? That guy works for loan sharks and collects the juice with a baseball bat and a throw-down ex-cop .38 tucked into the back of his pants. "Call me Vin," I said.

"Vin. Of course."

"I've got a few loose ends lying around. So, say early July?"

"Perfect. Your office will be down the hall. You're based at Andrews, right? So, we're already neighbors. Any questions you want to ask?"

"No, think I've asked most of them," I said honestly.

"Well, there'll be all kinds of letters and documents to sign moving forward, but let's make our contract simple — man-to-man. Ely stood in such a way that told me I should do likewise. He held out his hand. "Welcome aboard, Vince." We shook on it. As for the name thing, something to work on.

I also shook Willy Overton's hand, which was pudgy and a little sweaty. No judgment. So, he pushed a pencil and had overactive glands. This was a moment to celebrate. Hello, big salary and cushy hours. Farewell to scraping by and fuckheads sticking firearms in my face.

I relaxed on the sofa with nachos and a beer and then read aloud parts of the hand-delivered letters waiting on my doorstep when I arrived home. *"Dear Mr. Cooper, we are pleased to confirm your employment as Chief Security Officer...salary of $360,000 plus benefits outlined in the attached Schedule A..."* The thought of all that money tingled my nether regions. *"As discussed, your job specification will include managing company security resources and personnel, identifying and countering industrial espionage threats, overseeing our cybersecurity and related countermeasures, fieldwork...* et cetera, and so forth.

"The entire job specification will be outlined in a letter from our human resources department. There will be a week's induction scheduled in July, prior to you taking up your position with us. We would also like to confirm your commencement date of Monday, August 4th.

"Yours sincerely, William Overton, Vice President and Chief Financial Officer, Sands Aerospace & Defense."

An accompanying note from Ely Sands, Executive Chairman & President, was written with a fountain pen on personal stationery. It was brief and to the point. *"Dear Vince..."* Was I going to have to get used to being called someone else? Refocusing: *"I'm personally thrilled to have you joining our team. Having someone of your reputation and caliber as our head of security is a victory for SA&D. I have no doubt you will be a safe pair of hands. Come and see me on your first day, and we'll do lunch."*

Ely's signature was a careless flick of the pen, more a scratch, and reminded me of a fishhook, complete with barb. I took another swig of the Heineken. People like Ely didn't have lunch or eat it; they "did" it. This was the club I was joining. How did I feel about it? Actually, I felt...validated. Not a word I ever used on account of it dripped with the noxious toxic slime of woke-speak, but that kind of offensive nonsense was a child I was going to have to adopt if I was to survive in the corporate white-board world governed by HR weenies I was heading into. But hey, with a starting salary of over three hundred thou', plus bonuses and benefits, I could swallow the odd weasel word.

News time. I put the letters aside with an inner glow, aimed the remote at the wall, and pressed the red button. It was a minute or two past the hour, and I'd missed the headlines. My cell rang. The screen told me it was Arlen, Lieutenant Colonel Arlen Wayne, the soon-to-be-my-ex-supervisor. I picked up because Arlen was a buddy long before he became my boss, and he was also married to Marnie, a certain significant someone's kid sister. "Hey," I said.

"Have you seen the news?" he replied, skipping the polite banter part, his voice tense.

"Just about to. Why?" The newsreader was sitting at her desk, looking stern, and the word "Wikileaks" was hanging in the air beside her.

"I'll wait. Put me on speaker. Turn up the volume."

Intrigued, I hit the plus symbol on the remote.

The newsreader said, "...the mission report details the incident witnessed by an Australian SAS patrol at the Al Asad airbase in the early days of Operation Iraqi Freedom in April 2003, some hundred miles south of the Iraqi border with Syria. The top-secret document, acquired by Wikileaks, is a bombshell embarrassment to several administrations past and present. Sources in the Pentagon have launched an internal investigation to uncover the whistleblower's identity."

The report cut to some television analyst I'd never heard of: *"This goes to the heart of America's national defense,"* said the expert. *"What's next, the nuclear launch codes posted on Twitter?"*

Hmm, that was a stretch, but the news was nothing if not sensationalist these days, no matter what the channel.

"We'll bring you more on this breaking story as it comes to hand," he promised.

The image of a giant panda bear gnawing on a bamboo stick filled the newsreader's wall. *"In other news today, San Diego Zoo's most famous resident, the panda Mei Sheng, has just-"*

I thumbed the mute button.

"You missed it," Arlen said.

"You want to hear what Mei Sheng's up to? Could be important. I can unmute."

"No. You missed the meat of the SAS Wikileaks furor."

"And?"

"So, Vin..."

I'd had these sorts of conversations with Arlen many times — the urgent home call, a little incomplete back story, and then my name followed by a few dots. I attempted to bunt it away with silence.

"Hello...?" he said. "Look, I know you're still there. I can hear you breathing. You have to come in."

"Why?"

"I don't have to explain myself because I'm your superior, and that's what I want you to do."

I glanced at the letter on the sofa beside me. Do I tell him now, I wondered? It was easy to resign now that I was a civilian OSI special agent. "Just fill in the blanks for me a little, Arlen. You want me to come in, and it has something to do with the Wikileaks thing that I don't know shit about."

"This line is unsecured."

"So is the television news. Just tell me what I missed."

"I don't do this with anyone else, you know that, right?" he said.

"Do what?"

"Pander."

"I thought you weren't interested in Mei Sheng," I countered.

"What? Jesus, Vin..."

"Going now, Arlen. Sports is up next."

"Wikileaks has released a top-secret MISREP from the Australian patrol that secured Al Asad airbase. The early days of Operation Iraqi Freedom."

At last. "And?"

"The report details the sighting of an Iraqi convoy sneaking across the desert, heading for Syria before dawn."

"So...?"

"The conclusion reached by everyone is that the Aussies witnessed a cache of Saddam's WMD being spirited out of the country to Syria."

"How did they arrive at that conclusion?" I asked.

"The convoy had broken down, and the Iraqi Republican Guards riding shotgun were running around in full chemical warfare getup."

Not exactly what I would have called conclusive evidence, but with so many terrorist organizations in play these days, from nationalists to religious nutters, few things set Administration hearts aflutter more than the prospect of unaccounted-for WMD. "Arlen, you know I'm a team player," I began.

"No comment."

"Exactly. I'm not, which is why I'm not coming in."

"You're coming in because you don't have a choice."

"'G'bye."

"You hang up on me, Vin, and I'll have the MPs busting down your door within five minutes."

I knew when Arlen wasn't joking, and he wasn't joking.

"You haven't done shit since that thing with the Russian president," he reminded me.

"Except resign my commission and become a civilian," I reminded him. "But you're right. I am way out of practice, so maybe ask someone else to—"

"You draw a salary, so put on your best military bearing and get to the Pennsylvania Avenue address I'm texting you...within the next 30 minutes."

Pennsylvania Avenue? "But it's after hours." My phone *pinged* with the text.

"Vin!"

"Shit...," I muttered under my breath.

"I heard that."

The address on Pennsylvania Ave was a suite at the upscale St Regis Hotel, all marble and gargoyles. A couple of CIA toughs in off-the-rack suits for the underpaid stood shoulder-to-shoulder in front of the room's double doors.

"Are you keeping me out, or whoever's on the other side in?" I asked.

"Got an ID, wiseass?"

I held it up for him, and he opened the door. I walked into some kind of dining room with a large, gorgeously polished oak table. But more interesting than the furniture were the people seated around it. There was Arlen, of course, along with his boss, a one-star brigadier whose weapon of choice was a putter, the United States Secretary of State, and the White House Chief of Staff.

My heart sank. So, here's one thing I know. When powerful people invite a schmo into the room, it's always going to go badly for the schmo. In present company, I was the schmo.

"Ah, Mr. Cooper," said Aldus Picot, the president's Chief, a former Harvard Law School professor with no shoulders and a thin, high voice that made me think of a violin played by someone who shouldn't. "We've been expecting you. Take a seat."

Picot. All I knew about him was that he once had a popular podcast, now defunct, that aligned with the president's view of the world, which was that the United States would be number two in the superpower stakes over her dead body. He said, "You have possibly not met the Secretary of State, Dorothy Muirhead."

Correct. There was no Venn diagram where our circles intersected.

Muirhead was a stern headmistress type with a shortish salt and pepper hairstyle to match. She lowered her head to look over the thick black frames of her glasses like she was considering issuing a detention. "I read about your African exploits with those rappers in a magazine a few years back. But now I've had reason to review your file... Impressive. And on top of it all, you have a law degree."

So, no one's perfect, right?

Muirhead continued, "You may have fallen afoul of the previous administration, but I think we can put that right."

Oh, goodie. "Yes, ma'am."

"I'm sure you would like to know why you're here," said Picot.

In fact, I was hoping to be able to put that off indefinitely. "To serve my country, sir," I replied.

Arlen coughed discreetly.

"Can I call you Vin?" Picot continued.

No. "Yes, sir."

"The whole world has now heard about the MISREP from Iraqi Freedom illegally passed to Wikileaks, so I presume you're not in the dark?"

It had also been all over the radio, which I caught on the way in.

"No, sir."

"The leak presents us with a raft of issues. America and our coalition partners fought the war to capture and destroy Iraq's weapons of mass destruction. The war and what came after it cost American lives, the lives of our coalition partners, and well over a trillion dollars. While we can debate whether we achieved our aims in Iraq, what's not debatable is that we didn't find WMD despite credible intelligence to the contrary about Saddam's stockpiles. That we found nothing we could point to was, to put it mildly, a very public embarrassment both for the United States and our intelligence community. What's particularly uncomfortable about this latest development, as well as being potentially dangerous, is that this MISREP suggests — but does not confirm — that not only were we aware of the location of Saddam's WMD, but we also wilfully allowed it to slip through our fingers."

Muirhead summarized: "The leaking of the MISREP is a major public relations issue for this administration, domestically and geopolitically."

Picot wasn't down with the short form. "I think you're mistaken there, Madam Secretary," he argued. "The action outlined in the MISREP had nothing to do with the current White House. And there have been a number of Administrations since 2003, both red and blue."

"And yet it took a whistleblower to reveal the truth," Muirhead continued. "This casts Big Government, whether red or blue, in the same bad light. We appear to be just another Administration that has buried the SAS report. Why? Was it because it looks like we knew the WMD went to Bashar al-Assad's regime and tried to keep that a secret? We know that's not the case, but today's social media conspiracy theory is tomorrow's truth. And for all we know, these are the very weapons al-Assad has been using on his people. Now, because of the leaking of this MISREP, the whole world is asking if American-led Coalition forces knew about Iraq's WMD heading for Syria back in the day. Why didn't we try to stop it? We had whole armies on the ground at the time."

Muirhead was a formidable presence. She was angry, and it showed, especially in the waddle of skin under her chin that vibrated furiously for a long second after she finished speaking. I pictured her swatting naughty hands with a ruler. Maybe Picot's. In fact, one more interruption from Picot and she would have him writing out "I must not interrupt" a hundred times.

"We didn't stop it if indeed it was WMD because we had no mandate to invade Syria," Picot added with some sarcasm. Clearly, two of the most influential people in the president's inner circle didn't see eye-to-eye. "Again, going back to what I said earlier, I don't believe that this leaked MISREP confirms, unequivocally, the existence of WMD in Iraq."

I wanted to know if there were any more leaks about to sink the current Administration's ship.

More or less addressing this, Picot continued, "The joint chiefs have reviewed all the relevant MISREPS from the period of this incident. An Air Force colonel who was in command of an intelligence gathering asset close to the Iraq-Syria border back in '03 put together a mission profile looking for buried WMD in the area. This was in response to scuttlebutt on the ground that something untoward was going on. That mission was never approved, by the way. And even if it had been greenlit, the convoy in question would have been long gone from the area." Picot turned to me and reiterated his reiteration. "The point is, Major Cooper, the SAS story was never confirmed."

Clearly, the Chief of Staff had not received the memo that I'd been promoted from major to mister.

Muirhead was not impressed. "Well, it's hardly a story, is it, Aldus? *Story* implies a fictional component. But the SAS took photos of the convoy, time-stamped, and geolocated. I'd call that some kind of proof, wouldn't you?"

"It's proof that there was a convoy, but as to its cargo..." Picot shook his head.

Muirhead's index finger hovered over the control panel in front of her. The lights dimmed, and a series of green-on-green night-vision images played up on a wall. The images were electronically date-and-time-stamped, along with positional information. The snaps themselves showed low loaders and plenty of trucks accompanied by armed Iraqi soldiers in chemical warfare suits supervised by a sizeable contingent of workers in full, positive-pressure HAZMAT gear. It was all this chemical and biological protection that was at the heart of the current concerns. When Iraqis were wearing MOPP gear, surely that was a signal that they were in the presence of WMD?

"They could have been transporting fertilizer or defoliant," the brigadier suggested, just in case anyone was hoping for an alternative hypothesis.

Muirhead glanced at him like he was the slow kid in class. "Unlikely, General," was all she said. Any more suggestions that two and two could sometimes equal five, and the brigadier would be bending over in front of Muirhead's ruler with his pants around his knees.

"Madam Secretary," I said, raising my hand for permission to speak.

"Go on." Permission granted.

"You have three images. There have to be more."

"Indeed. And it's that kind of observation that serves to convince me that you are the right man for this job."

What was I thinking? Opening your mouth in these things suggests buy-in.

She fixed her gaze on me. "The president has multiple concerns here. Syria claims that its stocks of sarin nerve agents and precursor chemicals were destroyed in a U.S.-sponsored deal in 2014. But can we really trust that?"

No, we couldn't. If Bashar al-Assad were Pinocchio, the lying son of a bitch's nose would be worth substantial carbon credits.

The SecState continued, "Was a cache of undocumented WMD never declared to inspectors, the very WMD delivered to Syria by Saddam on that convoy? It goes without saying that if there is secret WMD out there, we want to secure it and destroy it."

I nodded with concentration furrowing my forehead because there are times when it pays to show some of that. But what I really wanted to do was walk out and leave a copy of the Sands letter of appointment fluttering in my slipstream.

"So, Vin..." said Muirhead, "this will be a very delicate assignment."

I decided to test its delicacy. Maybe if I was heavy-handed, that might convince them I wasn't the right person for the job after all. "Do you mind if I ask a question?"

"Of course," said Picot.

Did he mind, or did he not mind? I was unsure, but I asked anyway. "Was the leaked MISREP the original or a soft copy?"

"I believe it's a photo of the original unredacted hard copy. I'm told the soft copy has been deleted from the system. Or perhaps they just can't find it. The Pentagon is in a flap over it."

It surely would be.

"Permanent deletion of records is not supposed to be possible," added Muirhead.

I raised my hand again — it seemed the thing to do. "Also..."

Picot motioned at me.

"Can I ask why you're conducting this briefing in an unsecured, non-government facility?" I sensed Arlen squirming. Questions suggesting public officials were being underhanded didn't come from "team players."

"Good question," Muirhead said, which told me she didn't particularly care to answer it. "At the moment, we are merely hashing over a media story, right, Aldus?"

"Correct," he nodded.

Well, at least they agreed on covering each other's ass.

The SecState continued, "Nothing discussed in this room isn't already being dissected by CNN, Fox News, and the like. But I get where you're coming from. The CIA, the FBI, and the DoJ are all looking into various aspects of this. We want to know who was responsible for the leak and what the motive for it might be. The sensitivity of this investigation requires that it be off the books. Disavowed, if you want to be all Mission Impossible dramatic about it.

It's never pleasant to be told you'll be performing a high-wire act without a net.

"So naturally, we couldn't exactly have you dropping over to the White House Situation Room because then there would be a record of it and, perhaps down the track, an explanation about what was discussed at that meeting might be required by some committee or media group. We would like to limit the damage moving forward."

Weren't these people aware that Damage was my middle name?

She went on, "As such, you will be reporting progress to me and only me."

In short, Tweets keeping everyone up to date. Never mind what she was saying, what I was hearing was the only person going to get screwed if shiny went to shit was Mister Schmo here — me.

Muirhead and Picot began packing up their colored pencils.

"Colonel," said Muirhead with a nod to Arlen, "can you take the ball up from here?"

Sporting analogies. Not a fan, personally, but no doubt they'd be another thing I'd have to get used to at a company like SA&D, especially in group brainstorming sessions involving whiteboards. It was that kind of company. I thought about that $360k again and decided that, for all those lovely zeroes, I would happily ask the sporting analogy to sign my bare chest.

"Yes, Madam Secretary," said Arlen.

My turn for a Muirhead eyeballing. "Vin, it has been a pleasure and an honor. Your reputation precedes you, and I'm happy to say I'm not disappointed."

"Indeed," echoed Picot. "Major, thank you again for your time, your service, and your patriotism."

Mister. I rearranged my features into deep sincerity mode and replied, "Madam Secretary, Mr. Picot."

"Help yourself to the minibar," Muirhead suggested as if the shit sandwich being plated up for me would go down easier with booze. Maybe it would. Everything else seemed to.

"Gentlemen," the SecState said, her departing sayonara, and walked out trailing Picot.

I bet myself that if I met them in the lunch queue in the Pentagon Taco Bell tomorrow, they wouldn't recognize me.

"Well, I have an appointment," grunted the brigadier, standing and straightening his jacket. "I'll leave it in your capable hands, Arlen. If you need me, you know where to find me."

I figured teeing off at either Creighton Farms or East Potomac.

He departed, leaving Arlen and me alone with the minibar. I partook. "Arlen?"

"Fuck it, why not?" he said. "Smirnoff on the rocks."

I emptied three over a couple of rocks and harvested all the Johnny Walker Blacks into another glass. The SecState said to drink, and I follow orders. Mostly. "So, what is the brigadier leaving in your hands?" I still had no idea what I was being asked to do other than I wouldn't like it.

Arlen sipped his drink. "I believe the word capable was in there somewhere."

"Tell me where this is going because I know you know. What part of this am I handling?"

"Drink up first, Vin. And maybe have another."

"That bad?"

"I wouldn't say bad, exactly."

"Then what would you say?"

"You can't take on this case as a special agent in the OSI because it doesn't involve the Air Force."

"I distinctly heard mention of an Air Force colonel, didn't I?"

"That's no more than an interview with the retired officer in question but hardly germane to the core issue of there being WMD and a whistleblower on the loose."

"Maybe," I said. "Maybe not." I drank half of Mr. Walker's finest and felt the delightful sour heat hit my empty stomach a bunch of seconds later.

"You have to take this case as a federal agent working out of Langley."

I nearly choked. "What? You are fucking kidding..."

"I'll grant you it's ironic."

"You can't even say the words Central Intelligence Agency, can you?"

"I can, but only after you've taken the rest of that handy chilled anesthetic you're holding in your hand there." Arlen gestured at my glass.

"I resign, effective immediately," I told him.

"You know it's not that easy."

"I'll make it official in an email later today. I have another gig to go to. Money, benefits, travel, and no CIA."

"If it's a gig with a military supplier, I can tell you now the CIA is involved. They're like an octopus. Not one of the cute, friendly ones – more the type that drags ships under the water with all hands. Their tentacles are everywhere."

"Jesus, Arlen... Seriously, why me?" Equally depressingly, only gins were left in the minibar rack. "Is there any tonic in the fridge?"

"I don't know. Take a look."

"It's not like I'm the only special agent on the federal payroll."

"You were recommended to the Administration because you have investigative and combat experience on the ground in both Iraq and Syria."

Iraq and Syria, two of my least favorite words in the English language. I got up and had another look in the mini bar, just in case I overlooked a JW... Nope. Gordon's Gin was it. And no tonic. I picked up the Gordon's and mixed them into the scotch fumes hanging around in my glass.

"Up, down, up down...Just sit, Vin," said Arlen. "You're making me tense."

"You're tense. Who has it in for me? Who did the recommending?"

"You're the best man for the job."

"It was you, wasn't it?"

Arlen smiled. "You're welcome."

"Surely there's someone else on the books who'd love to fly to interesting places and try not to get killed."

"Now you're just being overly dramatic."

"Iraqi WMD gone to Syria, an administration that doesn't want to take any responsibility, a potential mole in the Pentagon, the nation's security apparatus compromised, expect to dodge bullets in

Iraq, Syria, and possibly both, and the CIA — an organization, let me remind you, that has tried to kill me on several occasions — is now your boss. Personally, I think overly dramatic undercooks it a little."

Arlen drank up.

"When does this mission start? And what is this mission?"

"What's the time?" he asked, glancing at the clock on the AV projector. "It's now fifteen hundred. So, let's say kick-off time is fifteen-thirty."

"What's the extra thirty for?"

"A leisurely drive from here to CIA, Langley."

"You haven't answered my other question."

"Hence the drive to Langley."

CIA, LANGLEY, VIRGINIA

Another boardroom. This one was small. Any smaller, it could be a shoe. A gray shoe. The carpet, walls, and corkboards were all gray. Even the used coffee mug down the far end of the gray table left behind from a previous meeting was gray.

An agent of around 50 years of age and married, according to the wedding band, was seated at the table, accompanied by a manila folder and an envelope. She had wrinkles in the places that told me she liked to smile. Maybe she liked jokes. Given that I was sitting in an orientation meeting at the CIA, maybe I was the punchline.

"Afternoon," she said as I sat. "How's your day been?"

"Peachy," I replied. "Yours?"

"Also a piece of fruit with the odd bruise. Rita Inglis." She slid her card across the table and then pressed a button on her phone screen. "I'll be your liaison here. I've just sent you a text with my details. Please add them to your contact list."

My pocket buzzed. They had my number already. "Will spyware be riding in along with it?"

Ms. Inglis looked at me blankly. "This is the CIA. We are not the enemy."

How naive can you get?

She went on to inform me that an office had been made available to me for when I was in the building. It was down the hall, the second door on the left, beside the men's head, which was the third door on the left, conveniently just next door to my door. In short, any closer to the john and my office would be in it. Unfortunate, Rita sympathized, especially given some recent plumbing issues, but space was tight. Great, I thought. Nothing focuses the mind like an occasional whiff of trough candy and urine.

She then presented my official CIA photo ID lanyard, which had to be worn around my neck at all times when in the building, and reminded me not to forget to take it off when I left, the CIA being a secret organization and so forth. To me, this seemed advice for the mentally challenged, like the tag on a toaster I bought recently showing the appliance with a big red cross through it, resting on the edge of a full bathtub. The ID included my photo, which was unsettling given that I had yet to pose for one.

Next came the Agency credit card and ten pages of rules about its use, a Company cell phone followed by rules about cell phones — where and when private phones could and could not be used and so forth, a Company laptop coded to my fingerprints and face and a slip of paper with login and password details to be memorized then burned and the ash crushed, where my security clearance would hit a wall, instructions on where to park my car in the lot, the location of the cafeteria, and how to log into the Agency intranet.

"What if I need to travel?"

"That's already been cleared."

"Do I get a CIA business card?"

"Yes!" she chirped and handed me a block wrapped in brown paper, an example card on one face of the block.

"Dr. Vincent Cooper, Ph.D., Biol. Ecological Systems," I read aloud. "I have a doctorate in Biology?"

"It's general enough," Inglis offered.

"Enough for who?"

"I doubt anyone will be quizzing you."

The embossed logo said I was working for the U.S. Department of Agriculture. Hmm...the sum total of my eco knowledge was that rain, not too much and not too little, was good for plants and that my recently acquired Chevy Impala, with its old premium-burning V8, was contributing to the demise of polar bears.

"You're on a trade mission if anyone enquires," Inglis continued.

I changed the subject. "Got a question for you."

"Shoot."

"What's the CIA's favorite game?"

"I'm sorry?"

"Whack-a-mole."

It took a moment, but then those laugh lines made use of themselves. "Wanna hear my current favorite?" she asked, getting into the swing of things.

"Sure."

"So, three guys are applying for a job at the Agency. The first guy is interviewed, and the key question is: 'Who killed Jesus Christ?' The first guy replies, 'The Jews.'

"The next guy is interviewed. He gets the same question: 'Who killed Jesus Christ?' His answer: 'The Romans killed him.'

"The third guy is interviewed, asked the question, and he says, 'Hmm, I'll have to go home and think about that for a while.'

"A little later, he arrives home, and his wife says, 'How did it go?' To which he replies, 'It went really well, honey. I've been assigned a case already!'"

"Not bad," I said with a grin. "Got another one. Two guys and a woman are—"

"Are you finished, Ms. Inglis?"

A couple of thick folders landed on the table, dropped from excessive height by someone unseen behind me.

"Thank you, Mr. Cooper." Inglis stood and gathered her possessions. "You need anything, please give me call."

The rest of the newcomer came around the table and hung his old sports jacket on the back of the seat opposite. I had a badly stained couch of that same material back when I left high school. "So, *you're* Cooper," he said. His scraggly beard was mottled brown and gray, biscuit crumbs trapped in the hairs. I guessed mid-to-late forties — not the biscuit crumbs. The name on his ID said Operations Officer Merle Ridge. He looked worn out for his age, but Ridge still managed to wear that CIA sneer reserved for federal agents Agency types considered lesser beings — everyone else, basically. Body odor drifted across the table, that jacket the prime suspect.

A woman followed him in. "Sidney Davidson," she said by way of introduction, reaching across the desk to shake my hand. "Welcome to the Agency."

"Vin Cooper."

"Yes," she said with a friendly smile. "Heard a lot about you."

Sidney was latte-colored, attractive, early 40s, and wore a wedding band on her finger. The sneer hadn't seemed to work its way into Sidney's facial vocabulary. I figured a close family member was probably in law enforcement and that she respected him or her. Sidney looked at Ridge and rubbed her chin at him. He got the message, located the crumbs, and brushed them onto the carpet.

"So, who's the cop?" I asked Sidney to get proceedings underway. "Your mother or your father?"

The question both perplexed and amused her. "Mother. New York's finest. Desk sergeant these days. Do you mind if I ask what inspired that intuition?"

"Lucky guess."

"We checked you out, Cooper," Ridge said with a New York Queens accent. "You and the CIA have some history."

There was nothing I cared to add.

"Well, you're one of us, now," said Sidney. "Just so you know, all is forgiven."

I doubted it. I would use the agency's resources but wouldn't be working out of the office next to the john or anywhere else in this building. The CIA thing was temporary. I wanted as little as possible of the place rubbing off on me.

"So, let's get to it," Sidney proposed, settled a pair of bifocals on her nose, and opened a folder. "There's not much to go on. You know something of this already." She slid a couple of sheets of yellow paper across the table. "It's the original written mission profile proposed by Air Force Lieutenant Colonel Mark "Grizzly" Adams back in oh-five, a couple of years into Iraqi Freedom. Adams was Air Force Intelligence, running surveillance ops in a one-off RC-12 platform code-named "Horned Owl." Adams was a good operator, widely respected. And Horned Owl was a big deal, cutting-edge technology tasked with hunting for IEDs. Seems he heard some rumors about something else and wanted to investigate."

I scanned the documents. There wasn't much new information. The request didn't mention WMD. The plan was to run the Horned Owl, a platform based on a medium-sized twin turbo-prop aircraft, down the border and see if anything pinged. Mission denied, according to the red stamp across the front page. "Where is Adams these days?" I asked.

"Rotated out of Iraq in '06, completed a tour of the Pentagon, retired in 2009 and moved to Berlin. He'd been stationed there in the 90s and liked it enough to settle down there. Bought a bar. His son runs it now — name of Richard. We have contact details for both father and son."

I liked Berlin. Fun town. The Agency Visa would be taking a hit.

Next across the table, a wad of redacted yellow duplicate paper. Sidney informed me, tapping the stack, "This is the mission report from the Australian SAS unit that secured Al Asad airbase and also witnessed the convoy in question."

Operation Iraqi Freedom was a long time ago. I asked, "I guess these guys have also left the service?"

Ridge's turn. "Warrant Officer Tom Wilkes, the unit's leader, retired in oh-five, rank of captain. These days, he owns a demolition company called..." He flicked through some notes. "...Road-Runner Explosives and Demolition. Offices all over. Must be doing well."

"Wilkes has a sense of humor," Sidney ventured.

"Huh?" Merle Ridge seemed lost.

"*Road-Runner* explosives," she said. "Get it?"

Her partner needed a rock dropped on him.

"You know, the cartoon – *beep-beep!* How many times did the coyote try to blow up the road runner?"

"I was a Tom and Jerry kid," Ridge countered.

Davidson turned to me, possibly for help. "Obviously, you need to speak with Adams and Wilkes. I would start with Wilkes. He's in Vegas, taking down an old hotel. Rita Inglis has all the details. And that's it, I'm afraid," she concluded. "It's thin, I know, but it's a start. You have to get moving on this, Cooper. Everyone up there," Sidney pointed at the ceiling, "is on edge."

"Anything further on the whistleblower?" I asked.

"Not your remit, Cooper," Ridge interjected.

Sidney clarified, "Merle is handling that side of the investigation."

"So...what am I doing exactly?"

"You're to ascertain whether WMD did, in fact, find its way to Syria."

At last. Seemed to me no one wanted this spelled out. "Tell me about WMD. There are lots of different types, right? What exactly are we talking about here?"

Sidney opened a folder and lifted a page. "Back in Desert Storm, '90-91, Saddam was shown to have stocks of mustard gas and sarin, as well as the precursor chemicals to make more. At the conclusion of the war, all stocks were believed to have been destroyed. Mustard gas was terrible enough and used extensively by all sides in World War One. Sarin, which came along after that war, is a whole other ballgame — possibly the most toxic compound ever created. It's a nerve agent. A tiny amount will lead to seizures, shut down your breathing, and lead to cardiac arrest. It's so toxic that it's more likely to be transported in its binary form — one part methylphosphonyl difluoride, often called difluoro or DF for short, and one part isopropyl alcohol. It's the DF we're after. It's probably more than likely what was being transported by that convoy if, indeed, it was WMD. Rita Inglis will send you the relevant notes."

"Okay, so what about the whistleblower? That might be relevant to my end of the pineapple."

"Why?" asked Ridge.

"Because if the leaking of files and the sudden emergence of the existence of Iraqi WMD are linked, which seems more than probable, then we're looking for more than one person. A conspiracy," I said. The legal type, not the social media fake-lunar-landing type.

The vagrant seated beside Sidney said, "First thing I said when this thing broke."

There's one at every meeting.

A knock on the door interrupted proceedings.

"Excuse me, just had to pop my head in. Cooper! Hey, I heard you were in the house." A hand landed on my shoulder. "Watch out for this guy; he's a total A-hole."

I looked at the hand on my shoulder and followed the arm to its source. Bradley Chalmers. He smiled down at me with his whitened smile, neat, streaked, JFK hair, and color-enhanced contacts like we were old chums reacquainting. "Nice to see you, Cooper. I'm sure I'll be seeing a lot more of you. Remember what I told you," he said and patted me on the shoulder again. "A-hole." With that, he left.

Davidson looked at me as if to say, "That was odd."

I asked, "What does the A stand for? Almond? Aardvark...? I'm confused." That raised a smirk from Davidson, but I was thinking about Chalmers. He was fake-tanned trouble. "Where is Deputy Assistant Director Chalmers on the CIA ladder these days?" I asked.

"*Mister* Chalmers is no longer with the Agency," Davidson informed me. "Retired, though he does seem to spend quite a lot of time in these hallways. He's an advisor."

"Who does he advise?" I asked.

"Secretary of State Muirhead," said Ridge.

I felt sucker punched.

"You'll be reporting directly to her...via him."

Not a great day at the salt mine. I made my way to the parking lot where I'd slotted the Impala between a couple of shiny black spy wagons — Suburbans with tinted windows. Though the lot was still relatively full, it was pleasing to see the Chevy now parked on its own, the scratches and dents in the old girl's bodywork sending a clear message of back-the-fuck-off. However, the Impala's statement didn't seem to deter Chalmers, who was leaning back against the doorsill waiting for someone. Me.

"I figured this pile of shit would be yours," he said.

I approached the door with a key. Where's a handy Sig when you need it? In fact, I had one taped under the glove box. A CCTV camera sat on top of a pole directly opposite, daring me. Chalmers moved to one side.

"I can't tell you how excited I am to be working with you," he said.

I said nothing.

"It's like old times," he added. "Or even recent times."

I opened the door. Once in the driver's seat, that Sig would be within easy reach.

"How's Anna?" he asked. "Do I come up in conversation between you two?"

"Mention your name and she throws up in her mouth so, no. What do you want, Chalmers?"

"I want you to resolve this case because that will make me look good. Alternatively, there's always the chance that you'll die trying. Either way, win-win."

We were nose-to-nose.

"I'm one of the good guys, Cooper."

"You need to start flossing," I said, "Or maybe go see a doctor. Could be something dead inside you." I slipped in behind the wheel and closed the door. The Chevy rumbled into life with a twist of the key. I pressed the accelerator, and the tires squealed. Chalmers may have wanted to tell me something relevant or important, and I hadn't given him the chance. Too bad. There would be other opportunities. As I drove away, I glanced in the rear-view mirror and saw him breathing into his cupped hand, checking his breath. Okay, so I have a low fun threshold.

Reaching the beltway, I checked my phone for messages. Just one. It read, *Please call when you get out.*

"Hey," Anna chirped after the first ring, her voice coming through the car speakers. "How'd it go?"

"I'll be reporting to Bradley Chalmers."

"What? No! Are you serious?"

"Deadly."

"Is he still with the Agency?"

"No. Government advisor."

"So, what are you going to do?"

"I informed Arlen that my letter resigning from the OSI, effective immediately, would be on his desk in the morning. And he informed me that it won't be accepted."

"Is the case a big deal?"

We both knew the rules didn't allow me to say.

"Can you give me a hint?"

"I'll do better than that. I have to locate Willy Wonka's Chocolate Factory before Doctor Nasty steals Willy's secret recipe for a new chocolate bar."

"But you're coming home first, though, right?"

"I'll be there in 20 minutes, traffic permitting."

"I'm just leaving Andrews now."

"How come so late?" I asked.

"Been updating my section's case files. Paperwork. Team leader stuff."

It was a relief to us both that Anna was released from the CIA's Special Activities Center. Returned to OSI duties, she was officially back in the land of no longer formally deceased. It had occurred to me that she also had the right qualifications for my current case or mission, or whatever the CIA called it, with combat experience on the ground in Iraq and Syria. "Have you had dinner?" I asked her, but only because there was a good chance that chit-chat about the evening's menu wouldn't encompass bumping off American citizens who'd thrown in their lot with ISIS — her last mission.

"No. But I feel like something spicy."

"How about a double helping of innuendo."

"I left you something on the kitchen bench," she said. "See you when I get home."

We said goodbye several times each, like love-smitten teens not wanting to be the first to end the call.

Around twenty minutes later, I was standing at the kitchen bench looking down at a plastic stick with two lines on it attached by a white ribbon to a red chocolate heart: I'm pregnant, love Anna.

My significant other arrived home ten minutes after me. We kissed, and then I took off all her clothes, followed by mine, and carried her to the bed. I wanted to carry her fireman style over my shoulder, but in her condition, maybe not such a good idea. We had sex, and then we made love. There's a difference, according to Anna, but we both mostly seem to arrive at the station on the same train no matter what she cares to call it.

We lay in bed after and decided dinner would be peanut butter on toast. And then reality entered the love nest.

"Are you excited about my news?" Anna asked.

"You know I am," I replied.

"Tell me the truth."

"I'll admit it's a shock. But it's a good shock."

"So... What do you want?"

"A yacht and a private jet."

"You know what I mean. If we have this baby, what do you want it to be?"

"What do you mean if?"

"I'm barely five weeks pregnant. Things can go wrong."

"Nothing's going to go wrong," I reassured her.

"No, but...assuming you're right, what will you be hoping for?"

"A successful tennis pro," I said. "The good ones have yachts and private jets, which I'm sure he or she would let us borrow."

"You're starting to annoy me."

"Sorry," I said. "Look, I really don't care. Boy, girl, something in between, or something either side... There are way more options these days, according to the available pronouns."

"So, as long as it has all its fingers and toes. Me, too."

Anna, pregnant with a child... In truth, the concept had yet to land. It was not something I'd considered. Maybe she had, which was why she was pregnant. "Tell me the truth, Anna. Have you been putting little holes in the condoms?"

"We don't use condoms."

"Right." She had me there.

Both of us thought our own thoughts for a time. My thoughts were on fatherhood. I was up for it, but was I up *to* it? "There's no chance the test kit could be wrong?"

"I've done it three times – same result," Anna advised.

"But you're not asking for pickled pepper-flavored ice cream with a side order of garlic shrimp, so that makes me wonder..."

"That sounds yummy."

"Then it's official," I said. "What about the morning sickness?"

"Usually starts after six weeks. That's what the pregnancy websites say. Something to look forward to."

I let it all sink in some more.

"When do you leave?" Anna asked me, breaking the spell. "I sense you're leaving to go somewhere."

"Tomorrow, honey, though not before at least three orgasms, four if you're lucky." I spanked my own butt.

"Can you be serious, please?"

"You don't think I can do four?"

"Vin, I want you to put my mind at rest, but it sounds to me like you're just being evasive. Do you expect trouble?"

"I'm flying business class, so only if they get my drinks order wrong or lose my suitcase."

"Just stop." Anna sat up on the bed, kneeling by my side. "You do this when you're nervous."

"Do what?"

"Make unfunny jokes about everything."

Unfunny? Surely not. I looked into her eyes, resisting the temptation to let them slip to her smallish but rather perky breasts. The one on the left — Anna's left — carried the scar tissue of a skin graft, which covered a significant exit wound. I believed the wound had been fatal. Nothing subsequently convinced me otherwise. The plastic surgeon had done a remarkable job, but my heart skipped a beat every time I looked at the scar tissue. "I'm going to Europe to see a guy who bought a bar. I think I can say that much. At the moment, it's just fact-finding." I let my eyes fall.

"Focus!" she said, lifting my chin.

"Sorry, but you make it difficult," I told her honestly, "asking me to focus when you're sitting there naked."

"Can I ask what facts you're hoping to find?"

I reached down by the bed, found my pants and then my wallet, and extracted my new business card. "Here," I said, handing her the card. "This should put your mind at ease.

"U.S. Department of Agriculture?"

"The big guns," I told her.

"Doctor Vin Cooper, Ph.D. Biologist... What do you know about biology?"

"Seriously? *You're* asking me that?

"Vin."

"Okay, almost nothing, but I've been doing some research."

"Really. Do tell."

"Vulture bees. Heard of them?"

"I know I'm going to regret asking."

"Vulture Bees originated in Costa Rica. The *carnobacterium* in their gut allows them to feed on dead things and turn them into honey. Fascinating, right?"

"When did-"

"Research suggests that due to changes in weather patterns, mutant varieties of vulture bees are making their way across the world and turning up in cornfields instead of graveyards. I'm keen to see, for my peeps at the U.S. Department of Agriculture, if these little devils have migrated to Europe and what the implications are for U.S. corn farmers."

"As I was about to say, when did you learn this nonsense? And why?"

"Online. In the ten minutes or so before you arrived home. As for why — it's my cover. But if vulture bees don't do the trick, I've also studied the life cycle of the Candiru."

"Wonderful."

"The Candiru, otherwise known as the penis fish, can—"

"No need to expand." Anna climbed on top of me. "Things are going to have to change around here now. You know that, right?"

She had me pinned. "Do I tap out now or wait till the train pulls into the station?"

Anna scribed circles on my chest with her nails, "I have absolutely no idea what you're talking about."

Maybe not, but Little Coop was sure getting the message.

"How long will you be gone?" she inquired.

"Too long. A week, maybe two. What will you do while I'm away?"

"I don't know... Got any socks with holes in them? I'll just sit at home and darn 'em for you."

Anna positioned herself over me just so. I moved, and she sucked in a breath as I entered her. Her breasts were close, and they smelt of soap.

"None of my socks have holes," I rasped, "but I do have some undershorts that could use some help."

Her breathing was coming in short, sharp gasps. "Shut up, for fuck's sake. You're spoiling it."

I leaned on the kitchen bench, eating a slice of toast in a little patch of sunlight coming through the window, listening to the noises Anna made as she prepared for the day. Anna didn't know what I was doing, and I had no idea what case or cases she was working. We were together, but the sharing had boundaries. I felt that last night, and I was thinking about it again as I munched on the toast. She walked in, toweling her longish wet hair, dressed in the standard non-uniform of the OSI, khaki pants and a navy polo shirt that never seemed to look good on anyone except her.

"Morning," she said.

I toasted her with the toast.

"How do you feel? I didn't get much sleep last night."

"Me, either. You wouldn't leave me alone," I reminded her.

"Is that how you remember it?" Anna came into my arms, and we kissed. "Mmm... A peanut butter-flavored kiss." She opened her mouth for the rest of my toast, which I surrendered. "I see you have a bag packed. What are you taking?"

"Tanning lotion, swim fins, a face mask, and three Hawaiian shirts. Doh, gave it away. You should be an interrogator."

"I meant, hot or cold-weather clothes?"

"Both," I told her.

"And you think you'll be away a week?"

"Or two. You're fishing."

I couldn't say what I was working on. I couldn't even reveal to her *who* I was working for. "Tell me more about this team leader gig," I asked her. "Paperwork at midnight? Really?"

I looked into Anna's electric, greeny-blue, gold-flecked eyes, and she looked deep into mine.

"Your whites are bloodshot," she told me. "And you're starting to get bags."

I couldn't find a single comeback, damn it.

"Your case has something to do with this Wikileaks thing that's all over the news, doesn't it?" Anna said nonchalantly, moving to fill a glass of water at the sink. "WMD spirited into Syria under the Coalition's nose, and so forth?"

"What makes you think that?" I asked her.

"The timing. And, I don't know, it just feels like the usual kind of Hail Mary pass that always seems to come your way."

"You didn't answer my question," I said. "Which answers my question."

"If you tell me I have to back off my career because I'm pregnant... All I can say is, don't."

"The furthest thing from my mind," I said, but of course it wasn't.

"Let's just get past the first two months before we start thinking about what color to paint the spare room, shall we?"

"We don't have a spare room," I pointed out. "Unless you count the garage, which could do with a coat of paint. But sure, I get it. So, back to you and your current posting."

"I can absolutely guarantee you that I am not killing anyone today." Anna grinned. "Unless someone takes my parking spot. And I'm right about the WMD thing, aren't I?"

"I know you, Anna. There's stuff you're not telling me."

"And there's stuff you're not telling me. So that makes us even, doesn't it?"

She had a point. Maybe this was the only way it could be between us — secrets Uncle Sam demanded that we keep from each other. "In that case, given I'm going away for a while, can we have parting sex?" I asked her on the basis that if you don't ask, you don't get.

"Is there such a thing?"

"Yes. It can be quick."

Anna grinned. "Quicker than usual?" She checked her watch. "How long are you going to be away for?"

For the third time, "A week, maybe two."

To my surprise, Anna peeled off her polo shirt. "Okay, then, but you're on the clock, buddy. Don't just stand there; show me what you've got. I don't have all day."

There were things that needed to be said and questions that needed to be asked, but seeing Anna naked made the blood rush to a more urgent place that was pulsing and turning purple and wiped all that from my mind. But, of course, that was her intention.

LAS VEGAS, NEVADA

McCarran airport was crowded with the usual glut of hopefuls convinced they were just a lucky spin away from a bathroom with gold taps. I stopped at a slot, its seductive lights and bells promising said taps. The thing lied, of course, sucking my ten bucks and giving nothing back.

Outside, it was hot, even for Vegas. The heat caused the hairs in my nostrils to curl. I picked up the rental from the lot, drove the short distance to the Strip, and left it in a parking garage. I knew the city well enough, having spent time at Nellis Air Force Base, Vegas's next-door neighbor, on numerous occasions.

The sidewalks were crowded, even for Vegas. The squeeze was caused by the Flamingo Casino and Hotel, which had been roped off in preparation for its implosion, slowing Strip traffic both ways, pedestrian and vehicular, to a one-lane crawl. I noted that the Flamingo's iconic neon bouquet of red and orange vaginas, a feature of the Strip for decades, had been removed and probably stored to re-emerge to light the entrance of the casino's third iteration. I knew all this because the casino's mobbed-up Bugsy Siegal history, imminent demise, and ultimate rebirth were covered in *Hemispheres*, United's in-flight magazine. And I was interested to read about it because Road Runner Demolitions — Wilkes' gig post the SAS — was handling Flamingo's latest collapse.

I ducked under the warning tape and was immediately approached by two construction types wearing high-viz, hard hats, and wrap-around sunglasses. "I am sorry, sir. But this area is presently off-limits to the general public," said one of them, a shortish, deeply tanned Mexican with a roll-your-own cigarette defying gravity off his bottom lip.

I showed my OSI badge. "Not the general public," I countered. "Tom Wilkes. Is he on-site?"

"Do you have an appointment, sir?" asked the Mexican.

"Uncle Sam says yes," I told him.

The welcoming committee shared a glance and a shrug and led me to a portable office behind the hotel swimming pool, which had been drained and boarded over. The Mexican opened the door. Inside, it was cooler, the rattling air-con straining to bring down the temperature. Four desks were littered with papers, three of them occupied by the people running the show, their shirt pockets embroidered with Road-Runner signage, which included the bird. Two of the three were black. I cleverly deduced the one who wasn't would be Wilkes.

"Can I help you, sir?" asked one of the African Americans, looking up from a burger and Coke occupying his attention.

I showed the badge again. "Special Agent Vin Cooper for the guy leaning back in his chair."

The subject of my request was talking on his cell. He glanced at me and said, "I'll have to call you back later." He put the phone down and leaned forward. "We're getting close to pushing the big red button. You mind if we walk and talk?"

"Sure," I replied.

Wilkes stood and said, "Twenty minutes," to his colleagues, grabbing a spare hard hat and high-viz vest. "Put these on." He further explained, "Regulations."

I slipped into the safety gear and walked out into the Vegas oven.

Wilkes was in his early forties and cage-fighter fit. He walked with sure-footed purpose while still being light on his feet, retaining the quirk of career combat soldiers of continually checking all points of the compass as he moved, not consciously but habitually. His forearms were thick, his bare hands large and powerful — tear-the-armor-plate-off-an-Abrams-tank-without-tools powerful.

"I know you," he said with that unusual but not unpleasant Australian accent that takes some getting used to. "We've met, kinda."

I was pretty sure we hadn't.

"You wouldn't remember," he continued. "It was on a hilltop in the 'stan. Helicopter crash. You survived it. I was on the team that covered the rescue op – loaded you into another CH-47 that took a rocket up its arse soon after dust-off and crashed on the next hill over. I saw you hanging out the back of the helo, attached by a safety strap, swinging around like a practice tennis ball on a rubber band. Funniest thing I ever saw. A couple of my guys placed bets on you being chopped up by the rotors." Wilkes was grinning at the memory.

"I'm glad no one collected."

"You know how combat warps your funny bone."

I did, but this period of light entertainment, surviving two helicopter crashes in a single morning, had left me with nightmares and flying issues for years afterward.

Wilkes walked through an open doorway into a bare concrete space and headed for the stairwell. "Have to do a walkthrough, one of many checks," he explained. "We blow this turkey tonight. You gonna be around?"

"Maybe," I said.

Road Runner employees were checking det chord connections and explosive charges. Wilkes explained, "We have to drop this old girl straight and true. There's expensive real estate on three sides with anxious owners who I don't want any trouble from, if you get my drift."

"Any nerves about bodies that may turn up when you excavate the basement?"

"Nah, they were all removed long ago, or so I'm told. Dumped in Lake Mead."

I must have smiled because Wilkes added, "You think I'm joking. Start digging around in the sand in these parts and all kinds of skeletons turn up, and I'm not talking metaphors."

The floor was gutted — all carpet, fittings, furnishings, doors, plumbing, wiring, and glass removed in preparation for the implosion. The Flamingo was going to its grave a bare concrete shell.

"Actually, I've been expecting you," Wilkes offered. "Well, not you, but someone. Army intelligence, maybe, or CID, FBI, DoD... One of your acronyms. You say you're OSI, but I'm not and never have been in the U.S. Air Force, so more than likely, you're CIA."

"Nope — a biology expert currently working for the U.S. Department of Agriculture," I said.

Wilkes grinned. "Now I know you're a spook. Okay, well..." He ran his hand along a length of det cord and examined the charge nestling in a hole drilled into a concrete pillar. He was satisfied enough to move on without comment.

"Explosives weren't your specialty in the SAS," I said.

He shrugged. "I like loud noises."

"Let's talk about April 9th, 2003. Forget you wrote a MISREP, and I'll forget I read it," I said. "Tell me what happened that day and what you saw."

We climbed another flight of stairs.

"How much time you got?"

"Enough."

"So, who was your mystery guest on the convoy?" I asked him when he was done reminiscing. "There was no reference to him in the MISREP."

"No. At the time, we didn't know who he was or even if his presence was significant. But images of him were included in the report. They weren't provided to you?"

"No."

"I can't answer for that. The scope's record is tamper-proof."

"What was so special about him?"

"He stood out from the crowd — didn't look like an Iraqi. His skin glowed in the NVGs, so it had to be bleached white. And his eyes were black pits in a face that appeared to phosphoresce. Kinda creepy."

"Was he in a MOPP suit, too?"

"Yeah, but hood off."

"You got any photographs of that night?"

"No."

"Sure you do."

"That would be illegal," Wilkes said.

"The people I work for wouldn't have it any other way."

Wilkes considered the request for a moment and then pulled out his cell. "You don't know where you saw these."

"You have my word as an employee of an agency that doesn't feel good about itself unless it's breaking the law. I'm talking about the U.S. Department of Agriculture. Show me what you've got."

Wilkes swiped his phone a couple more times. " I kept these because the whole incident was unusual and probably the reason why we were in Iraq at all."

He passed me his phone, and I reviewed several photos of the convoy.

"And you included these images in your report?" I asked.

"Like I said, the scope was tamper-proof, but I can't speak for the record."

Data at the base of the pics placed the camera 623 meters from the subject matter, a line of heavy vehicles stopped in the desert.

Closeups captured men wearing full pressurized HAZMAT suits, Iraqi Republican Guards in defensive perimeter positions, and other guards with AKs in chemical fighting suits. All that, to my mind, pretty much confirmed the presence of WMD. Swiping right, I saw the photo of a man whose face seemed to light the way like a spotlight, with two deep black holes where his eyes should be.

Wilkes took back his phone and pulled up another photo. "A few years later, I'm pretty sure I saw him again. This was taken at Al Asad. A big man — at least six-four, 240 pounds, give or take."

The photo showed a man in his mid to late 40s walking around in the bright Iraqi sunshine, skin fluorescing like a tube light. He wore dark glasses and utilities with a camouflage pattern that wasn't American; the patches on his shoulder and chest were also unfamiliar.

Wilkes said, "Later, I came across him without those glasses. His eyes were pink. Like a big white freaky rabbit. Hard not to stare."

"You're certain it's the same guy from the convoy?"

"You tell me? They don't pop blokes like this out of a mold. His name is Andre Niemiec. I inquired. When this was taken, he was a lieutenant colonel in the Polish Army. So, I asked myself, what's a Polish colonel doing on a suspicious enemy convoy racing for the Syrian border?"

"What answer did you come up with?"

"Fuck knows," he said.

Good question, useless answer. "You didn't raise any red flags at the time?"

"It was a fair while after the convoy incident. And the guy could just deny he was there. So, no."

"You said you thought one of the trucks had a flat."

"Yep."

"You also said you thought the Iraqis looked like they were panicking."

"Yes."

"So, maybe their cargo sprung a leak?" I suggested

"Same thing occurred to us at the time. That was all in my MISREP. CENTCOM was fully aware. I assumed a specialty WMD team would turn up to take soil samples, but as far as I know, they never turned up."

"Did you or your men discuss this incident with anyone?"

"Just amongst ourselves."

"You're sure about that?"

"The SAS doesn't gossip."

"How long did you stay at Al Asad?"

"A few days. We turned the base over to your blokes, the U.S. Army 3rd ACR, after we secured the place. There was a rumor doing the rounds. Something about the convoy and a firefight with a Kurdish patrol. One of them was supposedly killed following exposure to WMD."

"Anyone follow up on it?"

"Not that I know of. Like I said, we moved out shortly after the Cav' moved in."

"You remember any details?"

"About the Kurds taking on that convoy? Not really. I heard about it from a U.S. Marines sergeant attached to the 3rd Cav. He heard it from a Kurdish fighter scouting for them. I put it down to scuttlebutt."

"You remember the Kurd's name?"

Wilkes searched his memory. "Nope."

"How about the sergeant's."

"Fredricks, Fredericks...something like that."

"First name?"

Wilkes shook his head. "Sorry."

"Unit?"

"Bravo company rings a bell."

I made a mental note.

"What about Niemiec? Did you come to any conclusions about his presence in the convoy?"

"We concluded well after the event that the guy was probably on some kind of black ops assignment. All kinds of weird shit goes down in a war, right? No doubt you've been involved in some of it yourself. I know I have."

No comment.

"I got nothing else to add about that night," Wilkes told me. "And I only saw this Niemiec bloke once at Al Asad."

"But you said you asked around about him."

"Yeah. When you look like that, it tends to draw attention. Anyway, I never came across anyone who actually served with the guy. According to some Poles I shared a transit flight with, Niemiec came and went to Al Asad several times a year. He was never in-country on a standard deployment rotation. He was a mystery to his own people."

"How'd you end up with these personal pics?" I asked.

"Took photos of the scope's screen," Wilkes replied. "You gonna arrest me?"

"I'll think about it. How long were you involved in Iraqi Freedom?"

"I did three more tours hunting insurgents. On my last, I got caught up in the Battle of Fallujah. Other than that, nothing further to report."

Niemiec. I asked him to spell it. At least I had a name to follow up on. "Can you send me those photos?" I handed him my card.

Wilkes scanned it as his fingers worked his phone screen. "Biologist? Bullshit." After a moment, he said, "Photos sent, by the way. What do you do for them — the Department of Agriculture?"

My phone *pinged*. "World expert on vulture bees."

"Whatever the fuck they are. Listen, why don't you hang around?" Wilkes suggested. "We're gonna make some noise with this building at midnight, and then we're gonna go out and show the new Yanks we've employed how to get seriously fuckin' rat-arsed."

Aussies — my kind of people.

Road Runner Demolitions blew the building on schedule, and it came down straight. I made it back to my hotel seriously fucked as the sky was turning pink with the dawn. That much I recall. I slept through the 8am wake-up call, the phone alarm, and the concierge banging on the door. It was a presence in the room that ultimately raised me from the dead.

"You missed your flight."

Rita Inglis's face was in my face. I opened a crusty eye and sat up, which made the hammers in my head angry.

"Your profile says you drink too much," she continued.

"What's too much?"

"This," she said, gesturing at me.

"What are you doing here?" I asked.

"It's two in the afternoon."

"So?"

"You're booked on a plane to Berlin out of LAX at 8pm. You're already cleared through customs, but you have a connecting flight, and it leaves in...," she checked her watch, "fifty-eight minutes."

"I like you, Rita, but this is not how I work."

"And I like you, too. But you work for the Central Intelligence Agency; it doesn't work for you."

Touché.

"Remind me," I said. "What's in Berlin?"

"Not what, who. Retired Air Force Colonel Mark Adams. Horned Owl, RC-12. Ring any bells?"

No, but those hammers were denting the backs of my eyeballs.

"Take a shower and a handful of Motril. I'll drive you to the airport."

A short while later, we pulled into McCarran Departures. As I grabbed my bag from the rear seat, she said, "You have employment waiting for you at Sands Defense & Aerospace. For now." Her tone, coupled with a slight tilt of the head, conveyed to me elegantly how quickly that job would evaporate if I screwed up. "Neither of us wants that, but you have to know this job, the one for your country, is more important."

I really don't like the CIA. They know too much.

"And maybe your next gig isn't such a great lily pad for you to be jumping onto anyway. Could end up being quicksand."

I've never liked mixed metaphors.

Inglis continued, "Senate oversight committee just killed one of their major programs. The stock price is looking shaky."

"Is there a tail on me?" I asked, ignoring the investment advice.

"No, not technically."

"So, no, but yes?"

"No one is following you, but I was sent to keep an eye on you."

"By who?"

"The Secretary of State."

In other words, Chalmers.

Inglis continued, "The leaks, the WMD, the risk of further potential damage to America's reputation... People are nervous and impatient."

"Then are they sure they have the right person for the job?"

"Well, actually, the only person who thinks you're right for it is the DoD's new case management AI, and that's not a person."

"You tell the algorithm that if I think my own country is spying on me, I'm likely to go random."

"You can't blame the folks upstairs, Vin. Your record says you have a reputation for getting things done the hard way. I had to fly across the country to roust you out of bed, so..."

Point made.

Inglis glanced at the departure board behind the glass. "Go," she advised. "You're out of time."

I pulled up an image on my phone and pressed send. Inglis's phone *pinged*. "Take a look," I said.

"That's not a Company phone," she said immediately, nodding at the iPhone in my hand.

"Do you blame me?"

"As I informed you, using a private phone while working a case is against the rules."

"So, lodge a complaint with HR."

Inglis smiled. "Have your phone checked for spyware, Vin. And do it weekly. We all do."

Inglis produced her cell and performed a thumb dance on the screen. "So, who's this?" she asked.

"His name is Andre Niemiec. The photo was taken during the early days of Iraqi Freedom. He's wearing the uniform of a light colonel in the Polish Army."

"And?"

"You tell me. Plane to catch." I flashed Inglis a grin, pulled the handle on my suitcase, and left her behind as I wheeled into a queue of tired-looking Vegas tourists taking themselves and their maxed-out credit cards home to New York. I had some time to kill before boarding, so I called Anna.

"Hey," she said, picking up just as an announcement came over the PA warning people not to leave their bags unattended. "Where are you? Which airport?"

"McCarran."

"Vegas. You coming or going?"

"Going."

"Anything to report?"

"Honey," I reminded her. "You know the rules."

"The Agency's rules?"

"No, Vegas rules. What goes on tour, and so forth." I sensed Anna's eye roll in the dead air that followed. "Sorry," I said.

"No, you're not.

"I couldn't resist."

"Please try to next time."

"I met a guy who gave me a name, and now I'm going to Europe to meet another guy who'll give me another name, with luck. Plane leaves tonight."

"So you'll be catching a flight to JKF."

"Oh, you're good," I told her.

"Bon voyage. There's nothing at home for dinner anyway," she said. "Be careful, won't you."

"Nothing to be careful about."

"We both know you'll find something, and then ignore the careful."

"How about you?" I asked her. "Anything going on in your world today, aside from the biological miracle taking place within your reproductive organs?"

"Oh my god – more romance from Romeo."

To get some privacy, I turned away from a couple wandering into my space. "I read once that pregnant women get horny. Do you want me to talk dirty to you? I have a few minutes to spare."

"Call me when you get to wherever it is you're going."

"Is that a no, then?"

"I love you, Vin. Occasionally."

BERLIN, GERMANY

I caught CNN on the plane. The Wikileaks-Iraqi WMD coverup still had its teeth in the news cycle, but no new information had been dredged up. I could tell, though, that journalists believed there was more to see here if only they kept digging, which they intended to keep on doing. What kind of feeding frenzy would erupt if the image on Wilkes' phone of a senior Polish officer accompanying that convoy found its way onto an editor's desk? The thought raised a smirk. There is a point in everyone's life when government insistence on controlling the narrative begins to jar. That's when it's time to join Sands.

The flight in business class beat the hell out of a jump seat in a C-17, my former mode of intercontinental air travel. And it starts at the airport. The way airlines funnel passengers down a windowless steel box into a metal cylinder where booze, movies, and food await, you can almost believe that you never left the ground if you don't look out the window. I didn't. Those consecutive helicopter crashes that I'd survived back in the 'stan invoked nightmares of scorpion-clawed knife-wielding Islamists. I no longer endured the shakes, the sweats, and the hyperventilating that came with flying, but Wilkes had brought the memory of the dual incidents into the present, so why poke the bear? Let the airline alter reality. And so, 11 hours, three movies, and a power nap later, I stepped out of the cylinder and found myself, as if by magic, on the other side of the world, in Berlin.

As I said, I like Berlin. Like all great cities, it has multiple personality syndrome, being many things to many people. Or many things to the individual, depending on the individual's mood. Wandering along the *Kurfürstenstraße*, counting down the numbers to the bar owned by retired Air Force Lieutenant Colonel Mark "Grizzly" Adams and his son, the mood wears, among other items, bright pink plastic or red leather hot pants, white thigh-high boots, and tank tops. Two large women leaning against a sex shop, wearing false eyelashes long enough to comb their bangs, asked me if I'd be interested in a threesome. Perhaps just spinning the roulette wheel, they didn't wait for an answer and immediately asked the next man to come along, a balding older businessman, the same question. Maybe they just knew their customer when they saw him. A little further down the road, I arrived at *Die Barenumarmung* (or, in English, The Bear Hug — cute) and walked into the bar. It was around 1600hrs and maybe 60 degrees. Cold for this time of year. The sky was low and gray, the breeze chilling. But the three young women perched on stools, huddling quietly beneath the single element of an infrared wall heater, still wore next to nothing. One of them sat up as I passed and gave me "the look," the one that asks your wallet if it would care for a little stress relief. I said no thanks, and my wallet and I kept moving. A few lone customers drank at the polished concrete bar or occupied red, vinyl-lined booths conversing with their drinks. The place projected desolation. Maybe once the night came down, when the sound system began to pump and the neon signs flashed some warmth, it would be a different story.

A bartender in his late twenties with a circus mustache waxed into spirals leaned on the bar, doing a crossword. He saw me, straightened, and asked, *"Kann ich dir etwas bringen?"*

I don't speak German, but "Can I get you a drink?" is a universal language. "No, thanks," I replied, showing him my OSI badge. "Mark Adams. He around?"

"Is he in some kinda trouble?" the barman asked, his English perfect.

"Not from me., I said. "You must be Richard."

"Ricky, these days. The old man lives in an apartment not far from here. I guess I'll have to give you the address." He guessed right. I passed him a coaster, and he sketched a mud map. "First turn on your left. Two blocks down, take a right and walk another two blocks. I'll tell him you're coming. You're a long way from home. Must be important."

"Outstanding parking fines," I told him.

"Really?" he said in disbelief. "How many?"

"Three."

"You're joking. Come all this way for that?"

I shrugged. "Line item in some spreadsheet," and added the universal excuse for unreasonableness: "Bureaucrats."

"Right."

I left the bar, hurried along by a glance of bored disinterest from the girls under the heater.

There was not much to see on the Kurfürstenstraße that I hadn't seen in countless other redlight districts, daylight stripping all the faux excitement away so that only thin desperation remains, the bones of it watered-down drinks, petty crime, drugs, and $20 blow jobs. But those two blocks right and two blocks back revealed a spacious, clean world of modern concrete, glass, and steel apartment blocks with hanging gardens and high-end security systems. I buzzed Mark Adams's apartment.

"Hello?" said a voice through the speaker beyond the entranceway.

"Special Agent Vin Cooper, OSI," I replied.

The heavy glass doors *clicked*, and I pushed into the soulless foyer. The lift opened, and a stately German dowager in a fitted leather jacket stepped out. Giant hanging gold baubles stretched her fleshy earlobes. Her chihuahua, wearing a Swarovski collar carried in a pink leather Channel-branded bag, yapped at me. The dowager looked straight through me and kept going.

Five minutes later, I was admiring the district views beyond the weir-edge pool from the building's penthouse. The colonel was in his 60s but looked younger — tall with neat, gray hair and plenty of it, clear-eyed, and fit. He placed a glass of Jägermeister in my hand, an unexpected accompaniment to the usual introductions. Not my favorite drink, but I've had worse. I sipped it. Nope, maybe not.

"So," Grizzly Adams asked, "What can I do you for? Ricky called ahead and said something about parking fines. Kids these days will believe anything."

I hadn't come for small talk. "Back in Iraqi Freedom days, you were the CC of a unit operating a modified RC-12D called "Horned Owl. You ever fly any missions along the border with Syria?"

"Oh, right," he said. "The HO is still a classified asset. How do I know you've got the clearance to hear the answers to your questions?"

"Call the office of the Secretary of State," I said, "ask to speak with Dorothy Muirhead and tell her to get the Secretary of the Air Force on the line. After the SecAF has insulted you a bunch of times for wasting his time, he'll verify my bona fides. And then I'll come back."

"Okay...," Adams said, deciding not to go down that route. "Mind if I take a closer look at your badge?"

He asked, and I provided.

Adams put a pair of glasses on the end of his nose, bifocaled the badge into view for a few moments, and then handed it back, satisfied. "After thirty years on the 'Strasse, I can spot a fake at fifty paces. I reckon you're legit. You want a refresher?" He motioned at my glass.

"I'm good," I said, the original pour more or less still intact.

"Sit," Adams commanded like he was still in uniform. I settled on a white leather sofa that smelled like a luxury car's interior. "Go ahead and ask." He leaned forward and splashed a generous additional finger into my glass anyway, trying to get rid of the stuff, maybe.

I asked again, "Tell me about Horned Owl. What was it?"

"A flying ground-penetrating radar platform. The only one we had at the time. An expensive turkey kitted out to find sub-terranean magnetic anomalies. We renamed it the Ray Charles for reasons you can probably guess. After taking delivery, we put HO to the test on a known graveyard of Gulf War I tanks, maybe close to a hundred Iraqi T-72s buried under the sand. We got nothing. Other times, the system would go crazy, needles would jump, and sensors would sound off. Ghost returns, mostly."

"It can't have been that useless. In '04, you recommended the platform for a particular mission."

"By then, Ray had been upgraded some and stumbled around in the dark a little less. Which mission are you talking about? I put in quite a few mission requests."

"You wanted to run the Horned Owl along the Iraq-Syria border sometime in August 2003."

"That one. Right."

"Why?"

"I'm sure you already know. There were rumors that Saddam had buried his WMD there. There were many rumors about WMD."

"Where did you first hear this rumor in particular?"

"It was scuttlebutt doing the rounds at Al Asad. The Kurds also talked about it, and I met some Bedouins at a temporary strip up in the north who swore on the graves of their mothers... Anyway, mission denied."

"Why?"

"Why was it denied? Risk minimization?"

"Care to expand?"

"What if we did turn up something, and it was buried on the wrong side of the border? What then? What does the Commander-in-Chief do about it? If Iraqi Freedom was all about ridding the world of Saddam's WMD, do Coalition forces pivot, head north and invade Syria? Sometimes, it's best not to know."

"You weren't interested in satisfying your curiosity and flying the mission anyway?"

"Nope, not possible. The Horned Owl was considered a National Asset — same league as Air Force One. We lived in a fishbowl with that aircraft. One particular Air Force two-star used to pay us regular visits just to hang out and have photos taken with the HO for his personal album."

"And you never considered diverting from an approved mission?"

"I never took the HO anywhere it wasn't approved to go. Even if I wanted to, that wouldn't have been possible. The missions we flew were fine-tuned up the wazoo and down to a gnat's knuckle."

"You been following this Wikileaks thing?" I asked.

"I live in Berlin, not under a rock, Special Agent."

The front door burst open, and a woman of around 30 blew in: tall, Asian, possibly Vietnamese, hair dyed white, and wearing a miniskirt so short it barely covered Hawaii. Her legs were long and slender, the way I liked them. She breezed over to Adams, leaned over him, kissed him on the forehead, and said, *"Oh, es ist so kalt do draußen! Brrr."*

"Then put some clothes on if you're cold," Adams suggested with half a smile at me. "Joy, honey, we have a guest. From America."

"More clothes would spoil the look, don't you think?" she asked Adams, ignoring the guest, twirling, pouting, and bending over just far enough to show me Waikiki Beach.

I agreed with her. Minimalism had my vote.

"You're not out there competing, Joy. Not anymore."

"Ich geha nur duschen," she said. And then to me, on her way out of the room, "Hello, goodbye, guest from America."

"'Bye," I said.

"She's taking a shower," Adams translated with a sloppy grin and added, "What can I tell ya — life on the Strasse. You speak German?" he asked me.

"No."

"You're missing out."

That was hard to argue with. "So, Wikileaks," I said to get us both back to why I was here, "What's your take? Did we *knowingly* turn a blind eye to Saddam's WMD being spirited away?"

"We on or off the record?"

"The interview's over," I lied, sipping the Jäger and regretting it immediately.

"I don't know what I can and can't say to you," he said, repeating his opening gambit.

I went broad. "Iraqi Freedom was pitched on the back of ridding Saddam of his WMD. We didn't find any."

"Who says?" Adams jumped in.

"What I know is that we failed to find any. You saying we did?"

"Sorry, gotta stop there."

"Are you saying that we did find WMD, and you know that?"

"Like I said, I don't know what you're cleared to know."

"We failed to turn up any WMD after all kinds of intelligence guarantees that it was here. Looked like we'd concocted a reason to invade. Coalition partners like Britain and Australia also looked either misled or misleading or both. There were demonstrations. Governments fell. Insurgencies, civil wars, bombings, ISIS..." I was hearing myself talk, and what I heard myself describing was a shit show of show-stopping shit. I nevertheless continued. "This is, if we did find WMD, it would have been paraded around like the Second Coming."

"If you say so, Agent Cooper. Is there a question in your little speech somewhere?"

"If there were chemical and or biological weapons in Iraq, and we uncovered them, what possible reason could there have been for not announcing it?"

The colonel sneered a half smile. "Like I said, you know less than you should to be asking these questions, Special Agent. It's not my place to brief you."

"Then go hypothetical," I said.

Adams attempted to pour himself another Jägermeister and found the bottle empty. "You want that?" he asked, motioning at my glass. I handed it to him, and he poured the contents into his. "Waste not, want not, as my Grammy used to say. You been in a war, son?"

Several. "Yes."

"Seen combat?"

"Some."

"Well, then you know war is never neat. We made mistakes in Iraq, some of which kicked off the insurgency, and other mistakes poured gasoline on it. If we announced to the world that we'd found WMD, goes without saying the bad guys would've assumed there's more to be found. What would the insurgents have done to get their hands on it first? More than that, I won't say."

Did I buy that? I wasn't sure.

From somewhere close by, a voice called out, *"Ist er noch hier? Kommst du rein?"*

"Give me a moment." Grizzly called out, and then to me, "Joy wants to know if you're still here and, if not, am I coming to join her?"

I heard the shower begin to run.

"Well..." The colonel slapped his knees with his hands, a show of finality. "I don't know what else I can tell you and you know I've got somewhere else to be."

On cue, Joy called out something from the bathroom that I assumed was, "You coming?"

Adams stood, question time at an end.

"You did a tour of the Pentagon after Iraqi Freedom," I continued anyway.

"It's in my service record. Air Force Intelligence. Pushing paper around mostly. Not much to talk about there. Not much I *can* talk about. So..."

I stood and pulled my phone, and it opened on a pre-loaded photo. "Do you know this man?"

Adams's eyes slid across the screen like an ice skater with no grip. "No. Should I? Who is it?"

"A colonel in the Polish army," I replied. "Name of Andre Niemiec."

He barely glanced at the image. "No...got nothing for you, I'm afraid." He moved towards the door. "Sorry, I can't be of more help."

"Thank you for your time," I replied.

Joy made an appearance in a white towel little bigger than a washrag. "You coming?"

The words were for Adams, but she looked at me when she said them. She turned and walked away on tippy toes. My libido followed her out.

Adams cleared his throat.

"If I have more questions...?"

"Like I said, I think I've told you everything."

"Did you already tell me that?" I said as he herded me over the threshold.

'I did." Adams smiled pleasantly. *"Auf wiedersehen,"* and the door swung closed a little too fast.

I paused for a moment on the landing to process. Adams wanted me double-timing out of there. The invitation from Joy was reason enough, but his son had given him prior warning of my impending arrival. Adams could have worked out that little scene with his girlfriend beforehand. And his reaction to the photo of Niemiec had been unlikely to say the least. You don't see a specimen like Niemiec every day of the week. Even if you don't know him — in fact, *especially* if you don't know him — you're going to want to take a second look. In my line of work, you get a sense of when someone is lying, and what I knew for sure was that Lieutenant Colonel Mark Adams knew Colonel Niemiec.

I went to another bar on the Kurfürstenstraße to get the taste of Jägermeister out of my mouth. There were plenty of bars to choose from. I walked into "Moochers," a bar with lounges and modern décor and lighting that suggested it might serve a superior class of liquor. There was no Glen Keith that I could see, but there was a bottle of The Irishmans Single Malt sitting up there on the shelf behind the counter, all on its lonesome and two-thirds-full. I put the bottle on the Agency's card and drank my way through it while I noodled some thoughts on a napkin. But I drank too much, and the noodling turned into aimless boxes, stars, and spirals, mostly. The failure to find WMD in Iraq — the U.S. Administration had copped so much embarrassment and flak over it back in the day. I often wondered why the hell a CIA Special Ops Centre team wasn't tasked to salt a few gallons of WMD here and there if just to get the world off the president's back. Maybe such a plan had been suggested. Maybe the damage a conspiracy like that could do if the truth ever leaked out shelved it. Or just maybe there was another reason, the one put forward by Colonel Adams: that the Administration didn't want insurgents racing to find a cache of the stuff. But if there was no WMD, there was no race, and therefore no problem.

An interesting booze-fueled pile of nonsense but entertaining to think about. Three or four drinks later, nothing was any clearer. In fact, things were getting pleasantly hazy. I put a tip on the low table in front of my lounge — time to go.

"Gehst du weg? Ich hatte gehofft, Sie könnten mir einen drink anbieten?"

A woman was standing beside me. She was tall, had dark eye shadow to make her blue eyes pop, and medium-length golden hair that reminded me of a summer's day. She wore Swarovski-studded three-inch heels that made me think of a chihuahua in a pink handbag, and a tight, below-the-knee sky-blue sheath that matched the color of her eyes and revealed lean athletic shoulders, the barest hint of underwear, and all the right kind of bumps and mounds. A small black purse slung around her shoulders on a gold chain completed the ensemble. There wasn't much to the ensemble.

"Sorry," I said as I tried to align my eyeballs. "I don't speak German."

She switched to English. "I said I would like to buy a drink from you."

We looked at each other for what seemed a while, the cogs in my brain refusing to engage, the synchro out of sync. *Buy a drink from me?* "You'd like me to buy you a drink?" I offered to help clear things up.

"No." She gestured at the bottle of Irishman's. "This is what I drink, but the barman says you have bought it all, and so I ask to buy a drink from you... Before nothing is left." She produced a glass with rocks and added in perfectly mangled English, "Here, in case the answer from you is yes."

I pushed those mindless scribbles aside. "Sure," I said and poured the woman a double shot.

"How much is this?"

"On the house."

"Oh, very generous. Thank you." The woman said. She returned to the bar and took a seat.

I kept an eye on her because I'm a guy, and she definitely wasn't. She played with her phone, sipped the drink, glanced hopefully at the entrance as a couple of patrons entered, sipped some more, went back to her phone, toyed with it again, and then finished off the scotch. Her manner went from impatient to pissed. An empty glass was my cue. I went over to her with the bottle. "Same again?"

"Oh! Thank you, but no thank you. I have to leave."

"Some idiot stood you up." I could read the tea leaves.

"Yes." She produced a faint smile. "This dating thing on the phone. I hate it. Makes you feel like shit."

I wondered if the fool who left her waiting knew what he was missing out on. I waved the bottle over her glass. "Last chance..."

"Well...okay. Just a little bit."

I splashed the rocks but didn't drown them.

"And you? Are you waiting for someone?"

"No. Random bar for a not-so-random drink."

She smiled. "You are American."

Some women just know.

"The accent. You sound like an American movie person."

Maybe a compliment and maybe not — characters like Alvin the Chipmunk are in the movies, too.

"You look like a soldier."

"What makes you say that?"

"You have short hair, and you seem — I don't know — tough. Many American soldiers come to Berlin to see it because of the war."

"My grandfather came to Berlin in '45. But he wasn't a grandfather back then."

"There – you see? And you? What is your work? Soldier?"

"No, biologist. I work with bees."

"I would not have guessed this."

"How about you? What do you do?"

"I teach Pilates. I have a studio near here."

A Pilates instructor. Well, that figured. The woman certainly had one hell of a core.

She continued, "I am in the...I do not know how to say it in English, *der gesundheitszustand* industry."

I had no idea what that was.

My impromptu drinking buddy motioned at the barman for assistance, and they exchanged some words.

"She says she's in the wellness industry," he said and left us to go polish some more glasses.

"I am a...," she had to think about it, "...*die* Wellness consultant."

I had no idea what a wellness consultant might be. In my book, you're sick if you have a temperature and fever. When you don't, you're well. When you're well, do you need a consultant to tell you as much and give you a bill? I wisely kept these thoughts to myself.

"What is your name?"

"Vin," I informed her.

"Gisela." She held out her hand to shake. I took it. Her skin was cool and dry, the grip firm and confident. Gisela didn't seem the type that needed to lean on a dating app.

"Well, Gisela," I said, "nice to meet you, but now it's time for me to go."

"You are leaving?"

"Big day tomorrow," I explained as I slid off the stool. "You take the bottle."

"*Danke.*"

I placed it on the bar.

"So now it is my turn to play barman," Gisela said. "I offer *you* a drink, Vin. On the house, of course."

Gisela grinned, shifted on the stool, and held the lip of the bottle over my glass, an arch in one perfect eyebrow seeming to offer a challenge. She then recrossed her legs. An innocent movement, as movements usually go, but she made it seem both sensual and suggestive. Did any of that drive my capitulation? Maybe. "What the hell," I said and gave her a nod.

Gisela poured and we touched glasses.

I woke the following morning, sensing unexpected movement, and opened an eye in time to see a perfect ass wriggle into gossamer panties. The sheath was slipped on next, and then the woman turned to face me, held her hair back, bent down, and kissed me on the cheek.

"Auf weidersehen," she whispered. Another kiss and she was gone.

My mind was heavy with an unfamiliar fog, the previous evening a total blank. I remembered interviewing Colonel Adams. Then what? Some of the pieces fell into place, others didn't. I went to a bar. There was a woman. The woman just now. More memory shards returned. Her name was Gisela. Now that I thought about it, I could picture her pushing me back down onto the bed and then climbing on top. The memory came to me like I was a third person in the room, watching. Was I imagining the experience? A tight blue dress. It came off, pulled up and over her head. No bra. The memory stirred something even now. Damn, the imagination is a dangerous thing.

And then, as I reviewed these shards of the night before, the memory of seeing two lines on a certain pregnancy tester interjected. "Oh, fuck," I said under my breath. I got out of bed and looked out the window. The skyline was obscured by rain, and the street was a long way down, but what I could see was as unfamiliar as the room's décor. In short, this wasn't my hotel. My clothes were in a pile on the floor. I went through the pockets. My private phone was there, the Agency cell locked away with the laptop in a room safe at the Marriot. Wallet, check. Credit cards — all present and accounted for. A hundred and fifty emergency euros, give or take, were still tucked into the billfold. Gisela wasn't a thief. So, what was she? Before Anna walked into my life, I did okay with the ladies. But I'm no Brad Pitt; more like Jimmy Pitt, Brad's familiar but not so good-looking cousin. I went to the bathroom and ran the shower. I'd been picked up by a beautiful woman I'd never met before in a bar I'd never been to before and had sex I couldn't remember. There wasn't much right with that picture.

I turned off the shower, picked up my phone, and dialed Rita Inglis. It was just after 0800 in Berlin. The phone almost rang out before she picked up.

"Yes?" inquired a voice, sleep-addled.

"It's Cooper."

"I know. You're in my address book. Do you know what time it is in DC?"

"Just after two in the morning. Sorry, by the way."

"Why are you calling? Before you answer, remember this phone – this line – is unsecured."

"I need a blood test."

"For you?"

No, for my pet hamster. "Yes. For me."

"You're in Berlin?"

"Not sure," I replied.

"Please, it's too early — or late — for games."

"I think I'm in Berlin, but I'm not 100 percent certain. It's raining out and misty."

"Has the uncertainty about your location got something to do with the blood test?"

"Yes," I confirmed. "I woke up in a hotel room. It's not my room. I'm pretty sure it's not my hotel. I'm pretty sure I've been drugged. A woman is involved."

"Okay," Inglis said, relieved, like this was nothing new, like this happened every other day to folks in the CIA.

"I will text you the contact details of a clinic. If you haven't showered, don't. Maybe they can harvest some worthwhile DNA. Do you feel drowsy?"

I yawned. "Yes."

"Have blanks in your memory?"

I couldn't remember hitting a home run with Gisela, assuming that's what happened when we were both naked beneath the covers, which I was pretty sure had been our sleeping arrangements. I glanced at myself in the mirror. Yep, naked. "Yes."

"Sounds like you've been roofied. I'll brief the clinic. You just turn up and they'll do the rest." The phone *pinged* with a text. Inglis continued, "Meanwhile, I've sent you some information on your Polish colonel. Interesting character. You might like to call me after you've read through the intel, but do me a favor – during business hours in DC and on a secure line."

The call ended. I got dressed and rode the elevator to the lobby. Logos here and there told me I was in the Hilton. Some passengers who rode the elevator with me spoke German, which was promising. I walked into the foyer, where an interactive information panel's home screen presented a Berlin Hilton logo. Relief — at least I hadn't been renditioned to some god-forsaken place, like a Best Western.

The clinic was a short Uber ride away. I showed the attendant at the front desk my ID. In exchange, a technician took blood, and Little Coop got a tickle under the chin with a swab. The odd adventure with Gisela thus bookended, I took another Uber to the Marriot.

Entering my room, I saw a brown envelope had been slipped under the door. I knew what it contained before opening it, but tore it open anyway. Five color prints. No note. The photos were as X-rated as any I'd seen. Gisela had a killer body. She knew what to do with it, and the images showed she was doing it to me.

Around twenty minutes later, showered and no longer drowsy, I was sitting on the bed in my room with the Agency cell, wondering who had honey-trapped me with Gisela and why, as in, why bother? Before Anna's return, I'd have shrugged this off and even, perhaps, considered it a type of performance bonus. But with Anna back on the scene and cooking up a kid for us, not so much. In fact, I was pissed. Was it connected to this case? If so, that pared the suspects down substantially. It had nothing to do with Wilkes, of that I was sure. The only other obvious contender was Colonel Adams, but I couldn't see his angle, either.

I fired up the Agency's phone, and it beeped with the arrival of two emails – one from the "Human Resources Department" at Langley welcoming me to the Central Intelligence Agency, "an equal opportunities employer," which I took to mean the Agency fucked everyone over equally, and the other from Rita Inglis — files concerning Andre Niemiec. I sent the junk mail from HR to the trash, opened the email from Inglis, and allowed the download, a dossier. Some of its contents were stamped with the CIA's Eagle and Shield logo and the word "Secret." The balance had been provided by *Agencja Wywiadu*, which a hand-written note in the margin informed me was the Polish Foreign Intelligence Service. The Polish was translated. I skimmed the material.

Andre Niemiec was born in '61 behind the Iron Curtain in Warsaw, the son of a Polish father and an East German mother. He joined the Polish military at age 20 and served in a rifle company. He went to the Iron Curtain's equivalent of ROTC and was subsequently posted to Riga, Lithuania, and then to Dresden, East Germany. Accepted into Polish Special Forces, Niemiec was posted briefly to Cuba before ending up in Moscow in 1989 as the Soviet world dissolved. He remained in the military, transferring again, this time to logistics, and stationed near Warsaw. Niemiec earned the usual citations, progressed to the rank of lieutenant colonel, and was then posted with Polish units attached to Coalition Forces in the first year of Operation Iraqi Freedom, 2003. At some point during this tour, Niemiec must have known that he would be passed over for full colonel and that his time in the Polish military was about to hit the wall.

There was nothing particularly noteworthy in the guy's record up to this point, but then things started to get interesting. The colonel resigned his commission early in 2003, gave up his Polish citizenship, and emigrated to Russia. He then turned up in the ranks of the GRU, the Russian military intelligence service, fighting Islamist separatists in Chechnya, where, according to the CIA analyst's notes, the colonel served with distinction. Then, in 2005, he was instrumental in the planning of the operation that assassinated Chechen Independence Leader and architect of the Beslan School massacre, Shamil Basayev, who was killed by a booby-trapped cache of weapons. For this, Niemiec was awarded the Order of St George, First Class, the highest Russian military honor.

A further unconfirmed report fingered Niemiec as the Russian official responsible for the mass abduction and killing of over 70 captured Chechen fighters. There were photos of a mass grave, followed by images of corpses and several autopsy reports. Several men had been tortured to death and bled white. The images turned my stomach, and it's not easily turned.

I sifted through a parade of photos showing Niemiec in the company of Valery Petrovich, the president of the Russian Federation most recently killed after being captured by ISIS fighters in Syria during a failed rescue attempt headed by Yours Truly. The images showed that the two men were pals, having met when Niemiec was posted to Dresden, where Petrovich was a mid-level KGB operative, a much-reported factoid once he became president of the Russian Federation. I looked at an image of Niemiec and Petrovich, suited up for some official function, sharing a private joke about something unknown. The two buddies fished together, went on hunting trips together, holidayed with their wives at Petrovich's Sochi dacha, and killed countless thousands in Syria, among other places. Plenty to share a joke about.

With the Chechen unrest put down and a Petrovich favorite, Niemiec was promoted to the rank of full colonel and awarded the management of the GRU's Fourth Directorate, which encompassed the Middle East. He spent most of his time there coordinating operations with the Iranian Quds Force, the Islamic Republic's special ops unit. He retired in 2014 as a two-star general. His next posting was a surprise — number two in a new security organization called the Wagner Group, a company employing mercenaries that quickly established itself as President Petrovich's private army of choice, dispatched to acquit the Kremlin's dirtier missions, the ones requiring deniability, recruiting former Russian Spetsnaz, Special Forces, former GRU operatives and criminals looking to shorten their sentences.

In 2015, Niemiec supposedly sanctioned the capture, torture, and killing of half a dozen members of the Syrian White Hats, the civilian organization set up to rescue victims of Syrian and Russian bombing campaigns absurdly counter-claimed by Moscow to be a terrorist organization. More photos and autopsies, torture and exsanguination the common features.

I already knew something of the Wagner group from various unrelated briefings, but I'd never had the pleasure of running into the organization on the ground.

Following the death of Petrovich, Niemiec retired to a castle in the Polish countryside and dabbled in the occasional arms sale for the Kremlin. There, the record ended.

The albino Pole was an interesting character with questionable morals and allegiances, but there was nothing explicit in the guy's record that explained why he was riding on that suspicious convoy in northern Iraq back in '03.

I closed the files and called Inglis.

"Vin," Inglis answered.

"Morning," I began.

"You read the info on Niemiec?" she asked.

"Yeah."

"So, what's your interest in this character anyway? Where does he fit in?"

Someone in the CIA had to know about Niemiec being on that convoy because Wilkes had included images of the guy in his report. But for whatever reason, that information had been withheld from the Agency's lower echelons. "I don't know yet," I replied.

"Are you going to interview him?"

"That's my plan," I said. In fact, I didn't have a plan. All I had were a couple of questions only Niemiec could answer if he chose to. Thinking about it, I couldn't make him do or say anything. Was he still even residing in his castle?

"I'll arrange for you to contact the Polish internal security agency, the *Agencja Bezpieczeństwa Wewnętrznego*. I'll send you the information."

"I got Agency. Can you spell the rest of it?" I asked her, a pencil poised over some scrap paper. She rattled off some letters, but my pencil got confused after the first zee — I jotted the letters ABW.

"What about Wilkes?" she asked. "Anything of interest there?"

"He said he was surprised a WMD investigation team never showed up to test the area. Maybe CENTCOM just didn't want to know."

"What about your incident last night? You go to the clinic?"

"Yes."

"And?"

"And what?"

"Any thoughts on why you were set up?"

"No," I told her.

"There has to be a reason."

"I can't think of one."

"And you're sure it's blackmail?"

"I don't know," I said. "It could have been a friendly hotel courtesy. This is Berlin, after all."

Inglis ignored the stereotyping. "You're not married."

It wasn't a question.

"Did the photos capture any deviant crap?"

"Such as?"

"We once had an ambassador from Japan who was into autonepiophilia."

"Which is?"

"Getting turned on by dressing up as a baby complete with pacifier, rattles, diapers, a cute bonnet. And sex toys."

I was going to comment, but glass houses.

Inglis continued, "The North Koreans found out about it and caught the guy on film acting out this stuff with a couple of willing partners. He was married with three teenage kids. Great leverage."

"As for my situation, nothing weird," I said. "Unless you count being asleep and no doubt snoring while a woman punching way above my weight division is partying on my bits."

"What the fuck are you talking about, Cooper?" said a voice in Inglis's background. "Can we get on with this?"

We were on speaker? So much for secrecy.

"Sidney and Merle have just joined us," Rita informed me.

Fabulous.

"The woman was probably a prostitute," Inglis concluded. "Someone paid her, probably with cash, so there won't be a paper trail. I'd forget about the photos," she advised. "Doesn't sound like they can hurt you."

You don't know Anna, I thought.

"You were drugged, Vin. It happens."

None of that made it okay. However, Inglis's questions and observations, though obvious were also clarifying because suddenly I knew exactly who was behind those pics and why. "Shit," I murmured.

"I'm sorry?" said Rita.

"Nothing. I'll make contact again in a few days." I rang off, but not before I heard someone else in the room, probably Ridge, squeal, "Cooper! Hey! What the fuck do-"

I picked up those pics and had another look. The angles didn't reveal much about my level of participation or lack of it. Gisela, if that was her real name, could provide a link to the brains of the operation. She was a Pilates instructor, if what little memory of our encounter served, and had a studio nearby.

I returned all the photos bar one to the envelope, tossed it into my suitcase and packed. Forty minutes later, I detoured to Moochers on the way to the airport, asked the Uber driver to wait, and promised a tip. It was still early; the bar closed, the lights off, and the door shuttered. Peering into the bar's window revealed movement. Cleaners. I tapped on the glass. An older woman; short, dark, alopecia, and of Middle Eastern appearance — Syrian, I guessed, and mid-thirties. She opened the door.

"*Ya?*"

"Speak English?" I flashed my OSI badge to make it look official.

Instantly wary, the woman wiggled her hand from side to side and said, "Little."

I pulled the photo from my coat pocket, folded to frame Gisela's face and remove the X-rating. The camera lens was somewhere around the level of Gisela's forehead. Her mouth was open, possibly moaning, and she seemed in either pain or ecstasy or maybe a little of both. It was an odd photo to be showing around, but it was the best of the bunch. I showed it to the cleaner.

"Have you seen her? This woman — familiar? Gisela. Her name is Gisela." I pitched the question a couple of ways to ensure it landed.

The woman frowned and shook her head. "No. This *frau?* No."

I beckoned the cleaner's partner over. He came to the door — bearded, dark complexion, large friendly eyes, mid-thirties. Also Syrian, probably. I showed him the photo, and the woman asked the question. After a few seconds, he grinned and rattled off a sentence I couldn't understand, but the woman clouted him over the head. "No...he not know," she snapped and closed the door. I figured that while her partner didn't know Gisela, he would like to. This detour was a dead end. The clock was ticking as far as Washington and the CIA were concerned, and time was running out to make my flight. I returned to the Uber.

"Airport?" the driver asked.

"Airport," I replied and settled back.

The driver turned left, then right, and it was then that I saw Gisela unlock the door of a business called *Der Toning-Salon, Pilates,* which, linguistics genius that I am, I figured meant The Toning Salon, Pilates. I was tempted to ask the driver to stop but concluded a face-to-face with the blackmailer's instrument wouldn't make things any clearer to me than they already were. The woman hadn't lied about being a Pilates instructor with her own joint; somehow, that was important. I sat back in my seat and thought about her perfect ass wriggling into that dress, and I have to admit the thoughts were far from unpleasant.

The Uber dropped me off at Brandenburg International with thirty minutes in hand, the flight to Warsaw delayed slightly. I hadn't eaten, so I found a restaurant, ordered a plate of bratwurst on sauerkraut, washed down with a *Krombacher* Pilsner, the beer half the bar was drinking.

A table near the window overlooked the wind-swept ramp. Gisela was dressed in a black puffy jacket, scarf, baggy black Adidas track pants, and Nikes, turning the key in a lock, arriving at work. I wondered how she'd been drawn into the blackmailer's scheme, but the wondering lasted only a few moments. I could see the screen of the TV monitor reflected in the window, and what I saw made me turn to look. It was the familiar image of Andre Niemiec riding on the Iraqi convoy, his disturbing white face glowing like the full moon on a cold, clear winter's night. The volume was low and in German, but I could make out words like Iraq war and WMD. Wikileaks also came up as a title on the screen beside the newsreader's head. It wasn't a difficult jigsaw to piece together. Wikileaks had released more of the information handed over by the whistleblower on the alleged Iraqi WMD spirited away to Syria. As far as I could tell, Niemiec's name hadn't been mentioned in the report, which suggested that the world's media didn't know who he was. But the ignorance wouldn't last. The instant his identity was known, Niemiec would be sought by all manner of organizations from various governments. He would no doubt make himself scarce. My phone suddenly vibrated. I wasn't surprised — Muirhead and the rest would be having kittens, and the kittens would be having kittens. I fished the phone from my pocket, but the name on the screen wasn't the one I expected to see. "Hey," I said. The sound of Anna's voice triggered panic. Why was she calling now? What did she know? How did she know?

"Hi."

"Hi," I replied.

"Everything okay?"

"I think so. Why?"

"I don't know. Something in your voice."

"You go that from 'hey' and then 'hi?'"

"Yeah, I did."

"How about you? All copacetic?" I asked her.

"Why wouldn't it be?"

"Bun? Oven?" I reminded her.

"Please don't define me by this pregnancy. I've told you that."

"Okay, promise," I said, avoiding the desire to point out that her hormones had to be zinging.

"Back to you. What's up?"

"Nothing. I was just watching the news. Have you seen it? Looks like there was a Coalition officer on that WMD-convoy-heading-for-Syria thing."

"What time is it there?" I asked her.

"Early."

I did the calculation. "Why are you up? It's 4am."

"You're changing the subject. That's what you're working on, isn't it? The WMD thing. It was a suspicion before, but now it's a certainty."

"No."

"Yes, you are. And, yes, it's early. I couldn't sleep. I had a feeling about something. You're sure everything's okay?"

Goddamn women's intuition! "I am having a ball," I told her. "I've just had some cotton candy, and now I'm off to the Chasing Rainbows Museum."

I could hear the news playing in the background.

"The anchor woman's right. He doesn't look at all Iraqi. He's definitely European. What's a guy like that doing on an Iraqi convoy? And all those Iraqis mopped up. There's WMD on those B-doubles, no doubt about it. This shit is gonna get wild."

The other phone, the Agency's cell, was vibrating in my pocket. I took it out. The number on screen was familiar.

"Anna, sorry, have to go. Uncle Sam's evil nanny on the other phone."

"Phone me back," she said.

"I'm about to board. I'll call when I land in a couple of hours, okay?"

"Where are you going?"

"Anna..."

"I know, I know..."

"Gotta go, sorry." I ended one call and answered the other. "Cooper."

"You've seen the news?"

It was Chalmers.

"You're an asshole," I told him, and hung up.

WARSAW, POLAND

"Warsaw, this quaint old city, has a tale to tell. And mostly that tale runs with blood," informed the tourist brochure. "Bombed by the Nazi Luftwaffe in 1939, bombed by the Wehrmacht in the subsequent Siege of Warsaw, rebuilt, and then raised again by the Wehrmacht during the Warsaw Uprising in 1944, what you see today is the old city's façade meticulously rebuilt, more often than not hiding a modern building within."

In fact, the old city reminded me a little of the Venice canals and the Eiffel Tower in Vegas. Like the real thing, if you've never seen the real thing. A sort of caricature, only unlike those two comical doppelgangers in Vegas, there was nothing even vaguely amusing about the punishment Warsaw had endured that caused it to be reminiscent of the original.

I pushed through the old double doors of what appeared on the outside to be a medieval six-story building, complete with archways, balconies, and fish-head gargoyles on numerous overhangs, into a world of polished concrete and naked steel.

Glancing around the foyer, I decided that although there was no signage, I had the correct address, mostly due to the multitude of security guards armed with PM-84 Glauberyts, the Polish-made submachinegun. This was the home sweet home of the Polish Internal Security Agency or, in local speak, the *Agencja Bezpieczeństwa Wewnętrznego.* Don't ask me to pronounce it.

A snappy young corporate type in a fitted tan suit and long pointy shoes turned up at the toes, like Turkish slippers only not, eyeballed me and came over. "Vin Cooper?".

"Maybe," I said. "Who's asking?"

" Leonard Gibbs," he said, showing me his card, which I took.

"And what do you do for the U.S. Department of Housing and Urban Development all the way over here in Warsaw?" I asked him, scanning it.

"Fact finding," he grinned. "Attached to NATO. Occasionally, I do some handholding for visiting dignitaries. I'll be holding yours upstairs, though I'm sure everyone will be speaking English."

"I'm a dignitary?"

He shrugged. "You're from Washington."

"You speak Polish?" Gibbs was black, his accent conjuring the Bronx.

"Adopted," he said by way of explanation as he took point for the security checks. "Adoptive mother was Polish American."

I wasn't carrying a briefcase or a weapon, and the checks would have gone off without a hitch, except that one of the scanners made an exception to my belt buckle. Once I convinced the security detail that I couldn't hold the building hostage with it, we slid on through.

"What do you think of Warsaw so far, Agent Cooper?"

"Reminds me of Vegas," I told him.

"Well, that's a first."

The elevator had no buttons to speak of and no other passengers, but it seemed to know where it was going and pulled up on the eleventh floor. We walked into reception, which was all white, aside from a receptionist with dramatic flame-red hair wearing an emerald-green dress behind the sweeping, smooth, brilliant white alabaster counter. Still no signage. *"Agent Strahovski zaraz będzie z tobą, Agent Gibbs. Proszę usiąść,"* she said with a smile and gestured at a white couch.

"Dziękuję, Zofia," Gibbs replied, following her nod to the seating arrangements. "Take a seat. We're expected," he explained in an aside. "Do you want to sit?"

"I'm fine. Been sitting in planes for days."

Agent Kazia Strahovski strutted in with the confidence of a catwalk model. I almost expected her to twirl. Tall, blonde, blue-eyed, nice legs. Not my type, according to Anna. "Mr. Cooper, Leonard," she said, shaking first my hand and then my babysitter's. Her hand was cold, her fingers bony, the grip try-hard, attempting to project strength or maybe a steely will. I was prepared to go along with it. "Agent Kazia Strahovski. Pleased to meet you. Come with me." I gathered she knew Gibbs already, at least professionally.

Gibbs and I followed her down a hallway and turned a corner. She swiped a card, and a door opened. We entered a pinched, windowless room with a half-size board table. I wondered where everyone was going to sit, all the people who would be speaking English. Maybe my body language conveyed this because she said, "Washington has requested security measures. Few know who you are or what you are doing. We will keep it this way."

In other words, Washington had had its pants pulled down around its ankles, figuratively speaking, and the fewer the number of people who knew what was up, the less the embarrassment. I smiled — privately, of course.

"Please, sit." Agent Strahovski said, leading by example. "Coffee? Water?" she asked, her finger poised above the refreshments button on the office intercom system.

"We're good, Kazia," Gibbs replied for the both of us.

She pulled a tablet from a folder, pressed a button, and got down to business. "You want to interview a Russian citizen living in Poland. His name is Andre Niemiec."

There is no need to say anything at this point. It was already established that I wasn't here for the coffee.

"This man lives not far from Warsaw. He has been under observation for two days now."

The agent tapped a button on the tablet, swung it around, and presented half a dozen different views of what appeared to be a restored medieval castle patrolled by several burly types in civilian clothes.

"Those aren't your men," I asked.

"No. Niemiec has private security," she replied. "Wagner."

Why did he need a small army for protection? Protection from whom? Or what? "Is Niemiec home?"

"We believe he is there, yes."

Belief is one thing; fact is another.

"Have you hacked into his security system?" Gibbs asked.

"No, we have our own cameras."

I stood. "So, the guy's at home. Let's go say hi."

"But—" Whatever objection Agent Strahovski was about to raise, she decided against it. "I have car."

"Shotgun," I told Gibbs, who vaguely smiled.

Agent Strahovski was surprised. "You have a shotgun?"

I could have explained that the term was coined back in the old west when a guard would sit up beside the Wells Fargo driver armed with a trench sweeper and repel boarders but instead managed to come up with a clever alternative answer on the spur of the moment. "No."

She gave me a look. I've seen that look many times before. It's the one that says I'll never make their Christmas card list.

Around twenty minutes later, driving along in her car, a newish Audi SUV smelling of pine, the city sprawl eventually gave way to a rural setting. The cows and horses were a dead giveaway. "How far away is Niemiec's," I asked Kazia.

"Twenty-minute drive, maybe more. What will you be asking him?" she asked me.

"You've seen the photo of Niemiec in a chemical suit on the Iraqi truck convoy?"

"Yes, of course."

"I'll be asking him what he was doing on an Iraqi truck convoy wearing a chemical suit."

Agent Strahovski glanced at me, clearly impressed.

"I also want to know if he's hiding a few barrels of sarin in the basement."

"You think he has that?" she asked.

Gibbs chipped in from the back seat. "Is that possible?

"It won't hurt to ask." I didn't for a moment think Niemiec was sitting on a cache of WMD, but he was obviously deeply involved in some pretty shady dealings. I just didn't know how deep or how shady. He was on that convoy for a reason, and I wanted to know what that reason was. Unless he was on some kind of operation for an allied intelligence service as Wilkes presumed, helping WMD across the border while an officer in Coalition forces would, at the very least, be treasonous, and a tricky path for any justice system. Niemiec was now a citizen of the Russian Federation, and I was confident Moscow wouldn't comply with any Polish legal statutes. Niemiec's record suggested that he wouldn't cave to pressure, but that wouldn't stop me from applying it. You never know what will pop from the acne of someone's past. And Pimples Niemiec clearly had a past.

Strahovski handed me a folder stamped, *Ściśle tajny* — Polish for top secret, I figured. I sifted through the contents. There was nothing I didn't already know. Various Western intelligence services had pooled their knowledge of Niemiec and passed it around. Everyone was up to speed on the guy, from my point of view, roughly the speed of an old man on a walker.

The in-car nav system eventually took Strahovski on a ramp off the freeway. Several more turns left and right, a couple of villages, the second more petite than the first, and then we were on country back streets between low grass-covered hills dotted with those cattle I mentioned. I'd seen farms like these in Britain, France, Germany — all over Europe, rolling emerald fields, hedgerows, stone walls, barns, and mist. I glimpsed Niemiec's castle between a gap in the trees, a dramatic towering, red brick and white stone structure complete with fairy-tale-like towers, the kind you expect to see an angry mob storming with fiery torches and pitchforks.

We stopped on a bridge over a river that meandered close to the castle and offered a good view of the surroundings. I noted a dredge and an accompanying barge hard at work, keeping the river navigable, one of the few hints that we were in the 21st Century and not the 12th. The castle incorporated a wall complete with battlements. From the overhead photos of the castle I'd already seen, I knew there was a deep ditch between the battlements and the front door, which could only be reached by a drawbridge. Filled with water, the ditch would become a moat. The ye olde worlde defenses were impressive, but nothing a couple of hovering Blackhawks, a Special Forces unit, and rappelling ropes couldn't deal with. And those architects in the Middle Ages thought they had all bases covered. For us at that moment, though, even ringing the doorbell might prove a challenge.

Strahovski pulled off the road and stopped behind a set of heavy steel gates hanging off tall stone pillars, the only break in a wall of double brick crowned with jagged shards of glass that circled the castle's vast grounds. I got out of the car and went to have a closer look at the setup. The gates themselves were impressive – some grade of non-corrosive steel plate, each more than a quarter inch thick, interlocked and riveted, and at least 12 feet tall. A main battle tank could punch through these things, but the gunner might consider pumping an HE round into them first. A couple of CCTV cameras angled down on us, positioned where they could easily be seen atop the brickwork pillars on which the doors were hung, featured small blinking red lights. We were being watched. A dull stainless-steel panel recessed in the left-hand pillar included a "press to talk" button and a keypad. I pressed. An instant later, a burst of Polish came through the speaker. "Hi," I said. "Do you speak English?"

"What do you want?" came the heavily accented reply.

Behind me, two police vans arrived and disgorged cops wearing body armor and carrying Glauberyt submachine guns.

"Is Rapunzel home?" I asked the speaker.

"Who?"

"You know, the girl with the long golden hair kept prisoner in one of your towers. Rapunzel."

"There is no one here with this name. Go away."

At that moment, I became aware of a mechanical whine growing in intensity.

"Okay," I said. "Then I'll settle for Andre Niemiec."

"He is not here."

The speaker went dead. I turned to Strahovski and Gibbs, who were standing around with the cops, wondering what to do next. The whine changed pitch, and I suddenly knew what it was. We were too late. Another change in pitch and a large gray helicopter climbed slowly into the sky, appearing from behind the castle. It angled toward us, gathered a little forward speed, and came to a halt overhead, the downwash from its blades whipping up dirt, twigs, and leaf litter that lashed exposed skin. Its nose then dipped sharply forward, gained speed and height, and the aircraft disappeared soon after, obscured by the tree canopy. Have I mentioned I don't like helicopters?

"You couldn't find a reason to detain him?" I asked Strahovski while I tried to blink away some grit lodged against one of my eyeballs.

"What is the charge?" she replied, brushing herself down. "This is not your Wild West." Strahovski dismissed the cops with a nod and stomped off to the car, Gibbs gave me a shrug and followed.

Inglis called on the ride back to town.

"You know how they say a man's home is his castle?" I told her. "Niemiec's home is a castle, and I left my battering ram back at the hotel."

"Leonard Gibbs briefed me. Turns out he wasn't there anyway. We thought he was, and so did Polish intelligence, but he's just been positively identified in Idlib, Syria."

"So, you've got someone covering that?"

"Yes, you. There's a NATO aircraft departing Lotz Air Base tomorrow, early. You should be able to get there in plenty of time."

"Lotz?"

"It's an hour and a half drive southwest of Warsaw."

"And where is this aircraft going?"

"Incirlik. You'll catch a ride incountry from there and pick up a U.S. Army escort. Also, we're sending you additional resources."

"What sort of resources?"

"Manpower resources. The SecState wants additional muscle on the case."

"What outcome is required with Niemic."

"She wants him in a room on American soil, seated naked on a chair with a hood over his head, but you didn't hear that from me. And don't miss that flight. Won't be anyone there to roust you this time. Good luck."

In this game, when people wish you good luck, the good variety is likely to be thin on the ground.

"And, Vin, one last thing regarding Niemiec. You asked me to background him before the world knew he was on that convoy."

"Yeah."

"Sharing is a two-way street. You must have seen certain photos of that convoy before they were leaked but chose not to let me in on it. We both know that whoever has those photos is holding onto them illegally. I don't have an issue with that. What I care about is trust. If you want me to be your backstop, you need to tell me what you're pitching. You with me?"

"Yes, ma'am," I said. "No more curveballs with two out and bases loaded."

"I have no idea what that means, but I think we understand each other."

The line went dead. Sporting analogies, a habit SA&D shared with the CIA. I picked over the call. Trust between me and the Agency was wafer thin, but I was going to need someone on the inside with access to intelligence; that much was clear. "Okay, Rita," I said quietly. "I'm game if you are." I settled back and watched the countryside drift by. About the manpower she told me was being sent — please let it not be Ridge and his protein-stained jacket. I called Anna to pass the time, but she didn't answer, so I left a message that I missed her, to pretend that I was coming home early and to prepare to get naked. The thought got me all worked up. And then I thought about the events in Berlin and got worked up all over again, but in a different way.

Arriving back at the hotel, I took a shower. Dinner was taken in a glass with ice, after which I hit the hay. Lying in bed, I thought about Syria. The two of us didn't get along. With some of that good luck Inglis mentioned, maybe I could assemble a team of experienced bushwhackers, have Niemiec in Muirhead's chair within twenty-four hours, and then Anna and I could get down to making seriously sure of that pregnancy in a range of positions. Good plan.

The taxi ride to Lotz at sunrise was uneventful. Arriving at the apron at the scheduled time with my wheelie suitcase, I watched the Air

Force C-17 land. A few minutes later, it dipped to a stop in front of the ground handler and his paddles, the engines shut down, the rear door lowered, and the loadmaster trotted down with several enlisted men and women, preparing to offload cargo. "When are we leaving?" I asked the loadmaster as he walked by.

"Mr. Cooper?" he asked.

"Yep."

"Enough time to visit the john. We're just offloading some vehicles."

As he said this, a couple of Humvees drove down the Moose's — the Air Forces pet name for the C-17 — ramp.

Following behind the Humvees trotted a woman dressed in faded, well-worn utilities. She turned and strolled toward me. And, just as I recognized the walk, the words "Special Agent" followed by "Masters" above the shirt pocket came into focus.

Wait, what...?

What was Anna doing on the apron? And why was she looking like she was getting ready for deployment?

Anna opened this unexpected meeting with a casual smile and went straight in for the hug. "Hey, you," she said, and then her lips and tongue found mine. I wasn't going to fight it, but a couple of key fuzes were shorting out in my brain.

"What's with the utilities?" I asked when the kiss had run its course. "Don't you have a towering in-tray to get through?"

"I'm your new partner."

"No, you're my *old* partner," I reminded her. "And now you're my other partner, the one I sleep with and got pregnant."

"I'm going to stop you right there, Vin. *We* got pregnant. And I've got a womb, not a disability. I've already told you this technical pregnancy will not stop me from doing my job."

"Technical?"

"It's early days and anything could go wrong."

"Especially in a war zone like Syria where they're known to perform terminations with whirring pieces of flying shrapnel."

"You don't know what's going on, Vin. You've been in the air the last eleven hours. While you were watching movies and sipping whiskey in business class, Bradley Chalmers has gone missing."

"I travelled coach, and you've just made my day. Let's hope his body turns up somewhere soon so that we can celebrate." I visualized him chopped into pieces and fed into a garbage disposal. But the happy picture didn't last. I had a pretty good idea where he'd disappeared to.

Our conversation had attracted an audience, two airmen and the loadmaster.

"We're not doing this now," Anna insisted, looking around, self-conscious.

"Anna, c'mon..." I really didn't want her getting on that plane.

"Oh, for fuck's sake, Vin. I've spent more time on the ground in Syria than you. And if it wasn't for me, you might not have made it out last time you were there."

"So now what?" I asked her, stalemate reached.

"Secretary Muirhead assigned me personally just as she assigned you. I'm read in on this case. I know as much as you do."

"Does she know about us? About your...condition?"

"No, and no. Because neither is significant."

"No?"

Back from the head, the Moose's loadmaster beckoned, impatient.

Anna gave me a friendly punch on the arm and pivoted. "C'mon, look at us, on the same team. No secrets. No need for cover stories. No lies. We can *talk*. Feels good, doesn't it?" She went for the handle of my wheelie suitcase.

"I've got that," I said, beating her to it. "Got a broken wheel." It didn't, but what it contained was potentially explosive — a certain incriminating set of photographs. Anna was blissfully unaware of them; otherwise, I would've been met with a loaded 45. So, she didn't know *everything*. Sometimes, secrets are good.

"Well, I've bought everything you need: body armor, M4, utilities, new toothbrush. Take out what you need from that and leave it."

Great idea, but no way was I going through my dirty laundry with her peering over my shoulder. I dropped the handle and gave the case to a passing local ground crew. He looked at me quizzically. "Burn it," I said.

SOMEWHERE OVER EASTERN EUROPE

Space in the Moose's hold was cramped, stuffed as it was with several towering pallets and two AH-84 Apache gunships. Passengers were an afterthought, seating arrangements the jump-seat kind, a bare metal frame covered over with stretched nylon material bolted into the side of the plane. The service other airlines possibly have nightmares about was provided by a young, chubby loadmaster with pink cheeks and an orange mustache who presented Anna and me with khaki-colored cushions and two pairs of headphones jacked into the aircraft's intercom. The air in the hold was icy and smelt of dust, kerosene, and machine grease. Flight time to Incirlik Air Base, Turkey, just under three hours.

There wasn't much talk, not until the pilots throttled back and the plane settled into the cruise.

"Have you met Davidson and Ridge?" I asked.

"They briefed me. What did you make of Tom Wilkes?"

"You ever need to blow shit up, he's your man, the Rembrandt of demolitions."

"I'll keep it in mind. Aside from that."

"He also drinks too much."

"Says you."

"He's blunt, tough, confident, and Australian. You'd like him." I added, "So, don't expect an introduction."

"Spare me his Tinder score. What did he have to say about Niemiec, the convoy...?"

"He kept copies of the images taken that night in Iraq."

I showed Anna the images Wilkes had forwarded.

She scrolled through them. "These are classified. Holding onto them — he could go to jail."

"I'm sure it keeps him awake nights."

"Did he say why he copied these images?"

"I think at the time, he couldn't believe what he was seeing."

"And he sat on them?"

"To be fair, what was he going to do with them?"

"Delete, for starters. What else have you got?

"I've been thinking about my new office."

Anna looked at me. She wasn't smiling.

"I'm going with stainless steel, wood highlights, and maybe a feature wall."

Still no smile.

"So, how's D.C. at the moment, by the way?" I asked to prove that I wasn't wholly glib.

"Deep in damage control, for obvious reasons. Interpol is also after Niemiec, as are the Poles."

"We're a sideshow. Great. Pressure's off."

"Maybe for you, Vin, but I am committed to this."

Another White House scandal... I was having trouble firing up commitment, but I was chained to Anna, which, under different circumstances, I would enjoy.

"Tell me about Berlin?" Anna continued.

How did Anna know I was in Berlin? "Not much to tell," I said maybe a little too offhand, aware that a minefield potentially lay under my next footstep.

"What happened there?"

"Could you be more specific?"

"Did you interview Colonel Adams?"

"So, you know about Adams?"

"Like I said, I've been briefed, read in. I know what you know."

I hoped not.

"Well...?" She asked.

"Well, what?"

"Vin...c'mon."

"He played dumb, but he's not a great actor."

"What does that mean?"

"I asked him about the mission request, and he bunted it. Told me he heard a rumor from some local Kurds about WMD being ferried to Syria, wondered if a cache had been buried up on the border, and wanted to see if there was anything in the scuttlebutt. The plane he commanded had some fancy ground-penetrating radar suitable for that purpose. Mission request denied, end of story according to him."

"And you believe him?"

"I've got nothing that tells me otherwise."

"But you've got a hunch."

"He's got money, a beautiful young girlfriend, and he's no underwear model. Where did that come from? The money, not the squeeze."

"So, basically, you got nothing out of Berlin?" Anna asked, but with a raised eyebrow that seemed weaponized.

Did this third degree have something to do with a certain Pilates-toned ass? Did Inglis speak out of turn? "Not a total loss. I showed Adams a photo of Niemiec on the night of the convoy. He denied having met the guy, but from the reaction, I was pretty sure he recognized him."

"That's it?"

"What do you mean?"

"You got nothing else to tell me?"

"No."

"Nothing at all?"

"Nope."

"You're acting weird, Vin."

"No more than usual, though, right?"

"Maybe it's me — the hormones." Anna sat back in her seat, arched her spine, and stretched out her legs. She glanced at her watch. "Two hours thirty to go. You know, I thought you had the jump on me with this case, but I might even know more than you, just from watching the news."

"I've spent most of the last four days at thirty-thousand feet, so gimme a break."

"You're right. I'm sorry."

"Don't worry about it."

"You must be tired." Anna edged closer, presenting her shoulder and padding it with the pillow. "Here, lean on me. Get some sleep."

I put my head on her shoulder but was reluctant to close my eyes in case I drifted off and blurted out the one word that could get me killed — Gisela.

INCIRLIK AIR BASE, TURKEY

The Moose touched down and taxied to an apron where a Black Hawk was waiting, rotors chopping the cool desert air. A petit crew chief wearing an enormous helmet that looked half a dozen sizes too big for her head accompanied us to the helo, climbed in after us, and took her position behind the M134 minigun in the doorway. Another crew chief, a skinny guy in a baggy flight suit, face obscured by helmet and visor, handed us our flight helmets with integrated headsets.

"Where are we going?" I asked once I was geared up. I couldn't see his eyes behind the visor but sensed him glancing down at my shirt. The name tape said "Cooper," and the shoulder patch announced the United States, but my utilities were otherwise devoid of rank and unit identification. The angle of his helmet tilted towards Anna. He saw that her name was "Special Agent Masters." His helmet squared up to me again. "Vin Cooper, U.S. Department of Agriculture," I said to clear up any confusion.

"If you say so, sir," he replied.

Anna chose not to engage, but at least he knew where I was from, and it wasn't the department of bull shit and growing stuff. "Where are we going?" I repeated.

"Sir, we've got a rendezvous with an Army unit a little east of Idlib. I can't tell you much more than that, sir."

I nodded.

"What's our flight time, Specialist?" Anna inquired.

"'Bout an hour and forty-five, ma'am. Takin' the long way 'round. Can't go as the crow flies. Russians on the ground and in the air. Gotta thread the needle, if you know what I mean."

He was talking about jinking left, right, up, down, some High-G turns, and the possibility of the MRE I'd eaten on the Moose coming

110

up to say hello and staying behind all over the floor. "Any barf bags handy?"

"All out, sir, sorry."

Great.

Anna settled back against the bulkhead and closed her eyes, calm. "We're also meeting a guy I know."

"Who?"

"His name's Kaamil Bin Alzhur. You'll like him."

"Why?"

"The Russians have a price on his head."

Already, I wanted to buy him a beer.

IDLIB, SYRIA

The rendezvous was ten miles east of Idlib. The Black Hawk, which smelt of my puke by then, landed in the usual vortex of desert grit and purple smoke.

Off to one side of the LZ were three beat-up Land Cruiser pickups and a few Army Humvees. Anna and I slipped out of the helo and half ran at a crouch toward the welcoming committee, a mix of Syrians and U.S. Army infantry. One of those Syrians dressed in chinos, a blue check flannel shirt, and a New York Yankees ball cap stepped forward to meet Anna. He was mid-forties, bearded, under six feet, and with a deep scar that ran under his chin, up the side of one cheek, and disappeared briefly under longish graying hair before reappearing at an ear with the bottom half chewed off.

"Kaamil! It's great to see you." Anna said as the noise and the dust dissipated. "How are you?"

"It is good to see you too, Anna," he replied as they embraced. "Allah must love me because I am still here."

No, I thought. If he really loved you, you'd be sucking on a Margarita at a resort in Bali.

Anna continued, "This is Vin Cooper from the U.S. Department of Agriculture."

"Mr. Cooper. I am pleased to meet you."

"*Assalaam 'Alaikum*," I replied, ever the diplomat.

"*Wa 'alaikum assalaam*," came the standard response. "May I present my son, Maali."

The kid was on the skinny side of rangy, islands of dark peach fuzz on his chin and cheeks.

Anna, who could maybe see something I couldn't, told Bin Alzhur, "Your son has grown into a handsome man."

Bin Alzhur beamed, proud of his boy.

I shook the hand Maali offered. It felt like a 12-year-old's, diminutive and kinda dank. His eyes were large and brown and uncertain, reluctant to make contact, eyes that had seen too much and much too often. He carried an American M-16 that had seen plenty of wear and tear from the black-oxide coating worn off the barrel, as did the half dozen other young men roughly Maali's age loitering around their vehicles.

The Black Hawk sandblasted the vicinity on its way out.

"Let's get you folks mobile," shouted a U.S. Army staff sergeant over the rotors, "Maynard" on his nametag. Maynard's 10-man squad, having formed a cordon, closed in a semi-circle around us, their attention on the surrounding horizon while they shepherded us toward the vehicles. The sergeant may not have been expecting trouble, but he was ready for it.

Meanwhile, I was experiencing that fear rush that starts in the balls, runs up the spine, and ends in the throat, vaguely constricting it. If there was a head available, I might have taken a nervous crap. That initial adrenalin pump always hits when I arrive in a combat zone. I figure it's my conscious self informing the subconscious me that both of us could be killed at any moment. It's not a good feeling, and it passes, but it does heighten the senses. "Do you think there's a crapper handy anywhere close by?" I asked Anna under my breath.

Looking elsewhere, and without moving her lips, she replied, "I've come to the conclusion that you're on the spectrum."

Some of the best people are.

Anna informed Maynard, "If it's okay with you, Sarge, we'll ride with the White Helmets and get briefed on the go."

"Yes, ma'am. We've got orders to take you into Idlib, and then you're on your own. Unless you call me over the tac' radio, or the world goes to shit."

"You will not be on your own," Bin Alzhur reassured Anna, handing Maynard a slip of paper. This is where we are going."

The staff sergeant grunted. "Google's got it."

Minutes later, the four-vehicle convoy was dodging potholes in the dirt road that snaked around and over low hills, past skeletal shepherds herding emaciated goats. After so many years of civil war, Syria's rib cage and hip bones were showing.

Anna leaned forward between the front seats. "What can you tell us? Have you seen him?"

"Personally? No, I have not, but others have seen Al Shaytan Al'abyad. He is here."

"You call Niemiec the White Devil?"

Bin Alzhur turned to look at her. "He has many names. You speak Arabic now?"

Anna shrugged. "A few words and phrases."

"And you, Mr. Cooper?"

"Just the important stuff like, *'Telhas teeze,'* and *'Ya ibn el sharmouta.'*"

Bin Alzhur grinned. "Ah, your pronunciation is terrible, but son of a bitch and kiss my ass are universal sentiments."

"What about Niemiec's buddies from Wagner," I asked him.

"The Russian barbarians — their compound is in Homs, but Niemiec comes to Idlib to see what is left to destroy."

"Word is he's retired," Anna pointed out.

"Men drawn to destruction and death never retire. The pain Al Shaytan Al'abyad can inflict on Syria gives him joy. He is comfortable amid death and destruction. My country is a vacation resort for Andre Niemiec."

The drive to the outskirts of Idlib across the arid sun-baked ground was uneventful; despite passing numerous Syrian Arab Army units driving a variety of vehicles, safe passage was assured by the presence of the U.S. Army Humvees. Well beyond the city limits, we went through two roadblocks manned jointly by Russian and Syrian soldiers. One of the Russians flipped us the bird. Other than that, the level of hostility was low. Russian and the American forces that remain are wary of each other and no one wants to light the fuze.

Small clusters of mostly abandoned cinderblock hovels on abandoned tinder-dry farmland quickly gave way to a ruined city pulverized beyond repair but not yet forced into submission. Idlib was one of the last holdouts of the Free Syrian Forces, or terrorists, depending on your point of view, receiving an irregular rain of Russian artillery shells to keep the place on its toes. The main streets had been cleared of debris, but most buildings were uninhabitable, the Russian and Syrian strategy of subjugation being wholesale and complete destruction. Inhabitants of the city, young and old alike, shuffled, heads bowed through the ruins on their way to nowhere. A couple of children defecated in a shell hole, water from shattered pipes covered in a slick of green slime collected in others. Emaciated, listless dogs lived out their days in the streets, nosing through trash heaps.

The smashed and burned city reeked of desolation and human shit. Whole blocks of buildings had collapsed, some leaving behind a scorched, pockmarked wall shredded here and there like a cheese grater. Other structures had lost their facades completely, pounded away by blast waves, torn by shrapnel and small arms fire, exposing shattered concrete slabs ending in tangles of twisted, rusting rebar. Trash was everywhere, combined with rubble heaps and intimate possessions blasted from homes and the lives of families. And yet people existed among it all.

The drive-through was sobering. No one spoke. There were no words.

The four-vehicle convoy pulled to a halt in a plaza surrounded by stands of mortally wounded business towers and apartment blocks. And in the distance, the regular dull *crump* of artillery shells going about their destructive work.

"Okay," Bin Alzhur said over his shoulder. "We are here."

Several young men carrying AKs loitered in the plaza. Beyond them, a noisy crowd of people tried to get inside the ground floor of one of the few buildings that hadn't been reduced to road base. A couple of the young boys waved at us.

Sergeant Maynard caught my eye and touched a gloved finger to the brow of his helmet. I returned the gesture with a nod as our security escort motored away slowly.

"What is this place?" Anna asked Bin Alzhur.

"A hospital. Once, it was a hotel," he replied. "A good one."

I noticed several vans parked nearby, kept under camouflage awnings.

"They are ambulances," Bin Alzhur volunteered as we exited the pickup. "We do not identify them with the red crescent because Russian drones will follow them, and then the artillery shelling starts. The Russians hate our hospitals. The only thing they despise more are our schools."

Anna and I grabbed our packs from the pickup tray and headed for the shade of the former hotel's lobby. Men, women, and children lay about in mostly makeshift cots. Other patients lay on the ground, some in the process of being triaged. The smells of disinfectant and ether fought a losing battle against shit and pain.

A van arrived in the courtyard, horn blaring, accompanied by several pickups. Armed fighters jumped out of them and raced to the truck. Several men and women ran from the hospital to assist. The van's doors flew open. Crammed into the back — a wounded, bloodied middle-aged man, two older women, and one girl who couldn't have been more than five or six. All were unconscious and bleeding from numerous cuts and wounds. The white helmets lifted them from the van and carried them into the hospital, accompanied by much shouting.

Anna, Bin Alzhur, and I followed the wounded into the building and found a space to stand that was out of the way. A middle-aged, sleep-deprived doctor shuffled up to Bin Alzhur and handed him a dirty, white, battered construction helmet, and the two men had a brief conversation. The doctor then placed his hand on Bin Alzhur's shoulder, nodded at us with a lined, weary face, and walked off shouting instructions.

"That is my older brother. He has asked if we would help move some patients around to make more room.

"Where are we moving them to?" Anna asked him.

"Under the building, there are several floors for parking. It is safer there."

At that moment, Bin Alzhur's son Maali raced in from outside, saw his father, and made a beeline for him. The kid was excited. He babbled with animated hand movements like a man drowning. He, too, wore a dirty white helmet like his father. I caught the word explosion before he raced back outside.

"I am sorry, I must go," Bin Azur informed us. "The Russians, or maybe it is al-Assad's men. They have shelled homes nearby. Gas cylinders have exploded. We will return with more casualties. Burn victims." He pointed at the fire stairs. Maali reappeared at the entrance and called out to his father again to hurry. "Help them," Bin Alzhur called over his shoulder as he trotted towards the daylight where Maali had been.

Anna and I shared a glance. It was impossible not to get involved. We headed to the stairwell, which was crowded with people racing up and down, some carrying patients on stretchers or with a "fireman's lift," others carting medical supplies, bundles of dirty bandages, plastic-wrapped packages of bottled water, and so forth. We came out on the first level, the spaces between the bare concrete pillars occupied by wounded civilians, militia, and uniformed soldiers, many of whom were in severe distress, either from pain or shock or both.

A young, heavily bearded orderly sporting a pair of blue-black shiners approached us. He pointed at a patient lying on a stretcher on the floor, one leg bandaged and splinted from groin to ankle, and then motioned at the stairwell. He mumbled something.

"He wants us to take the patient downstairs to the next level," Anna interpreted. The kid on the stretcher couldn't have been older than 16.

I took the heavy end, and the three of us carefully carried him to the stairwell while he cried out with every movement. He smelled bad. I knew that smell – the sweet, putrid smell of gangrene, like a dead animal rotting behind a kitchen wall. We managed to wrangle him onto the stairs and around the first corner without bumping his leg. But the space was cramped, and people were in a hurry. The patient screamed a couple of times when passers-by brushed his leg — nothing we could do about it.

The world suddenly shook violently as a pressure wave punched

—

I regained awareness in complete darkness and immediately began coughing, gasping for air, my throat raw and dry. Where...? What...? Was this my hotel room...?

No.

Something or someone heavy was sitting on my chest. My legs were jammed in different directions like a hurdler clearing a jump. Was I upside down? What the fuck? My heart began booming in my chest. The air was thick with smoke, concrete dust, and burning motor oil. I knew that smell: C-4. The building had been bombed. I moved my right hand or tried to move it. It was pinned. I was pinned. I jerked my arm, and the rubble shifted. I could move it, but only a little. Moving caused me some pain, but it was distant, like a faraway voice on a bad phone line. The rubble closed in around my hand again—more pain. I coughed and coughed and couldn't stop. Suffocating. No light. Utter darkness. Was I facing up? Or down? Was I upside down? More coughing.

A voice cried over and over. "*Anaha harq...Anaha harq... Anaha harq...*" It's burning. It's burning. It's burning. Maybe it was the young doctor, or the kid with gangrene, or someone else — there was no way to know. The voice was young, male, and frightened. The weight shifted over my head and back, pressing down. I heard whimpering, an animal sound. A man screamed somewhere deep below me as the reek of barbecuing flesh reached my nostrils, the smell that makes you want to turn vegan.

And then I remembered! God...Anna had been with me! "Anna!" I called out, my voice a hoarse, grit-filled whisper. I cleared my throat and spat, fighting the panic. The weight on my head and shoulders was crushing. ...Getting more difficult to breathe.

Somewhere close, a man moaned incessantly for his mother. "*Al'umu... Al'umu... Al'umu...*"

The darkness was complete. It had density — weight. All I could see were the bright floaters that drifted before my eyes. "Anna!" I fought the need to cough and called again. "Anna!" Nothing came back. No answer. I imagined her crushed, buried alive. Lifeless. Tears welled along with a wave of anger. Why had we come to this shit hole? I wanted to lash out, but there was nothing but darkness, dust, and pressure. "Hey!" I shouted, but the darkness swallowed my voice. "HEY!" The sound was entombed in darkness, the same as me. Something shifted under my legs. I dropped maybe a handful of inches, relieving some of the pressure on my head and chest.

I shut the voices out as best I could and concentrated on my situation. I was sore all over – battered and bruised, but nothing was broken. I moved my leg and twisted my body. The rubble moved, and my leg came free. I moved again. The rubble shifted again, and I was no longer in the hurdling position, mid-jump.

"Oh god...what..." Anna's voice came in quiet gasps.

I felt a hand brush against my leg and then grab my ankle.

"Anna...?"

"Vin."

Her voice was feeble. She was drifting off.

"Anna!"

"What happened?" she asked.

"Is anything broken? Can you breathe?"

She coughed and coughed. Something gave way, and I heard the vaguely musical notes of rubble shifting against concrete. I tumbled half a meter. Dust and pulverized rock showered my head and filled my mouth and nostrils. I gagged, tried to get air, and spat out a gob of grit. The downpour of concrete, dust, and crushed cinderblock tapered off. I spat again and caught half a breath of dust-free air.

"Are you okay?" I asked Anna, the question inadequate, the words insufficient. No, she wasn't okay. Neither of us was okay. Last thing I remembered was being in the stairwell. But now we were buried along with everyone else in the underground parking level. From near and far floated the muffled voices of those who hadn't been immediately killed by falling concrete blocks or impaled on rebar, calling out, dying slowly in their coffins of rubble.

"I'm alive, I think." Anna was calm, the calm that comes when the only alternative is panic, a calm enforced by sheer will. "I'm below you," she said with absolute clarity. "I'm reaching up." The rubble moved again. Anna's arm – I guessed it was her arm — hooked around my leg.

I noticed a green glow somewhere in the blackness, the dots on my watch and the hour and minute arms. "Ten past one," I said.

"We've been out only a couple of minutes." Above my head, I could make out a zig-zagging outline of concrete, part of a flight of stairs.

"Could also be 12 hours," Anna whispered. "Got a hell of an egg on my head. Feels like a 12-hour egg." A block of concrete tumbled and something jammed into my kidneys.

"What?" said Anna.

The pain had an edge to it. I angled the watch face a little.

"I see it," Anna whispered. "Rebar." Her hand reached up, outlined in the faint glow. "I got your back." Something jerked free, the relief instant.

"The corny lines are my job," I reminded her as I lay still and tried to think. I had my cell in my back pocket and the CIA one in my front pocket, but there was no way I could reach either. "You got a phone on you?"

I heard some movement. A light came on below me for a few seconds. Shadows danced, then the light turned off. "No service," said Anna.

Neither of us spoke for a while, assessing the situation. My assessment was bleak. We were trapped in a rubble coffin, the zig-zag shape of concrete stairs the low roof.

"They'll be looking for us, digging us out," Anna whispered eventually.

I wondered who "they" might be. If she was thinking Bin Alzhur and his white hats, for all we knew the explosion had killed them, but I agreed with Anna for reasons of morale — sure, rescue might come any moment. "What about the baby?" I asked.

'What about it?"

"Is it okay?"

"It's not a baby," Anna reminded me, breathless. "It's a collection of dividing cells about half an inch long. Let's call it a tadpole."

"This is why I didn't want you to come," I said.

"Do you really want this argument now?"

No. "Didn't your friend say it would be safer down here?"

"Maybe it is. We don't know what happened topside. What's that smell?"

"C4. A truck bomb, maybe. Welcome to Syria, and have a nice day."

I heard and felt rubble shifting, Anna trying to find a better position. A large block of something — I guessed concrete — pressed down more heavily on my shoulder. I tried to find ways to ignore it. "So...," I grunted. "Now I've got you where I want you."

"What?"

"There's no escape. Perfect time to tell me what happened?"

"When?"

"When you were shot. When you died."

"Now? You want to do this now?"

"Somewhere else you need to be? Come on, talk to me. The paramedics on the scene told me you were dead. I went to your funeral. And then, a couple of years later, you came back. Risen from the dead. You should start a religion."

"You know I can't say anything about that time," she replied.

"Not to be negative, but we may never get out of here. You can tell me. Promise I won't have you arrested for violating the Secrecy Act."

"I don't know what happened after I was shot."

"Paramedics were on the scene so fast I wondered if maybe they were listening at the door."

"A nuclear facility like Oak Ridge... It has a pretty serious medical response unit in case things go wrong."

"You were dead, Anna. I saw your heart beating in your chest, for Christ's sake."

"They kept me alive."

"They did more than that."

Silence, and then: "They gave me a new heart."

"What? In the ambulance?" Few things surprised me these days, but that got me.

"Don't be ridiculous. I woke up in a facility. They told me there wasn't much they could do with the heart I was born with. So they gave me a new one."

I had so many questions that I didn't know which ones to ask first. "There's no suture line where they cracked your sternum."

"I already had a big hole in about the right spot, remember?"

True. "Where are all the anti-rejection drugs you must be on?"

"Stopped taking most of them 12 months ago. I take one medication daily, and I keep that at Andrews. Look, heart surgery is no big deal these days. The surgeon who did the op' told me if you're going to have health problems, make it your heart. They can do anything with that these days. You sound upset they brought me back?"

"I'm upset because you disappeared for two years and neglected to inform me that you weren't pushing up daisies. A small oversight. Meanwhile, I went through the five stages of grief."

"What? Glen Keith, Johnny Walker, Vat 69, Dimple, and what's the other one?"

"Funny."

"Vin, I'm sorry. I've told you I'm sorry a dozen times. I'll say it a dozen more times if that helps. But I can't go back and change things."

"Then do the next best thing and fill in the gaps."

I heard Anna breathing. The nearby cries for help had stopped — not a good sign.

"A week after the surgery, I felt okay," she continued. "Within ten days, I was in rehab."

"Where did all this happen?"

"I told you – a facility."

"You can do better than that."

"A CIA facility."

"Like you said, I'm on the team now. Let's hear it. "

"It doesn't work like that, Vin, and you know it."

"Is the transplant a risk to our dividing cells?"

"No, we should both be fine. It's you I'm having problems with."

"Keep going. So, there you were in rehab, doing leg curls and squat jumps..."

"Swimming, actually."

"Whatever."

"Bradley Chalmers paid me a visit—"

"That asshole was in on it?"

"He approached me to volunteer for the CIA's Special Activities Center."

"Isn't that where they teach recruits how to color in without going over the lines?"

"Special Activities also does the dirty shitty stuff no one will admit to.

"What was Chalmer's sales pitch?" I asked.

"He told me the system had me entered as killed in the line of duty. I was a true ghost, a clean sheet, the perfect recruit for an outfit off the grid."

"But you had to agree to that."

"I was told the job was of national importance..."

"Patriotism – last refuge of scoundrels."

"They didn't have enough people to complete the mission."

"Which was to assassinate American citizens."

"Citizens who had joined ISIS. And when ISIS collapsed, all those citizens expected to come home, bringing their military training and their crazy ideas and hatreds with them. The Pentagon war-gamed their homecoming, and none of the outcomes looked good."

"There's always GITMO."

"These fighters weren't captured. No one wanted them incarcerated. Interminable, costly, and uncertain legal battles... Stories on 60 Minutes... Guantanamo was never an option. These Americans were dangerous and inconvenient. That's how they were described to me."

"How many Americans are we talking about?" I asked, distracted, my breathing becoming more labored.

"That's classified, but more than 80."

I had no sympathy for anyone who decided to join a group that believed the fastest way to paradise was to take the lives of innocent people with them as their bona fides. But that wasn't my issue. "We had something, Anna, but you let someone talk you out of it. And you left me with a lie."

"Oh, for fuck's sake, Vin. You've been watching too much Oprah. Look, from my perspective, I believed I owed them. They gave me a second chance. A new heart, another shot at life. That was a debt I felt I had to repay."

Anna's speech was becoming broken by short breaths, oxygen becoming scarce.

"People like Chalmers are heartless. By giving you a heart — they bought you and knew you'd see it their way because that's how they operate. You became their property."

"That's ridiculous," Anna snapped.

"Could you walk out on the mission?"

"No, but you wouldn't walk out on a mission either, so what's the difference?"

"Work ethic is different to being owned."

"You're still angry," she said.

"Mostly at Chalmers. I am gonna kill that fucker one of these days." I met the guy several years ago in Japan while working a case. He was climbing the Agency ladder, stepping on as many people as possible, including his wife, their two kids, his girlfriend, and his boss. He was also lucky not to have gone to jail using his position at the CIA as an instrument to defraud Uncle Sam. And more recently, he'd conspired to have me executed by Anna in Syria. Chalmers was an invertebrate with amoral personality disorder — a spineless jerk prone to all manner of corruption. He was also doing his damnedest to get Anna into bed at every opportunity. To recap, I am gonna kill that fucker one of these days — if I manage to get out of here.

"We're even, the CIA and I," said Anna. "The debt's repaid. I have my life back, and one of the first things I've done is create a new life with you."

I chose to ignore the obvious and immediate flaw in that statement — that the three of us were likely to die here from suffocation if not further building collapse. I tried to take a deep breath, but that only brought on another coughing fit. I felt Anna's hand tighten around my leg. We both knew where this was going. I was feeling drowsy. "Keep talking," I said.

"It's your turn. Tell me about your mom and dad. It bothers me that you don't talk about them. We're going to be parents. What's your parenting model?"

"Can we talk about the weather instead?"

"Sure. If your father was a meteorologist, and it's a segue."

I never talked about them because there was little to say.

"I've got all day," Anna said into the silence.

"We should conserve oxygen."

"Right, when it's your turn to talk. What's so bad that you don't want to go near it? And this is me — Anna — the soon-to-be mother of your child."

"I thought we were having a tadpole."

The weight on my back and chest was slowly increasing, my breathing restricted to short, shallow breaths.

"So, tell me. Think of it as a deathbed confession."

"Blunt," I said.

"Look, this is a time when important things need to be said. Now it's your turn. Whatever you tell me, I'll never mention again if we get out of here. Are they still alive? Your parents? What were their names, at least? Your mother and father's...?"

"Lana and William Cooper — Billy to his friends. I've only ever known them as pictures in photo albums."

"There you go. Was that so hard?"

The rubble shifted again, releasing a bloom of concrete dust that caught in my throat. I tried to hack it away.

"You okay?" Anna whispered when silence returned.

"Yeah...You?"

"I can move around a little. It's not so bad. So, you were saying...?"

There was no escape. "It's not much of a story."

"Tell me anyway."

"My uncle, Nathanial — Nat — Billy's younger brother, got drafted to fight in Vietnam in 1970. Billy was out of work then, so he enlisted in support of Nat. Both ended up in rifle companies but in different battalions. They did some dumb things, and they earned medals for them. My old man was killed attempting one of those dumb things — stumbled across a unit of would-be Viet Cong infiltrators outside the wire at the Bien Hoa Air Base. He took them on instead of alerting base security. His M16 jammed, but he had a Colt .45 which he'd taken off a dead VC while on an earlier patrol, the pistol probably souvenired from a dead American. Anyway, Billy was badly wounded but killed four before the rest ran off. He left the Colt to Nat. I've got it these days. Keep it in a floor safe along with a lucky rabbit's foot. Billy was killed December '72. I came along in '73. By all accounts, my mother suffered what today would be called post-natal depression. She ran off twice, leaving me with Uncle Nat. The second time she ran away, she was killed in a car wreck, the driver an ex-Vietnam vet high on heroin."

"Jesus...," said Anna. "I'm sorry..."

"I never knew her."

"Tell me about Nat."

"He wrote in a letter that he decided to go carer to honor his brother's sacrifice. I remember we moved around a lot."

"Did your uncle marry?"

"No. Succession of girlfriends."

"This explains so much."

"Like what?"

"Your commitment issues."

"*My* commitment issues!"

"Where is Nat today?"

"Died in '91 during Desert Storm. An accident when a load shifted in a C-130."

"In '91, you would have been eighteen."

"Seventeen turning eighteen."

"Gee..."

"Hey, the Army is great at parenting. I did okay at school, graduated, went to college, got a law degree, passed the bar, practiced law, hated it."

"Why'd you hate it?"

"Most of the so-called innocent victims the firm represented were guilty as hell. I guess I missed the military. I went to the OTC and earned a commission. I had a law degree, so they offered me JAG, but I didn't want it. Got streamed into special operations, then combat controllers. And then I fell out the back of a couple of CH-47s and decided on a career change. Met a couple of guys along the way from OSI. I guess they were a good advertisement. But you know the Air Force. It can bounce you around when it feels like it." That seemed to satisfy the beast — Anna's relentless questions dried up. "Did I put you to sleep?"

"No. And thank you. Tell me about the rabbit's foot."

"Another time, maybe."

"Well...that was a conversation we needed to have. Don't you feel better, lighter?"

No. "Floating away, here."

"I'm tired."

"Try to stay awake," I told her.

A deafening explosion. And then another. The world lifted and dropped a couple of times. Bricks, masonry, concrete. Choking dust. Pressure. Unbelievable pressure...

The next thing I remember was being pulled out of a small hole in the rubble, many hands around my wrists and forearms — people shouting, yelling, gesturing at others around them. Water was poured over my face and then wiped with rags to clear the dust. An oxygen mask was pressed over my mouth and nose, and then many hands lifted me and passed me over the heads of a crowd, eventually setting me down on a stretcher. The blue sky above was crowded with faces and more shouting. I pushed the faces away, managed to sit, and then swept the mask off my mouth and nose. "Anna!" I called out and then started coughing uncontrollably. Someone forced the crowd of rescuers back. I recognized Bin Alzhur and his dirty white helmet. His son, Maali, too. Others among the crowd also wore white helmets. More cries and shouts. Anna was being rushed to a white van carried by four men. Other survivors were lying on the ground on stretchers, medics moving among them seeing to injuries. I pushed one guy out of my face and saw that I'd left a bloody handprint on his shirt. My hand was slaked with fresh blood, a deep gash down the length of my thumb, the muscle popping out like meat from a split sausage.

"Mr. Cooper, Mr. Cooper, you will come with me, please. You have many cuts. Your hand..."

Bin Alzhur was herding me toward the truck. Anna was there, so I was happy to go. We saw each other and were immediately in each other's arms.

"Vin..." she said, the strength of the embrace a reminder that neither of us believed we would have this moment.

"You're under arrest," I told her.

"What?"

"For violating the secrecy act."

"You promised."

"I lied."

Confusion swirled around us — mothers screaming, fathers shouting. More people arrived by van, car, and motorcycles to clear debris. Bodies and parts of bodies were carried from the rubble along with survivors, haggard, bloody, filthy... At least ten deceased, some of them children, lay on the road, faces covered by articles of blood-stained clothing.

A white hat worked on my hand, pouring disinfectant over the wound. He then began to stitch the wide laceration with a needle and thread. I flinched because, well, it hurt. He shrugged an apology and explained, "No anesthetic."

Bin Alzhur was talking, but the words failed to register.

"...and so this is what they do, but we have learned," he said.

"Who's 'they?'" I asked him.

"The Russians." He looked into my eyes. "You are disoriented. I will come back later."

"No, please...," said Anna.

"First explosion was car bomb," Bin Azhur repeated for my benefit. "A white van. We thought it was one of ours, but it was not. As you can see, many people have been killed. We know it was the Russians doing this because they wait for us to start digging, and then they make a second attack. Two shells. Airburst — artillery. Both missed by a little way. You were lucky."

I registered the growing line-up of corpses. Not so lucky for others.

A small convoy of military vehicles rolled into the square, down their flanks the red and white strip identified the Russian Federation. The trucks squealed to a stop 20 meters away. I looked around to signal Bin Alzhur and warn him, but he'd already made himself scarce. There wasn't a single White Helmet to be seen. Now, I couldn't see a single white helmet. Doors opened, and Russian fighters hopped out, lit cigarettes, and gave the world a brace of surly looks. The lead vehicle's last man out the door was a tall, heavy-set character wearing oversized square-rimmed dark sunglasses, a broad-brimmed floppy hat, and a Russian combat uniform devoid of insignia. His cheeks were white, his lips enormous — red and fleshy, like a gutted animal's entrails lying in snow. He strolled toward the destroyed building in no particular hurry, slowly climbing a mound of rubble to better the vantage point, where he stopped to survey the ongoing rescue. His head pivoted slowly, taking in the devastation. He appeared to nod with approval. And then his sunglasses settled on me, and the satisfaction evaporated. After several seconds, he raised a hand to his face and removed the sunglasses, perhaps to see if his eyes weren't deceiving him. On the subject of those eyes, I was close enough to see that they were a disconcerting pink, the irises flecked with flashes of red as if sliced by a razor. The pupils, dilated by the sunglasses, were as big and black as watermelon seeds before narrowing to pinpricks. They were the eyes of an experiment gone wrong, bottomless sinkholes, pits that led straight to hell.

"Jesus...," muttered Anna beside me.

"I doubt it," I said. "I'm thinking the other guy." My phone *pinged* with a text. I checked the screen. Wilkes was the sender. I thumbed the button and read, *US Marines GySgt. Gerome Frederickson, 1MEF. Attached to 2nd Light Armored Recon Battalion, Bravo Company back in the day. Hometown, Savannah, GA. Asked around. Runs some kind of a cult these days. Working on an address.*

A photo of Frederickson accompanied the text. I'd seen countless photos like this — sitting up on a tank, grinning, tanned, shirtless, and as bald as the ball on a towbar. The guy seemed normal enough during Iraqi Freedom days.

"Anything?" Anna asked.

"Maybe." I put the phone away. Whatever Niemiec had come to see — and I had a fair idea what that might be — setting those horror movie eyes on us, he'd seen enough. Replacing the sunglasses on his lily-white nose, he turned and climbed into the vehicle, his men following.

"Handsome devil," she observed.

She had it partly right. "If I didn't know better, I would say that building collapse was meant for us."

"What makes you say that?"

"The Russians hit the hospital just after we arrived, and then Niemiec turns up to assess the outcome. He gets one look at us and leaves. What does that tell you?"

"If that's true, someone informed him we were in the building."

The world had gone into the crapper, so, as promised, Staff Sergeant Maynard turned up this time with an M1127 Stryker recon vehicle. He slapped its dusty armored flank. "Just in case we need us a little extra fuck you."

The drive to Homs — according to Bin Alzhur, the center housing the main Wagner compound in this neck of the woods — was uneventful. The accompaniment of an 18-ton armored 8-wheeler and its M2 heavy machine gun had something to do with that. There wasn't much traffic, but what there was seemed to be primarily Syrian Government forces using a variety of transport options, a little Russian military traffic, and the occasional pickup with a machine gun mounted in the bed. The pickup guys waved. The Syrian regulars ignored us. The Russians glared.

Anna and I were both sore from our untimely burial, both of us covered in multiple bruises, cuts, and abrasions. It was hard to get comfortable. My thumb throbbed. The rest of me felt crushed. Anna didn't look so great either. But we were alive while plenty of others weren't, which came down to a spin of fate's roulette wheel and nothing more. It turned out that a section of the fire escape stairs had come down over our heads and, saved us from being turned into jelly by a much larger concrete slab and many tons of cinder block.

At least a dozen checkpoints later, we arrived at Homs, a bigger center than Idlib, but like the lesser town, Homs had been pulverized by Bashar al-Assad's attempts at restoring his popularity. The place featured more broken multi-story buildings either collapsed or with gaping holes, and neighborhoods cratered by bombs. Here and there, the city's inhabitants were engaged in the clean-up, but most people — the elderly, women, and children — went about their business. Males of fighting age, which began somewhere around 14 years of age, were as rare as a thin Idlib rat.

We drove the streets slowly, taking in another Middle East success story, Google Maps leading the way to the Wagner HQ, which was situated in a former children's kindergarten. There was irony there if I was prepared to dig for it.

Our convoy pulled up outside the kindy in a neighborhood spared the way a tornado can blow one house to bits but leave the one next door completely untouched. The entrance was barred by jury-rigged steel gates topped with razor wire and flanked by sand-bagged pillboxes. Maybe Wagner was expecting the place to be stormed by angry toddlers. Painted across the gate in prominent red Russian Cyrillic characters was the word *"Музыканты."*

Anna and I shared a look.

"It says The Musicians," she informed me. "Richard Wagner was Hitler's favorite composer." When I still seemed perplexed, she explained further, "You missed that briefing. The musician thing is a private joke with these assholes."

Quaint. The gates rolled back, permitting entry, and our vehicles stopped in an open area surrounded by buildings painted in a kaleidoscope of pastels and big, cheery flowers.

Sergeant Maynard got his men out of the vehicles, except for the gunner atop the Stryker, who remained behind the M2.

Half a dozen Wagner employees in Russian utilities swaggered out of one of the buildings to meet us. No rifles, just sidearms. I noted the men occupying the pillboxes were now turned around, facing our way, as were their mounted light machine guns, barrels pointed down.

The men who came to greet us were all in their mid-to-late forties with deeply lined faces suggesting autobiographies of hardship and violence. Their apparent leader, pushing fifty with dyed blonde hair and a side order of male pattern baldness, gave us a grin, which, from the decay in a front tooth, told me nothing other than he was afraid of dentists. His hands came to rest on his hips, the top of his right hand tattooed with the skull of...it could be a ram or a goat enclosed in a pentangle. I noted the trigger finger on his right hand had been lopped off at the first knuckle. There were tattoos on his remaining fingers — letters I couldn't make out.

Niemiec, wearing his sunglasses but no hat this time, came out of a doorway framed by a giant daisy. Taking small steps for a tall man, he made his way to the front, white hair flaring briefly in the sunlight as he walked from one shadow to another.

Anna and I took a couple of steps toward him and were going to take more, but he put his hand out to discourage us. He stopped inside the last of the shade provided by the building behind him, like a vampire afraid direct sun would ignite his skin.

"I thought you'd be shorter," I told him.

Niemiec carefully removed his sunglasses and placed them in a top pocket with the deliberation of a man who loses sunglasses like the rest of us lose pens. Those distinctive and, I had to admit, confronting pink and red eyes of his stared at us from beneath a pair of bushy blonde eyebrows like something vicious hiding under the heads of used toothbrushes.

"Your name is Cooper," he said, head tilting briefly toward my nametag.

"You can read."

He countered, "No need. I know who you are."

"Are you saying you can't read?"

"You are a former special agent in OSI and now CIA."

"No, U.S. Department of Agriculture," I corrected him. "You want to know about vulture bees? I'm your man. You might have me confused with someone else of the same name."

Those grotesque red lips of his parted, revealing a brace of tiny milk teeth. Up close, he was a terrifying man-baby, one who used way too much aftershave, a tsunami of something sweet and kinda nasty swamping us.

"We have some questions for you, Mr. Niemiec," said Anna, not one for small talk.

He fixed those baby pinks on my partner. "You, I do not know, but of course, you are also CIA."

He looked Anna up and down like she was a menu board with attractive prices.

"You've recently flown in from Poland," I told Niemiec in my finest bureaucratic monotone. "Did you bring any agricultural products, or had you visited any farms before your arrival here? Syria has strict bio-security laws."

Niemiec ignored the question.

"Spectrum," Anna said under her breath.

One of Niemiec's immediate wingmen, a skinny guy whose black skin shined like polished shoe leather, leaned on an oily 55-gallon drum and puffed on a vape. Was that strawberry sundae fighting with Niemiec's cologne?

"What you lookin' at, *dhoofaar*?" he said, blowing a cloud of dense steam that obscured his face.

The example beside him was more typical of the mercs standing around attempting to look tough — Caucasian, with a rangy, slightly underfed body type. A long brown beard hung from his jawline like a curtain of brushed pubic hair. Chechens, I figured. Their uniforms, webbing, and weapons suggested Russian Spetsnaz. But the shoulder patch featuring a grinning human skull centered in crosshairs said PMC Wagner, the Kremlin's private army of mercenaries and criminals.

I asked Blondie, "So what were you in for? Rape, murder, armed robbery?" No reaction. "No, don't tell me...Pedophilia?" Still no reaction.

"I know why you are here," Niemiec informed us.

Not hard to figure, Einstein.

He continued. "You want to know about so-called chemical weapons taken into Syria many years ago."

"How'd you guess?" I told him.

He replied, "You have wasted your time. Everyone knows there were no chemical weapons in Iraq."

Nice try. "Why is a Polish lieutenant colonel, a Coalition officer, wearing a Hazmat suit and riding on an enemy midnight truck convoy racing for the Syrian border ahead of the Coalition invasion?"

"These photos. They are fakes. False flag games."

"There was an accident *en* route, a spillage of methylphosphonyl difluoride—"

Niemiec interrupted, "This chemical... It is used for fighting fires, yes?"

"No," I said.

Anna added, "It's hardly worth rushing fire retardant out of the country."

"Nothing that can be proved," Niemiec shrugged. "And it could be anyone in these photos."

"Yeah, you disappear in a crowd," Anna replied.

"I have nothing to say. You Americans..."

Here we go, I thought, one of those The-Trouble-With-You-Americans speeches.

Niemiec sneered, "You think you can go anywhere in the world and make your lies."

The speech ended. At least it was brief.

"I do not have to talk to you, answer your questions. Syria is not an American courtroom."

"You left your castle back in Warsaw in a hurry," I pointed out. "When you want to question someone, and they run, it tells you something, and it's not the word innocent."

"I am a businessman," Niemiec replied. "I travel often."

"Methylphosphonyl difluoride is a component of the nerve toxin sarin," Anna said, getting us back on message.

"You have been drinking your government's Kool-aide," he said with a grin.

"Do you enjoy torturing people, Mr. Niemiec?" Anna asked, increasingly frustrated.

"Bah! I do not have to listen to you," Niemiec said, waving a hand, palming us off.

"Just answer the questions, Mr. Niemiec, and we'll leave you alone," I said, not entirely truthfully.

"This is why you come with tanks and machine guns." He motioned at the Stryker. "I am Russian. I do not have to cooperate with you. When this country descended into blood, America stood by and watched. Russia was not afraid to come and make Syria stable once more. Russia is welcome here. America is not. "

That depended on who you asked. "Why did you try to have us killed this morning?" I asked him. "You did try to kill us, right?"

"I do not know what you're talking about."

"You came to inspect a building that was bombed this morning because you're the one who bombed it. You came to see us dead and buried. Instead, you killed and maimed Syrians you claim you're here to help."

"I know nothing of what your American arrogance is accusing me of. Yes, I saw you this morning at a place where the white hat terrorists have been doing their evil work, spreading lies and making terrorist plans against the lawful government. But there were no white hats. Perhaps they were buried under the rubble where they belonged. There was nothing to see, so I left."

"I thought you were retired, Mr. Niemiec," said Anna, still steaming. "What are you doing here in Syria?"

Niemiec glanced at me, then Anna. His temper flared, flushing his cheeks a pinkish color that matched his eyes. "I will tell you again; I do not have to answer your questions. You have no authority, and your tank does not frighten me. You should go. Syria is a dangerous place, as you have found out."

"Are you threatening us?" Anna cooed, enjoying Niemiec's seeming discomfort.

Easy, buddy. You've already got this gal pissed — best not to double down.

"Let us pretend it was me on those trucks many years ago, and the trucks were carrying whatever you say they were carrying. What do you expect me to do about it? What can *you* do about it? Go. Go home; you are finished here." Niemiec turned and took the shaded path back to the daisy and disappeared inside.

Niemiec's entourage also wandered off now that Elvis had left the building, except for the Somali and the guy with the hand tattoo who said, "You Yankee assholes are not welcome here. Leave before we fuck you up." I recognized that accent — South African. He signaled to one of the gunners in the sandbagged pill boxes, and the man cocked his machine gun.

Right about now, our overwatch up on the 8-wheeler would be responding, thumbing off the M2's safety.

"Okay," said Maynard behind us, pulling his men back. "We don't want this going pear-shaped."

Anna snapped some pictures of the kindergarten courtyard with her cell.

"Dhoofaar? Did I hear that right?" I asked.

"It's Somali for pig."

"You speak Somali now?"

"We had a Somali deserter from ISIS as a guide," she explained. "He swore a lot. Syria brings out the worst in people."

You couldn't argue with that.

U.S. BASE AL-TANF, NORTHERN SYRIA

With our dressings changed, the medic packed away his bandages, swabs, and torn plastic packages. "If you can, keep that hand dry for a couple of days," he advised. "I've put a waterproof dressing over the stitches in your lower back." He placed a bottle of ibuprofen on the desk. "Something for the pain. Y'all have a good day, what's left of it."

"Thanks," I said. A good day? I'd had better. I took the top off the Coors and explained to Anna, "Something for the pain."

Anna drank a bottle of soda water and juggled cell phones. Mine *pinged*. "That's me. I just sent you photos of Niemiec and stooges taken at the kindy." She slung the phone over to me.

"Who took these?" I scrolled through images of the guy with the tattooed hand and his buddies.

"The specialist on the M2. I asked him to. Thinking maybe the Agency could collect some IDs. And I saw a text from Wilkes on the screen. Who's Frederickson?"

I lay back on the rack and put an arm behind my head. The stretch in my shoulder felt sore but good. I didn't know too much about the guy, only what Wilkes had told me. I opened the text. "Back in '03, when Wilkes and his SAS unit handed Al Asad air base over to the 3rd ACR, there was a rumor about a WMD convoy. Frederickson was a Marine attached to Armored Cavalry who talked to him about it. There was a Kurd in Frederickson's unit who said one of the men from his village was killed from exposure to WMD after being involved in a firefight with the convoy. It wasn't given any credence at the time. Anyway, I asked Wilkes for Frederickson's contact details. He lives in Savannah, Georgia. That's pretty much all I know."

Anna nodded and took in our surroundings — two single cots, a cupboard, a desk, and a dart board on the wall with one dart suck in the wall beside it.

"So, what do you think?" I said. "Nice of the Army to give us the honeymoon suite, right?"

"It's a 40-foot Maersk shipping container."

"Not just any shipping container. All of the others are half the size of this one, except for the CC's. But only one has you sitting on a cot in a tight Tee and shorts. Come on, take a load off, lie down." It didn't take much convincing. I put the Coors on the floor, and we spooned. Anna's freshly washed hair smelt of jasmine. I wriggled in closer.

"Niemiec seems way too confident for someone who's been caught with his hand in the cookie jar. There's another game here — we just can't see it."

Anna, always business.

"We'll catch up with Niemiec," I reassured her. Time and place. Muirhead has plans for him."

"By the book, though, right?"

"Depends on which book."

"Oh!" She said, somewhat startled. "That's not your elbow, is it?"

"No."

She shrugged my hand off her shoulder. "Vin, not in the mood."

I ran my fingertips up her arm and then across her bare shoulders. "But it's the honeymoon suite," I cooed, my fingers continuing their journey down her back, over her hip, and between her legs.

After a few moments of no reaction but no further protest, Anna said with a big sigh, "Okay, get it over with, then." She rolled over, turned to face me, grinning, and reached down. It didn't take long to find what she was looking for — it wasn't my elbow.

Getting it over with took a while longer than usual... Maybe there really is something in the whole pregnant-women-are-horny thing.

A Black Hawk circling the base on its way out woke us at dawn. A rack is built for one, and Anna never made it to hers. We sat on either side of the cot and looked at each other. Anna had pillow hair. I had a purple bruise on the side of my face that looked like a squashed plum.

"How is it you can look so damn good first thing in the morning," she said.

We both laughed, then went for showers.

The hot water, followed by the cold, did me some good. Everywhere was sore, and there was still grit in places I never knew I had, along with the memory of feeling slowly crushed by tons of rubble. No doubt my subconscious would work through it and present a nightmare with these new experiences magnified. And for sure, scorpions — it's always scorpions — would feature somewhere.

I dressed as Anna walked in, toweling her hair. A tap on the door was right behind her. We were both decent. "Yeah?" I called out. "Come in."

An Army captain walked in — a squat, solid woman with almost no neck. Put arms and legs on a bag of cement, and you've got the captain. Cumberland, according to the nametag. Mid-30s, give or take, though the buzz cut and desert weathering probably added maybe another five years to the age estimate. "Special Agent Masters, Mr. Cooper, your ride is on the apron. It'll be good to go in twenty minutes. Just getting some gas into it. Sergeant Maynard will take you over shortly. I hope your stay proved fruitful." She looked at me deadpan. "I heard you were here looking for bees, Mr. Cooper. You find any?"

"Wild goose chase," I said, shaking my head. "Someone in Washington thought otherwise."

"My daddy has an almond farm back home. Bees are like kin. What kind of bees you after?"

"Vulture bees," I said.

The look on her face told me the words "vulture" and "bees" didn't go together where she came from. I explained, "They make honey out of dead things."

"No. Really?"

"Uh-huh."

"And we got 'em here?"

"They live in rainforests."

The captain shook her square head in disbelief. "Which we have a lot of here..."

"Washington," I said, the universal excuse for everything that didn't make sense.

"I hear you...Well, y'all have a good flight. Vulture bees, eh?" the captain said and left with a shake of her head.

"Practicing your cover again?" Anna asked.

"You have to admit, it's working."

Anna admitted nothing. "We're going somewhere?"

"Savannah."

"As in Georgia? Frederickson? Listen, you said that was all you knew. What about, 'Hey, by the way, we're heading Stateside first thing in the morning.' You might have told me about this."

"Didn't want to spoil the moment."

Anna was pissed. "Vin, I am not here for your recreation, okay?"

"I'm sorry. I am."

Anna surveyed our surroundings. "Well, I guess I'd better pack."

Sergeant Maynard arrived ten minutes later and tapped on the steel door with his helmet. A few minutes later, we were motoring slowly toward a Moose on the apron. "I saw Kaamil Bin Alzhur this morning," Maynard said over his shoulder. "I told him you were leaving."

"I would've liked to say goodbye," Anna replied, flashing some disappointment in my direction.

"He said you'll be back."

I hoped to hell he was wrong, but he was probably right. Shit rolls downhill, and Syria seems to lie at the bottom of every hill.

SAVANNAH, GEORGIA

The address provided by Wilkes took us to the area in Savannah where the other half lived, a square lined shoulder-to-shoulder with stately Civil War-era homes and towering Myrtle oaks hung with shrouds of Spanish moss.

"This is it," I said, standing at the foot of half a dozen semi-circular stairs, an old iron hand railing leading up to a front door painted black with polished brass features. The home was three stories, painted dark green with lighter green shutters on the windows. A CCTV camera positioned over the front door gazed down at us, its red light winking. A polished brass plaque on a pillar at the base of the stairs announced in black lettering, "The Aetherius Society."

A middle-aged couple wearing hessian smocks with hoods pushed past us, walked up the stairs, opened the door, and went inside.

"What is this place?" Anna asked.

A man's voice drifted out from within.

Anna took point, climbed the stairs, and swung the front door's brass knocker a couple of times, a Civil War cannon in miniature, each rap a mini boom. No answer. She opened the door and walked in.

The voice, a male voice, kept at it, his tone and volume rising and falling for dramatic effect. It was a lecture, a speech, or a sermon – maybe all three. We followed it to the source, arriving at a heavy oak door. Opening it revealed an auditorium where a crowd of around 30 people were seated, all dressed in smocks, hoods pulled up over their heads. It was some kind of religious gathering, the air heavy with patchouli and hessian. The walls were dark-paneled, and the light was dim. A single ceiling-mounted spotlight centered on a silver curtain drawn across a stage at the front of the room, the focus of the crowd's attention.

The voice we'd heard was coming through speakers in the ceiling. Bearings established, I listened to what it was saying: "...And so the Cosmic Masters, higher beings of vastly superior mind, left their home on Planet Jupiter and vibrated into Earth's dimension, intent on growing our collective consciousness in the direction of peace and love. It is an open secret within the Washington Intelligence Community that the United States is in partnership with these stewards of the universe to see that planet Earth and humankind reach spiritual and peaceful perfection."

"That's news to me," I whispered.

"Where's Frederickson?" Anna asked.

"I don't see him."

The celestial revelations from the speaker continued as two hooded individuals began moving through their fellow attendees with buckets into which fat envelopes were being deposited. As each envelope was accepted, some benevolence was murmured to the giver, no doubt something along the lines of, "There's one born every minute."

The voice continued, "The Cosmic Masters have, over the last century, bequeathed more advanced technology to our species than in ages past, but the human race will not reach a suitable plane of understanding for the effective transfer of knowledge — a knowledge that will allow us to vibrate to a higher plane and move through the universe — until the earthly powers accept the inevitable truth that we are all destined to become Cosmic Masters — pure energy. At that point, more worldly treasures, and even the Earth itself, will cease to have relevance."

"That's you," I whispered.

"What...?"

"A Cosmic Masters."

Anna smirked. "I think he just said we're all gonna die."

"I wish someone had told me sooner. I thought I was here forever."

"Is that Frederickson's voice we're hearing?"

"Maybe. This is his home, so..."

Dramatic music took over, playing through the speakers, which caused the audience members to lean forward with expectation. I figured the show was about to get underway. One of the bucketmen moved toward a wall-mounted control box. The spotlight on the curtain was extinguished as it rolled back. After a moment of dramatic darkness, a white light punched down from the stage ceiling, illuminating a large, polished aluminum saucer. An audible gasp rose from the room, and then the screaming started. People stood. Some craned their necks to get a better view, others reeled back.

The source of the consternation was that a large amount of blood had sloshed over the rim of the saucer and pooled on the floor beneath it, not usually part of the show from the audience reaction.

Once the violence implied by all the blood registered on the room, a noisy, anxious stampede for the exit began. No one wanted to be here. As the crowd rushed the doorway, a human logjam of pushing and shoving, I caught glimpses of the faces hidden by hoods. The age spread was impressive: young and old, male and female. Two of the faces in the crush I recognized, although it took me a moment to register how I knew them and where we'd met. I hadn't expected to see anyone familiar among this gathering. It was Adams and his girlfriend, Joy. My eyes met with Adams's. He was afraid. Why? Was it because he didn't expect to see me either, and I'd placed him in Frederickson's home? Or was the fear related to that saucer of blood?

The room emptied. Anna and I couldn't stop the exodus. We had no authority here.

I informed Anna. "I just saw Adams and his girlfriend in the crowd,"

"Adams?"

"The commander of the Horned Owl."

"I know who he was. Why was he here? How's he connected to Frederickson?

Yeah, they would be my first questions, too. We hopped up onto the stage.

"Jesus...," Anna murmured as we confronted the contents of that saucer. Or rather, it confronted us.

A heavyset male was lying in a deep pool of blood, his smock black, the blood drenching it coagulated. In fact, there was so much blood that the body almost floated in it. The victim's head was submerged beneath the surface. A thick mass of matted black hair, a wig, had drifted free of the deceased's bald skull. It was difficult to be certain, but this was more than likely Frederickson. His wrists and ankles were fastened with duct tape. Anna placed a 911 call to summon the local PD. Meanwhile, I went backstage.

At a glance, as far as I could tell, Frederickson lived alone. And he lived well. Too well for a former Marine who retired a staff sergeant, although the game he had going with this cult game was probably pretty lucrative. The home was modern and newly renovated. It was also completely trashed, the floors covered in books, magazines and records, clothes, feathers from torn cushions, art ripped from the walls, draws pulled from cupboards, and so forth. This was a pro job. Whoever killed him was looking for something. I wondered what that something was and whether it had been found.

Savannah PD homicide arrived with forensics. The lead officer introduced herself as Sergeant Purdue, a tall African American woman with a moon boot on her foot and bags like flaccid balloons under her eyes, the product of too many late nights and too much stress, I figured. She came to the immediate conclusion that multiple perps were involved, an obvious call, perhaps, given the level of violence visited on both Frederickson and his belongings. The deceased was a powerful man and wouldn't have gone down easy. I figured some hurried torture had been involved to extract the whereabouts of whatever it was that the perps were nosing around for. From the wreckage of his belongings, I took a guess that he held out on them. The amount of blood in the saucer told me Frederickson had died slowly, a heart attack brought on by exsanguination, his body drained of blood, the scene reminiscent of handiwork I'd seen in various images attributed to Niemiec.

Purdue questioned Anna and me separately and then together, but as ours was a national security investigation involving the deceased, there weren't many satisfactory answers we could provide. Frederickson was a potential key witness in a case the OSI was investigating —Anna and I both gave up that much.

"What were they looking for, do you think?" the sergeant asked us.

Anna shook her head. "Don't know. They?"

"One perp? Too much going on here. And the victim had to be close to two hundred pounds. Was there some specific information you were hoping the deceased could provide for this case of yours?"

"Names."

'What names? Whose names?"

Anna kept it general. "People Frederickson had served with in Iraq."

"Does his murder surprise you?"

"We didn't think he was particularly at risk, if that's what you're asking," Anna replied. "I'd have said he was peripheral to our investigation. Now, I'm prepared to think different."

"I'm in on this cold, and you're not, so help me out. Do any suspects come readily to mind?"

Given the M.O., Andre Niemiec, of course, but we couldn't go there. "No," I said.

Disappointed, Purdue turned to me. "So, what's the U.S. Department of Agriculture's interest in this?"

"Can't say," I replied. "National security."

"I hate fucking national security." The sergeant glanced at the business cards Anna had provided and pocketed them. "The Department of Agriculture." She sighed. "Really?"

I gave her my regulation blank look.

"You're free to go, but I may have further questions. How long are you in Savannah?"

"Not sure. A night, maybe two," Anna replied.

"Well, before you go anywhere, let me know." She motioned at the moon boot. "I can't chase."

"How'd you get that?" I asked her.

"Kicking my subordinates."

In other circumstances, the sergeant and I could be pals. She handed us each her card.

"Sergeant *Sunshine* Purdue?" I asked her.

"Yeah, you could put a little fucking ray of it in my life and give me something I can use instead of stonewalling." She then turned and took out her frustration on the room, "Can someone get me the fucking security footage?"

One of the forensics team materialized and handed Sunshine a plastic evidence bag containing a blood-soaked laptop, the apparent terminus of said security footage. I heard the man say that they'd recovered it from the saucer beneath Frederickson's body.

Anna and I walked out the back door to avoid the phalanx of gawkers lining up behind the police crime scene tape. "We need to find Adams and his girlfriend," she said, voicing my thoughts. "Any ideas?"

"The girlfriend is high maintenance. I'd be looking at Savannah's best hotels. "

"You're enjoying yourself now, aren't you."

"What makes you say that?"

"Not a single mention of the job at Sands for a whole day."

We found a motel for the night and started ringing around the finer accommodation establishments in the hope of lucking out and being put through to Adams. No luck, and no Joy, either. It was late when Anna's phone rang, interrupting our search. "I'm going to put you on speaker," she told the caller. And then, to me, "Purdue."

"Turns out the deceased has no next of kin and no relatives. He's all alone in the big bad world, and we need a positive identification. Frederickson is ex-military, and I think you'll be able to access his dental records faster than I could. Any chance you would consider providing us with those?"

"We'll see what we can do," I told her.

"This is a strange one. I've asked the ME to rush the autopsy, and she's a workaholic. I'll send a car for you first thing tomorrow. Where are you staying?"

Anna gave her the motel's address while I found a quiet corner and dialed Inglis.

"These midnight calls are not endearing," she said. "You know that, right?"

"Thanks."

"I haven't said yes. Who is Frederickson and why should I care?"

I briefed her on Frederickson's back story and our latest interaction with his corpse.

"You could have told me that upfront."

I asked her to send the records through to Savannah PD, Homicide. "One other thing. This might take you a little longer than those dental records."

"Great."

"There was a Kurdish scout embedded in Frederickson's unit in '03, when the 3rd ACR moved into Al Asad. Who was he, and where is he now?"

"Look, no promises on any of this. Especially overnight, I'll have to call in favors."

"I'll owe you one."

"Don't worry, I'm running a tab."

The call ended. Anna asked, "Can you put Adams and Frederickson in the picture for me? How are they connected?"

"No," I said.

"I'm going to bed."

"Me too."

"No, you're going to the sofa, buddy."

The squawk of a police siren in the motel's forecourt summoned us at 8 a.m. A short while later, an officer escorted us past a long, double-stacked row of refrigerator doors, the general ambiance tinged with formaldehyde and chilled death. I opened the door to the "Post Mortem" room on Sunshine Purdue and a woman in a white lab coat. They were locked in an embrace that ended quickly like two cats suddenly soused with water.

"Morning," Purdue offered, a little embarrassed, straightening her clothes. "Recently married," she explained, not that an explanation was needed.

"Congratulations," Anna said.

"We weren't expecting you so soon."

"The officer went lights and sirens all the way here," I explained.

"Really?"

"No, just kidding."

"This is my partner," said Purdue. "Doctor Alexa Milne, county ME."

Dr. Milne, a large white women, had a round cherubic face that seemed out of place in this environment. We shook, her palm as soft as chamois, the dead not exactly hard on the hands.

The usual greetings of polite society followed beside an autopsy table on which a body was laid out beneath an opaque plastic sheet. Before getting down to business, the doctor fixed us cups of coffee from a coffee machine on a benchtop shared with a half-eaten sandwich and photos from the crime scene. Sunshine's better half removed the sheet revealing a black male. His skin was pulled back away from a deep Y incision that ran from collar bone to sternum to pubic bone, revealing a partially empty abdomen, the organs lying in various buckets waiting their turn to be weighed. The deceased's ribs, cut off in slabs, covered his genitals. I sipped my coffee and looked him over — mid-40s, and fit, a large black-on-black snarling USMC bulldog across his right bicep, an appendix scar, and a little vitiligo on both elbows, bleaching them pink. There were also deep cuts in the skin of his upper legs.

"Have his dental records been sent through?" Purdue enquired.

I checked my phone screen. "No, not as yet," I said, "but that's Frederickson, all right." I showed her the military ID photo that Wilkes had forwarded.

"Yeah, we found his driver's license and it looks like him," said Purdue, "but those records will confirm it."

"Your victim died from drowning," said Milne. "There was a lot of blood in his throat and lungs. More than likely, the killer or killers held his head under. You saw his wrists and ankles taped. I also found adhesive residue on his cheeks, lips, and hair. I suspect he was gagged while they tortured him – those cuts across his legs. There were more cuts across the back of his legs that I think were less about torture and more about inexperience. Whoever killed him was looking for the saphenous veins and didn't get the incision right, and so had a number of goes at it."

"They tortured him and then bled him out?" suggested Anna.

"Some statement, eh?" said Purdue.

"I also found this balled up in his rectum." Milne held an evidence bag containing a stained, creased scrap of lined paper on which was hand-written a series of numbers — 33375935422. "The paper is high quality and 200gsm, so heavier than the paper usually provided on, say, a pad. My guess — it's torn from a notebook."

"We believe it's the deceased's handwriting," said Purdue. "Checked against other samples found at Frederickson's residence."

"Maybe it's what the killers were looking for," suggested the ME. "If so, they didn't find it."

Frederickson had held out. Proof that even crazy U.S. Marines are made of 100 percent Marines.

"The numbers have got us stumped. They mean anything to you?" asked Purdue us.

"No, nothing," said Anna.

"Could be anything," I agreed. "Account numbers, a safe combination... Thirty-three is the country code for France. Might be a phone number."

"We're checking, of course," said Purdue.

"You mind if I take a photo?" Anna asked as my phone *pinged* with a text. It was from Inglis. The news was good and bad. "Frederickson's dental records have been sent to your office," I told Purdue.

"Appreciate it. Thank you."

"But I'm afraid we have to leave town."

"When?"

"Kinda now."

On the way out, Anna asked, "What's happened? Where are we going?"

"Back to Syria. There's been a WMD attack on Idlib."

Shit had collected at the bottom of that hill, as it always seemed to.

IDLIB, SYRIA

Sergeant Purdue wasn't thrilled to hear that Anna and I were boarding an Air Force Gulfstream forthwith and leaving the country. I could relate. Given a choice, I would have preferred a grim crime scene in Savannah to a visit to sunny Syria any day. By way of compensation, Anna gave the sergeant a description of Grizzly Adams and his girlfriend Joy to follow up on. Purdue's first question ran to the connection between Adams and Frederickson. I told her I hoped she'd uncover it and asked if she'd share it with us if she did. Exactly how those two were connected was weighing on me. And when exactly did their connection begin? I explained to the sergeant that Adams was a person of interest in our investigation who was present in the room when Frederickson was found to have been murdered, along with at least 30 other people, and that we were surprised to see him and Joy there. Of course, Sunshine was pissed that we hadn't mentioned this sooner and wanted to know if they should be considered suspects? My answer was no, but that they could well be witnesses.

Around 20 hours after leaving Savannah, Anna and I arrived again at the dust bowl outside Idlib, met by Staff Sergeant Maynard and his troop, only this time, the welcome was supplemented with a briefing about how the unit would react to a suspected chemical weapons attack, and the location of protective clothing, respirators, and shots of atropine — the standard antidote to nerve gas exposure.

"We also have a gear package for you," Maynard said. "Turned up at the base." He led us to the rear of another Humvee. In the storage tray were a couple of black lockers. Snapping open the cleats and lifting the lids revealed his and hers sets of body armor, smoke, flash and HE grenades, night vision gear, tactical headsets, silenced M4s with infrared scopes on the rails, and other sundry bits and pieces.

"Who are you people again?" he asked.

"I'm the expert on vulture bees," I reminded him.

"Yeah, right. So...you should know we're infantry, not Special Forces. We've got your back, but my guys and I — we're not trained for any ninja shit."

"We hear you," said Anna.

Maynard's satellite phone sounded off. He turned away to answer it and, a moment later, passed Anna the handset. "It's for you."

After a moment, Anna put her hand over the mouthpiece. "Sergeant Purdue." She led the way to the far side of the RZ for privacy and put the call on speaker.

"Where are you?" Purdue asked, her voice crackling through the speaker. "I've been on hold, then passed through several operators with odd noises and squeaks...?"

"Can't say. Sorry," Anna told her.

"Uh-huh...thought you'd say that. Mr. Cooper with you?"

"Morning, Sunshine," I said.

"Sergeant, if you don't mind. Only one person calls me Sunshine, and you ain't her. Well, this case started out weird and is only getting weirder."

"Any luck with Adams and his girlfriend?" I asked.

"Yeah, and no. They were staying at Montage, Palmetto Bluff, an upscale hideaway across the river in South Carolina. Checked out half an hour before the PD across the state line could get to them. They caught a private jet to JFK. By the time we managed to get a hold of Immigration and put a stop on their passports, they were wheels up on a connecting flight out of the country. Immigration believes they used different identities and possibly fake passports, so now Interpol is looking for them.

"Try Berlin," I said.

"A little out of my jurisdiction," Purdue replied. "But I give you all that by way of small talk. I thought you might be interested, and perhaps it's relevant to what you're doing, whatever that is."

"Appreciate it," said Anna.

"We couldn't get anything off Frederickson's computer," Sunshine continued. "The hard drive was smashed. However, we checked the security footage of other establishments in the area. Seems there were two assailants, one tall, medium build, the other slight — maybe even a little undernourished. Both wore hoodies and baseball caps and kept their heads down. They wore surgical gloves, too, so I think we can forget about DNA. But they made a mistake. The assailants stopped several blocks up the road to put their gloves on; only they got their shit together in the driveway of the home of a former U.S. senator who'd recently been robbed. The CCTV footage failed to identify the perpetrator of that crime because the security system was antiquated. So, the senator recently upgraded it with the latest, high-def gear. Cutting to it, one of the killers had an identifying tattoo on his hand."

"Was it a skull?" I asked.

"So, you know the killers?"

"Not personally," I said. "A goat skull, right? In a pentacle?"

"Yes, and tattooed letters on his fingers — S-T-A-N. We think his forefinger, when he had one, probably had the tattooed letter 'A' on it. So...Satan. Can you give me a name?"

"No," I replied, "and the national security stuff has nothing to do with it. He could be South African. Our paths have crossed once previously in Idlib, Syria."

"As in overseas Syria?" Clouds suddenly obscured Sunshine's optimism for a lucky break.

"We have an image of him and the man who accompanied him," I told her. "I'll clear it with head office and see that you get included if and when we get positive IDs."

"Clear it with the Department of Agriculture?" Purdue asked.

"Yes, ma'am," I said. "We farm boys are the real badasses in Uncle Sam's inventory."

The inspector gave an audible snort. "You're as city as they come, Mister Cooper."

Purdue ended the call.

"That gives us a connection to Niemiec," said Anna as we headed for the lead Humvee. "What did Frederickson know, or have, that Niemiec had him killed for it."

"Numbers," I said as she climbed into the Humvee behind Maynard.

"What can you tell us," Anna, moving on, asked the staff sergeant.

"Not much, ma'am, other than they believe sarin was the agent." The sergeant pulled himself up onto the front passenger seat. The vehicle jerked forward. Over his shoulder, Maynard continued, "Rumor has it up to a hundred or so dead and twice that number affected with symptoms ranging from mild to severe."

"Anyone taken credit?" Anna inquired.

"Not so far. Al-Assad and the Free Syria Forces are blaming each other. ISIS has also been blamed along with Al Qaida. The usual suspects."

"Where are we going now?"

"That's up to you."

"Can we take a look around the site of the attack?"

"No problem," Maynard replied and had a word with the driver.

I had my phone out to make a call, but it had no bars.

"We'll coming up on high ground soon," said Maynard. "You'll get coverage then."

Around 20 minutes later, we crested a ridge, the rutted road turning to follow it through groves of olive trees and rising to crown another hill. The gray city of Idlib revealed itself on the far side of the ridge. I now had bars and thumbed the number on speed dial.

Inglis answered. "You arrived at al-Qusour yet?"

"Where?'

'The lucky district in Idlib the world is hearing so much about right now."

"Be there soon. You got Niemiec's Wagner buddies ID'd? Specifically, a balding blond I'm guessing is South African, and the man standing beside him in the images I sent you, who's possibly Somalian?"

"Wait a minute..."

I heard papers being shuffled.

"Yeah...we've got a little info on these two with more to come. You're right about him being South African. His name is Liam Van Zyl — originally from Joburg, he emigrated to England and joined the army. Dishonorable discharge in 2005 for common assault along with stealing and selling regimental equipment on the black market."

"What did he steal?"

"A low-loader carrying a Warrior — British version of the Bradley Fighting Vehicle."

You couldn't accuse the guy of thinking small.

"Subsequently served five years for armed holdup. A tourist souvenir shop."

Thinking small? Maybe not. The guy had all the right credentials for Wagner Employee of the Month. "Van Zyl has a tattoo on his right hand, the skull of a goat's head in a pentangle, and the letters s-t-a-n on his thumb and fingers. He's also missing his right trigger finger. If you're wondering what the missing letter is, altogether the word spells moron."

"There's no record of any tattoos in his military or prison files. Must have got them post-discharge. I'll get it updated."

"And the Somali?"

"Nigerian, actually. Former Boko Haram, but fought in Somalia. Wanted in connection to the abduction of schoolgirls. He has a number of aliases, most of which are variations of Abu ibn Jihad – Abu al Jihan, Abu bin Jihad, Abu Jihan Jihad, Abu Jihad, etc. Lacking in imagination, that one. Both men have been identified fighting in Syria and are known killers."

"They recently visited the United States."

"You asking or telling?"

"Telling. There's convincing circumstantial evidence they murdered Gerome Frederickson."

"What's the evidence?"

"They were caught on CCTV a couple of blocks from the victim's house, putting their game face on, ski masks and gloves."

I went into further details of the crime.

"I'll reach out to Savannah PD and Sergeant Purdue and brief them on what I can," Inglis said when I'd finished. "What about the bigger picture?"

"We have leads we didn't have yesterday."

"Well, it's safe to say that with this latest attack in Idlib, there is definitely unaccounted-for WMD in al-Assad's possession. He supposedly gave up all his stocks as of last year — 900 gallons — and we destroyed it. This latest chemical weapons attack in Syria is being seen as a personal fuck you to the current Administration, given the Wikileaks situation. The Russians probably put al-Assad up to it."

I asked, "Anything on Frederickson's Kurdish scout from back in the day?"

"Not as yet, but we're working on it. I'm told Muirhead put a rocket under the Secretary of the Army to get us some cooperation."

"What about Niemiec? "I asked. "Where is he?"

"As far as we know, still in his compound in Syria. The SecState is losing patience, by the way."

I wasn't aware that she had any to lose.

"Do you have a plan, Vin?"

"I've got something in mind."

"Care to share?"

"Best not to."

"I like the sound of it already. Be careful."

As in whatever it is you have in mind, don't get caught. I rang off.

Anna said, "Inglis might not want to know, but I do."

"I'm still noodling it," I said. "Meanwhile, you mind telling me who you're reporting to?"

"You know who."

"You haven't called him, not around me."

"With good reason. His name comes up even in passing, and you lose it."

"What are you giving him?"

"The same things you're reporting to Inglis... Look," she said, "let's do this later, okay? "

Later was going to be interesting, but I was already couch surfing. How worse could it get? I turned my attention to the view out the dust-caked side window — the usual procession of broken cinderblock monotony — and did a little private seething.

Ten minutes later, driving in silence, we stopped at a roadblock guarded by Free Syrian forces, men in a combination of civilian and military clothes, U.S. Army body armor, and a mixture of M4s and AKs. The barrier was raised when a couple of the men caught sight of the Stars and Stripes shoulder patches on Maynard's driver, along with Anna's badge held towards them out the window, and waved us through.

"This looks familiar," I said, motioning at the view.

Maynard nodded in the general direction. "Same area you were in last week. The collapsed building they pulled you out of is three blocks over."

We stopped in a typical square surrounded by the pulverized Syrian cityscape.

"This is it," said Maynard. "It's safe, at least as far as any residual WMD is concerned. Sarin doesn't hang around for long — it evaporates. There's not much to see."

"I want to see it anyway," Anna told him.

"I'll pack a picnic basket," I said, checking my M4 carbine.

Out of the Humvees, Maynard assembled his men in a loose formation around us, a version of close protection, and we walked toward a collection of signs emblazoned with biological and chemical weapons symbols and ignored the local version of "do not cross" tape, ducking under it.

Anna headed for a narrow alley lined with small shops. The place was eerily silent. No blaring car horns, playing children, arguing vendors, calls to prayer, or screaming scooters. The street was littered with personal effects — dropped bags of groceries, burst suitcases, dusty clothing, abandoned bicycles, and a child's doll. A donkey lay on its side on the ground in rigor mortis, still harnessed to its cart, legs stiff and thrust straight out in front. Clouds of flies buzzed furiously. The acrid stench of old death left out in the sun triggered a gag reflex. A little further down the alley, the road was dotted with dead dogs. A scooter had plowed into a pole, which was splashed with blood that had turned black, the stain laced with black hair.

"From what I know, a Mi-24 dropped a canister in a nearby square. There was a minor explosion that most ignored after so many years of war. Air pressure carried the agent down these narrow streets, and animals started to cough. And then they started to fall over. Sarin has no smell, and it's colorless. No one knew what to do or where to run. Nowhere was safe."

The alley turned sharply. Half a dozen people in white oversized hazmat suits came into view, ferrying body bags out of a building. Heavy black plastic bags were already lying in the trays of two three-wheel motorized vehicles parked in the alley. One of the ghosts noticed our approach, jogged toward us and stopped ten feet away. He gestured at us to come no further and removed his respirator. It was Kaamil, Anna's white helmet pal.

He was surprised to see us. "You have returned!"

The usual rounds of Assalam greetings began, after which Anna said, "Kaamil, I am so sorry. This is awful."

"Yes, this is al-Assad's Syria."

"Where have the injured been taken?" I asked.

"Many places, but not hospitals. The Russians will bomb hospitals to free the regime of uncomfortable evidence."

Two more bodies were loaded onto the back of a three-wheeler, its suspension nearly bottoming under the load. Kaamil explained, "Three generations of one family. They hid in a cellar. Grandparents, parents, and children as young as three. Twelve victims."

The three-wheeler drove away as the second vehicle took delivery of two tiny bodies, each placed in the tray reverently by mopped-up white helmets.

Anna showed distress, the deaths of children affecting her more than they ordinarily would. "Is anyone documenting this?"

"The Organization for the Prohibition of Chemical Weapons," Kaamil replied. They have inspectors."

"Where? We want to talk with them."

"I can take you," Kaamil said. "Please, I need time to shower — I have surely picked up sarin residue. Do not come further along this road. There is nothing to see, but there are perhaps pockets of this chemical. Be careful also not to touch surfaces. The risk is small now, but..." He shrugged.

Maynard agreed. We took the Syrian's advice and retraced our steps to the Humvees. Kaamil arrived a short while later in a battered Toyota pickup that chugged clouds of smoke and took point. He led us down a maze of narrow streets overlooked by multiple darkened windows, which had Maynard and his driver worried about a potential ambush.

We drove through an open square cleared of rubble, skirted around a towering bonfire of burning clothes tended by men in hazmat suits and respirators, and eventually stopped at a large auto body shop where crowds of people had gathered. Maynard took us to the street beside the body shop, which was covered over with dun-colored tarpaulins to camouflage it from Russian drones.

We found Kaamil waiting for us behind the crowd of distressed locals. He handed us a pack of N5 face masks and surgical gloves. "I must tell you something and apologize for this treachery."

Anna stopped taking in the general area. "I'm sorry...?"

"The bombing of the building. You were nearly killed." Kaamil's eyes were on the ground, his head bowed. "My son, Maali. The Free Syrian Army has arrested him for treason."

"No!" Anna said, her hand on Kaamil's forearm.

"Please," he said, seeming to reject the small comfort she offered. "You do not understand....it was Maali who informed Wagner of your presence in Idlib. He sent a text when you were in the building so that it could be targeted. It is all on his phone. I am ashamed."

"Kaamil..." was all Anna could say out of pity for his distress.

My reaction? "Where is the little shit now?"

"Vin!" Anna snapped.

"Where are they keeping him?"

"Do not concern yourself. He will face Syrian justice."

"Why did he do it?" I asked.

"Money. To buy medical supplies. It is not terrible that you must work for your enemies so that you can help the people they maim and kill? Again, I am sorry," he said, head still bowed.

"What will happen to him?" Anna asked.

Kaamil looked up, his eyes wet with tears. "There is only one sentence for treason."

Anna rested a sympathetic hand on Bin Alzhur's shoulder. I would have preferred to wring the kid's neck. Venus and Mars.

Kaamil wiped his eyes with the back of his hand. "This is one of many evacuation stations," he motioned at a crowded shop front. "They are scattered all around al-Qusour. There is limited treatment. The victims are washed, their clothes are burnt because there is sarin in them, and they are given other people's clothing to wear."

Two U.S. Army trucks accompanied by several Humvees toting M60 machine guns pulled up with some urgent brake squeal. The truck tailgates flipped down, and U.S. Army soldiers began racing boxes marked "medical supplies" into the body shop.

"God bless America," Kaamil volunteered.

No need to bless anyone just yet, I thought. It could be boxes of cotton wool buds.

It was pure chaos inside the makeshift medical center — young children, often several to a cot, crying or screaming, mothers and fathers shouting and wailing, overwhelmed amateur medical staff rushing around, teenage and adult victims coughing, vomiting, convulsing, passing out. The air was thick with the smell of shit and puke. Death was still finding more victims. Anna pointed out several people in yellow coveralls walking among the injured, the acronym OPCW in large letters across their backs. Respirators dangled from their necks. Some of them were talking with the harried local medical response. Anna led the way to the group of these officials, weaving through whole families struck down by the nerve agent. She presented her badge. "Special Agent Anna Masters, United States Air Force Office of Special Investigations."

A tall woman among the OPCW team gave her a tight smile and introduced herself as Ange Noordstrom. Swedish or Norwegian, I figured. Dirty blonde hair, blue eyes, and dry sun-damaged skin from too many trips to the Greek Islands. Dragging 50. No one shook hands — gloves or not, too much nerve agent around.

"Have you confirmed this was sarin?" Anna asked.

Noordstrom replied, "I'm sorry. Who are you again? Who are you with?"

'U.S. federal investigators," Anna short-handed.

"The site tested positive for isopropyl methylphosphonofluoridate so yes, sarin has been confirmed. Was it you who brought the medical supplies just now?"

"No," said Anna.

"Well, I thank your government anyway."

"Can you identify where the sarin came from? Which batch? When it was made."

"We think it's possibly the chemical weapon also used in the recent Khan Shaykhun attack."

"How can you tell?"

'DF is synthesised from methyl phosphonic dichloride, MD for short, which has a range of chemical fingerprints. We believe the sarin used in both attacks came from this same batch of MD, but what we have so far are only preliminary findings. To be certain, a full isotopic analysis is required using a matrix-assisted laser to ionize tissue, which is then examined by mass spectrometry."

Anna had better be taking notes; there were more syllables than I had fingers and toes.

She continued, "I believe the results won't change, but we need evidence, not gut feeling. If there is a silver lining, it's that the water supply hasn't been contaminated. Then all this," she motioned at the dead and dying, "would be much much worse." Noordstrom pierced me with those blue eyes. "Your president will be angry, no?"

Yeah, she'll waggle her finger at al-Assad for sure.

The woman exclaimed under her breath, "We have to take that motherfucker down."

I assumed she meant al-Assad and not the U.S. president.

As we walked back to Bin Alzhur's vehicle, Anna seethed, "This has to be Saddam's sarin, the WMD Niemiec chaperoned out of Iraq."

We didn't know that for certain and might never know, but given that al-Assad's stocks of sarin had all supposedly been destroyed, there was a good chance she was right. "That plan I mentioned. Wanna hear it?"

"As long as it involves stringing Niemiec up by his lily-white testicles," she murmured.

The solid steel gate was no match for 18 tons of rolling Stryker. As one made contact with the other, the sheet metal gate parted from its mounts. It threw sparks as it skittered and bounced across the kindergarten's forecourt like a Frisbee, taking out one of the two sandbagged machine gun positions and giving a machine gunner a close haircut that began a little above the bridge of his nose. Small arms fire followed as Maynard's unit kept mercenaries blasting away from various points of cover diverted. Meanwhile, throwing a handy prayer rug across coils of razor wire, Anna and I shimmied over a side wall adjoining a general store and dropped into the kindergarten. Once on the ground, our night vision gear revealed fewer Wagner guys in attendance than we expected — certainly fewer than on our last visit.

I'd pictured a torrent of fighters pouring out of the kindy doors like kids set free at recess but counted only half a dozen potential troublemakers. Make that two after Anna and I parked silenced rounds in the nearest brain pans. Spooked, the remaining fighters bolted to the surviving .50 cal emplacement and sprayed the Stryker before swinging the gun in our direction. The 8-wheeler's M2 answered the fire and turned the two mercenaries inside out. Messy. The operation lasted inside of two minutes. The place fell silent. A couple of neighborhood dogs barking at the disturbance quickly lost interest.

Maynard and his men came out from behind the Stryker, moved into the kindergarten forecourt, spread out and checked the downed mercs for signs of life. Anna and I began to clear the buildings. There were cots and sleeping bags enough for around 20 men in rooms lined with colorful naïve finger paintings. There was also a mess room and kiddy-sized toilets, but no mercenaries were added to the tally of former employees rapidly cooling off in the courtyard. I had to admit disappointment. It was over too fast for any real satisfaction, except that none of our people was so much as scratched. And so far, no sign of the main prize — Andre Niemiec and those lily-white albino gonads Anna was looking to slip a noose around. And then, off one of the rooms we were yet to search, a toilet flushed, and one of those bearded Chechens came out zipping up his fly, a set of headphones over his ears, a Metallica number leaking out. Our eyes met. He went for his sidearm; my M4 beat him to it and sent him backward into the toilet.

"Clear," I called over my shoulder.

Anna came in, shaking her head. "Fuck it," she murmured. "Do we have a mole? Is he being tipped off? We get close, he vanishes." She sniffed the air. "And what is that...that smell?"

Now that she mentioned it — there was something in the air that reminded me of an Abercrombie & Fitch store I once accidentally walked into.

"A high school crush used to smell like that," Anna said, her nose wrinkling.

Maynard appeared in a doorway. "Take your time," he said, enjoying the moment. "The place is secured. Feels good putting the training to use." And then, "What's that smell?"

It was coming from the room we assumed was Niemiec's office, our next port of call. I went in. Yeah, source found. The place reeked. I hitched the M4 to my webbing and checked the desk drawers. Empty. The trash was empty, too. Niemiec must have made notes of some description. I opened a cupboard and found a change of clothes and shoes. A small chest of draws held nothing of interest. Opening another cupboard revealed a genuine prize: a paper shredder. And it was full. I remembered seeing a roll of plastic trash liners in the mess. I ducked out and returned with it. "Bag everything," I said.

Anna held up a charging lead. "There's a laptop. Or was. He's taken it with him." She pulled out the desk drawers. "Vin..."

From the expression on her face, this was serious. I leaned over to get a better view.

"Leyland Morris," she said, "Class of 99. I swear he used to do backstroke in this stuff." The drawer was full of little glass bottles in the shape of a male torso, some empty, some half full: Jean Paul Gautier, Le Male. "Brings back memories — a nasty combo of lavender, shower grate, Leyland's menthol cigarettes, and his sweaty hands tugging at my bra strap."

"What Memory Lane doesn't have a dumpster?" I said and lifted out a bottle — there were a lot of them. Niemiec's aftershave. Eau de Bug Spray. I'd caught a whiff at earlier encounters. "Maybe he gargles with it," I suggested. A further five minutes of thorough searching revealed nothing of interest.

We regrouped outside. A corporal walked up to Anna and said, "Ma'am, found this in a trash bin." He handed her a notebook and illuminated it with a red light. "Useful?" he asked.

The book was severely scorched. Anna flipped it open. "It's his diary." She handed it to me. "Frederickson's."

Inside the front cover was handwritten in neat lettering: 1MEF U.S. Marines GySgt. Gerard Frederickson, att. 2/3 ACR. Alpha company. "Corporal," I said. "Can I kiss you?"

"No, sir," he grinned.

Later, back at the base, I took a night-time stroll and called Rita Inglis to debrief her on the raid.

"Was that the plan I didn't want to know about?" was her first question.

"Yes."

"Was the man in question there?" she asked with some expectation.

"No," I replied as I wandered the base, under the stars for privacy.

"Figures. That would've been too easy," she observed.

"Do you have a more positive lead on his whereabouts than the one you had yesterday?"

"We thought we knew for certain where he was — in Syria, and he still might be."

That was no help at all. Hollywood presents the CIA as all-seeing and all-knowing. Unfortunately, or perhaps fortunately, it's not. "We recovered Frederickson's diary from Niemiec's compound."

"'Right. The diary is a positive connection between Niemiec and his murder," she said, joining her own dots. "What's in it?"

"Anna's going through it now," I said. We also collected shredded paper from Niemiec's office."

"That's good work, Vin."

"You mean, good work Vin and Anna."

"Of course, Vin and Anna. Or should I say, Anna and Vin?"

"Let's not get ahead of ourselves," I said.

"On another note, I've been asked to tell you officially that Secretary Muirhead is not impressed with your lack of communication."

Movement in the shadows caught my attention. It was Anna on the phone, taking the night air like I was for privacy. "I'm sure she's getting the latest," I said.

"The SecState wants to get it from you."

"Via Chalmers," I reminded her.

"You're making me the messenger. And you know what happens to messengers."

"Wear a vest," I suggested. "So, Rita... I want to know where his passport has been over the last two weeks."

"Whose? Niemiec's?"

"No, Chalmers'. I also want to know what Niemiec's net worth is and where his money comes from. Bank accounts, investments..."

"We're doing all that as a matter of course. Much of his income is derived from Russian sources, government and private. Nine months ago, he was paid roughly $100 million over the space of a week."

"From the one source?"

"Multiple. But that's what it added up to."

"All Russian sources?"

"Some, but not all. We're checking on the companies involved, but digging through the corporate structures to find out exactly who owns what takes time. Anyway, whatever Niemiec's motivations are, money probably isn't one of them."

"Has he always been wealthy?"

"He's an oligarch, net worth over half a billion."

"Hmm... So, will you look into it?"

"Niemiec's accounts? Haven't you been listening?"

"No, the other thing — Chalmers. Has he been out of the country recently, and if so, where did he go and what was the date of his departure?

"You'll get me fired."

"If that happens, I know someone who'll hire you on more money, plus health benefits."

"Who's that?"

"Me," I said. "Sands Aerospace & Defense."

"I'll keep it in mind."

"It's important."

"I can't promise. In the meantime, I'll send a pickup for Niemiec's trash and get more resources on tracking Niemiec's movements."

About time, I thought. The call ended. Given how everyone said this job was so important, I would have thought resources would have been a no-brainer from the get-go. But that's government agencies for you, maximum application to the minimum. I kept walking, taking in the view — a line-up of Strykers and a few Bradleys, and three Black Hawks on the apron. Not much of a view. There was also a mess hall, various demountable sheds and cinderblock buildings, at least 30 shipping containers, a basketball court, a signpost pointing the way to the location of a favorite strip joint in Vegas, sandbags and razor wire, observation towers, and guard posts. Al-Tanf was no different from any other temporary base I'd been to. It could have been anywhere in the world — anywhere hot and dusty.

Music of different genres and from different eras drifted across the base from several sources: hip-hop from the mechanic's sheds, different R&B tracks from several accommodation containers, and a Beatles tune from somewhere else I couldn't place. Other personnel were out walking, taking the cooler night air, most wearing headphones. Music was a connection with home and helped tune out some of the monotony — monotony being the biggest career killer in the military, whizzing bullets aside.

I soon found myself back at our luxe, extra-length executive steel box, muffled music leaking out — Baby Love by the Supremes. Motown. Anna liked the old guard. I opened the door, went inside, and immediately picked a fight. "What are you telling Chalmers?"

She closed Frederickson's diary. "How do you know I was on the phone with him?"

I gave her "the look."

"Okay, yes, I was briefing him. So what? Were you spying on me?

"Are you spying on me?" I asked her. "For him?"

"Don't be ridiculous."

"Is it?"

"It's not always about you, Vin."

"No, it's about you — I'm just the schmo who happens to be in the way."

"I think the world has moved on in that department, Vin."

Things weren't exactly peach fuzz between us, so why not make them worse? Sometimes, you just have to. "Look, I don't buy the Operation Phoenix Mark Two crap," I told her. "You said everyone on that squad was like you, technically dead, a prerequisite, but every country was doing the same clean-up job at the time, and none of their assassination squads was off the books. It was common knowledge on the ground — Britain, Australia, New Zealand, the Netherlands, Germany, France, Italy... Everyone was assassinating their citizens fighting for ISIS."

"Monologue finished?" Anna asked.

"The excuses you've been trotting out are, well, let's call 'em thin."

"What do you want me to tell you?"

"I want to know what you were doing while I was trying to get myself killed to end the guilt of being the cause of getting you shot to death." I was breathing hard, and my voice was raised.

"Vin, I'm sorry. I truly am. And you know that."

"So then tell me. You're lying on the floor and blood is spurting from the hole in your chest. In my experience, no one survives that kind of wound. They take you away, there's a funeral, and then two years later, you turn up at the beach. I want those two years, Anna. Where were you?"

Silence.

"Well?" I asked her.

"Look, you know I can't fill in the blanks," she said.

"My security clearance is as high as yours," I reminded her.

"That has nothing to do with it, and you know it."

"After Oak Ridge, after rehab and recovery, but before the Phoenix thing, Special Activities sent you somewhere. Where and why?"

Silence.

"Anna. Come on. You're going to crack eventually."

"Cuba," Anna said. "They sent me to Cuba."

"Guantanamo?"

"No. Havana."

"Keep going. Why?"

"To learn the language."

"Spanish? Why Cuba? Plenty of other countries speak Spanish."

"Because the Spanish they speak in Cuba is unique – it's Cubano, a mixture of Spanish, Haitian, Creole..."

Cuba. Relations between the U.S. and Cuba were in a thaw. Fidel was ash. Fidel's brother Raúl was retired. What interest could CIA Special Activities have in sending someone who had technically died, someone who no longer existed, to Cuba to learn Spanish the way the Cubans speak it? The obvious answer — the CIA eventually wanted to pass Anna off as a Cuban. She had olive skin, chocolate-colored hair, and those eyes — a Russian father and Cuban mother, perhaps? But again — why? To what purpose? My mind ran through options and scenarios, but none of the fruits on the spinning reels lined up for a jackpot.

"So now I've given you something," she said, "it's your turn to come clean."

"Huh?" I said, having only caught the tail end of that.

"What happened in Berlin?"

I blinked, swallowed, and sucked in a breath, sending a fistful of tells all at once; a deer caught in the headlights, moments from becoming roadkill.

"It's all over your face. Something did happen, didn't it?"

It was a big, ugly question with a trip wire connected to a grenade. "This is Chalmers again, isn't it?" I said. "He keeps doing this to us, but you can't see it."

"You're avoiding the question," Anna said.

"He wants me out of the way. If he can't do it with a bullet, he'll do it with mistrust."

"I'm waiting."

"You're not even supposed to know I was in Berlin."

"Just like you're not supposed to know I was ever in Cuba."

"So, is this stalemate?" I asked her.

Anna breathed heavily and tossed Frederickson's diary onto the cot. "There's nothing in here. Pages are torn out. Maybe Niemic tore them out. I'm pretty sure Frederickson tore out one of them. The paper looks similar to the evidence Dr. Milne recovered. I'm going for another walk."

With that, we retired to our neutral corners. Anna wouldn't compromise her mission's secrecy, and I wasn't about to let the cat named Gisela out of the bag. Both of us now had a strategy for ending uncomfortable questions about the past, but it put a strain on the relationship, the working one and the personal one. Example: the following afternoon, the atmosphere frosty, I asked if she was giving me the silent treatment. No, came the answer, but it was said as she was stuffing her belongings into a pack like Mike Tyson hits the heavy bag.

I picked up Frederickson's diary and flicked through it. Yes, the paper looked similar. I went to the pages taken out. We'd only ever know what was on one of them.

After two days of the polar wind blowing across our shipping container, the following obscure text from Inglis arrived. *"Eylo Pedrad, Kurdish scout att. to Army in '03. Bravo company, Frederickson's company. Transport arriving 06:00.*

I showed Anna. "Cryptic," I said.

She looked at it and merely shrugged. Once upon a time, BG, Before Gisela, we would have talked through the possibilities.

The following morning, a little before sunrise, two Black Hawks circled the base and landed. A runner for Staff Sergeant Maynard came to inform us that one was to pick up intelligence and take it to Incirlik Air Base, Turkey, while the other was our ride to Al Asad Air Base over the border. I handed over the two garbage bags collected from Niemiec's office. Anna and I rode in silence to the apron, our Black Hawk's main rotor beginning to swing.

NORTHERN IRAQ

Conversation between passengers is not easy in a UH-60 at the best of times, especially when the person you want to have a word with taps their headset and shrugs at you when you attempt it. So instead, I watched the featureless desert creeping by: 220 miles of sand, sandflies, and camel shit — the distance, general topography, and biology between Al Tanf and Al Asad.

From a height of three thousand feet, Al Asad Air Base resembled a vast, concrete scar on a withered landscape. Ground level didn't improve things any. We were met on the apron by an Iraqi army captain — squat, mid-30s, and with a heavy black mustache drooping under its own weight. Think Cheech. Or maybe Chong. His name, Mohammad Abboud.

"So, we're here," I told him. "Can you tell us why?"

We climbed into the back of a Humvee, and the captain offered us sodas and Snickers from a cold box on the floor. He took a candy bar for himself and tore the wrapper with his teeth. Anna said no thanks and turned to gaze out the window. I opened a Coke.

As we drove through Al Asad and took in the surroundings, I recalled the interview with Tom Wilkes. A lot of American money had poured into Al Asad since his time here, much of the base newly built or refurbished. We stopped at an intersection to let some traffic through and, slightly off the road, a signpost pointed to various places of interest. The details were in Arabic, so whether there was a shoutout to a strip joint or, more likely in these parts, a belly-dancing joint, I couldn't say.

The captain turned in his seat, interrupting these meandering thoughts. "So, you have been to Iraq before?"

I nodded.

"In good times or bad?" he asked, chewing.

There were good times? "Bad," I told him.

"How long are you staying?"

"Not sure."

"You know where we're going?" Anna inquired, engaging at last.

"Yes, yes, of course. First, to Kubaysah, a village south of here. People will meet you there. Bedouins. I warn you — do not trust these Arabs."

"I thought we were meeting a Kurdish man," said Anna.

"Perhaps there will be Kurds, but if there are none, you are lucky. Kurds — you can trust them even less. The Bedouins do not speak English. I will translate," he reassured us.

We were so far off the rails that I couldn't even see the rails, but that's Iraq.

"Do you know anything about a man called Eylo Pedrad?" Anna asked him, her frustration growing.

"Who?"

Given that talking to the captain was likely to make things even more confusing, Anna pivoted to me. "So, are you going to tell me?"

"Tell you what exactly?" My throat contracted; I knew exactly what.

"What's her name?"

And there it was.

"We are meeting a woman?" asked Abboud, perplexed. "No."

"If you don't answer me, I'll think the worst," said Anna. "Actually, I'm already thinking it."

"You want to do this here?" Something in my stomach was practicing reef knots.

"It's okay," said Mohamad, not reading the room. "There is plenty of time before we get to Kubaysah."

"I was drugged and set up," I explained. "The toxicology report said roofies."

"I asked you a simple question. Her name."

"Gisela." It came out like a sneeze.

Anna sat back in the seat.

"Look," I said, "I wake up in a hotel room I don't recognize with a woman I barely remember having had a conversation with. I get back to my hotel, and there are photos waiting, shoved under the door. Take your pregnancy hat off and look at the facts," I told her.

"Oh, you are pregnant!" Mohamad exclaimed happily.

"Were you naked in bed with her?" Anna wanted to know.

I didn't even realize that fact until I saw myself in a mirror. "Kind of."

"So, yes. Are the pictures incriminating?"

"If you choose not to see that I'm unconscious."

I waited for the storm to break, for the torrent of abuse to pour out. "Say something," I said into Anna's ferocious calm. "Anna...I had no idea what was going on. Like I said, roofies slipped into my drink."

"While you were chatting her up, right? Don't tell me sleeping with her didn't cross your mind. Let's be honest; you have a history."

"We had a conversation. That's it."

"And, let me guess – she was old, ugly, and not your type. "

A memory flashed of Gisela prowling towards me, naked, on all fours. "Not exactly," I said.

"Then how, exactly?"

"It's not important. What is important is that Gisela must have followed me because I walked into a random bar."

"Gisela-la-la-la..." Anna said in a mocking, sing-song voice.

"Come on, think about it. Who put this woman up to it? And how do you know about it? Who told you?"

"Chalmers. He briefed me on the phone last night. A package arrived, addressed to me. It looked suspicious, so he had it opened. You want to see what he found?"

No, not really.

Anna produced her phone and showed me the screen. Gisela, naked. She was on top of me, her hands gripping the bed head, her right nipple brushing my lips. I was naked, my mouth slightly open. Her hair obscured my eyes. The photo kicked my testicles into the back of my throat. My heart rate soared. This had to be — the end.

"I have other pics. Chalmers was very sorry to inform me, of course."

What a cunt. "I have a theory."

"I don't want to hear it. You were in Berlin in bed with a naked woman, having sex. Any theory you might have will be tainted by your desire to avoid me leaving you."

"There was no sex," I implored her. "And that was confirmed by the lab that did the blood test."

"You talked to the woman, had a drink. Was the drink your idea or hers? There would have been flirting. You were flirting, am I right?"

I pictured Gisela holding the bottle of scotch. She was slim and tall and had all the other things I like a woman to have, if you get my drift. I'm a guy, so, of course, I had "thoughts." But you can't be canceled for that, can you? Biology does what it does, right?

"Excuse, please," said Captain bin Mohamad. "We are here."

Thank fuck for that. I glanced out the window as the Humvees squealed to a stop. "Here" was a stretch of vacant desert with the dun-colored mud-brick wall of a village on the horizon, which was, presumably, Kubaysah.

"Don't think for a moment we are done with this conversation," said Anna, getting out of the vehicle. She needn't have feared; I knew there was more pain to come.

Nearby were two old Bedouin tribesmen and a heavily bearded man in his mid-forties wearing Desert Storm-era utilities. Accompanying them were camels, seven of them.

"What's with the camels?" I asked no one in particular, and no one answered.

Captain Abboud handled the intros. The Kurd introduced himself as Royan Rashidi. I figured he was in his mid-20s. He told us he was from the same village as Eylo Pedrad, the man we were supposed to be meeting, but Eylo had been killed recently by a Turkish sniper. Afran Simco, an uncle on his mother's side who fought with Pedrad, was also dead, killed in the fight against ISIS. But we were not to worry, Royan said. His uncle Afran had told him many stories of the American war, and especially the search for WMD. I wasn't sure I had this all correct — Royan spoke with bursts of speed, and sometimes, the words bumped into each other and tripped over themselves. He went on to tell us that his father often told of attacking a suspected Iraqi WMD convoy with Afran and that one of the men died, overcome by chemicals.

Death is easier in these parts than living.

I returned to my earlier question. "So, what's with the camels?"

"They are for us," Royan replied.

"Why? We're going somewhere?"

"Yes." Royan seemed surprised to be asked this question. "We go to the place where Yado Guli, the man killed by WMD, is buried."

Anna excused us and pulled me aside. "If there's a body out there with traces of the chemicals on that convoy, we want it. It's potentially the missing link connecting the WMD on that convoy with al-Assad's more recent use of chemical weapons."

Anna's turn to womansplain, but the fact that she was talking to me at all was a step in the right direction. "Yes, you're right," I said, hopefully with not too much wonder in my voice at this insight.

Royan led us over to the Bedouins. There was a slight shift in the breeze — those camels smelled bad. Once the usual Assalams were behind us, a Bedouin whose head was wrapped inside a sky-blue turban offered me the reins to the tallest mount. Protest was useless. He shifted his ancient AK to the other shoulder, tapped the animal with a long stick, mumbled some incantation, and it got down on its knees, followed by its hindquarters. He motioned for me to climb up. I wasn't sure I wanted to.

Meanwhile, Anna vaulted onto one of the camels with ease. In fact, the ease with which I climb onto bar stools. Perhaps my mouth was open because she explained, "Primary transport. Nine months in Syria chasing and killing assholes..."

I climbed up onto my camel and turned to say something amusing but was stopped dead. "Don't talk to me," she said. "Need to think."

About us, I assumed. Not a good sign. We got underway and I killed some time, focusing my attention on the swaying vagina of the camel in front as we plodded over the endless landscape beneath a vast sky. Eventually, I called out to Royan, "So, the place where your uncle's friend is buried," I began. "Is it far?"

He fell back. "In a pickup, it is far. On a camel, it is further."

"Why?"

"The camel cannot be hurried."

"The Bedouin are our guides?"

"Yes."

"You don't know where he's buried?"

"We respect the Bedouin's land, and they respect ours."

Avoiding a turf war. So unusual in this part of the world. "What did your uncle tell you about the attack on the WMD convoy?" I asked him.

"He said many of our people were helping Americans find Saddam's men hiding in the desert. On this night, Eylo, Afran, and Guli are coming home when they see lights in the desert. Guli, he races ahead to see if it is Iraqis. Eylo and Afran hear gunfire. When they arrive, Guli is on the ground. They think he is wounded, but he is sick and in great pain. His mouth froths. He says to my uncles that he will shoot at them if they come near. There is WMD, he says. He says he was close to trucks fleeing, and he shot at them. There was a spray coming from a truck — in the air, a smell like gasoline, but different. Guli says he knows this smell. Guli dies. Eylo and Afran bury him where he lies. His family comes for the body to take home, and everyone who touches him is sick. Again, someone dies. So, they bury him again with a cousin. Later, a goat eating grass near his grave dies."

I wondered how much of the story was accurate. I doubted the convoy would've been carrying ready-mixed sarin; that would have been too dangerous. I knew from the briefing notes that one of the two chemicals that make up sarin, methylphosphonyl difluoride, is incredibly toxic, but that the toxicity rises to a whole new level when it's mixed with isopropyl alcohol — standard, easy-to-come-by rubbing alcohol.

"The goat is buried there also?" I asked him.

"Yes."

More likely was that the goat just up and died. Sometimes, they do that, like humans.

"You fight in Iraq war?" Royan asked, changing the subject.

"Yes," I said.

"You come back to Iraq for chemical weapons now?"

"Just looking," I said, playing it down.

"America says there was no WMD in Iraq, but the Kurdish people know this is a lie." He continued, "Of course, Saddam had WMD. It is obvious. He used this on my people many times. Now, Al Assad has Saddam's WMD, and he kills Kurds in Syria. Why do Americans let this happen?"

Before I could say, "It's complicated," he smacked his camel with a stick, and it bounded away forward. Royan had worked himself into a lather, but I understood his frustration. Politicians' denials don't change people's reality. Other than Niemiec, maybe the last folks to know the truth about Iraq's WMD was CENTCOM back in the day. Rejecting the existence of Iraq's WMD post-Operation

Iraqi Freedom underpinned the belief system of subsequent U.S. administrations. But now, it served someone's purpose to expose the truth. Why?

Two hours later, we were still hiking over dunes and ridges. And then excitement seemed to overcome the Bedouin guides as they let out a whoop and galloped off. We eventually caught up to them in the middle of nowhere, the destination. On the flinty dirt was a small pile of wind-blown stones, no distinguishing features to be seen in any direction, man-made or otherwise.

Anna pulled up beside me and asked, "What are you waiting for? He's not going to dig himself out," and slid down off her camel. "Oh, and by the way, mystery solved. Not a French phone number." She tossed me her GPS, our position highlighted: 33.37.59.35.N 42.26.49.44. E

The numbers on the paper Frederickson had taken to his grave: 3337593542. I'd completely missed this. A partial position — the latitude and the first two figures of the longitude. He hadn't had time to complete noting the coordinates down in their entirety, along with the relevance for doing so, before he was overwhelmed. He'd tried to give us this location, the supposed burial site of a man killed by Saddam's WMD headed to Syria, on a convoy chaperoned by Andre Niemiec, a senior officer in the forces of the Coalition. What we still didn't know — how Frederickson and Adams were connected and what their connection was to Niemiec.

With the overhead sun doing its best to broil us, Anna and I dug into the flint beneath the pile of stones with pickaxes and shovels while Royan and the two Bedouins watched on. An hour of sweating buckets later, a hint of brown cloth revealed itself in the dirt. A further 30 minutes of careful digging exposed the desiccated remains of a human, mummified by the dry heat of the desert. The corpse's beard was still on his chin.

"You have found him," Royan exclaimed, appearing graveside. "I have seen pictures of him. He looks different."

Yeah, the deceased was no longer a spring chicken.

We lifted out the remains with the shovels, laid a blanket over them, and then dug around some more.

"You have found other bodies?" Royan returned to ask after some time.

"No," Anna told him.

"There should be another body, a cousin — the story says so."

"No. No other remains."

"No goat?"

"No goat," she replied.

I never expected to find one, but the local lore had had the effect of preserving the grave. Royan walked away, taking his disappointment over the missing cousin and the goat with him. "If this guy has sarin or DF in his system, it's the confirmation we need about the contents of Wilkes' convoy. Refocuses the attention on Niemiec. Maybe that's what Frederickson intended."

"I get that, but what it won't tell us is whether the WMD made it to Syria."

"Yeah." I glanced over my shoulder. "Looks like we're staying the night."

While we were digging, the Bedouins had set up camp nearby, a couple of open shade cloths with rugs beneath them on the bare earth. They also provided food. It had been a long day. I'd have eaten a horse. However, it wasn't on the menu. But camel meat was to be washed down with warm camel's milk.

"Vegan. Both vegan," I said, attempting to excuse Anna and me from at least the beverage side of the meal. But our hosts pressed, and I, at least, gave in and sipped, taking one for the team, even giving myself a "Got Milk" goat 'stash to show some extra appreciation. Both of our Bedouins seemed to like this, but Royan somewhat less so. I know this because he pressed an M4 muzzle into the back of my skull.

"I am taking him," he said.

"Who? Me?" Was this now a hostage situation?

"Your hands," Royan snapped. "I want to see your hands."

I raised them a little.

Anna already had her Sig out and pointed at the Kurd. Perhaps he wasn't aware that women could be dangerous, especially this woman. "The remains stay with us," she told him.

I would have been happier with, "Put the gun down," given that the muzzle was still pressed into my head.

"My friends, they disagree," Royan replied.

He was speaking of the two Bedouins; their weather-beaten AKs also pointed in our direction. My third thought, following the naked surprise of being corpse-jacked by folks I'd believed were friendly and Anna's disappointing priority, was that I had a mouthful of camel's milk that I didn't have to swallow. So, I turned slightly and sprayed it in Royan's face. The automatic reaction to wipe his eyes with his shoulder changed the angle of the M4's barrel. I grabbed it and pulled hard. Royan, now off balance, stumbled forward between Anna and me and fell into the buffet laid out by the Arabs, his foot landing in a pot of the creamy but, to my taste, overly salty camel beverage, which made him stumble all over again.

At that moment, our campsite was suddenly overrun by half a dozen additional Bedouin tribespeople who seemed to materialize from nowhere. They jumped from their mounts and ran to surround us as Anna stuffed her Sig under a cushion.

The two Bedouins who accompanied us joined in with the new arrivals, shouting Allahu akbar and shooting into the sky. A couple of tribespeople located the body we spent the afternoon digging up and zipped it into a bag, which they had obviously bought for the purpose. So, this was no random attack. They knew what they were looking for and immediately secured it.

The Bedouins then went through our gear, looking for valuables. One of them pulled out a pair of Anna's underwear and stuffed it into his robes, deciding it was a keeper.

Rifles were waved in our faces, along with shouts of "*Amrikiun!*" delivered as an accusation and an insult, their version of "You Americans," I assumed. With Anna and I effectively neutralized, Royan took over and barked a stream of Arabic at the tribespeople, who quietened down.

"I am taking him."

"Why?" I asked.

"You think we are stupid. He is proof that America let Saddam's WMD escape. You spent much gold in the war." Royan patted the body bag. "I think he is worth much money to keep your secret, no?"

Captain Abboud had warned us.

It was then that the distant, rhythmic thud of helicopter blades reached us, carried on the breeze. We all turned as one toward the sound and squinted into the distance. The familiar shape of a Black Hawk shimmered in the haze, scudding low across the desert toward us. But whose Black Hawk? Iraq's. Syria's? Turkey's? One of ours? The Bedouins decided not to wait around to find out, jumped onto their camels, and fled, leaving everything behind they'd set aside to take, apart from Anna's souvenired underwear. Royan also disappeared in the confusion and without the body bag.

Anna pulled the satellite beacon from her webbing and showed me its small flashing green LED. "You're welcome," she said, allowing herself the faintest of smiles, and watched the approaching Black Hawk she'd summoned. "I set it off when we located him," she nodded over her shoulder at the body bag.

The helicopter landed in a sandstorm of its own making. The door slid open, and out stepped our savior, Bradley Chalmers. "Going my way?" he said, trotting over.

I looked around. Damnit, where's a camel when you need one?

"I was at Al Tanf when your beacon went off. Looks like I arrived just in time," he announced.

Did he want a medal? I ignored him and carried the body bag to the Black Hawk.

"What have you got there?" Chalmers wondered. "Can't be a body — too light."

"We'll debrief you on the way," Anna informed him.

As the helicopter lifted off, he said, "Okay, so what's happened? Tell me. Who do we have here?" He prodded the heavy black zippered plastic with his boot.

I looked at Chalmers, tapped my headphones, and shrugged.

"You can't hear?"

I shrugged again. It had worked for Anna, right?

He fiddled with the connection. "How's that?"

I shook my head.

"Still no good?"

Shrug number three.

"Annoying," he said, "Anna?"

"I can hear you."

"Good, off you go, then."

Anna briefed Chalmers, backtracking on the developments in the Frederickson murder and what led us to this find dug up in the Iraqi desert. Chalmers was excited — not necessarily by these developments but by the prospect of being the person who'd be delivering this news to Muirhead.

"Interesting," he said when Anna had finished her wrap-up. "In response to the Wiki revelations, a Facebook page has launched offering a million-dollar reward for solid evidence that there was

WMD in Iraq during the second Gulf War. The CIA believes a Russian troll farm has put it up to embarrass us. Our contaminated friend here – assuming he still is — would probably cash in that million."

"I wondered if Niemiec might have been behind the attempted theft," Anna said. "But the Facebook thing makes more sense."

"We know sarin degrades fast, so for all we know, that," he motioned at the body bag with a smirk, "could be a dead end."

I watched the landscape scudding by five hundred feet below us, and it occurred to me that I could just push Chalmers out. He wasn't attached to a safety harness. People fall out of helicopters all the time. Okay, so mostly, that happened in South American dictatorships, but the Middle East also has a history. The Black Hawk hit some turbulence and bounced around a little, tempting me with a good excuse to offer any future investigation: "I don't know what happened. We hit a pocket of bad air. I looked around, and Chalmers was just...gone." Anna would be the only witness. Would she testify against the father of her child? I could always indicate some feature on the ground and, when she turned to look, push him out the opposite door. My inner voice was workshopping the physics, timing, and excuses for doing away with the asshole when I heard Chalmers say, "Y'know, Anna, utilities really do it for you, especially your shirt button undone. You remind me of... what's that character in that movie...? You know the one. Wear a push-up bra, and you're Lara Croft."

"You can't say that sort of thing these days, sir," Anna replied, uncomfortable.

"Oh, come on. We're all friends here?"

"Says who, asshole?" I said out loud.

Chalmers turned to me with mock surprise. "Oh, Cooper, I thought you were out for the duration." And then, to Anna, "My apologies. Sorry if you think I overstepped." He opened out his hands, welcoming. "So, now that we're all back on coms — Niemiec. Where are we at with him?"

"You know where we're at," I told him. "One step further along than Anna's last briefing, which is zipped into that body bag. We want to know what the fuck the CIA is doing? The Agency has to be better equipped to track Niemiec down than two agents in the field. While I'm at it, where are the two Wagner killers who whacked Frederickson? Have they been found? And what about Adams and his girlfriend? You picked them up yet?"

Anna joined in. "You know, Bradley, for an investigation we're told is a priority for the Administration, we're not getting a hell of a lot of support."

"I appreciate your observations, Special Agents," said Chalmers, slipping into public servant speak, "however discretion is of the utmost importance to the administration."

In short, deniability. Just a simple push — that's all it would take. "Meanwhile," I said, " people are being murdered, Wikileaks is still drip-feeding information to the media last I checked, Niemiec is slipping under the radar, and Saddam's WMD, which we let slip through our fingers, is potentially being used today by the al-Assad regime on its own people."

"Quite a speech, Cooper. Let me give you one back from our perspective. What have you done so far except get people killed? You've done nothing to bring Niemiec into custody, the whistleblower is still whistling, and we have no useful information on the WMD to force Syria into admitting it's using them, let alone compel al-Assad into giving it up. And why don't you tell me about Gisela? How does she fit into all this?"

The next thing I remember was being pulled off Chalmers by Anna and the loadmaster. Chalmers' face was the color of sweating beetroot. My fingers had been locked around his neck. They pushed me back against the bulkhead while Chalmers pulled himself up off the deck, rubbing his neck, coughing.

"Jesus, Vin...!" Anna shouted at me; the phones pushed off my head.

Chalmers sat back against the bulkhead opposite and refitted his headset. Disheveled and breathing hard, at least his perpetually smug sneer was packed away for a while. "Muirhead wanted you on this case," he rasped. "I recommended against it. I wanted the best, your partner here." He lifted his chin at Anna. "Anyone but you, Cooper. You're an unfortunate side-effect. She provides the cure while you bring on the headaches, impotence, and nausea."

"The drug analogy's an interesting choice, Chalmers. What do you know about roofies? How much did you pay Gisela to set me up?"

"You and me, Cooper... it's a fight to the death. We both know it. I'm going to kill your career. Anna deserves better."

"As in...you?"

Anna, incredulous. "Wait...you're not denying you paid that woman in Berlin?"

Chalmers declined to answer, and that said plenty.

"Let me get this straight. Vin is working on a case that's vital in establishing the existence of rogue WMD and securing the integrity of the Office of the President of the United States. But you're more interested in destroying our relationship?

"Listen, Anna...It's about time you realized this man is a liability to you and to the service he represents."

"Why are you here, Chalmers?" I asked him. "Why here, and why now? You could have sent Inglis, or Davidson, or even the guy with the semen-stained sports jacket. You're a long way from home. Come to gloat? See how your plan is coming along?"

Chalmers looked at me and smiled. "Just doing my job, Cooper."

Fuck, fuck, fuck. I kicked myself for not kicking this guy out the door when I had the chance.

INCIRLIK AIR BASE, TURKEY

The Black Hawk landed beside several waiting Humvees manned by personnel wearing U.S. Army utilities. They were otherwise unidentified — Agency worker bees. They raced to meet the Black Hawk and transferred the body bag into a waiting bio-security vehicle. The long-dead Kurdish fighter would soon be riding on a Moose to Landstuhl Hospital in Germany and, hence, to some off-the-books nook in the U.S. defense network for batteries of tests.

Chalmers went with the Humvees, giving me a burst of glare from his Ray-Ban Aviators as he motored by. The Black Hawk crew shut the machine down and walked off with the loadmaster to a cinderblock office. Anna and I were left standing, somewhat stranded. From somewhere distant came the departing roar of a fighter jet, which quickly receded. A breezy silence filled the void. It was Sunday. Global defense takes Sundays off. If you ever want to invade the West, hang out till Sunday. Everyone is sleeping in.

"C'mon," I said to Anna, picked up my gear and most of hers, and took several steps.

"Where are we going?"

I nodded at some buildings. "Take your pick."

"I can carry my own gear, you know," she reminded me.

Anna curled a thumb behind one of the straps over my shoulder and pulled off a heavy duffle bag.

Fine.

"So you get that I was drugged?"

"You're not a hundred percent innocent."

"How do you figure that?"

"Chalmers knew you'd be an easy mark for a honey trap. Why do you think that is?"

So, even though Anna knew I was set up, in her mind, that very fact made me complicit? Half the world thinks that kind of logic is perfectly reasonable. And that's why the other half scratches its head and watches sports.

A couple of Humvees braked hard beside us. A staff sergeant leaned out the window of the lead vehicle. "Mr. Cooper? Special Agent Masters?"

"Who wants to know?" I asked.

"Yes," Anna replied, shaking her head at me. "That's us."

"Sir, ma'am, there's an urgent call waiting for you."

The humvee doors opened, and several airmen ran to take our gear. Minutes later, we were sitting alone in a bunker in front of a secure monitor, SecState Muirhead's face at least six feet wide, the blue and red blood vessels in her eyes reminding me of railway network maps.

"I heard you secured some interesting potential evidence," she said, her voice also filling the room. "Let's hope it gives us something we can use. Meanwhile, Mark Adams' lady friend was found murdered in his apartment this morning."

Anna and I exchanged a look. Another victim. "What about Adams?" Anna asked.

"No sign of him — our guess is he caught a lucky break, dodged a bullet. No witnesses, no suspects. The CCTV cameras were disabled. Berlin PD is saying it was a professional hit. "

"How was she murdered?" I asked.

"Her throat was cut. The assumption is that Adams was the intended victim. The apartment was ransacked but half-heartedly, made to look like a robbery gone wrong. Adams is on the run."

I felt sorry for Joy. Her only crime was boning the wrong guy at the wrong time. Frederickson's murder, and now an attempted hit on Adams, felt like loose ends being tied. We believed we knew why Frederickson had been whacked, but what did Adams know, or have in his possession, that made him a target?

"I read the homicide report," Muirhead continued. "The victim was mutilated. It wasn't pretty."

"Bled out?" I asked.

"Yes."

"That's Niemiec's M.O." But did he do the deed himself or send in the clowns, perhaps the South African with the hand tatt and his wingman, the strawberry vaper?

"Four hours after the woman's body was found, Niemiec was observed arriving by helicopter at his Warsaw residence so he could have been the killer, but the timing would be tight. Polish intelligence has his residence under surveillance — time to get serious. We're in negotiations with the Polish government to have him rendered to the United States. We want you both there when they take him down."

'What are the charges against Niemiec, ma'am?" Anna inquired.

"The DoJ is working on those at the moment, assisting the Polish government and Interpol. Given that it seems Niemiec was potentially involved in the transfer of WMD to Syria while an officer in the Polish defense forces, I'd begin with treason, move on to conspiracy, and then I'd add accessory to murder. But they're just for starters. Also, you've been off the grid for a while, so you're probably not aware...sarin was released in a train carriage on the Berlin subway. A dozen people were overcome. No deaths, but all twelve ranging in age from 5 to 70 are currently in ICU."

"Where did the sarin come from? Has anyone claimed responsibility?"

"We don't know as yet, Special Agent. We're hoping tests will reveal the source. And no, no one has claimed responsibility. I don't need to tell you that this is deeply concerning."

No, she didn't. Was it a coincidence that sarin was currently the number one topic of discussion on the media's lips?

"The amount of the chemical used was small. But does this mean there's more sarin out there, and if so, how much?"

I said, "Ma'am, because a small amount was used, and there has been no claim of responsibility, my question would be — what was the point of the attack?" There had to be one; I just couldn't see what it was.

WARSAW, POLAND

The case notes on the Berlin attack came through on the Air Force Redeye flight. Several unidentified males in hoodies, wearing respirators and armed with aerosol cans, sprayed the contents into the last carriage, departing just as the doors closed and the train left the station. They then disappeared into the tunnel behind the train as it departed, captured on security cameras. There was panic in the carriage as the passengers began to succumb to the nerve agent, fainting, vomiting, and convulsing. All passengers in the carriage exposed to the nerve agent showed varying degrees of the effects of exposure. None could later offer any worthwhile information — no one saw anything. The cans containing the sarin were left behind. The perpetrators departed the scene via a service tunnel to the street, where fake roadworks protected their ingress and egress. It was a simple, well-executed plan with no clues for local security forces to get their teeth into apart from the dispersal cans left behind. My conclusion...it was Niemiec; had to be. And if it wasn't him directly, he was involved in some way — I was sure of that. "You've read this?" I asked Anna when I'd come to the end of the report.

She nodded. "Terrible. Commuters, and moms and dads with kids..."

I wondered how much of Anna's empathy was generated by the activity going on in her womb. Best keep that thought to yourself, Vin, I told myself. So, instead, I ventured, "This is Niemiec's handiwork."

"On the basis of what evidence?" Anna asked.

"None, but consider the timing. Let's look at this from a different perspective. We keep narrowing our focus to one man, but what if it's a Wagner operation? Niemiec used to be Wagner's boss, and he still has deep connections with it, as we've seen firsthand. Wagner is guns for hire."

"The Kremlin's private army."

"Or was. The guy who used to pull Wagner's strings is dead, so unless he's doing that from the grave..." I was referring to former President Valerei Petrovich, who was killed on my watch. As much as I would've liked to take credit for ending that asshole's life, someone else had had the pleasure of putting a hole in the Russian president.

"So, the baton has been passed," said Anna. "The king is dead; long live the king. Who's to say the Federation's new president is any different from the last guy on the throne? Anyway, you're right. We've been hung up on Niemiec, probably because that photo of him on the convoy stole the show. That, and he dropped a building on our heads. But maybe he's just someone's tool."

No argument there. "And what about Adams and Frederickson?" I wondered. "Is there a Wagner connection?"

Anna was likewise stumped. We were still struggling to put Adams and Frederickson together, let alone figure how out they fit into the bigger picture. And now there was the attack in Berlin to reckon with. Sure, Adams and Frederickson were both stationed at Al Asad at the same time and shared a proven interest in the search for WMD, but thousands of Coalition servicemen and women were stationed at Al Asad at the time and everyone had an interest in finding WMD. Also, working against any possible association between Adams and Frederickson — both men were from different service arms. One was an officer, while the other was an NCO. If Adams had an open friendship with Frederickson, it would have earned the Air Force officer a reprimand. Still, was it totally out of court to imagine that Frederickson and Adams had met back in the day when both were stationed at Al Asad Air Base? There was a clear connection between them. Otherwise, why had Adams turned up at Frederickson's home in Savannah?

Here, the road came to an end: assumptions and questions, but few facts and no answers. I picked at these scabs for a while and only realized I'd drifted off to sleep when Anna nudged me.

"We're landing," she said, the Gulfstream's engines surging through low rain clouds. Taxiing to a stop a short while later and peering through small rain-streaked porthole windows revealed several black SUVs on the wind-swept apron. Waiting beside the vehicles beneath buffeted umbrellas were Davidson, Ridge, and Leonard Gibbs.

"Get much sleep?" Davidson asked Anna, giving her some shelter.

"Not really," Anna replied.

"Shame. Going to be a long night."

"Vin, good to see you again," said Gibbs.

Give it time.

"Special Agent Masters," he continued, introducing himself. "Leonard Gibbs. Call me Lenny."

We made for the vehicles.

"Lenny is from the U.S. Department of Housing," I explained. "Doing a little work for State. He speaks Polish." In other words, Leonard is CIA, he's a spy, and he'll be our translator.

Anna shook his hand. "Good to meet you, Leonard."

The welcome I got from Agent Ridge amounted to a vague lift of his chin. I returned the pleasantry, scratching at the corner of my mouth with a finger, suggesting something was caught in that beard. There wasn't, at least not this time. I have a low fun threshold. "Found the whistleblower yet?" I asked.

'Following several leads," he replied, which I took to mean they didn't have shit.

"Any of those leads brought you here?"

"Maybe," he replied.

More shit he didn't have.

"What's the feeling back at the Pentagon?" asked Anna, settling into the back seat and finding the seat belt.

"Everyone's guilty unless proven innocent," said Davidson over her shoulder as we got underway. "The interviews are interminable. Individuals with even the slightest access are being polygraphed. And many people have access to top secret files, more than you'd think."

"Someone will crack eventually," Ridge ventured.

I had my doubts about that. Whoever had managed to get their hands on hard copies of unredacted classified material and then deleted them on the government server was one cool customer with high-level access and world-leading computer skills. A few questions weren't going to smoke out the guilty party. "Where are we going now?"

"The operation command center," said Davidson, handing back passes on lanyards. "Polish intelligence is working with JW Grom, their anti-terror special tactics unit – SWAT, basically."

"What's our role?" Anna asked, slipping the lanyard over her head.

"Observers," Davidson continued. "If they get their hands on Niemiec, we're accompanying him to Andrews. After that?" she shrugged, "I couldn't say."

I could — straight to a towel over the head and a bucket of water down the throat, or whatever Uncle Sam's equivalent was to that these days.

"Is there a plan for storming the castle?" I asked Ridge and Davidson, who'd already been on the ground in Warsaw for at least another twelve hours. It was a reasonable question. Castles were built to resist being stormed. They were fortresses, which was probably why Niemiec had chosen to live in one.

"As far as I know," Davidson informed us, "a cut to the power followed by two SF teams deployed to the rooftop with a third Black Hawk standing off for overwatch. Sharpshooters on elevated platforms. They're also putting divers in the moat, which has recently been flooded, and covering all exits." Davidson added, "Nothing fancy. By the book."

I didn't know there was a standard SOP for breaching a medieval bunker. I wondered if Niemiec had filled that moat with crocodiles or maybe piranha fish. I wouldn't have been surprised. "What about secret passageways," I said.

"What secret passageways?" Gipps asked.

Ridge breathed a sigh of barely tolerant patience.

I wasn't being facetious. "It's a castle. Castles have those things." Watch any movie with a castle in it, and there's always a secret exit or two of last resort. On top of that, Niemiec was a crafty motherfucker.

"I guess a builder's blueprint for a 600-year-old building might be a bit hard to come by," said Anna, more or less agreeing with me. "Have any renovations been performed?"

"It's their turf. I'm sure they know what they're doing." Ridge offered.

The drive to the operations center, a farmhouse within sight of the castle, took half an hour, over which time the drizzle had become heavy rainfall. The farmhouse, attended by numerous military and civilian vehicles, was set in a sea of cloying mud. Anna, Gibbs, Davidson, Ridge, and I ran from the cars to the farmhouse in the downpour, dodging police and anti-terror personnel dressed all in black. Davidson lost a shoe, sucked off her foot by the mud.

It was an old farmhouse, cramped, a little damp, and noisy, bustling with various officers from numerous services and departments going about their business. Pinned on corkboards were printed images of different views of the castle, noting the entrances, the surrounding environs, the road network, airspace changes, and architectural plans of the castle's interior provided by a company that had completed several restorations and renovations on the building prior to Niemiec's occupancy. There were also plenty of images of

Niemiec in case anyone forgot what an outsized albino man-baby looked like — various historical shots of him and his Wagner units in Syria, the now infamous photos of his midnight ride on the convoy, and more recent wide-angle images taken over the previous 24 hours as he patrolled his battlements.

No one paid us any attention. There would have been at least half a dozen different law enforcement agencies operating in the farmhouse. The presence of yet more unfamiliar personnel went unnoticed. Anna and I walked around, getting our bearings.

Gibbs led us to an area with a bank of monitors watched by operators with headphones, where he introduced us to various Polish officials whose names I'd struggle to remember, let alone pronounce, except for the blond-haired, blue-eyed Agent Kazia Strahovski of the Agencja *Bezpi...Bezpiwhizz...Bezpiwhizz Whoopdeedoo* — fuck it, the ABW.

Kaz took some time out from staring at the monitor fixed on Niemiec's lit-up castle to acknowledge my arrival with a nod and the hint of a smile.

"Who's she?" Anna whispered in my ear, picking up on Kaz's flagrant display of affection.

"Polish security, Kazia Strahovski," I replied, and addressing any concerns, "Not my type."

"Not if you know what's good for you, she's not," Anna whispered.

On their way to the castle, several helicopters roared by low overhead, intensifying everyone's attention on those monitors. Show time.

Darkened screens lit up with multiple real-time videos — live bodycam action provided by the inbound Special Forces — along with various bio feeds relaying the squad members' heart rates, blood pressures, body temps, and so forth.

More uniformed observers gathered around to follow the action as it unfolded, the mood in the room tense. The operators talking into headset mikes went silent. The units in those helicopters knew what they were doing and didn't need their instructions finessed.

As per the plan, two Black Hawks unloaded Polish Special Forces who rappelled down onto the castle's rooftop, while helicopter number three hovered abeam of the LZ, its loadmaster covering the area with a waist-mounted mini gun. Standard SOP.

The bodycam footage showed the unit wasn't wasting time deploying into the castle. The sounds of multiple soldiers running and breathing filled the silence. Shouts from one of the men came through a speaker, followed by anxious phone calls from a couple of the Poles at the monitors.

"What's up?" I asked Gibbs.

"The power is still on," he replied.

Not so surprising. Backup battery storage. Made sense for someone like Niemiec to negate night vision.

The Special Forces units continued clearing the top floor rooms and hallways. No opposition revealed itself. Subsequent floors were cleared with speed the same way and with the same result. But where was Niemiec? And where were his men? Tension in the operations center gave way to frustration, mostly voiced in Polish, peppered with the occasional expletive. As in, where the fuck was everyone?

Another burst of Polish, followed by bodycam footage of the men running down a lit hallway, through a doorway, and down a narrow stone spiral stairway, winding down like a corkscrew...

I checked with Gibbs.

He said, "Maybe a breakthrough. A secret passageway."

How surprising.

The bodycams left the circular stairwell and entered what appeared to be a broad, dank room. The sweep of flashlights revealed the extent of it when the beams illuminated moss-covered walls.

This was a cavern, a vast underground space not noted on any plans. Still no sign of Niemiec or his men. The Special Forces fanned out. Perhaps there was another passageway...

Flashlight beams revealed old stone walls, wet green moss, and nothing else.

Sudden shouting and confusion came through the speakers as an unfamiliar roar built in intensity. It quickly drowned out the voices of the men in that cavern.

"What the—" murmured Gibbs.

More running. More shouting. Real panic.

And then a wall of churning, rolling black water burst into view and swept the men off their feet. Bodycam footage illuminated by brief flashes of light beams showed men tossed violently in a roiling wall of churning water that arrived from nowhere. Several monitor screens winked to black when bodies slammed into walls or columns. Vital signs flatlined. Operations commanders, out of a sense of helplessness watching their men get smashed, shouted orders at the unit being overwhelmed by a violent force that neither bullets nor stun grenades could defend against.

Crunching collisions ended the transmission of two more, then three, and then four body cams.

Anna's hand was against her mouth, eyes wide with horror.

Davidson whispered, "Oh my god..."

The water rapidly swamped the cavern. In the blackness, men could be heard gasping for breath in the few remaining airspaces beneath the ceiling. The speakers were silenced in less than a minute, and only one bodycam wearer continued transmitting. The video on the remaining monitor showed greenish-black water moving much slower, pierced by a fuzzy flashlight beam drifting slowly through it. The beam turned in a slow arc, illuminating a silhouette, which became a man's leg. The beam moved up the body, the bodycam inching close past webbing stuffed with rifle magazines and other gear, including a bodycam ripped from its mount, and finally passed over the camo-streaked face of a man whose mouth and eyes were open and very dead.

Chatter burst through several speakers.

Gibbs, stunned, volunteered the translation. "The divers in the moat. They're saying it's drained."

I pictured half a dozen men in wetsuits and fins flapping around in the mud like stranded catfish. I didn't have to guess where all the water had gone.

Anna, Gibbs, Davidson, Ridge, and I stayed on to do what we could, which wasn't much, at least at first. But then one of the divers found a valve cock that released the water into the nearby river via a set of ancient pipes. With the cavern drained and the castle checked over for booby traps and cleared, the recovery operation could commence. Anna and I volunteered to help recover the dead. Once access to the watery tomb was gained, we removed the bodies of fifteen men. No survivors.

At first light, impromptu emergency meetings were conducted at the headquarters of numerous Polish security agencies attended by emotionally and physically drained colleagues of the deceased running on anger and adrenaline. Anna, Gibbs, and I attended the debrief held at the ABW's HQ. Davidson and Ridge stayed at the command center in case something turned up there.

The bottom line — Niemiec had somehow managed to slip through the fingers of Poland's security agencies but still managed to drop enough crumbs before skipping out to bring on the raid. In short, the wholesale destruction of the assault team had most likely been his aim.

Polish breakfast shows were airing the first reports of the disaster, which were immediately picked up by the world's media services. Niemiec would be watching the TV, laughing, his fat lips pulled back against his milk teeth, his white belly shaking with amusement.

"I'm going back to the castle," Anna whispered during a break in the debrief. "Want to be there while they're doing the survey. Never know what'll turn up."

I stayed at ABW to review all the intelligence on Niemiec and all the other information the CIA and the ABW had collected on this case. The couple of folders I saw at Langley two weeks ago had swelled to nine boxes. The door opened to the office I was borrowing. Agent Strahovski stood in the doorway. "Do you need anything?"

"Answers."

"Will coffee do?"

It wouldn't. But maybe a glass with some rocks and a belt of something distilled might loosen the brain cells. I'd spent the day consuming the contents of those boxes, hoping something important might leap out in a shimmering nightgown and draw attention to itself. But all I got was the feeling in the part of me sensitive to these things tugging at the calloused-over part that there was something...a realization that hadn't yet dawned. "I'm gonna go for a jog; clear the head," I told her. Or, more accurately, walk swiftly to a bar and have a finger or two of memory jogger.

"You want some company?" she asked.

The old me would have said sure, but the new me was aware that doing so could lead to all my worldly possessions being thrown out the window onto the sidewalk. "Thanks. Need some alone time," I replied and grabbed my jacket.

It was dark outside. Where had the day gone? I glanced at my watch. Come to think of it, where had the night gone? The streetscape looked like it was closing down. There was a bar, but the shutters were being put up. Maybe there'd be another a little further down the road. I dug my hands into the jacket pockets and walked into a cold headwind. The interview with Adams came to mind. I could have done better with that one. Maybe it was the Jägermeister. Adams said he knew nothing. Deny, deny, deny. And I let him get away with it. Turning up at Frederickson's home told me he was more deeply involved than I'd believed. Frederickson and Adams getting themselves murdered iced that cake and put a cherry on top. As they say, three people can keep a secret if two of them are dead. What was their shared secret, and who was the third person? Niemiec? And what was the connection? I had a feeling it had something to do with the MISREP Adams submitted, which was subsequently denied. But what? Adams said he never took the Horned Owl for a sneaky peek along the border. But maybe he flew it anyway if that were possible, or maybe he flew another mission that turned up something, and that something went on to involve Frederickson. Both men lived high in a style that a military pension wouldn't provide, and that's where Niemiec entered the picture.

My pocket started ringing. I dug out the cell. "How's it going there?" I asked Anna.

"The whole thing was a setup, but I don't get why. Was it just about antagonizing the authorities here? Niemiec's got nothing to gain by doing that. Just makes everyone want to nail the son of a bitch even more. How about you? Anything your end?"

"Been thinking about Adams and that mission CENTCOM denied. There has to be more to it."

"Maybe." I heard her sigh. "It's been a long fucked-up day."

No argument there.

"I'm standing at the gateway to the castle grounds. There was a vigil here, people with candles, leaving cards, a mountain of flowers. Images of the deceased were pinned to the wall. There were young children, some crying. I guess they lost their dads..."

It was easy to visualize. Scenes like that played out at mass shootings back home on a daily basis.

"And then the ultra-nationalists arrived," Anna continued. "White wall haircuts, Nazi tattoos, waving pictures of Hitler. They kicked over the candles and flowers and tore everything up. A riot squad arrived with nightsticks, arrested some, disbursed the rest."

"Time to clock out for the day," I told her.

"Yeah. See you back at the hotel. I need to soak this crap out of my skin. I'll be in the bath. Hurry home and join me."

"It's a big bath. We can do laps."

"Vin..."

"Yeah?"

"It's good to hear your voice."

"You too... Does that mean I'm back in the good books?"

"Don't push it." Anna ended the call.

I pocketed the phone as I walked into a passer-by, clipping shoulders hard enough that it jolted me out of that hot bath filled with suds I was picturing. "Hey, sorry, I—"

Something slammed into my face, hard and brutal, causing bright orange planets to appear behind my eyeballs and then explode in a shower of fat droplets. I reeled backward, fighting consciousness, as a second man came on. In the darkness and side angle, I didn't see him. Out of nowhere, a brutal hit was delivered to my kidneys. And then another piledriver slammed into my jaw. I went down, the pavement reaching up for my face. Muggers? I sucked in the cold night air, the street dark, and rolled onto my back. Two men stood over me. One tall and skinny, one not so tall. I smelled strawberries.

"Stand up and get what's comin' to ya, bru," sneered the tall one. South African accent. "Call me a fuckin' pedo...

The cogs clicked into place — Idlib, Wagner, Van Zyl...

A turning vehicle's headlights briefly swept the area, enough time for me to get a look at them.

"Yankee mother fucker," said the other one, the vaper. "We been waiting all day for you, man."

"If you think back," I said, getting up slowly, painfully, playing for time, eyes on the South African. "I didn't call you a pedo. It was a question. A rising inflection. There's a difference." Something was hanging from his hand, a long, dark shape. It made a rattling sound. Another set of headlights caught the device: a Sawzall, a power tool with an all-purpose reciprocating cutting blade. "And my first choice, if you remember," I reminded him, eyes now on the power tool, "was murderer. Second was rapist. Both top-shelf quality crimes with plenty of prison cred."

He swung the clattering Sawzall at my head. A wild swing. The follow-through *zinged* the blade off a steel sign pole, sending out a spray of sparks.

The backswing. It jagged my waist, but no cut. Wrong side of the blade. Lucky.

I charged him before he could chamber another swing and hit him in the midsection. I drove him backward into the side of a building hard, and we both fell to the sidewalk, dazed. The power tool clattered to the ground. The shock passed, and we were wrestling for the Sawzall, one hand on top of the other. My finger found the trigger. The thing suddenly rattled into life, the blade biting into something. The man yelled an obscenity and pushed me away, breaking off the fight.

The vaper came again while I was on all fours and laid a boot into my ribs. Once, twice... *Fuck!* I rolled. His boot hovered over my face. The Sawzall was still in my grasp. I pulled the trigger, and it clattered to life as I swung, the blade catching something in the shadows, steel teeth sawing into something soft. The man screamed. I kept the trigger pulled and the pressure on as he howled, trying to break free of the clattering blade. A warm spray washed across my face. And then the blade was free. The man stood, resting against the pole of a street sign. The sounds he made were animal. Another set of headlights swung past, and, in the beam of light, I saw one of his legs swinging precariously, the flesh and bone below the knee no longer connected to anything substantial that I could see. I dragged myself up off the ground and saw that he was rummaging through a jacket pocket for something, a gun, I figured. He pulled it free as I charged him, lifted him off the ground, and drove him into the street sign pole so hard it quivered with a *bong*. Something substantial within him cracked, and the body went in my arms. I let him fall, a dead weight, and he rolled slowly into the gutter.

Meanwhile, the South African lurched off, doubled over, into the night. At my feet lay the vaper, a dull nothingness reflecting in his open, vaguely crossed eyes. One of his hands cradled a pistol; in the other, brass knuckles. Something was going on with my ribs — pain, but it was distant, almost as if it belonged to someone else. I bent down to pry the knucks off the dead fingers. Bad idea. The world began to spin. I sat heavily on the sidewalk beside the body, slumped forward, and drifted off.

The hard pencil light slashed across my eyes as I tried to figure out where I was, who I was, why I was hurting, and what the attractive blonde woman who then leaned over me and said she was my fiancé might look like with her clothes off. If she was my fiancé. I should know, so why didn't I? Troubling. But then, after a brief period, my memory came back, big chunks of it. She explained that the fiancé thing was just a ruse to gain access to my room without having to claim government credentials, and then I realized that the only woman I had seen naked in the immediate vicinity was the one walking toward me down the corridor with concern on her face.

"What's the worst of it? His injuries," Anna asked once the pleasantries were done.

The fake fiancé went through a list of various breaks, cuts, and contusions and finished with, "We go now to morgue. He killed a man."

Anna looked at me with an impatient, unspoken, again?

"If you're about to ask whether it was for work or play — neither," I told her. "Two of Niemiec's Wagner mercs jumped me, Van Zyl and his Nigerian pal.

Anna had more questions, but the drugs had yet to kick in, and I was too aware of how much I was hurting to recall specifics. A short while later, I was standing over the naked body of the vaper, the lower third of his left leg attached by a thin band of muscle, a blood vessel or two, and a narrow flap of skin. Though a full autopsy had yet to be performed, the ME had speculated that the cause of death was more than likely a broken back. She also believed that it would have been instantaneous. I had a flash of memory along those lines — the crunch, the sound of his body with my weight behind it crashing against the pole, and the sudden dead weight in my arms.

Anna commented, "So I suppose this is the other guy I should see?"

Conversations between U.S. and Polish authorities had been held at the highest level. The result — the story of a mystery corpse left parked at the base of a "No Stopping" sign had been pulled from local media. Investigations by local homicide authorities had also been headed off. The body on the slab had a toe tag labeling him the Polish equivalent of a John Doe. Anna's phone beeped. She excused herself and went to a corner of the room, leaving Kaz, the corpse, and me to get to know each other.

"She is pretty your partner," the Polish agent observed with a nod in Anna's direction. "You have slept with her?"

I ignored the question. HR, privacy issues, et cetera, and so forth...

"Do you love her, or is she a fuck for you?"

Okay, so what is it with these Europeans? Can't they have a healthy puritanical embarrassment about sex like us Americans? "Maybe both," I said, breaking under the pressure of this relentless interrogation. Also, maybe if I gave her the answers, the probing would cease, and we could move on to more normal conversation between law enforcement acquaintances — causes of violent death and so forth. "She's also the mother of our unborn child."

"What is that?"

"We're having a baby."

"Oh! Your first? You are excited, yes?"

Anna was still deep in conversation on the phone, beyond earshot.

The particular environment made the Q&A surreal. What the hell was that little pill they gave me back at the hospital for the pain? The vaper's eyes were open, and his mouth was set with a drunken smile like he was about to chuckle. He could be about to roll onto his side, prop his head on a hand, and say something like, "Seriously, though, are you ready to be a father?" My eyes were locked on the corpse's face. I missed Kaz's next question. "Sorry, what?"

"I said, are you ready to be a father?"

"Yes, and I can prove it. What did one wall say to the other wall?"

Kazia looked at me with a confused frown.

"I'll meet you at the corner."

She blinked.

"See?" I said. "Got the most important dad thing covered. Just ask Anna."

Speaking of the devil, she rejoined us and held her phone up so I could see the images on the screen as she swiped. "Your Nigerian, Mamadou Doumbia, aged 32." She scrolled through a series of photos shot in Syria of Doumbia posing with various small arms. "He joined Wagner in Syria in 2016 after fleeing his own country following a string of armed robberies, two of which involved murder. The White Helmets suspect he has been involved in at least two massacres of Free Syria prisoners." A photo of Doumbia grinning beside a dusty severed human head finished the slide presentation. "It's believed he transferred to Niemiec's band about a year ago, along with Van Zyl. And we've got more on him now, too." She held up an image of the familiar asshole with the hand tattoo posing with Doumbia, both adorned with ammunition belts and various small arms. Anna continued. "Van Zyl emigrated to England, joined the army, and wound up in 3 Commando, but he didn't fit the mold and was dishonorably discharged within two years of service for numerous charges including vehicle theft — the Warrior on the low-loader — and common assault. He was deported back to South Africa, where he married. Three years later, his wife was found murdered. It's a cold case. The only eyewitness to the murder was killed in a gas explosion in his apartment. Even though Van Zyl was in remand for robbery at the time — the tourist shop — law enforcement in Joburg believed he had a hand in the explosion. But again, no proof."

Calling this asshole an asshole was an insult to assholes. "So where does that leave us?" I asked.

"We can provide information to Detective Purdue in Savanah about Frederickson's murder that will give that case some closure. There's that, and Niemiec sent those two after you for a reason. Maybe we're close to something—"

"And don't know it," I said.

"Or because you're just plain annoying."

She kissed me on the cheek, the fractured one. Love and pain. Back to normal. If I had to take a beating to get there, it was worth it. "Did you find anything at the castle?"

"Computers and a server, but none of it was password protected. Niemiec would have loaded them with BS. It's the kind of thing he'd do."

"Find any more secret passageways?"

"The local authorities put a stop to further investigation. A heritage site or something. They think we're going to damage it."

"My suggestion — call Tom Wilkes and have him blow it into the river."

"Good idea. Text me his number."

Whatever they gave me at the hospital was wearing off, and the deceased was back to being very dead. Now I could look forward to pain that made me want to sit, or stand, or lie down or maybe just say fuck loudly.

As for Agent Kazia, she was so thoroughly thrilled by our impromptu work-in-progress meeting that she was yawning and glancing at her watch. "Can I give you ride somewhere?" she asked, eager to get moving.

Half an hour later, the three of us were standing on a riverbank, the spires on top of Niemiec's castle visible over the canopy of trees crowding the riverbank.

"What are we doing here?" Anna enquired.

"To begin with, helping to find us a boat,"

"Why?" Kaz demanded with growing impatience.

I motioned at the dredge dumping sludge into an accompanying barge. "Because I'm in no condition to swim."

A fishing boat was eventually hailed. It ferried us the short distance across the slow-moving brown water to the dredge. One of the vessel's workers stopped us at a rusty ladder and held a brief, puzzled conversation with Kaz until she flashed her credentials. He then led us to the wheelhouse and presented us to an overweight skipper with a ruddy face in filthy coveralls, sitting in a chair in a cloud of cigarette smoke. His feet were up on the dash, surfing what appeared to be underage porn on his phone. He looked up at us, surprised, which wasn't surprising. How many uninvited guests arrive on a working dredge, especially ones that look like Anna and Kaz? From the way he licked his lips, not many. He juggled his phone like it had turned into a slippery fish, found a pocket for it, and then got indignant.

"Who the fuck are you people?" he whined in Polish, but which I nevertheless understood.

Kazia broke out her ID once more and snapped a few terse words. Her attitude was my doing. I'd almost had to drag her here. But of the three of us, only one spoke Polish, and I was pretty sure that would come in handy.

Can I ask you some questions? I said, Kaz, interpreting.

"Yes. I am busy."

I ignored the palm off. "How long have you been dredging the river?"

"Forever."

"No, here. On this part of the river?"

He glanced skyward to do the sums. "Off and on, seven years. Yes, seven."

"Did the river ever require dredging before that?"

"Elsewhere, yes. Here, no."

"So why suddenly here? Any ideas?"

"No."

Putting it another way, I asked him, "What sort of events require a river to be dredged?"

"Silting up because of tidal flows..."

"But this is a freshwater river."

"Yes, there are no tidal flows here. Flooding is another reason. Again, silting. It's always about silt."

"Has the river flooded in the last seven years?"

"No."

"Can you think of any other reasons?" I asked him via Kaz.

"Rivers are alive. They change course, the banks move, and the water rolls this way and that, like a woman removing her stockings." Kaz shrugged at me. "That is what this troll says."

"What about landslips upriver?" I asked.

The skipper replied, "If the river holds silt when the water slows, silt will drop."

"What if the water is already slow-moving when it picks up the silt?"

"It won't pick up much silt; if it carries silt, it will not be carried far."

As he said, it was all about silt. "Thank you for your time, sir," I told him.

"What was that all about?" Anna asked as the dredge's punt motored us back to solid ground.

"Silt."

"Thank you. Don't be a dick."

"It's the ribs," I explained.

"No, it's not."

"Okay, look. Why is silt a problem at this location?" Niemiec's castle was adjacent, somewhere behind the trees. "Gotta be a reason. Maybe Niemiec's doing some excavation under the castle and secretly dumping the tailings here. Or maybe there's another reason. I'll be sure to ask him when we catch up with him."

My pants pocket began to hum. Langley calling. "Yes," I said after pressing the button. I motioned for Anna to follow and started walking to the back of the barge for some privacy.

"Not a professionally civil way to answer the phone, Vin."

"This is a CIA phone, so there's not always a professionally civil person on the line. Call back and we can start over."

"Never mind. The news is...well, I guess you'd call it disturbing."

"Wait, I'm putting you on speaker. Anna's with me... Go ahead."

"Results have come in on the body you recovered from the desert. The dry conditions mummified the remains, and that also preserved the chemicals in his tissue. DF killed him. Spectral analysis also revealed it's the same DF used in the sarin attacks on al Qusour as well as Khan Shaykhun."

"Okay," I said. Answers.

"Not quite ready to high-five yet. They tested the cans left behind in the attack on the Berlin train. It's the same DF."

"So, not all of Saddam's sarin made it to Syria."

"The news has sent everyone here into a tailspin. If the sarin used in Berlin was a sample, how much more is in circulation? Who's got it? And what are their intentions for it?"

The questions I had had earlier were now top of the list.

"Jesus," Anna whispered.

"While no one has issued orders to the effect, if I were you, I'd focus on tracking it down. A single drop of sarin on the skin is lethal. A bucketful could kill thousands. So, in the wrong hands..."

There was a big clock, and now it was ticking loud and clear.

"So...the wastepaper you recovered from Niemiec's office," Inglis continued. "We're still piecing it together, but it appears Niemiec doodled the word Zruba numerous times. Zruba is the nickname of Arcady Zrubarov, a Russian oligarch and the former director of Rosoboronexport, the Russian Federation's official supplier of all Russian-manufactured military armaments. If it's Niemiec who has WMD for sale, someone like Zruba would be a useful connection."

"We're chasing doodles now?"

"It's a place to start. We don't have much to go on, and our analysts are convinced this is meaningful." Inglis probed the silence, then added, "Big cases have broken on less."

"Niemiec could also have left that waste for us to collect, shredding it to make it seem like he didn't."

"Possibly, but not likely. That's the assessment."

"Do you know where we can find this Zruba?"

"On his boat. Currently berthed in Monaco harbor."

"As in Monte Carlo?"

"Yeah. Something else of interest in that paper waste. He sketched out the chemical structure of sarin, replacing the usual chemical symbols in that structure with different letters."

"How different?"

"Instead of various phosphorus and fluorine symbols, he penned in the symbols Ni, Zu, and Sd, all of which are meaningless because, while Ni is the symbol for nickel and Zr is zirconium, neither have anything to do with the makeup of sarin. And Sd isn't an element at all."

Was now a good time to inform Inglis that I failed high school chemistry?

Inglis continued, "But all this takes on a different meaning if Ni and Zr are symbols for Niemiec and Zruba, respectively. And if that's what we're looking at, then who or what is Sd?"

I had nothing, but then, neither did head office.

"Also, Niemiec was in the habit of drawing bull's eyes and putting your name in the center. What does that tell you?" Inglis said.

"Don't walk into buildings when he's around?"

"Good advice. You should heed it. And that's all I've got for you at the moment."

"Before you go, Anna and I want to get read-in on all the missions Adams flew in command of Horned Owl back in the day."

Anna looked at me quizzically, this being news to her.

"What are you hoping to find?"

"I'm hoping we'll know when we see it."

"Might be tricky. Horned Owl is still classified."

"Twenty years later?"

"I'll see what I can do. Right at the moment, the Pentagon will buy almost anything, even a fishing expedition, but I'll still need a solid rationale."

"Adams spent some time at the Pentagon after Iraqi Freedom. The Puzzle Palace would have a record of him accessing those missions."

"I can enquire, but why the interest?"

"Mine or Adams's?"

"Both."

"If Adams reviewed his missions, I want to know which ones he looked at, and then maybe the reasons why those specific missions interested him will pop."

"What's your hunch?"

"That he used the asset illegally, went looking for WMD, and found it."

"Okay, that's big, but it's also pretty thin. Maybe I can dress it up and put lipstick on it."

"Also, Adams would have had multiple crew members on the HO over the course of its deployment. Can you see if any of them end up at the Palace at the same time Adams did his tour there?"

"You've reminded me — there's no record of Adams entering the United States recently. The assumption we're going with is that he's traveling on a false passport. We doubt he's still in the U.S."

I wasn't surprised.

"So...where was I?" Inglis said. "Monaco, Monte Carlo. Tread lightly. Zruba is a Russian citizen and a Kremlin favorite. Muirhead doesn't want an international incident. It's Monaco's biggest week of the year and the reason Zruba's boat is in town. News cameras are everywhere."

"What's the occasion?"

"Motor racing. The F1 circus. I'll hook you up with local law enforcement." Inglis concluded, "Send me a postcard, will you?".

The line went dead, and then my phone *pinged* with our flight information.

Anna brightened. "I know I shouldn't say this, given where things are now, but Monaco! A last, a perk!"

MONTE CARLO, MONACO

Anna led the way with a Monaco police officer, our local liaison with the rank of sous-brigadier, a pleasant French-speaking middle-aged woman by the name of Therese. Our destination — the mega yacht Zorya, which towered over the playthings of lesser billionaires, moored at the far end of one of the piers. The boat was Zruba's red, white, and blue penis extension, a floating monument to excess decked out in the colors of the Russian Federation. It was hard to think straight with the sun flashing off all that ill-gotten money bestowed on the former head of Rosoboronexport by Kremlin favoritism. But maybe the searing high-pitched scream of practicing F1 race cars echoing around the harbor also had something to do with that, along with mind-melting decibel levels belting from sound systems energizing the parties on almost every boat.

"Did I mention I have a headache?" I said to Anna. She didn't answer. Not because she didn't hear but because she was distracted by the sight of Zrubarov dancing with a conga line of bikini models on Zorya's stern deck.

Two guards, cage fighters with cauliflower ears and full-sleeve tats, were dressed up in navy striped shirts, red scarves, and navy linen shorts. While they looked like a couple of extras in a Village People music video, they held the gangplank like it was the bridge at Thermopylae. Anna flashed her badge. The light caught it and danced in one of the goon's eyes. He ducked like he was slipping a punch, so Anna flashed it some more.

"Here to see Arcady Zrubarov," she said with a peaches and cream smile, sliding a calling card into his breast pocket and tapping it.

"Wait," he grunted and lumbered up the gangway.

"Nice cravat," I told the remaining guard. "Or is it a neckerchief? And the color is you. Matches the broken veins in your cheeks." No reaction unless the bunched jaw muscles counted as he ground his teeth.

Zruba appeared in the doorway at the head of the gangway. "What do you want?" he called out.

Anna replied, "Answers to some questions."

"What about?"

"Things that might embarrass you if I have to shout them out from here."

Zruba thought about it, then beckoned us forward. When we were inside the doorway, he hesitated. "I do not have to answer questions. You are American; I am Russian. You have no power here." He then beseeched our accompanying cop. "They have no power here." Therese ignored him.

"You got money in the States, right, bub?" I asked.

"What...?"

"United States Secretary of State Dorothy Muirhead sends her regards and says she'd like to know if you want that money of yours tied up with its hands tied behind its back and water-boarded?"

"We are here as the representatives of the U.S. Secretary of State," Anna translated. "And she would very much appreciate your cooperation."

"I know you. You are CIA," he told me.

"No need to get personal, Zruba. In fact, I represent the United States Department of Agriculture."

"My associate is one of our foremost experts on bees," said Anna.

"I know who you are," he told me. "You are American spy. No more games."

Three young women wearing almost nothing giggled and threaded their way between us, heading off to somewhere else on the boat. In fact, what they were wearing was closer to nothing than to almost nothing. One of them stroked Zruba's face on the way through and then pecked him on the cheek. I took a fresh look at Zruba just in case I had it wrong. Nope, still the man I'd seen beforehand in the files sent to us by Inglis — mid-50s, soft belly, man boobs, and jowls like old handbags. I'd put money on his liver looking like an alcohol-soaked pepperoni pizza.

"Would you stop ogling the scenery?" Anna whispered with a nudge.

I flinched, the nudge tickling an injured rib, and did as the lady asked. Zruba took us to Zorya's stern, where the party was in full swing. An African woman in skimpy lime-green bikini bottoms, matching lime-green lipstick, and nothing else other than a big smile ignored the sous-brigadier and handed Anna and me his and hers lime-green swimsuits. Behind her, 20 or more perfect human specimens splashed in the pool on the sundeck, most wearing the lime-green swimwear in the colors of the race team sponsored by the oligarch. At the same time, at least the same number swayed to the DJ's beats as they sipped champagne, threw back vodka shots, and gobbled caviar like it was their last meal from ice sculptures of F1 cars.

"*Nyet!*" Zruba snatched the merchandise from our hands and stuffed them back into the lime green bag hanging from the woman's shoulder. The smile remained, but the woman moved along.

Anna asked Therese to wait for us back on the marina, and we followed Zruba into the ship's superstructure. The Village People and I brought up the rear.

Three flights of stairs and two plush carpeted hallways lined with glossy teak later, we came to what I presumed was Zruba's office, but only because I spotted a desk. The rest of it was decked out like a Botswana hunting lodge, complete with the stuffed heads of big game animals hung on rustic walls of weathered wood paneling. A flayed lion skin rug was spread in front of a solid basalt stone hearth. Indigenous tribal weapons, including spears, knives, and cleavers, were set out in a locked display case, along with large caliber handguns, several scoped sniper rifles of various makes, and a couple of composite hunting bows. Zruba took a seat behind the desk and motioned us toward lounge chairs covered in zebra skins. The security kept the doorway covered outside. I glanced around the room. Were we still in Monte Carlo? The setting might have changed, but Zruba's resentment hadn't. "What do you want? I am busy man."

Right. He had a hot tub to get to.

"How well do you know Andre Niemiec?" Anna asked him.

"Ah," he replied as if now all was apparent to him. Perhaps it was. "You think I am involved in this WMD scandal hurting your White House?"

"Please answer the question, sir," Anna repeated.

"We have met, it's true, and on many occasions over many years. Why should I deny this? It is natural that Andre Niemiec should purchase merchandise for Wagner from Rosoboronexport."

At last, someone admitting they actually knew the guy.

"How long have you known him?"

"Long enough."

"How many years?"

"I cannot think. Many."

"Has he ever sold anything to you?"

Zruba appeared insulted. "I am seller, not buyer."

"Have you ever sold a quantity of the chemical difluoro?"

"What is that, di...diflur...?"

"We can wait while you phone a friend," I said.

Anna pressed. "Difluoro is used to make sarin."

"No, I do not deal in such things."

He was indignant. How dare we insinuate that there's a wrong way to kill people en mass. He was a man of principle.

Anna continued. "Have you met with Niemiec lately?"

"No. And your government knows nothing if it thinks this."

"I believe you sold a quantity of difluoro to the Syrian government back in 2003, the sale organized by your good friend Andre Niemiec," I said.

Zruba stared at me.

"Saddam's difluoro," I said, rubbing it in.

Behind Zruba's eyes, connections were snapping and sparking like naked electrical wiring.

"This is ridiculous," he blurted. "Did you not hear me? I do not trade in this."

Keeping the pressure up, I showed him a photo of Grizzly Adams. "Have you ever had any dealings with this man?"

He shook his head. "Who is this?"

A photo of Gerome Frederickson earned the same reaction.

"You're lying," Anna insisted. "You're Niemiec's middleman of choice. Has he come to you recently with more DF to sell? Are you looking for a buyer? Was the attack on the Berlin subway your idea, a public demonstration of the weapon's effectiveness to up the price for prospective buyers?"

He stood. "You are crazy. This is wild accusation. You have no jurisdiction here. I will throw you off ship."

We stood. "Going a little overboard with the threats, don't you think?" I told him.

"You've admitted to a relationship with Andre Niemiec," Anna persisted. "If there's another WMD attack, large or small, in a Western city, we will come for you, and we won't be so polite second time around."

"Приходить!" he shouted. A door opened, and the muscle in the sailor suits joined us. "Сопроводите их до пристани," Zruba demanded.

I took that to mean, "Get them the fuck outta here," because one of Zruba's goons went to grab Anna's arm.

She smiled. "Touch me, and I'll shoot you in the face."

Clearly, I'm a good influence.

The escort made sure there were no detours, herding us back the way we came. I caught glimpses of the party cavorting poolside. And that's when I saw Adams. He was accepting a pair of lime swim briefs from the African woman, the one with the smile. His eyes met mine. "Adams!" I shouted and jumped over a banana lounge while making a lunge for him. But I tripped over a couple lying on towels feeding each other shrimp. Adams also jumped, leaping off the back of the ship and into a tender, the one I guess he'd just arrived on, as it was reversing away from Zorya. He managed to make the distance, his front foot connecting with the last few inches of the bow and fell sprawling into the passenger area.

I heard him shout, "Go! GO!" at the tender's skipper, who pushed the throttle to the stops. The outboard's prop bit and the tender surged backward, taking in a wave of water that washed over the stern and Adams and half-filled the boat.

Other tenders were rocking behind Zorya. I vaulted for the nearest one, cleared the transom, and came down hard, my knee and shoulder crashing against the boat's windshield but sparing those damaged ribs of mine.

Anna landed beside me like a cat. "You okay?"

"Living the dream, honey," I panted as she slipped the rope connecting the tender to the Zorya.

"Hey! That's mine!" shouted an indignant guest on Zorya with influencer muscles and sculptured eyebrows, tossing aside a cracker loaded with caviar as we made off with his motorboat.

"Thanks," I called back to him, firing up the engine. I jammed the throttles to the stops, and the boat surged forward as Anna dropped into the passenger seat beside me.

"That was Adams? You're sure?"

"I'm sure."

"Where'd he get to?"

I gestured at the general area ahead. Adams was headed for the crush of vessels tied up to each other four and five deep off the marina. The waterway in the confined protected area of the cove was choppy, churned by countless tenders plying back and forth between parties.

"There!" Anna pointed to a small blue powerboat disappearing behind the bow of a ship almost as big as Zorya.

I spun the wheel around and nearly rammed another speedboat motoring beside us. Adams had changed course and was now attempting to lose us in the caverns created by the towering hulls of pleasure boats almost the size of destroyers. We came around behind the speedboat, and I gunned the engine at Anna's last sighting, weaving around the traffic. Throttling back, I took us into the shadows between two giants, both hulls pulsing with muffled internal beats. But Adams was nowhere to be seen. Coming out into the light, I spotted the guy heading for a gap between the hulls of a giant catamaran.

I pushed the throttles and we smashed through the chop, racing to head Adams off at the other end of the cat'. We came around the bow as he turned in towards the marina. We were gaining on him. The gap closed as we carved through a slalom course of piers. Out of the shadows and again into the sunlight, it was then that I noticed the police launch powering towards us, throwing up a massive bow wave, red and blue lights blazing, horn sounding. Adam's launch glided up to a marina ladder, and he scampered up the rungs like a frightened squirrel. Reaching the top, he kept running. The police launch, meanwhile, bore down, officers glaring at us from the bow. *"Arrêt! Tu dois arrêter!"* a voice boomed at us through a PA with squeals of feedback.

"They want us to stop," said Anna.

I figured as much.

Partygoers on all the pleasure boats in the cove stopped their self-absorption for a few moments to gawp at the unexpected show happening in the bay. The launch slid alongside us, and two officers jumped down.

"What's the problem?" I asked after he barked something in rapid-fire French.

"You are speeding," his partner snapped in English. "Four knots! Four knots. You make twenty knots!"

"You're arresting us," I asked.

He slapped a ticket in my hand and added a safety lecture. The handcuffs only came out when the owner of the tender arrived and with him the charge of stealing. But then Sous-Brigadier Therese turned up to straighten things out and explained to the equivalent of the desk sergeant that the government of Monaco was aiding the United States with a criminal inquiry of national significance to America and that Anna and I were part of that. We were then released, but not without plenty of grumbling. Outside the station, Therese gave us one of those The-Trouble-With-You-Americans lectures. At least, I think that's what she gave us before walking off because it was delivered in French.

Anna and I returned to our hotel along streets packed with racegoers. The cars were back out on the track, filling the city with sounds like howler monkeys in heat.

"You're sure that was Adams?" Anna asked again.

"Positive," I replied.

"What's he doing here?"

"You mean, other than confirming to us by visiting Arcady Zrubarov that both of them are up to their necks in this?"

"Yeah, okay. I agree. So, how do we find him in this?" Anna wondered, motioning at the festival of horsepower warships cramming the streets.

My Company phone buzzed against my leg. I pulled it and checked the screen. There was no caller ID. "Hello," I said, answering it nevertheless.

"There you go, a pleasant tone," said Inglis.

"That's me, all joy and light."

"Your hunch about a crew member from the Horned Owl who also served under Adams at the Pentagon paid off. A captain, Dexter Foord, an operations research analyst with a doctorate in computer science. There's some crossover time when both men served at the Pentagon."

"Where does he live?"

"We're trying to locate him. You can't just look these people up in the directory. Folks like Foord aren't easy to find, especially when they don't want to be found. Why Foord? What's he got to do with this?"

"Can't say just yet. Maybe nothing. Maybe everything."

"Well, keep me posted. Meanwhile, your Lieutenant Colonel Adams. He reviewed all 403 Horned Owl MISREPs. Get this — after his tour serving in Iraqi Freedom, he was posted to the Secretary of the Air Force's department to review the performance of the Horned Owl. What a gift." Inglis continued. "The MISREP hard copies are located at Central Command, Tampa. Adams had all 403 of them boxed up and sent to him at the Pentagon, along with access to digitized paperwork. All MISREPS were returned, by the way. I checked."

"Thanks," I said. I'd hoped it would only be one or two missions Adams reviewed, but that would make it too easy for someone like me nosing around his history. "Our theory is that Adams came to believe the HO found a cache of WMD during a mission, and he needed some information about that find, possibly the coordinates."

"So he could dig it up and sell it?"

"That's your mystery sarin showing up in Berlin — a sample."

The silence on the line told me Inglis was letting it sink in. "Wow." Then, "Okay, I've sent you copies of all HO's MISREPs. There's some redaction — can't be helped. The other line is calling. Sorry, gotta go."

The call ended.

"So, this is *our* theory now?" Anna asked, pissed.

"What's mine is yours, remember?" I replied. "Look, you must be toying with either the scenario I just outlined or something like it because you asked Zruba if Niemiec had come to him with WMD. The thing is, we have to start making some assumptions about the people we know are involved in this and apply pressure. Otherwise, this nut's never going to crack."

"Well, I'll come along for the ride, at least for now, but don't speak for me until we've spoken about it first."

"Deal."

We found a computer shop and bought a printer, a shredder, and a couple of reams of paper. Booze was next on the list — to help us through the night. Once back at the ranch, we printed out the mission reports, all 403 of them, and got to work.

Anna flicked through her stack. "Telling Zruba he was going a little overboard when he threatened to throw us off the boat..."

"Just limbering up the dad jokes," I said.

"Keep that in mind at 2am when Junior needs a bottle and his or her diaper is full of last night's dinner."

"I'm skipping that part and going straight to Junior winning Wimbledon." I was only half listening. There was something buried in Adams MISREPS. I had no idea what that something was, but I didn't want to miss it. He was the sole commander of the RC-12D, code-named Horned Owl, operational from January 1st, 2005, to June 25th, 2005, after which the asset was benched, along with Adams, who then went off to do three years of hard labor, pushing paper at the Pentagon.

The HO missions made for dry reading. They contained times, headings, personnel, weather data and observations, basic flight information, and plenty of map coordinates. After five hours of review, I came across something that seemed like nothing, but the more I looked into it, the nothing was possibly something. I printed out another copy and passed it to Anna. "Take a look at this — mission number 386." I read through the MISREP again. On May 4th, 2005, Horned Owl departed Al Asad Air Base for a routine sortie following Highway 12, surveying the section between the cities of Hit and Albaghdadi, a 43-kilometer stretch of the main north-south road route linking Al Asad to Ramadi, Fallujah, and hence to Baghdad. Army Intelligence believed insurgents had buried IEDs along the route, hence the call to Horned Owl to pinpoint them. But then, early in the afternoon, a dust storm that defied weather forecasts swept up from the southwest, affecting air traffic in the area. Al Asad was closed. Lieutenant Colonel Adams abandoned the scheduled mission and, waiting for the storm to pass, took the opportunity to align the aircraft's more sensitive instruments. The HO flew a grid pattern east of the base, doing 12 passes roughly northeast to southwest. Precise course headings and each pass's duration were noted, along with altitude, ground speed, and other details. I freshened up our glasses with another finger of Glen Keith.

"No, thanks. You keep pouring, and this mother-to-be keeps refusing."

"Just being inclusive," I said.

"And then you pour mine into yours."

"Don't want you to feel pressured."

"I love how you're always so considerate."

"I try," I said.

Anna scanned the MISREP and handed it back. "Nope, don't see anything here that's even remotely interesting."

"Look, it's the one mission out of 403 that's random, the sole instance Horned Owl searched a pattern that had nothing to do with the mission's approved parameters," I insisted. "Remember, HO is a national asset with its every movement planned, and to quote Adams, 'up the wazoo.'"

Anna looked up from her pile of paper and stifled a yawn. "Keep digging."

Perhaps she was right. I put #386 aside and reviewed another half-dozen missions, but I kept coming back to it. Something wasn't adding up. But what? The grid pattern flown by HO was nowhere near the convoy geolocated by Wilkes, the location of the buried Kurdish fighter. HO's search pattern was to the east of Al Asad, while all points of interest were to the west.

I checked the MISREP's supporting information – the intelligence assessment and the weather report. The dust storm rolled in from the southwest — wind speed 30 mph. Typical, though late in the season.

I went back to the MISREP and the coordinates of the HO's grid search, then back to the weather data. Wait a minute... "The MISREP says they searched this pattern because the dust storm prevented them from flying the mission."

"What?"

"MISREP 386."

"Let it go, Vin."

"No, look. According to the weather data, the HO flew its grid pattern over the storm's footprint."

"Really? Give me a look."

I handed over the sheaf of paperwork with the relevant info circled.

Anna checked through it, her frown deepening. She scribbled a few notes, went back to the data, and scribbled some more.

Eventually, she said, "You're right. Did Adams make a mistake when he made out this MISREP? Is that possible?"

"No," I said.

"Then is it possible the HO's mission data has been altered after the fact?"

"I wouldn't have thought so."

"Then what have we got?"

"Something that's a hundred percent wrong. Either HO flew its mission in the teeth of a dust storm that closed Al Asad, or it flew its grid pattern somewhere else, and the information on this MISREP has been falsified. There's no way on earth HO searched a grid in the teeth of a dust storm."

Anna went back to her notes. "Keep the stated latitude lines in MISREP as they are and shift the longitude coordinates, say, 50 miles to the east; where's the Horned Owl?"

I opened the computer's mapping function, Anna looking over my shoulder, and overlayed the revised coordinates. The pattern was close to the Al Asad base, maybe five clicks to the south and west. "Here is the position of the convoy identified by Wilkes and the Aussie SAS patrol," I found the point on the desert floor and marked it. "And here is where we dug up Pedrad's buddy." I indicated that point also — both now under the Horned Owl's revised grid search.

"Check the weather data in the MISREP," Anna suggested. "Maybe that's wrong. Then the HO's coordinates on the original MISREP will make sense,"

A few minutes later, we had the dust storm's severity and footprint confirmed. The weather report in the MISREP aligned with the historical data. That, at least, was true and accurate.

"This is exciting," said Anna. "It's *something*! But it's going to upset a few people. Somehow, MISREP 386 has been doctored. And you'd never know it unless you went through this exercise."

"It's late," I said. "Want to hear a bedtime story?"

"Does anyone turn into a pumpkin?"

"Adams hears rumors about buried WMD up on the border. He believes in them enough to put in a mission request to check it out. Request denied. He forgets about it while Horned Owl is flying out of Balad Air Base, but then operations are shifted to Al Asad where rumors about buried WMD have assumed local legend status. Only now, they're more pointed — there's a potential location. There are even rewards of up to $200,000 being offered to Iraqis for information that will lead to the unearthing of chemical and biological weapons. So, when that dust storm hits, Adams takes advantage of it and runs Horned Owl over the area — the focus of the rumors about WMD around Al Asad. Adams isn't a technician, but he hears something. Maybe he hears it from Foord or another crew member. Let's say it's Foord himself. Maybe they shoot hoops together, or play computer games, or train hamsters — I don't know. But information is exchanged. They're all on the same team, stuck on the same base. And a few years later, both Adams and Foord meet up at the Pentagon. And there's Marine Sergeant Gerome Frederickson, who's also based at Al Asad."

"There's a lot of pumpkin here, Vin. It's all supposition. Also, Adams and Frederickson...an officer hanging out with an NCO? One Air Force, the other Marine? You're suggesting oil mixing with water."

"There's a war going on. Stanger things have happened. Maybe the two cook up a plan. After Iraqi Freedom, Adams lucks out and goes to the Pentagon, where he wants to be. He does his job and, as part of it, legitimately accesses his missions. He hit the jackpot, handed the perfect cover to access the one mission he was truly interested in. This one." I waggled number 386. "He notes the coordinates of the grid search and makes a few educated guesses based on those rumors. Then, years later, once the insurgency has settled down some, he returns to Iraq, luring Frederickson with promises of a big payday. They visit the most likely coords of that anomaly and dig up a fortune."

"You've used the word 'rumor' at least half a dozen times in the last twenty minutes. More pumpkin."

"The theory fits the facts."

"I thought this was a bedtime story, but now it's a theory, and the assumptions are facts?"

"Wait, I'm not finished turning mice into footmen. The original MISREP submitted by Adams after Mission #386 has been deleted and replaced with this one by Captain Dexter Foord."

Anna guffawed. "Now it's a fairy tale. What you're suggesting is just not possible."

"Who was it who said when you've eliminated the impossible, whatever remains, however improbable, must be the truth?"

"Wasn't it the prince? You know, when he found the gorgeous owner of that glass slipper was really an urchin covered in soot?" Anna took a breath. "I could really use a drink right now. This is doing my head in." She massaged her temples. "Okay, let's keep going."

"So, look... There's a lot of impossible that we know has happened here – this altered MISREP, for example. The stakes are high with big money to be made. And there are billionaire terrorists out there who'd pay top dollar for WMD. Nothing else I can think of fits what we know." I held up the offending MISREP. "You want hard evidence? We know this here is pure fiction. Someone has made this shit up."

"If you're right, and let's pretend for the moment that you are, the Pentagon will cease to have any confidence in the authenticity of its records."

"Not our problem. But there's something about this guy," I said.

"Which guy?"

"Dexter Foord." I went back to the computer, pulled his record, and put his service ID photo on screen. Pasty complexion, 160 pounds, nerdy. "He could've been a multi-millionaire by the age of 30 — certainly had the body type." I scanned his record, much of it redacted. "A wizard with computers and data. Earned his doctorate from probably the world's top computer science college — Stanford — and won the Edward F. Codd Award for..." I read the note verbatim, "...significant contributions of enduring value to the development, understanding, or use of database systems and databases..." Make that a billionaire, except that he'd chosen to serve his country instead. Or maybe disservice it. "Foord is a one-man Anonymous, or could be if he turned his mind to it. And I think he did exactly that."

"What?"

"I think this guy could be our leaker."

"You're that sure?"

"If you wanted someone capable of hacking into a secure server and altering docs, he's got the perfect CV."

There were other notes and documents — a marriage license, wedding photos (he married late in life to a large French woman fifteen years his junior), driving record (a single speeding fine), health records (he was a mild asthmatic), and so forth. No recorded convictions. Lived a clean life. Nothing to see here, move on. "With assistance from Frederickson and Foord, Adams had the means to find WMD. I believe he found it and chose to keep that a secret for financial gain. And that's where Zruba and Niemiec enter the picture."

"There's so much 'I think' and 'I believe' in all of that. Aside from that single MISREP, where's the hard evidence for any of it?

"Feel like a swim?"

Anna examined the boat through the scope. "What are we looking for?"

"A relationship between Zruba and Adams. And if we can tie in Frederickson, even better."

"Please don't tell me you're only going to accept evidence that confirms your Cinderella theory."

"We find evidence that refutes it; we'll throw the baby out with the bathwater."

"Can't you find a less offensive simile?" Anna said, handing me the scope. "It's 4:30 in the morning, and the party's still going strong."

Zorya was moored on the end of an arm of the marina that afforded a clear view of the back of the boat. Couples were in the pool, doing what couples do in the pool at 4:30am. Retiring the scope to my pack, I lifted my shirt over my head and then slipped down a ladder between two yachts into the black water. Monte Carlo was quiet, the city catching some zees before race day. Music was still in the air, beats drifting across the cove from some of the boats entertaining die-hards. I breast-stroked toward the ship, which had a stern platform lapped by the waterline, and hoisted myself up onto the smooth teak platform. Zorya was written on the stern in large gold and black letters, Sevastopol, its home port in smaller gold lettering, beneath.

"Hey," Anna whispered, swimming up to the boat. "Thanks for waiting."

I gave her a hand up.

"That's more like it," she said.

I peeked over the transom. "C'mon," I said and hopped over the teak railing.

The mood lighting in the pool area faded in and out through the colors of the rainbow, accompanying some South American lothario softly crooning his way in Spanish through Sinatra hits. As far as we could make out, two couples were in the pool, and two were in the adjoining hot tub. All were steaming up the water. No threats that I could see. On a bench seat within reach was a familiar lime green bag. I reached over and grabbed it.

"What's that?" Anna whispered.

I dug around in the bag. "Here, put this on."

Anna held a few strings up to the light. "I can't wear this!" she hissed. "I'm pregnant."

I ignored the protest and exchanged my shorts for a swimsuit that was little more than a tourniquet. "If I can, you can."

Anna got to work building herself a cat's cradle to slip into. When she was ready, I stood up and crept into the hot tub. Anna followed. As far as I could tell, no one noticed our arrival. The water was hot. I took hold of Anna and suggested we adjust ourselves to the environment.

"What are you doing?" she whispered into my ear as I maneuvered her onto my lap.

"When in Rome," I told her.

"This isn't Rome." And then... "What's that?! Listen, I'm getting out if you can't control yourself."

At that moment, the two Wagner types we'd met earlier walked out onto the pool deck, doing their rounds. It was like getting whacked with a cold spoon. "Rain check," I told Anna and waited for security to turn their backs and head for the superstructure.

"What are you going to do?" Anna asked.

"Wing it," I whispered.

"No."

"Shh..."

About a minute later, one of them returned, paused to take in the action happening on the pool deck, sweeping a flashlight beam over it. Satisfied there were no threats, he took a few more slow steps and stopped to admire Monte Carlo, glittering like a Vegas chorus line girl.

At that point, I hopped out of the jacuzzi. The splash made him turn, so I stopped to press the button that fired up the hot tub's water jets, which seemed to allay any warning bells. He turned his back on me and started moving again. Before I knew exactly how I was going to wing it, I was double-timing across the deck, the noise of the bubbling water jets covering the sound of my wet, padding feet. On the way through, I grabbed a handy unopened bottle of champagne from a bucket. The bottle was over my head in the striking position almost directly behind him when he turned. I was caught cold, but he was distracted by Anna, topless, wearing not quite enough to truss a chicken, strutting toward us. I completed the downswing, the Veuve putting a sudden end to any fantasies that might have been about to take root.

"That's the mother of my child, buddy," I said as I frisked him, turning up a switchblade and a 9mm Ruger in a shoulder holster with a full mag and a round chambered. "Take your pick," I said, offering both weapons to Anna. She took the Ruger. Good choice. I stripped off the guy's padded vest and handed it to her. "In case you need someplace to hide the gun." She stuffed her phone in a pocket.

Anna doubled back and returned almost immediately with a handful of swimsuits, tying his hands with bikini strings and stuffing a couple of men's bathing costumes in his mouth. "His pal won't be far behind," Anna advised as another flashlight swept the pool deck. There was nowhere convenient to stash the guy sprawled on the floor. I grabbed the champagne bottle and took up a position behind the door. Anna had nowhere to go, so she opened the jacket to her navel and leaned drunkenly against the polished paneling.

The Wagner guy stopped when he saw her. His eyes had enough time to register the semi-nakedness and the lump on the floor, his buddy, but then Veuve turned his lights out before any of that made sense. But these two weren't the only security. It wouldn't be long before the alarm was raised. I dropped the bottle, dragged the guy into a deep shadow area and patted him down, but he wasn't carrying. I left him and we headed for Zruba's African Safari lounge, up three flights of stairs and along two corridors.

There were many rooms. I wondered who occupied them as we passed countless doors. Zruba's themed office announced itself with a double entrance. I twisted the handle. Locked. Resistance ended with a suggestion from the switchblade.

Once inside, I relaxed and headed for the desk. It was completely cleared, except for a phone charging station. Two drawers revealed nothing except for new stationery. Zruba was either careful or organized. Another way to look at it—empty desk, empty mind.

Anna headed for the adjoining suite. A handful of seconds and her head popped around the door. "Come and see this," she called out.

Anna stood before a glass cabinet. "Taxidermy is Zruba's thing." Opening it, she lifted out a gold trophy, examined it briefly, and then tossed it to me.

I read out the engraved plaque. "Arcady Zrubarov, First Place, World Taxidermy Championship, 2012."

In the cabinet, a photo accompanied the champion's trophy — a stuffed mountain lion on the branch of a gnarled tree, hung with a beard of fake snow. The winning entry was also here in the room. The big cat was bounding off the branch, both paws outstretched, teeth bared as if leaping toward prey, the animal seemingly snap-frozen in that moment. Three tiny mountain lion cubs nestled into each other at the base of the tree. Nature's power, along with her fierce beauty and protective maternal instinct. So completely lifelike and yet so totally dead.

Beneath the glass cabinet were shelves stocked with a reference library of taxidermy books and a leather-bound box lined with red velvet containing various picks, brushes, combs, and scalpels kept on hand, I figured, for touching up the displays.

"Take a look at these pictures," Anna murmured as she snapped away with her phone, capturing the room's contents. There was a door between us. I opened it, checking the space beyond — a short, empty hallway ending in a T-intersection and a broader hallway.

"What an asshole..." I heard Anna say almost but not entirely to herself. She handed a framed photo to me. It showed a grinning Zruba holding a high-powered rifle, accompanied by shirtless former Russian Federation president, the late Valeriy Petrovich, both taking a knee behind the carcass of a rhinoceros they'd recently shot. The animal's tongue was hanging out of its mouth, lolling on sandy ground, covered in giant red ants. Seeing Petrovich took me back to the man's death — nailed to a cross, a dagger in his shoulder, and a bullet in his gut. I got a nice warm feeling over it.

Zruba had other memories of animals hunted to death on the display wall, shot from a safe distance by him and his pals, who saw glory in killing from a distance when the animal had no chance to defend itself. And then came a photo of a lifeless mountain lion sprawled across the hood of a 4 x 4, three dead, blood-stained cubs beside their mother. "Jesus..." I muttered, sickened.

"I couldn't look at it," Anna said, adding, "I'm liking this guy less and less. And I didn't like him at all to begin with." She lifted another framed photo off the wall. "Maybe this is what we came here to find."

The image was a little blurred, but there was no mistake. A black and white photo of Zruba with a rifle, kneeling on another dead animal, a giraffe, this time. Accompanying him were two pals cradling high-powered scoped rifles and grinning like fools. One of them was Niemiec, much of his face hidden behind oversized reflective sunglasses and a broad-brimmed hat, but the size of the man, the pallor of his skin, and those lips stretched tight against the ridiculous baby teeth were unmistakable. Then there was shooter number three in the picture. His presence took me completely by surprise. I peeled the backing off the frame and gave it to Anna. "You've got pockets."

"So, who's the other guy here with these two?" Anna wondered. "You recognize him. Who is he?"

The main double door banged open without warning on a scrimmage line of security guards. Quarterback Zruba stood behind them in a flowing purple silk dressing gown, barking the play in Russian. I frisbeed the picture frame at the lineup, which caught one guard in the chin. Anna opened the door in the display room as the guards surged in. They waved their pistols around and were about to fire, but Zruba stopped them with a shout of *"Nyet!"* and a bunch of expletives. A stray bullet or two might bury themselves in his handiwork. Shooting an animal when it was alive was fine, but dead? Watch out!

I followed Anna, slammed the door shut behind me in the face of two guards, and flicked the lock. We were a long way from the pool deck. Anna raced to the T-intersection, turned left, and kept running. More security materialized behind us, the help now less cautious with their weapons. They blasted away as they ran, the shots coming nowhere close.

Anna followed the exit signs until we came out through a hatchway into the night air, the lights of Monte Carlo bouncing off the dappled black water 50 feet below. A charging phalanx of pissed security types was coming up fast behind us.

"At least we're dressed for it," Anna said, looking over the railing at the water several stories below.

The faces of several guards appeared in the hatchway door's glass panel. Anna fired a couple of discouraging rounds into the hatchway's woodwork, then vaulted the railing into the cool night air. I followed.

Slugs drilled the blackness around us as Anna and I kicked for the depths, away from the deadly burrowing lead. Zorya's underwear lights came on, and scything blue and white beams reached out to fix us for the shooter. By then, Anna and I were out of range.

We surfaced in darkness 30 meters from the Zorya, now lit up like Gravman's Chinese Theatre for a premier. There was no risk of discovery despite the boatload of eyes scanning the water for us. Off to our right, Monte Carlo was starting to come awake, no doubt with a hell of a hangover from the night's partying. Out to the east, over the Med, a blush of orange tinged the sky at the waterline. It was getting lighter by the moment. Anna tapped me on the shoulder, and we swam away.

"Are you going to let me in on the secret?" Anna asked as we dressed, one eye on Zorya and the security guards now patrolling its mooring at the far end of another arm of the marina.

"What secret is that?" I said, pulling on my pants.

"How many do you have?"

"Why don't you tell me about Cuba."

"Focus. The photo, Vin. Who's the third man? There's Zruba, Niemiec, and someone you know. I saw the look on your face. You'd make a terrible poker player. "

"What's my tell?"

"Your eyes kind of bug out."

"That's the salt water."

"Who is it?"

"Chase Overton."

"And he is?"

"My soon-to-be new boss. Vice President and Chief Pencil Pusher at Sands Aerospace & Defense."

That got Anna's attention.

"You're fucking kidding."

"Now it's your eyes bugging out. And I know what you're thinking. That I've agreed to work for an asshole who shoots defenseless animals for kicks."

"No, it's not his hobby, which is appalling enough, but the company your future boss keeps — Zruba, Niemiec, Petrovich... That's a conflict of interest if ever there was one."

"You think I should recuse myself? Or let Sands know that the deal between us is off? Strictly speaking, Overton's not my boss; it's Ely Sands. Overton just signs the checks. And all we know for certain at this moment is that he's an asshole, and I've worked for plenty of those over the years. What's one more?"

"That photo connects Overton and through him Sands Aerospace & Defense, with Saddam's WMD."

It did, and no matter what I was saying to Anna, I was mentally seeing my big office, company car, and $360,000 plus bonuses sailing off into the sunset without me.

"We have to interview him," she continued as we left the marina.

Goodbye, cushy corporate retirement.

"One more thing, honey..."

Oh, shit. *Honey?* Trouble ahead. "Yes?"

"You keep going through doors first, jumping over railings first, heading into danger first... You're shielding me. That has to stop. We're partners. That means we're exposed to danger equally. If you take a bullet for me, I'm going to be really pissed."

"Okay, I promise not to die before you."

"That's not what I mean, and you know it. We do these things by the book."

"All right, I apologize. But I'm finding it difficult to separate the woman I love and the mother of my child from the person I share donuts with."

She took my face between her hands and kissed my lips. "I get it, but you have to."

"I'll try," I said as we resumed the battle against early birds cramming the sidewalks, hoping to snap up the best vantage points for the day's events.

Arriving at our Airbnb, a one-room studio above a convenience store with the scenic view of a parking lot brick wall that cost a month's salary for two nights, she asked, "So... leaving Overton aside for the moment, what's the immediate plan?"

I unlocked the door. "Two plans. Number one is to find Adams. I don't think he realizes turning up at Zorya is putting his head in the stuffed lion's mouth."

"And Number two?"

"Take a shower, wash off the salt, and you never know your luck in the big city," I said as we walked in.

"I don't like your odds," said the man sitting on the sofa opposite, a to-go latte in one hand and a Glock in the other. He waggled the pistol in such a way that said, "Come in, close the door, and don't do anything stupid."

Adams.

"We've been looking for you," said Anna. "Thanks. You've saved us the trouble."

"Your snooping around got Joy killed," Adams replied. "Sit down." Anna and I took the two armchairs set up opposite. "I read she died badly. Who killed her?"

"We think we know, but we don't know for sure," I told him.

"It was Niemiec, wasn't it?"

"Or Captain Stubing parked out there on the love boat. Given his hobby, he'd be pretty handy with a knife."

"Zrubarov? No."

"Why not?" I asked.

"Not his style."

"What's his style?"

"Theatrical."

"And Niemiec's M.O., murder by exsanguination, isn't? Either way, the same thing will happen to you unless we get you taken into protective custody."

"This says you're not taking me anywhere," he assured us with a convincing movement of the firearm.

"A lot of people want answers you can provide," Anna said. "Almost as many people don't want you providing them. But only one of those groups wants you alive."

"You know it's bullshit, don't you?" he countered. "The organization I used to work for, the system you work for now. The lies, the deceit, the government cover-ups, the—"

"Look, just because you're waving around doesn't mean we have to listen to a The-Trouble-With-You-Americans speech, especially one from an American. We're both tired and salty and, as you also probably gleaned from my innuendo, my partner and I have better things to do in the shower. So, Anna?" I got up from the chair.

"Frederickson and I located a cache of methylphosphonyl difluoride in the Iraqi desert, and we recovered it," said Adams.

The confession made me sit back down. There it was, the connection between them that had eluded us, along with the reason for it.

He continued, "I bought out Frederickson's share for five million and offered to sell it to Niemiec, the asking price being a hundred million. Niemiec took out an option on the chems for the $5 million to cover my out-of-pocket expenses. The idea was to partner with me and pitch the sale to Zrubarov. Whatever Zrubarov paid, I believe they cut me out of the deal."

Adams was running off at the mouth and I was struggling to catch up, my mind still processing his bombshell. "Wait...You have WMD?"

"I did. But now I think Zruba has it."

"On his boat?"

"I doubt it. Niemiec will have it stored somewhere — I don't know where."

An avalanche of questions piled up in my brain. Washington was concerned about WMD that had escaped from Iran to Syria during Operation Iraqi Freedom. The attack on the Berlin subway informed the world that there was some sarin out there on the loose, but not that there might be barrels of the stuff floating around in private hands, looking for a buyer.

"How much DF are we talking about."

"Ninety gallons."

Anna shot me a glance. Ninety gallons of DF could be turned into 180 gallons of sarin. I did the math. I said, "That's enough to kill around seven million people, enough to wipe out New York City or Los Angeles."

"Is that why you approached Zruba's boat yesterday?" Anna asked, also incredulous. "You wanted to check the selling price?"

"Sounds like you've got a case to take to the Federal Trade Commission," I added, "which I'm sure the Federal Bureau of Prisons will be more than happy to let you conduct from your cell."

"Look, I'm just the middleman. I'm not responsible."

"That's bullshit and you know it's bullshit. If that sarin gets used, your name will go down in history alongside other mass murderers like Hitler, Stalin, Pol Pot, and—"

"I don't care what you think. Bottom line. I'm not going to jail, and I'm not turning myself in. That is not what this is about," he said, "this" being his surprise appearance in our Airbnb. "I want money for information. That's my offer."

"You didn't answer my question," Anna pressed. "If Frederickson had sold out of your scheme, why did you pay him a visit?"

"Yeah, Joy and I saw you both at his place, which is why we didn't hang around. Look, thanks to the Wikileaks story, everything was falling apart. I wanted to see if Frederickson had been approached."

"Approached by who?"

"Someone like you, or maybe Niemiec or even Zruba. I wanted to know how much time I had to get things sorted out."

"Frederickson was approached all right," I said. "Tell me about your pal, Dexter Foord."

"Yeah, well, the lieutenant got cold feet and messed things up big time. Other than that, I've got nothing more to say until Uncle Sam and I come to a mutually beneficial arrangement."

Anna and I looked at each other, and she laughed. "No one's going to want to make a deal with you, asshole. The Office of the President of the United States wants to bury you. Not only have you embarrassed the nation, but you're also dealing in weapons of mass destruction. That's one of the biggest crimes there is. On top of which, you've sold it to some very bad actors who'll no doubt sell it on to fanatics who've got some big ideas about how to make a statement with mass murder."

"Adams, throw in the towel before you get killed and, trust me, the way these people do murder, not very pleasantly."

The retired Air Force officer finished his coffee, coolly placed it on the low table in front of him, and stood up. "Give me your door key," he said.

"Why?" asked Anna.

"Give it to me. Now," he said, waving his pistol at us and cocking the hammer.

Anna placed the key on the table and pushed it toward him.

"I want WITSEC and six million, putting me a million ahead. In the scheme of things, that's the bargain of the century." He took the key and moved to the front door, covering us with the pistol. He opened the door, put the key in the door lock, turned it, and then brought the butt of the gun down on the key, breaking it off in the lock. "Guarantee that in writing, signed by someone meaningful in Washington, and I'll tell you what's going on with the difluoro. I'll also give up Niemiec and Zruba. What you're getting in exchange for my demands, trust me, I'm selling it cheap."

He pulled the door closed. Anna rushed to it while I went for the window over the kitchen sink and pulled it open. I crawled through the small opening and tumbled onto the landing. Anna did the same half a second behind, only without the tumble.

"There!" Anna shouted, pointing out Adams hurrying to a small white Audi hatchback. This guy needed to be suitably detained and properly questioned. Millions of lives probably depended on it. We sprinted down the stairs onto the sidewalk and stood in the Audi's dust as it sped away.

Anna shattered a car window beside her with the butt of the Ruger, then handed the pistol to me. "You're shotgun." She opened the car door, jumped behind the steering wheel, and ripped out the wires from under the steering column as I took the passenger seat.

The engine kicked; she jammed the stick shift into gear, floored the accelerator, and stalled it out. "Say nothing," Anna warned me.

"Farthest thing from my mind," I replied.

Another flick with the wires in her lap, and we were moving. All four tires tore at the asphalt, and my neck muscles strained with the acceleration. "What is this thing?"

"A car."

"Thanks."

On the horn boss were the letters STi. Whatever, this rice burner had some poke.

Anna jammed on the brakes and swerved around a group of racegoers tumbling off the crowded sidewalk onto the road. Ahead, the Audi hooked left. Adams was heading for the hills up behind Monte Carlo, where the congestion thinned out.

Anna downshifted and took the turn, the STi sticking to the road like a bad reputation. We were closing on Adams. A small yellow vehicle darted from a side street between us and the Audi. A shooter leaned out the passenger window, fired a silenced pistol at the Audi, and its rear window exploded in a shower of crystals. No doubt some of those people Anna mentioned didn't want Adams to provide answers.

"Behind us!" Anna said, her eyes flicking to the rear-view mirror.

Sure enough, on our tail was some Euro job driving dangerously.

"They're shooting at us," I told her as our side mirror disappeared, the victim of a lucky shot.

Anna snapped, "You've got a gun, too, right?"

Firing from a randomly swerving platform at another randomly swerving platform with a handgun was a waste of bullets, and there weren't enough in the mag to waste. Still, I leaned out and peeled off two anyway because, well, happy wife, happy common-law life.

Anna kept the STi weaving across the asphalt. She snapped the wheel left, left again, and then hard right, following the Audi and its yellow tail as the road ahead became a series of tight, ninety-degree switchbacks. The backside of Monte Carlo shrank below and behind us as we climbed. Beyond the city, the bay.

Two tour buses coming down the hill in front of us cut a corner, forcing us sideways into the dirt. Anna ignored the diversion and kept her foot on the gas, correcting the oversteer like a pro.

"You always drive like this now?" I asked her.

"Only when there's a sale I don't want to miss." The STi fishtailed out of a tight bend and slammed hard against a stone mile-marker.

"This has to be Zruba's people following us and Adams," I observed.

"Mansplaining."

"Any time."

The road ahead snapped a one-eighty to the right before climbing steeply toward France. As Adams' tail climbed away from the corner and we approached it, our vehicles would be side-by-side for a brief moment. "Stay left and keep it steady," I shouted as the Audi and its tail took the sharp bend ahead. I leaned towards the rear passenger window behind Anna, took aim at the yellow car as it climbed out of the switchback, and fired three quick shots two-handed into the passenger door area. One of its windows shattered. The car swerved wildly and crashed into the stone blocks edging the road. It bounced over them, pitched down the incline, slammed onto the road behind us, and kept going, smashing through another row of edging stones. It was then airborne off a cliff, hit a rock outcropping, burst into a fireball, and dived into a deep cleft in the rock, where it stopped suddenly, jammed as snug as a cork in a bottle.

A couple of tour buses came creeping toward us in low gear down the hill. Anna blew by them and took another tight corner. "Where'd he go?" she snapped. "Where's Adams?" The Audi had disappeared. "Did he miss a bend?" Anna wondered. "Did he go over the edge?"

I checked behind us, looking back down the hill, ahead of those buses. Accelerating away was the white roof of Adams's Audi. Tricky bastard. "There he is. You see him?"

Anna glanced over her shoulder. "Yeah." She wrenched on the hand brake and spun the steering wheel. The STi's back end lost traction and whipped entirely around. In one fluid movement, the brake was released, the accelerator pedal stomped on, and we rocketed down the hill, just as Adams had done, putting a bus between us and our own unfriendly tail.

"You must love a sale," I told Anna. She was enjoying herself. "Seriously, where'd you learn to drive like this? Cuba?"

We flew past the lumbering tour buses, the STi eating away the distance separating us from the Audi. A few more turns and, once again, we'd be in the back blocks of Monaco.

The STi slowed. "What are you doing?" I asked her. "Go!"

"Trust me," Anna said, checking the rearview mirror.

"What are you gonna do?"

"Wing it."

"Can you give me a hint?" I pulled the pistol's mag: five rounds and one in the spout.

"You ready?" she asked.

"That's your hint?"

Anna stamped on the brakes as she wrenched the steering wheel hard over, throwing me violently forward against the seatbelt and sideways into the door. The STi swerved across the road into the path of the shooters coming up fast behind us. The tailing vehicle suddenly skidded sideways to avoid a collision with our trunk. As it sailed by, I pumped three slugs into the cabin. Blood sprayed the inside of the windshield as the vehicle blew through a low wall and kept on going over the edge. It sailed through mid-air, rolled inverted, and landed upside down on the roof of an apartment further down the hill, where it tumbled a couple of times and ended right way up, rocking on its suspension, smoking and steaming, tangled up in a clothesline.

Anna selected second and stomped on the accelerator. I was thrown back into the seat like a ball smacking the meat of a glove. "You're in the wrong game," I told her.

She smiled at me. "I'll take that as a compliment."

"You got a barf bag handy?"

Ahead, Adams was taking significant risks with civilian traffic. Had he been watching his rear-view mirror, he'd have seen two of the vehicles giving chase come to unfortunate ends. We were well into Monte Carlo now. People were everywhere. Roads were blocked off.

Adams ignored the signs, plowing through a barrier sealing off the race circuit area from street traffic and skittling half a dozen traffic wardens.

Anna turned into a hotel driveway, providing us with a view of the city below.

The white roof of Adams' Audi was visible from our vantage point, weaving dangerously through pedestrians.

"What the fuck is he doing?" Anna murmured.

The Audi burst through another barrier.

"Jesus..." Anna said. "He's on the racing circuit."

Race marshals were swarming onto the track, waving at Adams to stop. He didn't. The Audi accelerated down a short straight, crashed through another barrier, down a flight of stairs, and found itself on the marina. People were leaping out of its path into the water. The Audi kept going, picking up speed. It butted a service cart out of the way as more people jumped for their lives. And then the Audi sailed off the end of the marina and splashed into the drink.

Anna and I shared an unspoken WTF moment.

The Audi hit the water at the very spot Zorya had been moored, only the boat was now anchored further out in the bay with several other larger vessels. Maybe our nocturnal visit had something to do with the move.

Anna observed, "He still believes the people trying to kill him are Niemiec's people when it's Zruba's people."

"I think they're all the same people."

The Audi sank fast, the roof almost immediately level with the water's choppy surface, and then it disappeared beneath the surface with a burst of bubbles. People crowded the end of the marina. Several dived in, attempting a rescue.

There was so much going on around the Audi that Anna and I failed to realize several police vehicles were joining us, their emergency lights flashing. Officers jumped out armed with sub-machine guns. They started shouting at us, or more specifically, at me. The pistol in my hand — I can read the room. I tossed the weapon into a garden bed and lay face down on the pavement, fingers interlocked behind my head, alongside Anna doing the same.

The desk sergeant was unbelievably thrilled to see us again. Anna confronted him with a barrage of French and plenty of hand and arm movements. I caught "WMD" and "incident international," but the rest of it was Greek to me. Maybe it was to the sergeant, too, because he brushed us aside with a disinterested flick of his hand, sending us both to separate holding cells for a couple of days despite loud protests from both Anna and me.

On the third morning, we were reunited and shown the back door, which was slapped shut behind us. The parking lot was empty except for three black Suburbans. A Secret Service agent opened the rear passenger door of the center vehicle.

Secretary of State Muirhead leaned forward into view and said, "Get in."

I'd already observed at our meeting at the St Regis Hotel that the SecState's resting face was somewhere between sour and a Saturday morning detention. But that would have been an improvement. She was not a happy camper.

"Cooled off?" she asked.

Anna began, "Madam Secretary, we—"

Muirhead cut her off. "What the fuck are you two doing?"

"If you mean the situation with the white-"

"You know exactly what I mean," Muirhead continued. "And you, Special Agent Masters. You're here to inhibit Cooper's worst impulses. Seems to me you're enabling them."

"But we—"

"Stop," Muirhead snapped. "I'll do the talking."

The SecState composed herself. "Brief me, and I'll decide whether or not to let the authorities here eat you alive."

"Madam Secretary, we've been reliably informed that there's a large quantity of sarin in existence and that it could well be in the hands of terrorists."

After a moment of wide-eyed shock, Muirhead asked, deadly calm, "How much sarin are we talking about?"

"Around 180 gallons."

The SecState worked silently through the potential consequences of that much sarin released in a major city. "Is that why you were involved in this running gunbattle that brought Monaco to a standstill?"

"Yes, Madam Secretary."

"Take me back to the beginning," she said, somewhat mollified. "Put it together for me. I'll have to brief the president."

Anna and I began with old ground — Wilkes's photo shoot and the Iraqi convoy ambushed by the Kurdish fighter whose mummified corpse we recovered, Adams's deal gone sour with Niemiec and Arcady Zrubarov, aka Zruba, former chief of the Russian arms bank Rosoboronexport, and ended with the real possibility that a former crew member of Adams', Dexter Foord, was the leaker.

"So, is your feeling that the Kremlin is involved in this?" Muirhead asked.

Anna replied, "Zrubarov and Niemiec are Russian connections, and we know that the late Russian president and Niemiec were more than acquaintances, but we haven't come across any official Russian engagement."

"Yet," I added.

"How sure are you that this Foord is our leaker?"

"Reasonably, ma'am."

"Madam Secretary," she corrected me before concluding, "Well, you're making progress, but the matinee exhibitionism you're indulging in, shooting up foreign cities, dangerous car chases, interrupting international events for the amazement and entertainment of global television audiences, is testing trans-Atlantic patience...to say nothing of mine. It has to stop. Turn the goddamn volume down. We're fortunate I happened to be in Paris for bilateral talks so I could be here to straighten things out. The French, if you remember, refused to join the Coalition of the Willing and have little sympathy for our dealings in Iraq and anything to do with WMD. Now, do you know where these chemical weapons are?"

"No, Madam Secretary," said Anna.

"And Niemiec? What about him? Do you know where he is?"

"No, ma'am. We're working in concert with Langley to pin him down," Anna told her.

"In your view, is the threat of a major WMD attack real?"

"Yes, Madam Secretary," I said.

"And the target or targets?"

Anna's turn. "We have no information on that as yet, Madam Secretary."

"Then you'd better get busy, hadn't you?"

"Yes, ma'am. Was Adams' body recovered from the submerged vehicle?" Anna enquired. "The police kept us in the dark."

"I haven't been informed officially. All I can tell you is what's been reported in the media. It's a mystery. There was no body recovered. He just disappeared."

"And Zrubarov's boat?" Anna enquired.

"Sailed after the conclusion of the race on Sunday. It's being tracked, currently off the coast of Sicily. It doesn't seem to be in any particular hurry. Its home port is Sevastopol, Crimea, so it could be heading there. But satellites have observed helicopters shuttling to and from the vessel. So, as to who's on the ship, we can't be sure."

"Would you consider greenlighting a mission to board it, ma'am?" I asked.

"Zrubarov is close to the new Russian leadership. After the business with President Petrovich, another incident is something we'd like to avoid. And we certainly wouldn't risk without probable cause. Now, if you tell us the WMD is aboard that ship, that's something else entirely. Is that what you believe to be the case?"

"No, Madam Secretary," said Anna, "we can't be sure."

"That's what I thought."

The SecState lowered her window and gestured at her driver, who jogged around the vehicle and opened the door beside us. "Assuming the threat is genuine, tens of thousands of civilians and possibly more are about to die from the first terrorist use of WMD. It would be helpful to know where and when, don't you agree? Meanwhile, you've wasted enough time behind bars."

Anna and I took the hint and got out.

The driver closed the door, jogged back around the vehicle, and the convoy moved off.

Anna wasn't happy. "No more winging it. You're going to get us dishonorably discharged."

"Me?" Should I point out that it wasn't my winging that landed us in jail? No, not unless I wanted to return to the sofa.

Anna hailed a cab, and a few minutes later, we were back at the Airbnb, which was a lot messier than I remembered. "Do you always leave your dirty washing scattered around?" I said, unhooking a bra from a lampshade. "This is something you're going to have to work on."

"What were they after, and did they get it?" Anna asked, surveying the ransacked apartment. Even the sofa cushions had been cut to ribbons and the stuffing pulled out.

"Maybe it's this," I said, taking a folded photo from my back pocket of Niemic, Zruba, and Chase Overton from my back pocket. I was surprised it had survived the dunking in Monaco harbor.

Anna nodded. "Yeah, maybe."

I took in the destruction. "I think our deposit is toast." I went to the bedroom to check the safe. The cupboard it was in no longer had doors, and the safe itself was scorched and battered, but it was still anchored to the floor. Whoever had come calling — I assumed Wagner types sent by Zruba or Niemiec — had either lost patience or been disturbed. The keypad responded positively to the combination. The Agency laptop that I'd been carrying around unused for the duration was undamaged. Given the level of encryption, even if it fell into the wrong hands, it would be useless, but I could do without the grief I'd get from Inglis if it had been stolen. I plugged in the phone, which was out of juice.

"Something Zruba said keeps raising its head and waving at me for attention," I said as I righted a lamp. "You were telling Zruba about my expertise with bees, and he said to me, 'I know who you are.' How would he know? We've never met."

"So?"

"Niemiec also said more or less the same thing after he dropped the building on us. We thought we were both targeted, but what if it was me he was after?"

"Why you?" Anna dismissed the question with other concerns. "I noticed you didn't mention Chase Overton's relationship with Zrubarov to the SecState in your wrap-up?"

"Is Overton a suspect?"

"No."

"There's your answer. We don't know if he's relevant."

"We don't know that he *isn't* relevant." Anna countered.

"Overton is in the armaments business, and so is Zruba. They would have met at countless defense shows and expos. Just because Overton has been indulging in a grotesque pastime with a key person of interest to us is no reason to sic Muirhead onto him."

"But we are going to question him so that we can discount him...?"

"Of course. I'm not protecting him."

"Good."

"Not unless he doubles my salary."

"What?"

"Just kidding." Now, with a little charge, my phone began pinging with messages, the latest ten minutes old, from Rita Inglis. I clicked that one. "Call me. Urgent," it read.

"Rita," I said when she answered.

"Oh, you're back. How was jail? I hear the uniform in a Monte Carlo lockup is a smoking jacket." "

"Yeah, and they give you a little bell to ring for room service."

"There was a lot of citizen reporter footage of that hatchback breaking onto the racing circuit and then doing a leap off the pier. It was all over the news here. I heard you had a visit from the SecState. How'd that go?"

"I'm still breathing. What's urgent?

"We've got a lead on the possible whereabouts of Dexter Foord. He retired to the south of France and lives with his wife and their two young children on a vineyard near Aix-en-Provence. He's gone to great lengths to hide his digital footprint, but we're close. The town is not far from where you are now — an hour and a half's drive. By the time you arrive, we'll be able to put a pin in the exact location. If he's not home when you get there, we'll jump on that BOLO with Interpol. One other thing... Eighty-five gallons of DF has just gone up for auction on the dark web."

AIX-EN-PROVENCE, FRANCE

Captain Dexter Foord's address, a vineyard, featured rolling pillow-shaped hills laddered with rows of vines, and at the foot of the hills, beside a manicured garden complete with sundial, a rustic two-story farmhouse with just the right amount of weathered patina on its soft peach paintwork. Chickens wandered around pecking at morsels on the grass, and a large pond fed by a stream provided a home for ducks, ducklings, and a couple of geese. On the way in, we even passed an old beret-wearing French cliché on a bicycle with a couple of bread baguettes tucked under his arm. But this postcard also included a few spoilers, namely, a semi-submerged SUV in the pond, a half dozen police vehicles parked in the forecourt, their flashing blue emergency lights beginning to take over in the dusk, and about 100 yards of crime scene tape.

It took some convincing for the gendarmes at the gate to allow us entry, but Anna's command of the local lingo eventually prevailed, along with her OSI credentials. One of the gendarmes accompanied us to meet the officer in charge, a brunette with dark eyes in her mid-thirties, wearing navy-colored slacks and a sleeveless black padded vest. I could go further with the description and note that those dark eyes of hers were of the smoky bedroom variety, the lips full and pouty, and that when she walked, her butt bounced in those slacks like a sports coupe at the drive-in, but notes like that would see me sleeping on the sofa for a week, so...

The officer's name was Dubois, as far as I could tell, given that was the only word I picked up with any certainty in the conversation between her and Anna. Eventually, the two women shook hands. I watched the coupe walk off and tried not to be too obvious about following its departure, but then a large van with "Police Scientifique" in large letters across its side came to the rescue, driving between us and cutting off the view. "Police Scientifique...," I said, "CSI?"

"Triple murder-suicide," said Anna. "According to the inspector, Foord had a brain snap, strangled his wife, drowned his two kids in the duck pond, then hanged himself."

I was surprised. Not so much about the acts of murder but how they were executed. "Why didn't he just shoot them?"

"They don't have guns here like we do back home."

"Okay, stab them. Or club them to death with an ashtray or a five iron."

"Is this going somewhere?"

Maybe, but it seemed a complex assortment of ways to go about killing your family if the reason for the violence was a sudden lapse into darkness, but I wasn't going to argue about it because then I'd be wrong. "Forget it," I said.

"He left a note."

"What did it say?"

"'I'm sorry.' No signature."

"That's it?"

Anna nodded.

"Who's he saying sorry to?" I wondered.

Anna shrugged. "The attending cops? The in-laws? The universe?"

I wasn't buying it. The timing was too convenient for Adams, Zruba, and Niemiec. "Foord, who doesn't have any history of violence, strangles his wife, then drives his two kids into the duckpond before tying a rope around his own neck?"

"We going back to this? And it was an electric iron cord from a coat hook on the back of a door. Your point is...?"

"There's no blood. Strangulation and drowning both take time. He has to look into his wife's dying eyes with his hands around her neck while she struggles and then listen to his kids screaming in terror as the water rises. Leaving motive aside, so much quicker and painless for all concerned to use a gun, a knife, or that five iron. Get it over and done with."

"Still not following the logic," said Anna.

"We both think this is Wagner."

"It had crossed my mind," she agreed.

"If you were Wagner and didn't want us to think Wagner did this, wouldn't you do the deed in a non-Wagner way? They're guns and knives people. But not this time, not here. Zip the corpses into bags, pull the vehicle from the pool over there, put the flowers back in the vase, and you'd never know what went down."

"So, the fact that this doesn't look like a Wagner operation proves it was?"

"You know how much hand strength it takes to strangle the life out of someone, right? The chief suspect was maybe 160 pounds of solid dweeb. The guy would have trouble wringing a doorbell. And his wife, she had to be 200 pounds. I've seen photos. She's an offensive tackle."

"That's offensive."

"I try."

"So, what you're saying — this is a stage play, and Foord's wife and kids are just props, murdered to convince law enforcement that Foord went suddenly berserk...?" Anna sighed with dismay.

"Yeah, Food was murdered, and the rest is window dressing."

Movement behind my disturbed partner's shoulder distracted me. It was the old guy on the bicycle with the breadsticks. He was now on the other side of a hedge, beckoning us to come join him, the flashing blue police lights strobing through the gathering darkness, adding urgency. "What does he want, do you think?" I don't have much patience for rubberneckers at crime scenes, but I was prepared to do my bit for trans-Atlantic amity.

"*Parlez vous Francise*?" he asked as I approached.

"Nope. Can I help you?"

Ah, you're American," he said in perfect English.

"What gave it away?" I asked him.

"If I'd asked a local copper, he would have said, *"Va te faire voir."*

Who knew what that meant, but it sounded so elegantly...French.

"Which means to fuck off," The old guy continued.

Right.

"I saw the forensic van just now. What's happened?" he asked.

"So, who are you?"

"Gordon Smith-Wandsworth. I'm...I'm the neighbor. It's Dex. He's been murdered, hasn't he?"

The neighbor's apparent insider knowledge stopped me. "What makes you say that?"

"Because he lived in fear. You get a nose for these things. "

Especially when you're nosy.

"I'm right, aren't I? Foord has been murdered."

"The police think he killed his family and then himself."

"Good lord, no. How perfectly awful. The children, too? I... I don't believe it. We—" The old guy choked up. "The Foords bought this winery from me a couple of years ago. I live in a cottage just over there." He gestured a lightly shaking hand at a stand of trees behind another hedgerow. "They've become my family."

Then it's lucky for you that you're not looking at the inside of a body bag with the rest of your family.

"I'm sorry for your loss," said Anna, who'd joined us, the empathy side of our double act.

"You're CIA, aren't you?" George asked me.

Another pivot. "Who?"

He continued, a finger like a bent tree root pointing at my chest. "That is you, isn't it? The CIA?"

Was it tattooed on my forehead?

"He said if things went bad, you'd turn up. Come."

Anna and I glanced at each other and then followed. "So, you're English...?' she asked when we caught up.

"When I was a lad, I got into a spot of bother and had to leave London in a hurry. I needed protection, so I joined the only gang I knew that wouldn't ask questions, the French Foreign Legion."

He pulled up a shirt sleeve, revealing an old smudged furry tattoo of what appeared to be a golden flame on his forearm. The Legion's insignia, I figured.

"Thirty-five years I served," he continued. "Saw action in Cambodia, Somalia, the Central African Republic, Rwanda, the Congo, and the First Gulf War. Along the way, I took up French citizenship. Retired with the rank of lieutenant colonel. So, might sound English, but in here," he thumped his heart with a fist half the size of a Thanksgiving turkey, *"Vive la France."*

"How well did you know the deceased?" I asked, more interested in another backstory.

"Dexter? Like I said — family. We had an affinity, both being ex-military, but there was always a barrier, something Dex didn't want to talk about, something I'm positive is connected to the awful events next door and the reason you're here."

We let him run with it.

"Dex would pop over to my place to use the computer. Wouldn't have one in his house. No mobile phone, either. That's strange these days, but I never pressed him about it. I know he was in your Air Force and served in the Second Gulf War, but he wouldn't talk about his wartime experiences. Unlike me," he said. "A few cognacs, and you can't shut me up."

I believed him.

The former Legionnaire's home was small and gingerbread-house-like. Gordon opened the front door and turned on the lights, revealing a memorabilia museum commemorating thirty-five years of service with one of the most formidable outfits in the military world. In his prime, the lieutenant colonel would've been badass. I guessed him to be around 70 years of age, but a life in the military had left him fit and strong. He motioned for us to sit at the kitchen table.

"Speaking of cognac, can I interest you...?" He didn't wait for an answer and grabbed a bottle and three glasses off a shelf.

"A bit early for me, thanks," said Anna.

"We've all had a shock." He pulled the cork. "Trust me, this'll help," Gordon assured her and poured. "Maybe not the first one, but you get to the fourth and, well..." He licked his lips.

Now, why couldn't Anna and I have neighbors like Gordon?

"Just give me a sec', would you?" He walked out of the room, rummaged through something noisily out of sight, and returned with a plain brown envelope. "Here," he said, handing it to Anna.

"What is it?" she asked, turning it over.

"That's what Dexter asked me to give you if anything happened to him. I don't know what's in it and didn't ask."

"Do you have a plastic bag?" Anna inquired.

The hotel room in Aix-en-Provence was a tight fit but serviceable. Wearing surgical gloves, Anna removed the envelope from the plastic sandwich bag with tongs and slit it open with a knife.

"Any surprises?" I asked.

She up-ended the envelope, and a thumb drive dropped onto the plastic bag along with a scrap of paper scrawled with a line of symbols. "Where's your laptop?"

"I'm not sure you're allowed to play with that?" I said.

"I'm certain of it. Now, go get."

I don't argue with that tone of voice and returned with it. After a raft of authentication checks, the CIA symbol disappeared, leaving behind an empty desktop.

Anna pushed the drive into the slot, and a dialogue box opened on the screen. She tapped in the note's collection of hand-written symbols, numbers, and parentheses and explained, "It's a SAP algorithm."

"Which is," I said.

"A Special Access Program."

"A Cuba essential? "

"Along with sunscreen and a bikini."

A window on the desktop opened, displaying an MP4 file.

Anna hovered the cursor over the icon and clicked.

Another window opened, revealing a heavily bearded Foord, framed head and shoulders, the background out of focus and non-descript. *"If you're watching this,"* he began, *"it means I'm dead."* He took a deep breath and exhaled, taking his time.

I glanced at Anna. He'd certainly gotten that right.

"Tell my wife I'm sorry," Foord continued. *"Tell her I loved her. And the kids. They're too young to understand, but tell them anyway. I'm giving this to you. Do that much for me."*

Another glance. Did the killer or killers make him watch when they murdered his family?

"I fully intended to give myself up. Naively, I never realized the full extent of the terrible things my actions would set in motion. Not at the time. Back when all this began, I believed it was about truth. Fucking naive."

Foord collected his thoughts. *"I served my country during the Second Gulf War, Operation Iraqi Freedom. I was proud to serve. As I'm sure you know already, I worked as a computer programmer and data analyst. The job entailed reviewing data in real-time generated* by airborne systems designed to identify sub-surface anomalies. The integrated platform for these systems was code-named Horned Owl. I helped develop some of these systems. I also updated some of the software code. HO wasn't particularly effective at first, but it got better. I got better. The team got better. And we saved lives.

"My commanding officer in Horned Owl, Lieutenant Colonel Mark Adams, callsign Grizzly, was more in tune with the aircraft side of the equation, but he came to have a working knowledge of what we were doing, even if the specifics escaped him.

Foord paused to sip a glass of water. He continued, "Adams assured us that HO's primary task was to hunt for IEDs, which would then be dug up and defused or detonated. We never went looking for WMD, not that I was aware of at the time.

He sipped again, collected his notes, and the tape ran uninterrupted.

"HO was pulled after six months. By then, we'd scanned almost every square meter of the Iraqi desert north of Baghdad. I got transferred to the Pentagon, a special unit put together to harden the Pentagon's servers against outside attacks, hackers from Iran, Russia, China, and North Korea — the usual suspects. I was in the elevator one morning when Adams walked in. I was surprised to see him. There was no contact after our mission ended, and suddenly, there he was, working in an Air Force intelligence group out of the office of the Air Force Secretary. We met for coffee a few times. Had lunch. Played golf. Became pals.

"Then, out of the blue, he shows me a MISREP from back in the day. It's marked 'Confidential,' so even though I was present for that mission, the rules say I'm not supposed to see that document. A line crossed. Anyway, I remembered that mission because it was so non-eventful. We got snookered by a dust storm. Balad was closed, Al Asad, too. So, Adams had us working a grid east of Al Asad to calibrate our instruments until the storm passed. That was the reason he gave us *at the time. But I came to realize that was BS. Anyway, flying the grid, we hit an anomaly. Not a big one, and getting returns wasn't unusual. There's so much junk from the First Gulf War as well as WWII buried in the Iraqi desert; if you don't have the settings right, the systems light up like a pinball machine with all the hits. Our feeling at the time — maybe this was just some of the usual crap, nothing to get excited about. A couple of years later, in the Pentagon's cafeteria, Adams tells me he's convinced it's WMD we found that day."*

Anna paused the video, "Please don't be smug about this."

"No 'I told you so?'"

"Not if you want to return to the couch." She squeezed my arm. "This is incredible."

Foord continued, *"Adams believed CENTCOM knew there was WMD in the vicinity but didn't want to do anything about it. And he said he could prove it. At the time, I'd only been at the Pentagon a few months, so I was nervous about staying in my lane, but, as Adams pointed out, I'd already gone way outside it when I looked at the Confidential document, just as he had by removing it from his section and showing it to me.*

"He told me about an Australian SAS patrol that destroyed an Iraqi truck convoy near Al Asad, loaded with WMD headed for Syria, in the early days of the invasion. I told him that had to be fiction, but he said he could prove it if I were half the systems guy he knew me to be. All I had to do was hack the server, download it, and then cover my tracks. I was part of a team working on making the Pentagon's servers impervious to attack and told him what he was asking was impossible. But conversations along these lines continued for about a month. Eventually, curiosity got the better of me. Could I beat the world's toughest security protocols? And do it so that the Pentagon would never know?

"Adams gave me the date range for the SAS patrol's MISREP, and I had a crack at it. I had to figure out how to mask my searches,

which took time. Hard to explain in detail how I managed this, but essentially, I created a fake employment record on the system, identical in all but the minutest detail, for someone with a top security clearance already in existence — think replacing a semi-colon with a colon. That duplicate fake employee with a top clearance then requested the document, and I tapped the correct security authorization into the dialogue box. I also had to hack the authorizations. I'm making it sound easy — it wasn't. With the documents printed out, I wrote an algorithm for the system to create hundreds more duplicated employment records to make the one I used to hack the protocols all the more difficult for the internal data police to sniff out.

"Given the level of clearance of my false persona, I got the full unredacted document Adams was talking about, and the story about the SAS unit more or less stood up. The unit observed a truck convoy they believed could be carrying WMD because the Iraqi guards were mopped up. The convoy was stalled in the desert, the security detachment handling some emergency with the cargo. The SAS didn't destroy the convoy, and it continued its journey north toward Syria.

"I realized that this single MISREP would be a disaster for the United States if it ever fell into the wrong hands. I took photos of the MISREP and then made the soft copy disappear by altering its filing code — like a document that has slipped down the back of the filing cabinet drawer. It's still there, but unless you move the whole cabinet, in a digital sense, you'd never find it."

Interesting that Foord didn't realize *his* were the wrong hands. He was blinded by professional pride. Ego had everything to do with it. Like so many traitors, the guy was a narcissist. If he'd ever come before a judge, he'd be handing out blow jobs in Leavenworth for the rest of his life.

"I gave Adams the MISREP. I was nervous about having it in my possession. He had a safe deposit box and would keep it there. He wasn't surprised that he had his facts wrong about the SAS destroying

the WMD. I think he knew what happened all along. We talked about destroying the document, but Adams said he didn't want to be responsible for wiping history.

"There was one other task Adams handed me — hack into the server holding our MISREPS, revise #386, and reposition our search so that there was no connection between HO and the potential location of the WMD and, by extension, the two of us. I was already nervous about being discovered. We'd uncovered a secret that could do enormous reputational damage to the country. Again, I agreed. I was in too deep by then to back out."

"So much for pumpkins," I said.

"Didn't I warn you about saying I told you so."

"For years after, I was nervous about being discovered. There'd be a knock on the door, and I'd end up in GITMO. Or maybe I wouldn't hear the knock. But ten years passed and...nothing. And then, almost to the day, a courier arrived with an envelope containing instructions with an address, a set of numbers, and a return ticket to the Caymans. I was curious. I took the flight. The address was the main office for the Trident Trust Company, and the numbers an account with a balance of $ 1 million. Adams solved the mystery with a phone call. He told me he returned to Iraq with a Marines' buddy and dug up two drums of DF — methylphosphonyl difluoride, enough to make around 180 gallons of sarin. He told me he intended to sell the DF, and the million dollars was to buy out my share. That million-dollar payout was buying my silence. I withdrew the cash and spent it on disappearing. You're watching this, so the million bucks wasn't enough to do the job right.

"My conscience wouldn't give me a break. I couldn't eat, couldn't sleep, I lost weight... The reports of Bashar al-Assad's sarin attacks against his own people made it worse. Was this the DF that I'd let loose on the world made into the sarin now killing people? If Adams had already sold it, who was the buyer? There are only wrong hands you can put a weapon like that into. And now, the sarin attacks in Berlin."

I noticed the slightest jump in the video, the only edit up to this point. *"When I gave Adams the original SAS mission report, I swore it was the only copy, but I've seen enough movies. I made a soft copy and sent it to Wikileaks, changing my mind about keeping this information secret.*

With all that undocumented DF now in circulation, putting the world on notice is more important than sparing America embarrassment."

Foord lifted his eyes from his notes. His tone changed, ad-libbing. *"Adams will know I'm the leaker, and he'll come after me."* He seemed uncertain about what to say next, fidgeted with a remote, pointed it at the camera, and the screen went dark.

"A little more to it than 'I'm sorry,'" said Anna after a few seconds of silence. "Wow... What do we make of that?"

"Which part?" I asked, also shaken.

In his video confession, Foord, confessed leaker, had admitted to a wide range of crimes not limited to but including wire fraud, espionage, being part of a criminal conspiracy with Adams, as well as being an accessory to the trafficking of weapons of mass destruction. Neither Niemiec nor Zruba had been mentioned. Maybe Adams kept them at arm's length. He worked in intelligence and would have been familiar with compartmentalizing information.

"The video is one take with a cut," Anna said. "Did you notice that? Why cut it? Why cut it *there*? And what's on the cutting room floor?"

"This is a deathbed statement," I said. "Foord only ever thought this would be seen if he took the eternal nap. There's no good reason to hold anything back. Another point: if Foord didn't have a computer, what did he cut this on? If he used the neighbor's computer, why didn't the old guy mention it? And, thinking about it, Foord was a whiz with computers. He could easily have masked his IP address while monitoring the web for any developments, especially any attempts to find his whereabouts. That would give him time to run if he saw the risks of discovery increasing."

"So...was that Foord's killer we had a drink with this afternoon?" Anna wondered.

My thought, too. It was a leap, but we'd arrived at the same place. "We'll go back tomorrow morning," I said. "I'll call Detective Whatshername."

"Were you too busy watching her ass to catch her name?"

"I don't know what you're talking about," I said.

"Brigadier Faurot."

"Right," I said, looking busy. "I'm going to brief Inglis and Muirhead on this."

"What are you going to tell them?"

"Their leak has been plugged."

Anna sat back, let out a breath, and massaged her neck. "You do that. Meanwhile, I'm hungry," she said. "And I need sex."

Inglis and Muirhead could wait a while. "I've got something you can eat."

We pulled up beside a marked police car at the front gate, crime scene tape still barring entry. Anna and I shook hands with Brigadier Faurot. My assessment of her appearance from the previous day held.

"My department has been instructed to lend you every assistance," she said with a heavy accent.

"You speak English," I said.

She smiled. "*Oui.* So do you. Incredible, *non*?"

I glanced at Anna, who replied with a don't-look-at-me shrug. "Are you still thinking this is a murder-suicide case?" she asked the inspector.

"There are inconsistencies. The autopsy will tell us."

One immediately obvious thing, the bruising on the deceased's neck would have to be consistent with Foord's hand span. There would also be the usual forensic investigation of any DNA evidence, and especially with close contact crimes of violence like these, the scrapings beneath the fingernails of all the deceased would be given the works. That takes time, even with a rush order.

"What is your government's interest here?" the inspector asked.

"It's largely routine," Anna deflected. "Dexter Foord was in a sensitive position in the U.S. military. We're just chasing up some paperwork. But all this...," she waved an arm, "took us by surprise. Just terrible. We'll be filing a report. Mental trauma following active duty is something the United States military is tracking big time these days. And what appears to have happened here could have had its roots in Foord's service."

The heady mixture of truths, half-truths, and blather — essential tools of the trade.

Brigadier Faurot nodded along like a seasoned pro, no doubt used to the bullshit. We walked toward the house, the gravel driveway crunching underfoot. Curls of mist slid through the rows of vines lined up across the hills, hints of jasmine suffusing the cool morning. Elsewhere in a local morgue, bodies with rigor mortis, removed from this idyllic setting, were beginning to soften.

"Have you found cell phones or computers?" Anna inquired.

"No. No computer or phone. Strange, no?"

Yes. "Have you managed to interview the neighbor?" I asked. "We met him yesterday. He's aware of what's happened."

"You told him?"

'Yes.' Anna and I were walking a fine line here. We had no formal right to question potential witnesses and could easily be charged with obstructing justice, or whatever the French equivalent might be. But I was confident we'd get a pass—blundering around uninvited and ignorant is what we Americans do.

"You questioned him?"

"We had a drink," I said, sticking more or less to the facts. "He told us about his time in the French Foreign Legion."

"A gendarme knocked on his door, but there was no answer."

Anna suggested, "Shall we try again now?"

"*Oui.*" The inspector changed direction and picked up the pace a little. A short while later, the three of us crowded onto a porch as she rang the front doorbell.

Nothing.

Babette rang again.

Silence.

The old guy's bike was leaning against the back of the house where he'd left it yesterday. Come to think of it, I didn't recall seeing a vehicle parked in the driveway, so maybe he didn't own one. I took a peek through a window shrouded with lace curtains and saw, well, lace curtains. The place looked and felt deserted.

The inspector shrugged and started to walk off. "We will come back," she said, just as a vehicle's nose appeared at the end of the driveway, which became a Citroen of some vintage that rolled to a stop adjacent to us. A man somewhere in his early 70s opened the door and got out. *"Puis-je vous aider?"* he asked before reaching back into the vehicle for a carry-on-sized wheelie case.

Detective Faurot threw him a question, which he answered, then asked several more.

Anna frowned.

"What's up?" I asked. "Who is he?"

"You're going to love this," Anna said. "He lives here."

She was wrong. I didn't love it.

"He is not the man you spoke with yesterday?" the inspector asked me, surprised.

"No." Though he could have been. Similar height, dark eyes, once dark features tending to gray...

The inspector confronted the old guy, this time in English. "You have identification?"

"Driver's license?" he replied, his accent polo-playing English gentleman.

"Show me."

He presented it.

"Gordon Smith-Wandsworth," she read off the card, but the inspector wasn't satisfied. "Passport?"

"What's this all about?" he asked, justifiability nervous.

I had the same question but from a different perspective.

"Passport," the inspector repeated tersely.

"Of course," said this new Gordon. It's inside. Please," he said, gesturing that we should follow him.

We filed into the sunroom stuffed with memorabilia. "You've been away," I said.

"Yes. Spent the last five days in hospital with gastro," he said, rummaging in a dresser drawer and coming up with his passport, which he handed over. "Ghastly. Worse than Congo Bongo. Most unpleasant. They put me on a drip."

"You are French?" the inspector asked, surprised, as she flipped through the passport.

"Mais oui," he replied.

"Quel hôpital?"

"Centre Hospitalier du Pays d'Aix," he said and presented the hospital discharge papers.

"You have an excellent accent," she told him.

Gordon's absence cleared up, baring a call to double-check the alibi, the brigadier briefed him on what he'd missed. The news about the Foords shook the guy badly, if the ensuing flood of tears was any indication. He was especially close to the children, who had become surrogate grandkids. His own, along with his only son and daughter-in-law, had been wiped out in a car accident several years ago.

The waterworks eventually dried up, and I asked him about the Legion. An executive summary followed that felt like déjà vu, down to the faded flame tattoo on his forearm. Whoever had been impersonating the guy had stolen his life's experiences.

"Do you have a computer?" Anna inquired when the remembrances dried up.

"Yes."

"Did Dexter ever use it?"

"No. He had his own setup. Impressive, too."

Brigadier Babette frowned. Where was Foord's "impressive setup?"

"Did Foord ever give you anything to pass on to authorities if anything happened to him?" I inquired.

"Like what?"

"Anything."

George considered this carefully as was, I noted, Faurot. "No, nothing I can think of."

"Have you been bitten by anything lately?" I inquired, moving on with one eye on the inspector. "Perhaps working in the garden?"

"Mr. Cooper is an apiologist, an expert on bees," Anna informed Gordon in case he was wondering. He was.

"Why is a bee expert investigating a murder?" he asked.

"Perhaps Mr. Cooper can explain," said Anna, throwing to me with mischief in her eyes.

"Insects interact with the deceased in all sorts of ways," I said, which was true, but not for regular bees. Vulture bees, maybe.

"Oh, well, I do have a bite on the back of my arm that's been damned itchy," he said, scratching it.

The inspector spoke to Smith-Wandsworth in rapid-fire French and then impatiently ushered us all out the door, including the old guy carrying an overnight bag. I picked up the word forensic several times. I figured she would be calling in CSI and wanted the place vacant. Smith-Wandsworth drove off in his Citroen without protest, and the inspector walked us to our rental.

"Can you provide me with a statement of your meeting with the imposter yesterday?" she asked us.

"Of course," Anna replied.

The inspector also asked if we could include a detailed description of him. I suggested that she take a photo of the genuine article, the George we'd just met, and add maybe ten pounds because a slightly heavier frame was all that distinguished one from the other.

Babette Faurot also picked over whether Smith-Wandsworth had been intentionally poisoned to remove him from his home.

Well, of course he was. I was surprised he hadn't been murdered just to make sure of it, murder at the vineyard having been splashed about so enthusiastically. I figured the inspector would have the real Smith-Wandsworth tested and get that bite he spoke about looked at, although I doubted anything of substance would be revealed.

The inspector then asked the one I knew was coming — whether the imposter had given us anything. If not, why had I just now put this question to George? What had prompted it? My response was vague — George and Dexter were close. "Family," according to both Georges. If Dexter Foord felt threatened, wasn't there a slim chance he might have left George with a letter, something more than "I'm sorry?" Detective Faurot was prepared to buy it, but only because we both knew that without evidence to the contrary, she had no other choice.

Finally, the inspector asked again how we happened to be at the scene of the crime so conveniently, an American law enforcement officer and a representative from the U.S. State Department who probably knew less about bees than she did. What was our government's interest in this man, and was it relevant to the murders? Fair questions but impossible to answer without crossing lines of secrecy, so Anna repeated the vague story about missing paperwork from Foord's time in the Air Force. The inspector bought it even less the second time around, but it permitted her to move on. She released us on the proviso that we would be willing to answer more questions if required.

As we drove off, I kept an eye on Brigadier Faurot in the rear-view mirror, watching us depart. Anna's diplomacy hadn't put the inspector's mind to rest. What seemed to have been a straightforward murder-suicide case was now something else entirely, something mysterious, trickier, and of an international scope that was impossible for her to fathom. To begin with, as Faurot pointed out, Anna and I were snooping around, agents of the American government, and we happened to be on the scene fast, as fast as the local cops. We must have had forewarning, *non?* Or perhaps we were somehow involved. As for the mystery man posing as Smith-Wandsworth, he was clearly involved in the killings. Were they his hands around Mrs. Foord's neck rather than her husband's? And the flash drive. He clearly doctored it and gave it to us to lead us down the garden path. And where was Dexter Foord's missing computer? And that was another puzzling question.

"I'm struggling to find anything about this that feels right," Anna said, thinking along the same lines.

I put the question to Anna. "So, what changed Foord's mind?"

"What do you mean?"

"At one point, he felt the information he'd uncovered, the SAS MISREP, would embarrass the United States so completely that he was determined it be kept secret. But then he released the intelligence to the whole world via Wikileaks? Something big changed his mind. What was that thing?"

Anna had other issues. "We're denying Foord, his wife, and his kids justice by not revealing what we know to the police."

I didn't care so much about Foord, but his family was a different matter. Not everything about this job makes you want to do jumping jacks. And there was that other big question: what had been cut from the video?

The drive to our hotel in Aix-en-Provence could have been a pleasant meander through the south of France, but I barely noticed the scenery. Too much to process. Three weeks into the investigation, the universe was still expanding. Washington now had its whistleblower, and the condition he was in guaranteed the leaks would stop. But we were no closer to the WMD or Niemiec. The whereabouts of Zruba and Adams were also unknown.

We pulled into the hotel's guest parking to see Merle Ridge leaning on the back of a rental, arms folded, waiting for us.

"I hear we're too late," he said as we got out of the car. "And he did his wife and kids, too. What an asshole. You got something for me?"

"Abuse?" I suggested.

"What?" he snapped.

I peered at the hedge around his face. "Lemme guess. For breakfast, you had eggs over easy and a side order of bacon. You need to lighten up on the ketchup."

"What's that got to do with anything?"

Anna asked, "Where's the rest of the CIA? Where's your partner?"

"You're here, I'm here. How many officers does it take to pick up a thumb drive?" He jutted out his chin, although I couldn't be sure he had one under all the foliage.

"The Administration is falling over itself to pin down the whistleblower. We find him, and the only thing Washington's interested in is this?" I pulled the drive from my pocket, safe inside a clear evidence bag.

"We're coordinating with the DGSE." He glanced at his watch. "I'm also visiting the crime scene to get a briefing from your contact, Inspector Clouseau..." He glanced at his watch. "Soon."

"Going through the motions?" Anna asked.

"It's called being professional — take notes," Ridge replied. "I'll have that evidence now. And, as for who found Foord, I think that was us at Langley."

"Don't include yourself, Ridge. Most days, you can barely find your mouth with a fork," I told him.

"The drive." He held out his hand.

"Has Niemiec showed up?" I asked. "Got any leads on him?"

"That's your job, Cooper. I've done mine. Give me the fucking drive."

I glanced at Anna. She nodded, and I handed it over. "It's encrypted. Open it, and you'll get nothing."

He held the bag up to the light. "This the original?"

"You think I'd make dupes?"

"There's been some talk about you back at the ranch, Cooper."

"That I make copies?"

"That you're not a team player."

"Depends on the team," I said.

"I'll ask you the question again. You haven't made copies of this."

"Technically, not a question, Merle. More a statement."

"You're an asshole, Cooper. If you've made copies, shit will get real."

Anna weighed in. "That's not a threat, is it?"

"Now that's a question," I informed him. "Hear the difference? The rising inflection?"

"Expect a call from head office." Ridge stuffed the evidence bag into his pants pocket and took the few steps to his rental. "One day, you'll need the Agency, Cooper, and it won't be there for you."

"Now you're just trying to reassure me."

"Asshole," he said, getting into the vehicle and slamming the door shut.

"Was the pissing competition necessary?" Anna wanted to know as Ridge drove away.

"Well, I feel better," I said.

"Whose dick is bigger?"

"Do you have to ask?" I held two closed fists towards her. "Choose one."

She looked at them, frowning. "You didn't."

"Don't spoil it."

She gave me a sometimes-you're-so-tiresome sigh and tapped the wrong fist.

"Okay, I give in," I said. "You're too good at this," and opened the other fist to reveal a thumb drive.

"You lied about making a copy?"

"He took the spare I bought at a gas station in town. So, no. I didn't lie. No copies were made."

"What do you want me to do with this?"

"Hang onto it."

"You're making me an accessory to withholding evidence."

"No, that there is key to a case we're building," I said. "There's a difference."

"Sure, but a case against whom?" Anna replied, leaning down and rolling the drive into her sock.

"I don't know yet. Meanwhile, are you getting the sense that Langley's losing interest?"

"What do you mean?"

"They've got their whistleblower. Case closed."

"I don't see how it can be." Anna showed me her phone screen and swiped through photos of the imposter George Smith-Wandsworth taken without his knowledge after we'd been inside his home. "You trust Inglis?"

"So far so good."

"Send her these images. Run them through the system, see what spits out."

The following morning, French Intelligence had replaced local police homicide at the winery. Anna and I were refused entry. The section of the driveway I could see was clogged with unmarked plain white vans, their anonymity preparation for the claim that they were never here if anyone should ask in the future. People in disposable puffy blue CSI coveralls were in the garden poking and prodding at various spots around the pond while a steady stream of other blue-suited blobs filed in and out of the house.

I felt a tap on my shoulder — Brigadier Babette, her police vehicle parked across the road.

"*Bonjour,*" she said with a forced smile.

"*Bonjour,*" Anna replied for the both of us.

"Things have become — the word in French is *obscurcie*. You know this word?"

It wasn't hard to guess.

"In France, when something is made to be hidden, we say it is *mettre sous le tapis*. You know this?"

With a hint of a smile, Anna repeated, "*Mettre sous le tapis*...Put under the rug. We say swept under the carpet."

"*Oui*, there is much sweeping going on here."

The three of us watched the blue people wafting about their secretive business as cold drizzle fell from a low sky. Anna, experiencing a "fuck it" moment, said, "Look, inspector, you know we're not really who we say we are. And you also know we don't just happen to be here now to look over some lost paperwork. You know I can't tell you why we're here or what both our governments' interest is in Dexter Foord, but it is important — thousands of lives could be in danger. We came here to speak with Foord about that threat. His murder is without a doubt related to that. But as to who murdered him and his family and why, we know no more than you. I promise."

Babette stared at Anna briefly as if seeing her anew. "*Merci beaucoup*. I appreciate the honesty."

"If anything happens that you think might be useful to us..." Anna gave the inspector a card.

"We do not have the autopsy report, but there was food in the refrigerator, some fruit and vegetables, the freshest of it two days old," the inspector said, adding, "I met another person from your State Department yesterday. He was very...American."

"Rude?" Anna suggested.

"*Oui*. The DGSE let him into the crime scene. I think there is much you are not telling me about this, despite what you say, but this is not my problem now. I think it is yours. If I have more questions for you and *Monsieur* Bees...?" She grinned at me.

"You know how to reach us," Anna said.

The inspector gave us an "*Au revoir*" then jogged across the road, climbed into her car, and any justice for Foord's wife and kids drove off with her.

"We're done here," Anna said, turning back towards our rental.

Several hundred yards down the road, she pulled to a stop beside a row of pencil pines.

"What are we doing? I asked.

"Babette slipped something into my pocket just now." She dug around and produced tightly folded sheets of paper.

The top sheet was a CCTV image of a man filling his car at a gas station. There were facial recognition crop marks around his head. A set of meaningless codes accompanied the crop marks. A second printout was a mug shot taken with a telephoto lens and a wider image captured several years ago showing the location outside a wrecked building. A Russian T-72 tank was parked nearby. I went back for a closer look at the face.

"It's him," Anna said. "It's George. But not yesterday's George. It's George the first, imposter George."

The real George could have been brothers with this one, a few pounds here and there aside. The black eyes and brows were identical, and the coloring was similarly gray. However, this George, according to the rap sheet included with the close-up, was a sniper in the *Qawat Al-Nimr* or "Tiger Force," an elite Syrian Special Forces unit. At 67, he was three years younger than George the second, the "real" George, and currently an agent of al-Assad's General Security Directorate, the *Mukhabarat*.

"Whaaaat...? Anna exclaimed quietly, confused. "You sent the images of the imposter I forwarded to you off to Rita Inglis, right?"

"Yes."

"So, is the DGSE more on the ball than the CIA? Why aren't we getting this from Langley?"

I couldn't answer that, but replacing the real George with a lookalike stood up to zero scrutiny if the DGSE could turn around the imposter's true identity overnight. Maybe whoever or whatever was behind the switch didn't seem to care. It had served its purpose, and Foord wouldn't be telling any further tales. While these latest aspects of our investigation were murky as hell, what was clear to us: George the first, a Syrian government asset, most likely killed Foord and his family, edited Foord's video statement, took his computers, and then sat around waiting for us to arrive so that he could pass on that doctored statement and gloat.

"What are we not being told?" Anna wondered. "Ridge turns up to claim key evidence, tells us nothing, and leaves. And now this. You got the same bad feeling?"

I did. Washington had its whistleblower secured and the leak silenced, but the WMD, Niemiec, Zruba, and Adams were still out there. People were being murdered. And now there was direct involvement from Bashar al-Assad's regime to figure into the mess, which the CIA must have known soon after I uploaded Anna's pics of the fake George but had chosen to keep us in the dark about for reasons presently unknown to us.

Anna put the shifter into drive and eased back onto the road.

My phone started ringing. The screen said, "No caller ID." I don't answer those because it's usually some corporation I'm trying to avoid, but this was my CIA phone and, therefore, unlikely to be Netflix accounts payable. "Vin Cooper speaking," I said, answering it.

"Please hold," said a female voice. "Secretary of State Muirhead on the line for you."

"Muirhead," I told Anna, covering the mike.

"This'll be interesting," she said quietly.

I waited a bunch of long seconds for someone to speak, and then:

"Agent Cooper, is Agent Masters with you?"

"Yes, Madam Secretary," I replied.

"Put me on speaker, would you?"

I thumbed the icon.

"The case you're working on is officially closed," the SecState announced, "and I wish to personally congratulate you both on the fine job you've done tracking down the source of the leaks."

Anna and I shared a glance, and it wasn't one of fulfillment.

"The Administration is indebted to you both, and your efforts will be recognized in no uncertain terms in the future. So, come on home, and please stop by Blair House for some genuine Georgia hospitality. I'll have my executive assistant sort out the details. So, again, well done. When do you think you'll be able to get on a plane home."

Anna reminded her, "Madam Secretary, we still have no idea where eighty to ninety gallons of DF is..."

"Are you sure it exists?"

"Berlin, ma'am. The attack on the train?"

"Well, we now believe Berlin was a stunt to convince the world that there was more and bigger in store. We doubt there's any more WMD in circulation."

What the fuck? "Madam Secretary," I said, "we have separate statements from Adams and Foord corroborating the existence of the DF, and there's also the auction on the dark web."

"We're not convinced. We think it's a stunt."

The SecState could not have been more dismissive.

I tried a different tack. "And Andre Niemiec, ma'am?" I asked. "We don't know where he is."

"Niemiec is a Russian national. He's not the United States' problem, Special Agent. We can't be going around fixing everyone's mess."

The Muirhead I knew was a tough, no-nonsense head kicker. This Muirhead I didn't recognize. "We also have a Syrian government connection to the murder of Dexter Foord, the whistleblower, and his family."

"The Syrians? Really? Do you have evidence of that, Cooper?"

I replied, "We have the positive identification of a Syrian asset occupying a domicile adjoining the Foord property, impersonating the resident of that property at the time of the murder of Foord and his family."

"Do you have anything more substantial to corroborate that claim, Cooper? Something we can wave about in the International Court of Justice or even the UN? Do we have fingerprints, DNA, CCTV footage, eyewitnesses?"

We had photos of the imposter from Tiger Force at the crime scene, along with a positive identification provided by the DGSE. Was that enough? I thought so, but Muirhead didn't wait for the answer.

"Give yourselves the night. Go to the best restaurant in Aix — there must be a Michelin-star-rated restaurant nearby — and get on a plane tomorrow. If the Syrians have become involved in this, all the more reason to leave what appears to be an expanding Charlie Foxtrot behind. Polish Intelligence can take it from here. You've broken the back of this thing. I'll be seeing you soon. Stay on the line for Virginia and your travel arrangements."

Neither of us spoke for a while as we drove on, processing Muirhead's dangerous bullshit. If she was wrong, the consequences were potentially catastrophic. Eventually, it might have been me who broke the silence, and what I think I shouted was, "HEY!" because a tractor was parked across the road, blocking it. And standing on the tractor's roof was the South African pedo with the hand tat. And on his shoulder was a rocket-propelled grenade launcher. And maybe I just thought about shouting a warning because the instant I registered the threat, our world was filled with flame and heat as our rental was launched into the air, spinning, cartwheeling, and—

THE ZORYA, SOMEWHERE

My gummy eyes opened, the world blurry, taking its time to come into focus, but when it did, I found myself staring into a horror show — pink, blood-flecked eyes above a white nose, the skin dimpled with dirt-filled pores and the occasional blackhead. I smelt his aftershave, sweet and sickly, and then his breath, yeasty and sour. My head pounded. My ribs sent pain spikes through me with each shallow breath. I was seated. What did Niemiec just say? Whatever it was, he didn't appreciate my lack of response, so he punched me in the side. Not hard, but hard enough to send a grenade of exploding pain through my chest, the sharp intake of breath I took in reaction to it not helping either.

"Cooper, you seem to have picked up an injury or two," said Niemiec, tut-tutting with mock concern and in that disturbingly high-pitched voice of his. "Bruises, cuts, many old scars, so I am sure you are used to this. How are you still alive? You survived a collapsed building, the efforts of two of my best men, and now an unfortunate collision with an RPG."

I must have said Anna's name because Niemiec replied, "Ah, enquiring after your partner? Yes, this woman was not included in the work order. You want to know if she is alive or dead? He shrugged.

Work order?

"I would say she is dead, but then I would say that because you are my enemy, and it is my job to make your every breath a misery." He jabbed me in the side again to prove the point. The pain sent me again to the brink of unconsciousness, and he savored it with a smile.

My brain changed channels. The South African, the skull tattoo, a shouldered RPG... I was still alive and kicking. I had to believe Anna would be, too, and that she was still pregnant. But were both outcomes likely? I felt a surge of anger. Niemiec was close. I lashed out at him but didn't get far, maybe a half-inch or so, as heavy leather straps held me securely in a heavy steel chair bolted to the floor. My wrists were pinned to the armrests with zip-ties, ankles likewise immobilized, and my waist pulled down tight by additional webbing across the beltline. I wasn't going anywhere.

"Yes," he said, realizing I'd launched a failed attempt to engulf him with physical violence. "As you Americans say, good luck with that."

"What do you want?" I spat, not because I was in the least interested, but because I needed time to get my shit together.

"Many things," Niemiec replied, standing in front of me with arms folded. "But from you, for the moment, captivity is enough. At first, my orders were to eliminate you when the opportunity arose, but certain interests have grown curious..."

I switched off at that point and focused instead on my surroundings. I was on a boat. The one oddly curved wall in the shape of a bow told me that, along with a row of rectangular-shaped porthole windows. Through one of those portholes, I could see a pier, large bollards for tying off big ships, a heavy lift crane, and behind it, other cranes and gantries. This had to be Zruba's tub Zorya, and if that were the case, the facility I could see beyond would have to be in a non-Euro-zone port to avoid a visit from a NATO boarding party. Given Zruba's last known speed and heading, I put that somewhere in the Black Sea, a Russian port — Novorossiysk? Sochi? Sevastopol, the boat's home port?

Taking in the immediate surroundings more closely, the room I was being held in was some kind of medical facility. The surfaces were mainly stainless. A whiff of ether tinged the air. What appeared to be an operating table occupied center stage, a large multi-adjustable surgical light positioned above it. I turned my head still further and saw Niemiec and I had company. Zruba and his award-winning ensemble of the taxidermized lioness and her cubs were present. The Russian was engrossed in the presentation, busily working on it and improving it. The lioness, fangs bared, was no longer as I remembered it, leaping off the branch into mid-air toward an unseen quarry. The big cat's prey had since been added, and Zruba was making some final adjustments to the ensemble. Soon-to-be the feline's lunch was a Daniel Boon-type character complete with a raccoon-skin cap and flint-lock rifle. One of the lioness's front claws was sunk deep into Dan's shoulder as he reeled back in terror. Zruba adjusted the position of Dan's cap and then stood back to better admire his handiwork, which provided me with an unobstructed view of the new addition. Boon looked familiar. And then I recognized him. It was Grizzly Adams. Zruba had taxidermied the guy. It was amusing for roughly a second before I realized I was probably next in line.

I turned back, wondering if I was still dreaming, as Niemiec slid a hypodermic needle into my forearm. A warmth rushed forth from that point and enveloped my body, giving me enough time to say, "Are you licensed to do that?" which I mumbled as I fell backward off a black cliff.

MOSCOW, THE RUSSIAN FEDERATION

My head was pounding, and it was some headache. I must have drunk plenty because I couldn't remember where... My eyes opened. I drew breath, startled. It was no longer Niemiec's face in mine but that of a severe-looking creature with short orange hair, a black monobrow, and purple lipstick. She was dressed in a white coat and holding a hypodermic in a raised purple-rubber-gloved hand. You finished with that syringe or about to start? The usual where-am-I question circled my mouth, which was as dry as a sandbox. "Wat-," I said, the word breaking off in my throat. The woman nodded some satisfaction to herself and placed the syringe in a plastic kidney tray; the plunger was all the way in. She gathered up the tray and departed, which was when I noticed an audience in attendance. Also worth noting, I was no longer in a taxidermy workshop on Zruba's boat but held in a dull, dirty-cream-colored windowless cell with a single gray-green steel door, heavy bolts top and bottom. The air was cold, dank, old, and this time around, smelled of urine. I preferred ether.

The woman walked past three balding middle-aged men dressed in expensive suits and a guard in a blue camouflage pattern battle dress. The suits ignored her. The guard opened the door, and she slipped through the gap. I caught the guard's shoulder patch, three horizontal stripes — white at the top, red at the bottom, and blue in the middle, the flag of the Russian Federation. Russia? I've been renditioned to Russia? How long had I been out cold? "Water," I croaked again.

One of the suits snapped, *"Voda,"* at the guard. He almost jumped out the door and returned with a small plastic bottle of water. I opened my mouth, and he poured some in, waited for me to swallow, and then poured in some more.

"Advil?" I asked him but got nothing back. "That a no?"

Thirst more or less quenched for the moment, I noticed other features of my current situation. I was secured to a different kind of chair with thick leather straps and brass buckles. I also recognized one of the suits—the chatty, demanding one—as the relatively new president of the Russian Federation, Yevgeny Suvorovskayev, the former director of the FSB, which was the current incarnation of the KGB.

Suvorovskayev leaned in towards one of his suit pals and muttered something, and the man came over and slapped me around some. He grabbed a handful of my hair. "You assassinate President Petrovich."

I honestly wished I had, but in fact, I'd rescued the asshole because that was my mission. Unfortunately for the both of us, when I was distracted, he was shot by someone I didn't think I had to watch. So, my bad, I failed to do my job. But was I sorry? No. Petrovich's existence was like ticks, mosquitoes, and those penis fish that lived in the Amazon whose name I'd forgotten that live in the Amazon — totally indefensible.

"Answer me!" he commanded, "or it will be bad for you. You killed President Petrovich."

Newsflash, pal, it's already bad for me.

"You are American spy. Your government sent you to Syria to kill president. For this, you will be killed. So, tell truth, American."

The truth is that ISIS had nailed Petrovich to a cross to end his life slow and symbolically, a promotional stunt to crowdsource more fighters for their Jihad. But others were lining up to have a crack at Petrovich because, as I found out, he was even more evil than I thought. I only received the mission to save his ass because I happened to be in Syria when the Russian president's helicopter was shot down. I did manage to bring him back, but, unfortunately for him, along the way, and as I mentioned, he picked up a fatal gunshot wound to the heart. His corpse was then mutilated by an angry woman with a large knife looking to take revenge on the narcissistic motherfucker for repeatedly raping her while her drugged husband slept beside her. *That* was the truth. Did they want to hear it? "Your President died because what goes around comes around," I said.

The answer earned a few more slaps that made my ears ring.

The door opened. Niemiec and his aftershave walked in, ducking to get his head under the doorway. The four men shook hands and exchanged hearty pleasantries.

The fog had well and truly lifted by now, but I was no clearer on how I was going to avoid whatever was coming next. The presence of these officials suggested I was located in either St Petersburg or Moscow. President Suvorovskayev dropping by narrowed the choice to Moscow, and given he was formerly the long-serving boss of the FSB, made the location likely to be in the basement of the FSB head office, the Lubyanka, the infamous prison and torture capital of the KGB. They were giving me the personal tour.

The four men went into a huddle, apparently to discuss something, the president breaking focus a couple of times to glare at me. When they separated, Suvorovskayev held a pistol. He walked up to me, the weapon aimed at my face. Sweat bloomed cold on my skin. He placed the muzzle against my forehead and cocked the hammer. Here, in this place, the Russians could do whatever they felt like doing, and clearly doing me was high on their agenda. I regretted that I wouldn't see Anna or our baby.

"Valeriy Petrovich was my friend," Suvorovskayev whispered. "This is for him."

I took a breath and felt strangely calm, even warm. I conjured an image of Anna's face, her smell, my fingers running through her hair. The skin around his index finger whitened as he brought pressure to the trigger.

BOOOOM!

I ducked, tried to bury my ears between my shoulders. The wall of sound ripped through my head. I opened my mouth wide in an effort to clear the aftermath, a sharp ringing. The Russian delegation and Niemiec were chuckling, releasing the fingers from their ears, enjoying the shared joke of my momentary terror. Smoke curled from the muzzle pointed at the corner of the cell behind me. Suvorovskayev's grin hardened. Sudden body movement. A backswing. The world slowed, and everything became the dull black metal heel of the pistol's grip as it arced toward my hea—

PARTS UNKNOWN

I stiffened and then recoiled; a shock delivered to the brain through the nose. My eyes opened.

"Ah, a little ammonia and ethanol, and here you are, back with us," said Zruba, removing the bottle of smelling salts. His face pulled sharply into focus, inches from my face. "He is awake," he called out and then walked from view.

As the ammonia dissipated, other smells took over — ether, formaldehyde, and Le Male. Then, the usual questions began to pile up: what, where, why... I hunted for the source of the vile cologne, and there he was, sitting at a desk in a corner, engrossed by a laptop computer. He didn't look up or acknowledge Zrua, who appeared in front of me again, examining my face. "You have green eyes," he said, as if that were unusual, and continued the examination as I got my bearings. Another venue change. The Lubyanka had been replaced by walls that were soft and khaki-colored and moved a little in and out as if breathing. I was in a large tent. But where? Zruba kept talking, but I wasn't listening; I was trying to figure something out something else. And that something was... the complete absence of pain. It had been my constant companion for days, always in my mind, stealing my attention, robbing my sleep: the busted ribcage, every breath accompanied by a sharp stab in my side. But not now. Now, I couldn't feel a thing — at least, nothing below the neck.

A bottle of water appeared in my face. "Drink," said Zruba.

I hesitated.

"Your hands are not tied. Drink."

I wanted to take it, but I couldn't move. Worse than that, I had a new, frightening sensation of nothingness. My hands, arms, and legs were non-existent. I looked down — that much I could do — and everything was still where it should be. I was dressed in some kind of surgical gown.

"See? Ha! It is impossible. Good."

I ignored him and tried to command those hands of mine to take the bottle. Usually, they just did the things I wanted them to do without me having to think about it. But both of them remained in my lap — immobile, heavy, dead weights, as useful as lumps of modeling clay. My legs, too. And then I realized that I was completely naked. What the fuck...?

"I thought buprenorphine, but no. Many side effects," Zruba continued. "Andre wants you conscious. So, I go with bupivacaine. A local anesthetic. Women have it in lower back when giving birth," he explained. "I could saw off your arm, and you would feel nothing. Ha! Why is this important? No struggling from you when I begin. Pressure sores, lesions on wrists, ankles. No, these I can do without. I could touch up with paint and make-up, but trained eye sees these things. Judges — they know all tricks. I have more appropriate injuries planned for you.

The asshole prattled on like a hairdresser. "Once heart stops pumping, you are the best you will ever be, and then death, it takes over — lividity, rigor, decay... No, I want you in best condition. In return, I will provide immortality. You will be young forever."

What the fuck was this guy on?

The stream-of-consciousness continued as he checked me over. "Hmm, plenty of scars. Bullet entry and exit wound, maybe two of these. You have been stabbed. Several times. Sutures on hand palm — I will remove them. And three ribs." He tut-tutted. "Was painful to breathe before anesthetic?"

I braced myself as Zruba pressed the skin bruised purple, black, and yellow around my ribcage.

"But now, nothing, *da*?"

He was right about that; I let out the breath I was holding. It was as if the rest of me below the neck belonged to someone else.

"I will accentuate injuries, work with them. Yes! Exactly."

He seemed to be experiencing something of a eureka moment. Meanwhile, I tried again to move, but I wasn't going anywhere.

Zruba took a metal skewer and jabbed various points in my legs and arms with it, raising blood spots but no pain. "Good, good," he said, nodding with appreciation.

He poked around some more with the sharp implement while I sat immobile and silent. He might as well have been sticking that skewer into his own leg for all it affected me.

"Andre wants you to feel when I cut, but there is no drug for being immobilized and conscious at same time, with exception of exotic poison from Amazonian frog species. But these you cannot get on eBay." He chuckled and called out to Niemiec: "We argue back and forth about this, Andre. *Da?*"

Niemiec didn't acknowledge, lost in whatever was happening on his laptop.

"So instead, you are just conscious. For everything I do to you! Imagine! But first Niemiec, he make me buy you from him. And you were not cheap. You'll be most expensive display ever, but worth it."

Display? "Where are we?" I asked, able to get a word in at last.

"Idlib, Syria. Secret compound. Very private. We will not be disturbed," he said.

"This where you've been hiding all this time?" I called out to Niemiec, but he gave no indication that he heard me.

Zruba laid stainless-steel instruments onto a tray. Surgical instruments. A couple of different saws, forceps, scissors, scalpels, and a long blade with a rounded tip. I didn't like the look of any of it. Zruba was resuming where he'd left off when I'd last seen him before my side excursion to Russia. I remembered Adams, dressed up as Daniel Boon, frozen in the moment of becoming a big bowl of Friskies for the lioness and her cubs.

"Ah, I see you have interest," said Zruba, bringing me back to the present. He took the knife and gave me a closer look at the blade etched with dark, wavy lines like a topographical map. "Damascus steel. A present from friend." He pointed the blade at his buddy, Niemiec. "Wootz steel, many layers, heated, folded, beaten. It is work of art. Syria's gift to world. In other time, a knife like this would make death of thousand cuts. You know this torture? Imagine the terror of such a death, to watch life force drain away over weeks, longer if person who gives torture is expert. A cut here, a slice there, over and over until body is big, lacerated scab, nerve endings exposed, enough blood for heart to beat, but mind gone." For added effect, he motioned blowing out his brains with a forefinger. "This was Andre's plan for you. But when I buy you, Andre give knife as present. Shame to waste, he say to me." Zruba called out, "But I will give it good use, Andre."

Niemiec lifted his pink eyes from the screen.

Zruba continued, "But death I plan for you, Cooper, you do not have to worry. It will be quick—maybe six to ten hours. I am not sadist." He laughed. So, you see this knife. Blade is unusual shape. Tip is round, but edge is sharp, to cut skin, slip beneath, and separate skin from fat and muscle." He examined my face. You seem confused."

No, actually I was shitting myself.

"I will demonstrate."

"That's fine," I said. "I think I get it."

He was concentrating, no longer listening. He placed the rounded end of the blade against the skin over by broken ribs and made a slice. The rounded tip cut through my skin like it was butter. The blade began to disappear inside me. I felt nothing. I watched it happen like a spectator. The complete absence of pain made the experience bizarre. I even started watching with interest. The blade slid deep beneath my skin and then deeper still until maybe ten inches of cold steel was inside me.

"Then you move the blade from side to side like this," said Zruba, demonstrating, "the blade making a perfect cut between the epidermis and musculature. You have little fat, and this calls for precision with knife." He wiggled the blade left and right a few more times, cutting from side to side, the blade moving easier with each movement. "There is little blood. Why? The anesthetic stops this." He removed the blade slowly, as if pulling it from a scabbard, the steel slicked red with a thin film of blood. "So, this is taxidermy. I will do this all over. I take skin, preserve with chemical, and place on hard form. I use mannequin for this." He gestured at a corner of the room at a store dummy.

Zruba swabbed the blood oozing slowly from the cut in my side with a sponge and then applied several stick-on sutures. "There. Good as new," he said and spun the chair 180 degrees. I wasn't thrilled about having my back to Niemiec. Nothing I could do about it.

"You see tiger?" he asked.

Yeah, I saw it. The big, stuffed cat was hard to miss as it was maybe three meters long and snarling and...what was a tiger doing in a tent in Idlib, Syria?

Zruba flung back a cover revealing a clothes rack with various odd items hanging off it, including an unusual steel helmet with a steel grate over the face, a short, thick sword, a shield, and a few other items. "Can you guess?" he asked me. I wasn't playing along. I just looked at him, attempting to keep as much fear and anxiety out of my face as possible.

"Are you not intrigued?" He lifted the helmet off the rack.

I'd seen helmets like that in movies — ones set in ancient Rome with gladiators.

"I have incredible idea for you. You will be *murmillo*. Wait, I get picture," he said, moving to resolve the comprehension issue I seemed to be having.

He snatched something from an open cabinet drawer and held it in front of my face — a crumpled page from an old magazine.

It was an illustrated image of a Roman gladiator on the ground, savaged by a monstrous tiger like the one currently sharing the tent, wearing a helmet like the one in Zruba's hand. He then explained that in the moment caught by the display he was hoping to achieve, the gladiator would have a good chunk of his shoulder hanging from the animal's mouth. As I attempted to digest this, my mind lagging in shock, Zruba prattled on about winning some taxidermy championship conducted on the dark web. Essentially, he explained, I was to be frozen in the act of being fatally mauled by the tiger after failing to subdue it with my sword, a pastiche recalling the games they played in Ancient Rome. Chunks of flesh would be torn from my legs, the tiger over my prone body, its claws raking the intestines out of my shredded belly. These depredations, Zruba told me with delicious intricacy, he would do to me himself, crafting them with his array of instruments, all while I was conscious and watching for Andre Niemiec's entertainment. From the neck up, I was terrified. From the neck down, I couldn't feel a thing.

With Zruba having concluded describing his ambition for me, Niemiec got up from the computer and sashayed across the floor towards me, singing in his soft girlie voice, "M-I-C...see you real soon...K-E-Y... Why? Because we like you... R-E-E-D-Y..."

Was I losing my marbles? Was he losing his?

The oversized lily-white man with yellow hair the color of urine-soaked snow and dressed in khaki sweats, skipped over toward me in the best of moods, paused to pick up that skewer, did a spin on his toes and then jammed that metal spike down into my thigh with some force. The skewer stuck out of my thigh at 90 degrees like a mini flagpole. I couldn't move.

"Good. This is good, Zruba," Niemiec told his pal as Zruba hummed to himself, lost in the preparation of more surgical instruments. "How are you feeling, Mr. Cooper?"

I bit the inside of my lip to get some good, wholesome pain going. I replied. "When I get up off this chair, I am going to take that Damascus steel knife you gave Zruba and hand it to you along with your balls."

Niemiec flicked the skewer sticking up out of my bare flesh so that it *twanged* and observed, "But you are helpless, Cooper, see?" Blood pooled around the base of the metal. It was almost a relief, confirmation that my flesh was still alive.

"Where is the WMD?" I demanded to know.

"I owe you nothing, Cooper. No information. Nothing. You are only here so that I can enjoy seeing your end. No other reason."

"Why do you care? I'm just a government employee."

He chuckled. "So modest. You killed my friend. I have motive to care."

"Which friend?"

"Valerei Petrovich. The Kremlin has motive too."

The anesthetic had numbed my body, but not my mind, and the tumblers in my head were beginning to make some sense of things: the shared connection between the deceased Russian president Valerei Petrovich and Niemic, the side excursion to Moscow, and there was that odd comment from Niemic after Anna and I had managed to escape being buried alive. "When last we met, you said to me, 'I know who you are.' How? How do you know me? I'd remember you if we'd met. I'm not so great with faces, but I never forget an asshole." Zruba, a complete stranger to me, had also said those exact same words — I know who you are.

Niemiec's grin faded to a snarl. "Everyone wants you dead," he said. "Me, I did not care so much at first when the Kremlin placed a contract on you for your role in killing President Petrovich. But you have cost me. You have killed my men, you have insulted me, and you won't die. So now I will fulfill my obligations to the Kremlin and reward myself at the same time watching a master craftsman turn you into a permanent exhibition of agony."

"Let me get this straight," I said. "The work order thing. Yevgeny Suvorovskayev put out a hit on me and then asked you to take me to Moscow so that he could enjoy my capture?"

"The president wanted to look into the face of the man who killed a great Russian patriot. I like to keep my customers happy — they come back for more."

"What has any of that got to do with the WMD?" I wondered.

"Nothing. The United States would intervene if news of Saddam's WMD ever surfaced. This we knew. When my presence accompanying the WMD became known, everyone also knew I would become a target for American agents. My clients took the opportunity to even the score when you appeared on the case. So, to answer your question, Mr. Cooper, killing you became a parallel purpose — icing on the cake."

"Your clients, the Kremlin. What was their other purpose? Are they involved in the WMD deal?"

Niemiec smiled or, at least, he showed me his milk teeth. "Why should I give you the satisfaction of answering your burning questions?"

"I tried to return Petrovich alive," I said, attempting another tack.

"So you say." He shrugged.

Did Niemic have other friends? The Syrians, maybe? He undoubtedly had a good relationship with al-Assad's regime, but why involve Damascus in this business by having them silence Foord? And, come to think of it, why would the Syrians agree to become involved? Any Syrian involvement would inevitably be exposed and acted on. But something significant was distracting me from raising these questions, robbing me of concentration: it was the rapidly growing realization of *pain.*

"Andre, come see!" Zruba called out, poised over Niemiec's laptop. "What are they doing?"

Niemiec joined him behind the computer.

Something was up.

Zruba toggled a keystroke several times. "They are everywhere — look!"

Niemiec went in for a closer inspection and then dismissed Zruba's concern. "Ah, see? They are leaving."

I heard and saw this exchange out of the corner of my eye, but I was more focused on the fact that the skewer sticking up out of my quad was starting to give me some serious issues, as in it was beginning to *fucking hurt*. The return of feeling was something I had to hide from these two bat-shit crazies. A cold sweat bloomed on my forehead and across my back. I bit the inside of my lip again to give another location some authority over the pain in my leg, but I wouldn't be able to hold on much longer. I tried to move my right index finger, and it... *moved!*

Niemic and Zruba pushed back from the laptop. Niemiec said, relaxed, "So, let's begin."

Zruba hurried to a mobile stand, wheeled it over, and positioned it beside me, surgical instruments and several kidney basins on a tray. He then turned on a tiny pump and handed a tube attached to it to Nurse Niemiec. "Here. There will be much blood."

The grin was back. Niemiec replied, "I am looking forward to it."

Zruba lifted my right arm and was pleased when it flopped rag-doll-like with gravity, bashing against the seat's arm.

No reaction to this crept into my face, *but I felt it!*

"Good," Zruba observed. He then took one of several hypodermics from his tray, held it to the light, and squeezed the plunger until a thin stream of clear liquid squirted from the tip of the needle. "We must keep him numb," the Russian explained. He chose a spot uncomfortably close to my groin and inserted the long hypodermic deep into the muscle. Zruba and Niemiec leaned in.

I had no idea whether my limbs would answer the call, but I lashed out. One of my hands smacked Niemiec in the nose. The other found the skewer, gripped it, and wrenched it free. I took a swing at Zruba. The skewer smashed through his front teeth, exited his jaw behind the point of his chin, and spitted his Adam's apple. Blood gushed out between the gaps in his shattered teeth. He reeled away, grabbing the skewer with both hands, desperate to pull it out. Niemiec recovered from the punch in the nose, lunged for the long, rounded-tip knife, and got a hand around the blade. But I already had the handle. I jerked it away from him, and his thumb plopped onto the floor like a crooked sausage. He shrieked and gazed disbelieving for a long moment at his butchered hand.

A *BOOM* sounded that shook the floor and rolled across the tent walls. Were we being shelled?

Right, I forgot. This is Syria. Of course we were being—

The floor suddenly became liquid, dissolved, and fell away. Then, the air blew apart as a churning, boiling, unstoppable fist of water smashed into the tent, ripped me out of the chair, and swept me away in darkness. I fought for breath, bashing into walls, tangled in the tent, rolling along with debris, carried violently along by a savage current, an undeniable, unstoppable force that came from nowhere.

What the fuck was happening? I needed to breathe. Water surged into the back of my throat, filling my nose and ears. One leg was useless, the other less so. I covered my head, the surging current hurling me into unseen objects, tumbling, rolling... And just as suddenly, the violence stopped. All was quiet. I was floating. No, sinking. I gulped, desperate to breathe — the desire overwhelming. There was light below me. *Reach for it.* Was the light above or below? Confusion. Desperation. *Which way is up?* Struggling. I started to gag. Lungs bursting...

My hands reached for the light. I was starting to dream, my thoughts cloudy. *Just stop...*, the voice in my head soothed.

My arms and hands didn't listen. One leg kicked, the other dragged. *Stop. Just stop. It's okay...* I wasn't going to make it. Darkness closed in around me. *Breathe. It's okay...* Darkness...sliding...slipping...down....

A weight pushed rhythmically against my chest. Water gushed and spouted, spewing and bubbling from my mouth as I coughed. My lungs, my throat...on fire.

"Vin, Vin..."

Hands pawed at my face. I began to struggle, to thrash against the noise, the sounds of desperation. Faces were floating over me, and behind them, blue sky and clouds. I recognized one of those faces, the nearest one. "Anna..."

"Vin!" Her dripping hair hung down, brushing my forehead. I was shivering.

"Take it easy, take it easy," she said.

My lungs ached. Another coughing fit. I sat up with Anna's assistance and looked around, bewildered. Syria sure had changed — a lot. "Where are we?" I whispered; my throat stripped raw.

"Warsaw," she replied.

A paramedic wrapped a silver blanket around my shoulders. I was on a barge, on a river. None of this was adding up.

I could make out a flagpole over the tops of a familiar tree line. Several police boats were motoring toward us, emergency lights flashing. The barge swarmed with police and paramedics. A police helicopter hovered nearby. Divers were in the water.

I saw a body in a bag, the zipper yet to be pulled over the man's pale face. It was Zruba. A chrome skewer shishkebabed his jaw to his Adam's apple. His eyes were open, but there was nothing in them. Niemic was sitting on a low part of the barge's superstructure and far less intimidating with a silver blanket wrapped low around his hairy white shoulders. A freshly bandaged hand short of a thumb was in his lap, the other hand handcuffed to a pipe. Police suited in body armor armed with Heckler & Koch submachine guns flanked him. The expression on Niemiec's face was blank as if he had shut down mentally, unable to process the sudden and unexpected change to his fortunes.

Leonard Gibbs discussed something with Agent Kazia Strahovski. Unfamiliar plainclothes agents in body armor stenciled with "ABW" loitered. The barge's captain was seated and cuffed to another pipe and nervous. In the dark green river water beside the barge, four police divers bobbed to the surface, joining two others. What had happened here?

"Vin," I heard a voice behind me say, the twang familiar. "You had us fuckin' worried, mate."

Wilkes? The Australian was picking his way through the crowded gangway, coming towards us with a broad grin. What was he doing here? I wasn't in Syria — I got that much. But how the hell did I get to Poland? Things weren't adding up. If I seemed dazed, that's because I was. Much of the drug-induced numbness was wearing off, except in the leg most recently sedated, and my body was suffering from a severe case of pins and needles. Perhaps my brain was, too. And those fractured ribs of mine were beginning to reassert their presence and my breathing was starting to catch. A line of fresh butterfly sutures secured a neat cut below the bottom rib. Zruba, and that fucking round-tipped knife... A paramedic finished peppering my skin around those sutures with a hypodermic, reached for another hypodermic and went to work on the holes in my thighs.

He said, "Sir, you have many injuries. You will be in pain for a long time when anesthetic wears off. Here." He put a plastic pill bottle in my hand. "Pain killers. Strong. Take only when needed."

I looked at the bottle. "Berry burst flavor?"

"You can chew them."

More police were boarding the barge. Fingers were pointing at the Australian. Two uniforms approached him. One patted him down while the other waited with cuffs."

"Can you fill me in?" I said to Anna as I watched them lead him away. "You're okay, right? And junior?"

"We're both fine," she said, kneeling in front of me. She had two black eyes, the bruising gone yellow at the edges.

Relief made the skin on the back of my neck tingle.

"What did they do to you?" Tears stained her cheeks.

They scared the living shit out of me. "The rocket attack... Do you remember what happened?" If I survived it, there was a good chance Anna had, too, and I'd held onto that. We'd been lucky. The warhead must have detonated under the engine block, taking the brunt of the explosion.

"I got thrown from the car," she said. "Woke up in the ambulance. Concussion, a couple of shiners, a few bumps and bruises, but otherwise, nothing to worry about..." Anna patted her tummy. "The paramedics said there was only one person injured at the scene — me, which felt weird, but I couldn't put my finger on why. I spent a day under observation in the hospital. Brigadier Faurot paid me a visit. It's not every day people get blown off the road in the south of France by an RPG, she told me. Then she asked about you, and I suddenly remembered you were in the car and who fired that rocket. It was like the lights turning on."

Yeah, I was familiar with that sensation.

"Wagner had taken you, or maybe taken your corpse — I had no way of knowing."

The bruising around her eyes gave me a timeline. "Was that around a week ago?"

"Six days ago. Do you know where they took you?"

"A Russian naval port. I figured Sevastopol."

"More likely Novorossiysk. That's where the Zorya is now. Satellite images picked up Zruba and Niemiec on deck, but then the trail went cold. The CIA passed on the intel. Thank your friend."

"I didn't know I had one."

"Inglis. The CIA's not all bad."

Maybe she just hadn't been there long enough. "They renditioned me to Moscow."

"Moscow?!"

"I had an audience with President Suvorovskayev. He wanted to congratulate me man-to-man for handing him the top job."

"What?"

"I got the blame for Petrovich's death. Suvorovskayev, or maybe the Kremlin, put a contract out on me and gave it to Wagner."

"So, the building collapse, the other near misses..."

"Just as well I don't take these things personally."

Anna produced a wan smile. "Maybe you should."

"Niemiec mentioned the Kremlin has a parallel purpose — his words. One purpose was the contract. I don't know how or why, but I think the other purpose is wrapped up in the WMD."

"We've got Niemiec now so we can question him."

"Also, I found Adams."

"Alive or dead?"

"The word 'lifelike' more accurately describes him these days."

"Where is he?'

"Forget it, he's stuffed."

"I'm sorry...?"

"Zruba turned him into a taxidermy display."

"You're kidding?"

"He was about to turn me into a scene from Gladiator."

"I love that movie."

"I'm serious."

"Was that skewer embedded in Zruba's face a gift from you?"

"From the both of us. How did you know I was in there, by the way?" I asked, motioning in the castle's direction.

"You remember I spent some time at Niemiec's castle looking for secret passageways?"

I did.

"And how the Polish government pulled us out over concerns we might damage a national treasure?"

"Uh-huh."

"Agent Strahovski and I had the servicing utility company monitor the castle's electricity consumption. I figured Niemiec would be in the house when the consumption spiked, or *somebody* would be. The usage shot up the day before yesterday. We sent some agents in there disguised as electricity service employees. They found nothing, but the power consumption didn't lie. So where did everyone go? And how did they get in without us knowing? Then I got to thinking about this dredge. Remember the lecture we got about silt? How the captain has been dredging for the best part of seven years? Turns out, seven years is how long Niemiec has owned the castle. Coincidence?"

Attagirl.

Anna continued, "So, we had the water depth tested. The rest of the river is around fifteen to twenty feet deep. Here, it's fifty. Why?"

Several more divers surfaced in the river beside the barge, and then a long tapering steel tube popped up.

"Well, that just stole my thunder," Anna guffawed. "I wondered whether the deep water and the dredge keeping it that way had anything to do with Niemiec's comings and goings. The mini-sub was ferrying him and his goons in and out under our noses. That's how you got moved in. The helicopter arrivals and departures were decoys. When we thought Niemiec was here, he wasn't. And when we thought he wasn't...you get the picture."

"You've still got it," I told her. "Baby brain and all."

"You can give me a kiss and a thank you later."

"I've got something else in mind."

"Easy, Tiger. You've been through a lot."

"Don't mention the T-word," I said.

Two divers were man-handling a sodden taxidermied. They rolled it into a net.

"Anyway, I might not have figured it out without your excursion to question the barge captain."

Nice of her to say, but I didn't believe that for a second.

"I wasn't going to get any help locally, so I took a chance and called your friend, the Rembrandt of demolitions. Wilkes was in Birmingham, bringing down an old power station. He jumped on the company jet and flew straight over. Kazia got us the plans of the castle they had on file for the inquiry into the disaster with the Special Forces team, and Tom did his thing. He was worried about the water pressure after what happened the last time the basement was flooded, but I guess he figured it out."

"Why's he in custody?" I asked.

"Attempted destruction of a heritage-listed building. We knew that would happen. Better to beg forgiveness, right? Kazia's people will get him off the hook, especially as the operation netted us Niemiec. And you, of course."

"Any word on the WMD??"

"Sold for $10 million, buyer or buyers unknown."

"So cheap?" I was thinking it would sell for ten times that.

"Yeah, doesn't make much sense."

"What about Muirhead and Chalmers? Heard from them?"

"I've stalled the former and hung up on the latter three times. Fuck 'em, we're seeing this through."

I must be contagious. "So, is Muirhead back on the team?"

"I wouldn't say that. I can't figure her out. Her primary concern seems to be bad PR."

"Any good news?"

"Your CIA phone is junk, destroyed by the RPG."

"Silver lining," I said.

"And there's these. I recovered them from the car wreck. Keep 'em as a souvenir," Anna swung the pack off her shoulder, rummaged through it, and pulled out a pair of knuckledusters.

Divers were surfacing with more evidence washed out of the castle. One of them reached up and handed Gibbs a laptop. Kazia took it out of his hands, and Gibbs snatched it back.

"Is the rest of the castle being searched?" I asked.

"They're waiting until engineers have surveyed the place. Wilkes' explosives and all that water damaged the foundations."

Kazia, accompanied by two uniforms, confronted Gibbs. He handed over the laptop, pissed.

"Refreshing to see allied intelligence agencies getting along," Anna commented.

Gibbs, hand on hip and pacing, made a brief call on his cell, then came over to us. "How are you feeling?" he asked me.

I looked at him.

The stab wounds in my thighs, the broken and cracked ribs, and Zruba's demonstration with his rounded tip knife all throbbed away beneath my skin like a five-year-old bashing away on a drum kit.

"Dumb question," he said. "Well, rest up when you can."

"Send me a get-well-soon-card," I suggested, opened up the bottle in my hand and popped a couple of berry bursts.

"I'll do that," he said, his expression pensive. "Thought I'd come and tell you — no drums of DL on site. We've got all kinds of tests for it in the event of leaks. The place is clean."

Anna observed, "We've got the next best thing — Niemiec and his laptop."

Gibbs forced a smile.

"We do have the laptop, right?" Anna asked.

"In a manner of speaking," Gibbs said, glancing in Kazia's direction. "Intelligence is a competitive game. They're our allies. I trust them."

But did our allies trust us? A phalanx of Polish police accompanied our chief person of interest — Niemiec — to a waiting flotilla of police launches.

"Where are they taking him?" I asked.

Niemiec caught my eye as the police escort eased him over the side. I saw him smirk. The smirk troubled me. It was a so-you-think-you've-won smirk.

The observation area was standing room only, the tight space crowded with various uniformed and plain clothes law enforcement, curious to see the unusual specimen on the other side of the glass. Kazia barked at them all to beat it.

"She's turned out all right," Anna murmured as the room emptied. The various officers and agents grumbled as they left, filing past us.

Niemiec was alone in the gray room, sitting upright, one heavily bandaged hand on the desk in front of him, manacled wrists chained to a ring on the desk's underside.

The observation room door opened, and Gibbs slipped through the crack. "He talking?"

"No," Kazia replied.

"How long can you hold him?"

"He's a terror suspect, so fourteen days without charge."

"What about the laptop?" Anna inquired.

Gibbs looked at Kazia. "It wasn't running when we recovered it, so the motherboard and hard drive should be okay once they dry it out."

"Rice," I suggested.

"Spectrum," Anna hummed quietly in my ear and squeezed my hand.

Gibbs continued, "It'll be password protected, though, so there's that."

Kazia agreed with a nod.

The speaker above the glass came to life: "Cooper. Are you here yet? I have been waiting. Come."

Niemiec had turned his ghastly rabbit eyes toward the glass. He was grinning, lips like a couple of 16oz sirloin steaks pulled back to reveal those yellowing milk teeth. Creepy.

"Go," Kazia insisted. "If he will talk to you, good."

Niemiec had been trying wholeheartedly to kill me, and he didn't care if Anna and the future Cooper Junior, who she was carrying, were included. So, rather than talk, I was all for turning his face inside out with a couple of hollow points or, failing that, working him over with those knuckledusters, which, fortunately for Niemiec, I had to leave at the security station in the foyer.

"You okay?" Anna asked.

"Geronimo," I said, standing.

"Stay cool."

"Call me Mr Popsicle."

Moments later, I was seated opposite the world's most wanted man.

"You have questions?" he said after at least a minute of silent staring.

I had plenty, a pile-on of questions beginning with why he thought it necessary to kill an entire unit of Polish Special Forces. I wanted to know what his role aboard that Iraqi truck convoy was and if Zruba had handled the sale of its WMD to al-Assad. I wanted to know where the 80 gallons of DF was, why it sold so cheap, and what the mystery purchaser intended to do with it. I wanted him to confirm the facts of Adams' story, that he purchased the DF from the former Horned Owl CO after he and Frederickson had dug it up in the Iraqi desert. I wanted to have him confess to having his people kill Frederickson. I wanted to know why the Syrians had stepped into the picture with the murder of Dexter Foord. I wanted to know if Niemiec knew what was on the deleted section of Foord's video confession. I wanted to know about Niemiec's relationship with Sands Aerospace & Defense, given that he and Zruba had a mutual friend in Chase Overton. I wanted to know what Niemiec's laptop password was. And I also wanted to know why he overdid it with Le Male. So, yeah, I had questions, but I kept it to a statement. "Gonna be problematic jerking off without a thumb, but you'll find plenty of help inside."

Niemiec leaned forward. "Something you will not like is coming, Cooper. You know this. Many so-called innocent will die, and there is nothing you can do to stop it."

"I'm sensing you get pleasure out of killing innocent people," I told him.

"They are the best kind to kill when you want to make a point," he lectured me. "The more innocent, the better. Women, children — the senselessness of their death will provide a cause with momentum."

Was I hearing Niemiec's sales pitch to prospective buyers for the WMD?

He continued, "And it is preferable if you can cause their deaths when it is least expected. For example, when these so-called innocent people are doing something playful."

I wanted to call him a monster, but that wouldn't be fair to monsters. "Who are the 'so-called innocent'?"

Niemiec leaned back and took his time answering, considering whether or not to continue. He examined my face, and I felt his gaze crawling across my skin like a cold shadow. And then he said, "There's no such thing as an innocent person, Cooper. Given the right circumstances, everyone is guilty."

"Guilty of what?"

"Cruelty."

"I don't get it."

"Of course you don't. My parents could not stand to look at me, so I was sent to military school. Can you imagine the other boys, the taunts, the bullying, the cruelty? My tormentors were considered innocent, and most of them continue to be innocent into adulthood. Innocent people have innocent children, and around it goes. But inside, they are far from innocent. Everyone is cruel."

"So let me get this straight: you're happy for hundreds of thousands of people to die because back at school, someone short-sheeted your bed?"

"I knew you would not understand."

"Oh, boo-hoo, diddums," I said, standing. "Are you going to tell me where the DF is?"

"Of course not."

"Then why get me in here?"

"I don't like you. I wanted to see hopelessness and anger on your face, and you have given me that. Thank you."

I reached for the door.

"Cooper, what do you think will happen now?" he asked. "To me?"

"To you? Easy. First, various authorities here will take turns roughing you up. You might even get a visit from the buddies of the Special Forces team whose members you slaughtered, and that would be fun to watch. And once everyone has lost interest in stomping on your ass and things settle down to inane mind-numbing monotony, you'll rot in a Polish prison until you die."

Niemiec had no intention of telling us anything that wasn't in his interest for us to know. And, given there was no way he would be able to cut a deal, there was no incentive for him to cooperate. Knuckledusters might have given him a reason.

He replied calmly, "No, you are wrong. There will be a prisoner swap. Soon, sooner than you think, I will be relaxing in a dacha in Crimea."

I thought about this for all of half a second and realized Niemiec was probably right. His sponsors, the Russians, wouldn't want to give American intelligence agencies unfettered indefinite access to whatever secrets he may possess, and neither would their pals, the Syrians. Deals would be done, and Niemiec would walk free — free to parade around Moscow with a Hero of the Russian Federation on his chest for his disservices to humankind. I remembered that smirk on Niemiec's face when he was getting onto the boat, and now I had a context for it. "Why sell the DF at a discount? You would have had other offers?"

"Yes, there were other buyers, but it's not always about price. Intent has a value. Intent matters."

What the fuck? I left the room and tried not to give Niemiec the satisfaction of another burst of anger.

Walking out into the hallway, I found the air being sucked out of it by Merle Ridge having a rant at Anna and Kazia.

"Cooper had half an excuse, but not you," he hissed at Anna.

"An excuse for what?" I asked. "And what are you doing here? I don't think you were invited. Kazia, was he invited?"

"You were wanted back in DC more than a week ago," Ridge steamed. "Ignoring directives, not answering phones..."

"I got diverted," I told him, grabbed Anna's arm and kept walking. Ridge, Gibbs, and Kazia could duke it out. We had work to do.

"Cooper! Where are you going?" He called after me. "COOPER!"

'You're going to get me suspended or discharged," said Anna as I shepherded her into the elevator.

"You're welcome."

"Vin, Jesus...!"

"All's forgiven when you crack the case. There are too many unanswered questions. Washington might be happy the leaks have stopped, the leaker identified, and Niemiec behind bars, but I was just informed that a lot of innocent people are going to die if we don't find it. And fast.

"Where do we start looking?"

"The only place we can. We go back through everything. Review our notes, the Agency's info dumps, interviews, and so forth. There's got to be something we've missed."

Anna hit the sack at 3am. Nothing popped. I joined her at 4. She pushed me away at 4.05. The day began at 7. Agent Ridge pounded on the door at ten and again at 1:30pm. He threatened to huff and puff and blow the house down. Then he picked the door lock, but the chain held. He eventually went away, and therein lies a lesson for those three little pigs — just don't answer the fucking door. Simple.

Gibbs and Kazia rang Anna's phone and left a message that Niemic remained silent and that his laptop's security key was voice-printed phrase, which Niemiec refused to provide and that, without it, the computer was a useless box of plastic and circuitry.

Gibbs phoned in again to inform us that Langley was pissed and considering sending the FBI over to arrest us for disobeying orders. And Kazia rang again, this time to notify us that the charges against Tom Wilkes had been dropped.

Not long after receiving this news, I was back in the interrogation room with Niemiec. I was dreaming. It was one of those dreams where you know you're dreaming. I was seated opposite Niemiec. He was silent, just staring at me with that sly, off-putting grin. But then he opened his mouth, and a black scorpion crawled out, picked its way down his chin, and then dropped off, turned into a shiny black bubble, and floated toward the ceiling. It swelled as it climbed, growing bigger and bigger. And then it popped. And when it popped, it made a musical note.

Gross, but intriguing. And all the more so because, as I said, I knew this was a dream. What was my subconscious trying to tell me?

Niemiec opened his mouth again. Another black scorpion crawled out, followed by another. They both fell off his chin, turned into black bubbles, rose toward the ceiling, and popped, making musical notes. It was gross, but I watched, enthralled.

Those scorpions start scuttling out of his mouth faster, rising into the air and popping one after the other so that the notes create a tune. I recognized the tune from a memory I'd been trying to forget, back when I was in that tent, looking at the wavy lines on a Damascus steel knife with a round tip, Niemic on his computer humming this same tune.

"Vin... Vin... Wake up."

My eyes opened on Anna leaning over me. I lifted my head off my arm, which was a dead weight, gone to sleep, a feeling reminiscent of Zruba's anesthetic. "I just had the weirdest dream," I told her.

"You were making some odd sounds. I've found something," she said, placing her phone on the desk. On-screen was an image of

Zruba, Niemiec, and Overton. They were standing beside their Toyota Hi-Lux, cradling scoped high-powered rifles, dressed in hunting gear. Just the boys having some fun after a hard day killing things. It was one of the images Anna had snapped when we were aboard Zorya the second time. "Look," she said when my attention drifted.

I looked again. "What am I missing?"

"You see the photographer reflected in the driver's window?"

My fingers made the image larger. The angle of the reflection caught the photographer almost in profile.

Anna and I exchanged a glance and said nothing. And the fact that we said nothing said everything.

There was a knock on the door. "Vin, Anna... You home?"

It was Wilkes.

Anna got up to let him in. "You have to admit, that is fucked up," she said along the way.

It certainly fucked my plans up. "I think I might also have something."

"What?"

"Could be nothing. Can I use your phone?"

Anna nodded and opened the door.

"Hey," said Wilkes. "The world is going nuts looking for you two."

"Slucham..." a female voice answered on the phone's speaker.

"Kazia?" I said.

"Helo? Kto to jest?"

"It's Cooper."

"Oh, it's you," said Kaz, switching to English. "Where have you been? What do you want?"

"Have you cracked Niemiec's computer password?"

"No. Niemiec won't cooperate."

"Got something for you to try."

"What?"

"You might have to sing it. Better still, get Niemiec to sing it."

"Sing what?"

"Karaoke is not my thing, but here goes. M-I-C...K-E-Y...M-O-U-S-E."

Wilkes agreed. "Karaoke is definitely not your thing."

"DEVIL'S "SWAMP," MISSISSIPPI, UNITED STATES

At zero-two-thirty, half an hour after the moon had set, we moved forward to recon the whereabouts of that WMD. Drone footage taken at last light suggested we'd have to contend with twenty or so farmers, storekeepers, mechanics, clerks, barbers, and so forth. They called themselves the Patriot Brothers; people united in a belief that the government was waging war on their freedoms and that society had gone down the toilet. America had failed them, and they were going to take it back by making a statement. If our intel was good, they were going to make it using sarin.

I watched from a distance of around 75 meters as two thirty-somethings in hunting camos met, shared a private joke, and lit cigarettes, the lighter flaring in my optics. A few of these people probably had some level of military training. We weren't going to underestimate them. Surprise had to do more than just even the odds; it had to push them firmly in our favor. The moonless night and a fortunate breeze in the treetops to cover extraneous noise would help.

Anna and I had the path to the north covered. Armed with an AXSR sniper rifle, Wilkes covered the remaining entrance from a high point halfway up a tree.

We'd geared up for this off-the-books recon with a trip to a Walmart, the retailer having everything we needed except hollow points and body armor. What's this country coming to, right? Maybe these Patriot Brothers really did have something to gripe about.

So, why was this recon of ours "off the books?" Because Kazia (and the service she worked) for didn't trust our government and had decided to delay intelligence sharing. The WMD that supposedly wasn't found in Operation Iraqi Freedom, or maybe was found but allowed to slip away to save the U.S. embarrassment, had them spooked. Lack of trust is a common theme these days. But Kazia and her fellow conspiracists at the Agencja Bezpieczeństwa Wewnętrznego trusted Anna and me enough to leak us some useful details. Inglis believed we had a six-hour head start at best.

Niemiec's laptop had been woken up by an artificially generated version of him singing the Mouseketeer theme. Once cracked, the device revealed that the WMD buyer was a Louisiana-based private militia led by a fitness instructor (unemployed) named Jimmy LeFranc. The guy had a rap sheet, which Inglis sent through along with his mugshot. LeFranc had previously been charged with stiffing his wife on alimony payment. There were also two counts of common assault filed by his former wife. The mugshot revealed a man with dark features accentuated by a black beard trimmed the length of his buzzcut and a badly broken nose, an old injury. This asshole had come straight from Wife Beater Central Casting. His Facebook page featured a stream of rants involving his children, girls aged eleven and thirteen. The courts, which he referred to as "the goverment," had taken away shared custody and, ultimately, visitation rights. The other side of LeFranc's coin — he was just your average baseball nut, a loveable Mississippi Braves fan, with more than a few images showing him dressed up in the team's merch.

Accompanying social service interviews of the children revealed a father with a violent temper. They were scared of him and scared for their mother. LeFranc blamed society for their fear. He looked and acted like a top-shelf shithead, a fact to which his ex and kids would no doubt attest. But where would a currently unemployed fitness instructor find $10 million?

The target LeFranc had chosen on which to make his anti-establishment feelings known was still being determined, but Disneyland seemed the obvious choice. I recalled what Niemiec had told me: *It is preferable if you can cause their deaths when it is least expected. For example, when these so-called innocent people are doing something playful...*

The laptop's security password suggested Disney, but which Disney? Six of its theme parks were dotted around the U.S., and how would the sarin be disbursed?

There wasn't much time to plan, so the plan was to keep it simple — scout, check for WMD, question a couple of the Patriot Brothers if the opportunity presented itself, and leave.

Anna tapped me on the shoulder. It was time. "Moving," I said into the comms, alerting Wilkes, who would be getting into position.

We kept low, using the shrubs for cover, staying off the beaten path. Drawing closer, the night vision optics picked up a fine, straight, bright-green line in the bushes just ahead. I gave Anna the signal, crept forward, found a steel cord with my fingers, and followed it to the source, a Claymore — six hundred steel balls of warm welcome packed in C4, enough to turn more than a couple of humans into ground meat at this range, body armor or not. The anti-personnel mine told me these people were serious. They either had something to hide, were nervous by nature, or had been tipped off. Maybe all three. I safed the mine, added it to my pack, and gave Anna the unnecessary signal to keep a lookout. Where there was one Claymore, there were usually more.

I popped a couple of berry bursts to take the edge off and slipped into the black water to avoid the path. A slick of algae swirled up around my waist, and foul-smelling swamp-gas found my nose. Anna, about to follow, was delayed by a second Claymore, which she added to our stores. We then tracked the edge of dry land to the planned waypoint.

Two militiamen had placed themselves at a choke point we couldn't avoid. They were good ol' boys, overweight and early 50s — a couple of bearded Elmer Fudds. Pairs rather than individuals handled the guard duty — someone had done their homework. It would be challenging to silence both simultaneously unless we silenced them permanently. But while this group was allegedly plotting a terrorist act with a chemical weapon, most of them would probably be more comfortable hunting wabbits in wabbit season. We weren't here to kill folks.

Anna and I circled back until each of us had a militiaman covered. I signaled to Anna to wait while I slipped my pack and hooked a strap onto a tree root. She spotted a third Claymore and took a minute to disarm and recover it.

All set, I crawled out of the water, across a muddy finger of land, slithered into the bushes, drew my Sig, and waited. I could smell the guy's body odor — old wet gym socks and ashtray. When Anna was in position, she nodded, and we both moved on our respective marks. One moment my guy was thinking red-neck thoughts, and the next, I had that neck in the crook of my elbow and the Sig's muzzle buried in his cheek, where he could see it.

"Move or make a sound, and I will blow your head off," I whispered in his ear. "Understand?"

He nodded feverishly and raised shaky hands.

Anna had her man face down on the ground. He was out cold. Laying aside the Ka-Bar she probably used to render him unconscious, Anna put her knee in the small of his back, pulled his hands behind him, and restrained them with zipcuffs. She rolled him onto his back, cut the laces off one of his boots, pulled off a sock and stuffed it in his mouth, which she then taped with duct tape, winding the roll around his head several times. She then did the same to his ankles. Poetry in motion. Cooper Jr. was in a world of trouble if he/she ever gave his/her mother lip.

"Count yourself lucky," I murmured to my guy as, wide-eyed, he watched Anna efficiently complete the processing of his buddy.

Anna brandished the Ka-Bar in my captive's face and motioned him to stand. He grunted his way up onto his feet. I cuffed him, taped him, and had him sit with his back against a tree. We then pulled the man she'd hog-tied up into a seating position beside him and taped both of them to the trunk. I whispered to my guy, "Make a sound, and she's the one who'll come back to remind you to shush. Got it?"

He nodded with some intensity.

Anna and I returned to the swamp and kept working our way 'round to the central clearing, on which a collection of sheds had been erected. There were substantially fewer than the 40 militiamen who'd been present before sunset. I counted another five militiamen. Perhaps the terrain was masking others from view.

I came out of the swamp onto the edge of the clearing on which the sheds had been built. Three men were sitting on crates, smoking, huddled around a coffee pot on a gas camping burner. They had rifles slung across their backs. The other two I counted were walking the perimeter. I signaled Anna to focus on them while I dealt with F-Troop on a break. She crept silently off through the tree, weapon raised. Once she was clear, I let my rifle hang by my leg, reached into my pocket, and walked into the clearing. "I'll have a latte, thanks. You can have my lumps."

There was a moment of shock from them, and then one got to his feet, reached around for his rifle, and said, "Who the fuck are you?"

I figured he was the tough guy of the group, and he was going for his gun, so I cracked him one, a left hook to the jawline with the knuckledusters. Not hard, but hard enough. He went down like a ten-dollar hooker on a dead president.

The other two said, "Hey!" and went for their weapons, but I already had mine leveled, covering them.

"I'd think twice if I were you," I warned them. "Better shots than me have got their eyes on you." I motioned at their chests. The fight left both of them when they saw the red laser dot bounce from one sternum to the other. "Drop the mags, empty the chambers, and toss those rifles where I can no longer see 'em," I said. They followed the instructions reluctantly, shaking their heads, muttering, and then throwing their ARs into the bushes. "Now, do me a favor and put these on." I tossed a couple of zipcuffs at their feet.

"You a government man?" one of them asked as he bent to pick them up.

I cannot lie. "Yeah."

"CIA? FBI? Or one of them black ops, off-the-books outfits."

"Department of Agriculture," I said.

"Bull sheeee-it."

"I agree it's a stretch. Where's LeFranc?"

"He ain't here."

Anna marched the two guards into the clearing. "On your knees," she said. They did as they were told. She tossed them zipcuffs. "You know what to do."

Tom Wilkes walked in. "Where is everyone?" he said, lobbing a Claymore under a tree.

A couple of the militia shared sly grins. "You're too late," said one.

The other added, "Come high noon, our nation under God will have new lords of chaos, and true Americans will flock to our standard of hope."

Back to the first one: "Tell these gov'ment scum nuttin'"

"What's happening at midday, fellas?" I asked.

Neither had anything further to say. I checked that the cuffs were tight and dragged them into a row. "Move, and it'll be your last."

It was then that the sound of multiple helicopters approaching pierced the night.

"Vin!" Anna called out. She was standing in the doorway of one of the sheds, waving her flashlight around the interior. I joined her and found a storehouse stacked mainly with boxes of tinned food, medical supplies, clothing, ammo, and spares. Drums of WMD were absent. Anna danced her beam of light over a costume; outsized, soft, and foamy, the type a football team mascot might wear. From what I could make out, it was some kind of bird. The beak gave it away.

"It's a costume," said Anna, rummaging around it.

"Thanks. And?"

"You don't know who this is?"

"Should I ask for an autograph?"

"It's Orange bird."

"Who?"

She held up a lanyard to the light. "And this is an employee pass for Disney World Resort, Orlando..."

The air was suddenly full of the roar of jet engines and rotor wash. I left the shed. Peering up, I couldn't see a silhouette of a helicopter against the black night sky, but I knew it was there above the thrashing treetops. Thick ropes tumbled out of the heavens, along with a sudden whirling maelstrom of leaf litter, twigs, and flying grit.

Black shadows descended on those ropes. I laid the AK on the ground and assumed the position on my knees. A moment later, my face was pressed into the dirt while unseen hands padded me down and removed items of varying lethality. Whoever they were, they were efficient, stealthy, and they meant business. I just wasn't sure whose business.

The helicopter departed as a troop of other forces raced in by land, red laser-sight beams knifing through the dust kicked up by the helicopter rotors.

"Get up."

I knew that voice. I got to my feet as Anna was being helped to hers by Merle Ridge, dressed in black, wearing black body armor and a black combat assault helmet. Sidney was also here, questioning one of the Patriot Brothers. Flashlight beams danced around the encampment, a search underway. From what I could make out, this was an FBI operation with the CIA tagging along for the ride as observers.

"So, you got here before us, Cooper," said Ridge. "Congratufuckinglations. What do you know that we don't?"

That left plenty of room for a range of insults, but it just isn't the same when it's that easy. "We have a lead on the target," I said.

"Well... Don't keep us in suspense."

"Disney, Orlando."

One of the FBI agents was holding up the Orange Bird suit, patting it down, maybe for hidden birdseed.

"Really? That all you've got, aside from a handful of rednecks?" Ridge rewarded my agreeable nature with a smile that had smug written all over it. "Counter-terror FBI teams are already on the ground there, a no-fly-zone over the area. I think we can take it from here."

"Disney World is a big place. They know where to look? There's the Epcot Center, Magic Kingdom, Animal Kingdom—"

"Would you like me to pick you up some Mickey ears, Cooper?"

"What delivery mechanism are they going to use for the sarin?"

"Jimmy LeFranc has a pilot's license, and his brother runs a crop-dusting business. Hence the no-fly zone."

"Have you picked up LeFranc?" I asked.

"No, but law enforcement agencies in four states have a BOLO on him. Got it covered. Now—"

"What about his brother's aircraft?"

"Jesus H. Christ, Cooper," Ridge said with a labored sigh and a shake of the head that freed a breadcrumb from his beard. "Todd LeFranc is in custody on suspicion, and his aircraft impounded, okay? Leave it to the professionals."

Insults are what you get for playing nice. "So, what now?" I asked him.

"Why don't you just head on back to mediocrity? And take your friends with you."

"That's it? No inconvenient jail time to teach me a lesson?"

"Have you killed anyone today, Cooper?"

"It's early. What are you doing later?"

"Asshole."

I asked him, "So, why are you here if you know Disney World is the target[?"

"Same as you, checking for WMD."

"If you know the target is Disney World, Orlando, wouldn't it be there?"

"Piece of advice regarding jail time. Fuck off before someone around here — me — changes his mind."

ORLANDO, FLORIDA

Great reasons to own a private jet. No lines. No lost luggage. No plastic knife that can't cut overcooked pasta. And no overcooked pasta. That's what my waking-sleep was processing, along with information about Disney World gleaned from various websites during the two-hour flight. My power nap ended abruptly as Wilkes's company Gulfstream switched from cruise to descent. Opening my eyes, I saw Anna on the seat across the aisle, on her cell. I was about to say something when she held up her hand with a gesture that said, "Don't interrupt."

"What's happened?" I asked anyway.

She pressed the phone into her shoulder and said in a low voice, "It's Inglis. Niemiec's been murdered."

"What?" I countermanded Anna's hand gesture with one of my own. Anna handed me the cell. "Rita."

"What happened with Niemiec? How'd it go down?"

"Poison, they think. The autopsy will tell us."

"No CCTV?" I asked.

"No. There was some malfunction, apparently."

"Does anyone believe that?"

"What do you think?"

"Any suspects?"

"No. And we checked the visitor roster for the days he was held. Various law enforcement officers."

"Anyone we know?"

"ABW, CIA... Kazia, Gibbs, Ridge, Davidson, and a few other ABW anti-terror personnel — law enforcement working this case." Inglis continued, "Bright side? At least we can close the book on that whack job."

I wasn't ready to do that. Not now.

"Anna says you're heading to Disney World Resort."

332

"That's the plan."

"Try not to get in the way."

I ended the call.

"Can you believe that?" asked Anna, retrieving her phone.

I could. Niemiec was all too conveniently gone, and with him, too many unanswered questions.

We arrived at the theme Park's main entry a little after ten thirty in the morning. It was a Sunday, and the queues were long. Two unmarked police vehicles were parked on the side of the road on the way in, and there were also a couple of police helicopters in the sky, one hovering stationary at about five hundred feet, the other a couple of hundred feet above it, moving in a slow arc across the sky. No other obvious clues that trouble was in the air.

"This the right gate?" asked Wilkes, driving.

Welcome to the Magic Kingdom said the sign overhead.

Anna replied, "We're going to the Sunshine Tree Terrace. The map says that it's in Adventureland, and we can get there via the Magic Kingdom, so we're good. We have to take the monorail to the entrance."

"This isn't the entrance?" I asked.

"Yeah, to the parking lot."

"This is making me nervous," Wilkes offered.

"Don't like monorails?"

I scoped the general area and observed several people doing ordinary people things a little too obviously and were, therefore, probably FBI. "We know it's going down, and we think we know where. So why is this place not crawling with cops?" Disney had its own police and even special forces, but frankly, I couldn't understand why the park wasn't closed until further notice.

Wilkes continued, "How do we think they're going to do it? With aerosol cans like in Berlin? Artillery shells like in Idlib? How?"

None of the above, probably.

A short while later, we passed through security, where personnel who were more than likely law-enforcement stand-ins were thoroughly checking bags. Of course, the bad guys were going to wheel the stuff in through the front gate in a shoulder bag.

The FBI, the agency handling this counter-terror operation, believed the situation was well in hand — Merle Ridge's claim. Anna and I used our OSI IDs, which got us entry along with our concealed firearms. Wilkes had to stop and pay and leave his Glock 43 in a gun safe before being permitted entry.

We made our way through the morning crowds toward the monorail station, joining the throng. Then we stood in the monorail carriage brimming with excited kids, music from a Disney flick playing through the speakers.

"Surreal," Anna and I said simultaneously.

She smiled. "Jinx!"

Adventureland. It was a hot day, the temps above ninety. The queue for Splash Mountain was a long snake winding through the gates. I watched some kids standing in a fountain, hurling water at each other. A couple of youngsters ran past, shooting each other with water pistols.

Eventually, we arrived at Sunshine Tree Terrace, where Orange Bird was walking around and interacting with the smaller children. It seemed like a typical day at the park — Mums, dads, kids, merch.

Wilkes shoved a couple of liters of orange juice in my hand. "I'll never get over the way you Yanks supersize these things."

"Land of plenty," said Anna absently, scanning our surroundings, looking for trouble but not finding any.

"So, now what?" said Wilkes. "We're here, assuming here — the Terrace — is significant."

More kids were engaged in a running water battle.

It was a little after eleven. *Come high noon, our nation under God will have new lords of chaos, and true Americans will flock to our standard of hope.*

"It's officially a stinker," said Wilkes, flicking sweat off his forehead with the swipe of a finger. "And where I come from, an average summer's day melts roads, buckles railway lines, and fries eggs on your car's bonnet."

"We call it a hood here, and wouldn't it be easier to use a frying pan?" Anna asked, still surveilling the general area.

I wasn't engaging in the weather report. How was LeFranc going to pull it off? Niemiec had been murdered after only a couple of days in confinement. Was he murdered to minimize the risk that he'd give the plan away? He'd sold the WMD to a third party. Would that third party share their plans for the weapon's intended use with Niemiec? My thinking — one of the conditions of sale was that the WMD would be deployed against the right kind of innocents — the more innocent, the better. And what was more innocent than the targeting of children, especially children engaged in having innocent fun at the capital of innocence — Disneyland. Back in the tent, when Zruba was on the verge of turning me into a gladiator, Niemiec had got up from his laptop, danced across the room, and sung, "M-I-C...see you real soon...K-E-Y...why? Because we like you..." inadvertently telegraphing his laptop's security code. That same tune had also led us, ultimately, here. I went over to Anna. "Do you know the Mouseketeer theme song?"

"Who doesn't?" She casually sang, "M-I-C...K-E-Y...M-O-U-S-E..."

"You've got a nice voice. Who knew," I told her, and Anna did have a good voice, but that's not exactly what Niemiec had sung.

There was more to it, and I only just now realized it. What was it, exactly?

Two boys chasing a third unloaded their Master Blasters. One of the boys miss-fired as they ran by, and I collected a squirt to the side of the head. "Hey...!" I called out, but the kids didn't hear me, and nor would they care if they did. My mind was rambling, the thoughts jumping around, attempting to land on something solid. Lots of "innocents" here. Niemiec would be pleased. The sarin attack at Idlib came to mind, the dead donkey on its side with its stiff legs in the air an enduring image. There was something the investigator from the Organization for the Prohibition of Chemical Weapons had said. What was her name? Ange Noordstrom... *"If there is a silver lining, it's that the water supply hasn't been contaminated."*

I went over to Anna and Wilkes. "So, what Niemiec sang, all of it, went like this — M-I-C...see you real soon... K-E-Y... Why? Because we like you... R-E-E-D-Y"

Wilkes frowned. "I've changed my mind. You absolutely should do karaoke because tone deafness lives at karaoke."

"Reedy, Reedy...That rings a bell." Anna pulled out her phone and went to work with her thumbs. "I read something about that on the plane. Yeah, Reedy... Reedy Creek. It's the municipality owned and run by Disney." Her thumbs were a blur. "Here it is...Reedy Creek is where Disney gets its water. The location of..." Anna looked at me in horror. "...its water treatment facility. Oh my god, they're going to put it into the water!"

"We have to get the park evacuated...like now!" I watched those kids frolicking in the fountain. If sarin-contaminated water began flowing through the pipes, all those children were dead. Splash Mountain would become a killing zone. Every bubbler and water fountain would be lethal. "We need a radio.

"The Park Security people use them," said Anna.

Wilkes climbed on a bench to get a better view. "None around."

"There's got to be," I said, scanning the area. Orange Bird had borrowed a blaster and was feigning recoil as he squired it. "I'll get them to come to us."

Wilkes was dubious. "How you gonna do that?"

I went up to Orange Bird, pulled the blaster out of its odd-looking wing hands, and emptied the canister into its face, or rather the mesh covering the face of the human inside. "Hey...!" came the muffed cry. I pulled the Orange Bird's head off, threw it aside, and then pushed the young guy wearing the costume down on the ground.

A toddler, a little girl, pointed at Orange Bird's decapitated head sitting on the grass, a big smile on its beak, and burst into a flood of tears.

A couple of Park Security Guards and Disney cops materialized miraculously out of the shadows and raced to what they thought was a confrontation with a park mascot. "Sir, what seems to be the problem here?" asked the more senior of the two as they approached the unfortunate twenty-something in an orange onesie down on his back.

"Hey!" The younger of the two guards said as Anna snatched the radio out of her hand.

Holding her badge up so they could see it, Anna said, "You know what's going on in the background, right? You've been briefed?"

The Disney enforcement folks exchanged a glance. "Yes," said the more senior of the group.

"What just happened here was us catching your attention so that we could access this." Anna waggled the radio. "The park has to evacuate immediately. We have new information. The threat is credible, it's significant, and it's now!"

"Who are you with, ma'am? The FBI?"

"We're federal agents."

"But you're not FBI. If you were, you'd have your own radio. So, who are you, and what about him?" the officer motioned at me.

The Department of Agriculture probably wouldn't cut it. "CIA," I said, "and we are assholes. Just ask him." I motioned at the unfortunate half-suited-up kid still on the ground, then pulled the pistol from the small of my back. "So, if you don't want me to start shooting into the air to get this park evacuated in a hurry, you'll get on your radio, contact your control center, and give the code word or phrase I know you guys are gonna have for a terror attack and get this place shut down, pronto."

"Yes, sir," said the officer, responding well to threats.

I returned the firearm to its hiding place and helped Orange Bird to his feet. "Sorry, kid."

"Asshole," he said. He brushed himself down, gathered his big head off the ground, tucked it under his arm, and stomped off toward the Terrace.

One of the guards spoke into his radio, walking a few paces away. Did I trust him? Any minute, we could find ourselves surrounded by FBI agents believing a mass shooting was about to happen and that Anna, Wilkes, and I were the shooters.

The music, playing through the loudspeaker system that I wasn't even aware of till all went quiet, went quiet. Then a loud warbling attention-getting tone sounded on the PA system, followed by a reassuring female voice. "Ladies, gentlemen, and children, due to an electrical malfunction, Disney World is regrettably forced to close until the fault is rectified. A full refund will be made available. Please make your way immediately to the nearest exit."

The message repeated. It was pre-recorded. That made sense. The risk assessment folks would require that the park could respond immediately to a terror threat with an announcement that wouldn't induce panic. To the younger security guard, I said, "See those kids playing in the fountain. You want them to die; let them keep playing." The two security guards raced off to put an end to the potentially lethal fun.

Anna, Wilkes, and I were also on the move. "How far is Reedy Creek?" I asked.

"Technically, we're already on it, but the water treatment facility is five or six miles from here on service roads," said Anna, breaking into a jog.

Eleven-thirty. Midday was zero hour. We were out of time, especially if I had to get there on foot. I saw a revolving yellow warning light and, beneath it, a golf cart. Goofy was in the passenger seat beside a driver. "There!" I said, breaking into a sprint. I caught it as it slowed at an intersection and jumped in front of it. The driver hit the brakes and looked at me, more than a little nervous. "Police business," I told him, holding up my badge. "We need to commandeer your vehicle."

Anna, arriving beside me, added, "Do you know a shortcut to the water treatment facility?"

"Er, yeah..."

"Can you take us?"

"Um..."

"You're taking us," I informed him, eliminating uncertainty and climbing into the back seat. Anna and Wilkes piled in beside me.

"Apologies," Anna said, leaning forward, 'but we need to stop some bad people, and we're in a hurry."

"Okay." The driver, a young kid with glasses and a lisp, stamped on the pedal. The buggy surged forward and settled into a leisurely pace.

"Can you go any faster?" I asked.

"Sorry," said the driver. "This is it. Probably overloaded."

"Want me to get out and push?"

The park was emptying, though maybe not fast enough. There were overhead misting sprays on some of the concessions to keep the customers cool. If people were in the area when they started spraying sarin, the death toll would multiply. A group of law enforcement types were arguing with park staff. What about, I wondered? Did the park have to be shut down? Who gave the order to do that? There would be confusion up and down the communications chain, for sure. If the threat materialized and people died because the evacuation hadn't been timely, there'd be an inquiry and a reckoning. And if the threat proved to be a false alarm, there would be a significant compensation payment. But who would be liable? Any way you looked at it, heads would more than likely roll, and if they did, my neck would probably be one of the first on the chopping block.

Reading my mind again, Anna warned, "Vin, I hope you're right. If you're wrong, this is going to go badly. We need to tell someone what's going down. They haven't figured it out."

There was no one on the ground we could brief. We had no authority. "Call Inglis. Tell her where we're going and why. Maybe get us some backup."

Anna pulled out her phone, made a call, and turned away for privacy as the kid with a lisp asked, "So, the water treatment plant? How come? What gives?"

"Sorry. National Security," I said to cover for the fact that we had no firm idea what we were heading into. Goofy turned his big head in my direction. "Let us know when you want to get off, buddy," I told him, which earned me a big dopey foam-and-plastic grin.

The golf cart turned away from public areas to "cast only" zones and then ducked through a maze of service tunnels beneath the park, seeing daylight again at an exit adjacent to the golf course. Goofy tapped the driver on the shoulder, we stopped, and the mascot hopped out.

"Sorry about the inconvenience, sir," Anna told him.

The Goof said nothing and continued giving us that big dopey grin, which, to be fair, he couldn't do anything about.

"I'll take you to the service road. It's just off the green of the 15th; from there, the treatment plant is around two miles."

Anna glanced at her phone. "No service."

Wilkes checked his screen. "Same."

Whatever came next, we'd have to manage analog.

We bounced over the drive, hit the access road, turned onto the course, and scattered a group teeing off. Within a couple of minutes, we turned onto the access road. The time — 11:26. The cart pulled to a stop.

"This is it," the driver said. "Just through those bushes and take a right. Might be a little overgrown. Not used much. There's another track off to your right about halfway along. Ignore it. Follow this one all the way to the plant."

"Thank you," Anna said, giving him a reassuring smile and replacing him behind the wheel. "You might just have saved many lives."

"Okay. Well, have a Disney day," he said with a half-hearted wave. Anna hit the accelerator pedal, and we left him behind.

"We've got two Sigs between three," Wilkes ventured, leaning over the front seat between Anna and me as overhanging branches slapped against the bodywork. "Not keen to go in unarmed. So... Scissors, paper, rock?" He held a closed fist.

"You win." I pulled my pistol and handed it to him. "Try not to get it dirty," I said. "Just cleaned it."

Wilkes checked the chamber, a round in the spout, then dropped the mag. "Ball. Would have preferred hollow points against these fuck-knuckles. Hmm... No safety."

"Compensates with heavy trigger pressure."

"Thought you blokes used the M9 Beretta."

"Hated that thing. No, the Sig 229. I like the weight."

"Would you and your guns like to get a room?" Anna asked over her shoulder. "Here's that road coming up on our right."

"Pull into the bushes," I told her.

Anna drove the vehicle into the dense shrubbery. We jumped out and placed broken branches against the yellow panels to conceal them.

The time: 11:44.

"How do you want to do this?" asked Wilkes.

"Keep off the road. We have no comms, so we stay visual and reassess once we get some threat assessment."

Wilkes and Anna nodded. I led off. The ground underfoot was waterlogged, the bushes thick with a heavy canopy. The three of us had to be reasonably close to remain in sight of each other. The heat and humidity were oppressive, sweat already running down my forehead and stinging my eyes. Clouds of mosquitoes whined. We hadn't crept forward more than a hundred meters before a soft whistle from Anna drew my attention. I signaled Wilkes to remain in place and then made my way towards her.

"What?" I gestured.

She pointed forward at the ground. I couldn't see what the issue was, not at first. Then I saw it — a tripwire. I took a couple of paces forward, went into a crouch over the wire, and looked along its length — a Claymore. I shouldn't have been surprised, given their use back in the swamp. Anna had done well to spot the wire, its length obscured by the foliage. I went to the curved flat face, reached behind, put it on safety, and harvested the thing. There were bound to be more. And, of course, the presence of the mine confirmed not only that we were right about the Patriot Brothers' plans but that there was likely to be a gunfight in our future.

I kissed Anna on the cheek for not getting herself blown up, wondering how I ever let her and our unborn come on this mission, and then remembered I had no say in it whatsoever, retraced my steps back to the center, then made my way across to Wilkes and handed him the mine.

"You've made my day," he said with glee.

Moving through the trees, I could see the smooth sides of a couple of large water storage tanks up ahead. The treatment facility had to be behind them. Since we'd arrived without setting off any alarm bells, there was a chance we would have the all-important element of surprise. But what we wouldn't have — any opportunity to look into the facility before we attempted to gain entry. We'd be going in blind and in broad daylight.

Heading back to the center, I checked with Anna. She signaled the presence of a guard, pointing him out, and I smelled the tobacco smoke before I saw the guy. I circled behind him, the bushes providing good cover. The ground was soft but noisy, with plenty of rotten sticks to sound a warning. Lucky for me, and unfortunately for him, he was wearing earbuds. I watched him flick his butt into the middle of the track and continue patrolling, coming closer, step by step. He was a big guy whose hobby was beer, if the belly was any indication. He also had a hard-on for military gear, being fully outfitted with the latest in urban warfare: an AR-15 with laser sight, webbing stuffed with magazines over compact Kevlar body armor, some kind of flashy revolver on one hip, and a Ka-Bar strapped to his opposite thigh. A Kevlar helmet topped off the package. His AR was pointed at his feet, one hand on the grip. He didn't look like he was expecting trouble. Maybe he thought that as long as the road was clear, the Claymore would provide fair warning from the flanks.

He strolled past, whistling along to something, then stopped. I wondered if he'd heard me, but then he took his phone out, changed the song list, and started walking. The whistling resumed. I came at him from the side, bursting out of the bushes, leading with a right cross to his jawline, my body weight behind the punch. He crumpled like a pleated skirt. I caught him before he hit the ground and dragged him into the cover. Anna went to the edge of the road to keep watch while I stripped him. A radio was clipped to his shoulder, a cheap walkie-talkie. I turned down the volume and pocketed it. Next, the ammo — eight mags for the AR, the contents hollow points. More joy for Wilkes. Attached to the webbing was a gas mask in a pouch and thick rubber gloves bulging in a thigh pocket — minimum essentials around sarin. The body armor came off next, along with his phone (no service), belt, water bottle, Ka-Bar, four speed-loaders with ball, and a pearl-handled, nickel-plated S&W 686 from off his hip.

"Son," I informed the unconscious, "don't you know only pimps in Louisiana whore houses pack a pearl-handled revolver?" No answer. Clearly, his pappy hadn't passed down that piece of wisdom from General George S. Patton Jr.

Patting him down turned up his wallet. It contained a few cards, a rewards stub from a café with nine out of ten cups crossed, his next, a freebie. There was also a receipt for the AR, the Ka-Bar, and the hollow points. His license said Willard M. Pritchard from Pearlington, Mississippi, age thirty-four. I could return all the gear tomorrow, tell the shop assistant they didn't fit, get a refund, and grab a free coffee while I was in town. In a back pocket, I found gold — a Google Earth printout of the facility. I held it up to show Anna. We wouldn't be going in blind after all. I removed his shirt and cut off one of the sleeves with the showroom-sharp Ka-Bar, pulled off his boots, and then his pants. Shit, this asshole was going full commando. He wore his politics on his skin — the tattoo of a Nazi dagger on one side of his rib cage and a Luger pistol with a swastika on the handgrip on the other. He was also circumcised. How did those things happen to come together on this guy's body?

The tats caught Anna's eye. "Asshole," she whispered.

Wilkes joined us, a torn plastic bag under his arm. "Handsome specimen," he observed. "That's a lot of gear. And I don't mean what you think I mean."

I picked up the body armor and helmet and held them out to Anna. "No argument."

She accepted them but with a look that said expect the argument later.

"And take these." I gestured at a separate pile of gear that included the webbing, revolver and speed-loaders, gas mask, and gloves. I then handed her the revolver. "Won't hurt to have a backup."

She took the revolver. "Flashy."

"Tom, I'll swap you my Sig for the AR."

"Fair trade," he said, handing back my pistol.

I flattened the map printout against a tree trunk.

Tom whispered. "That asshole got a kitchen sink on him too?"

The storage tanks shown on the map were the ones visible through the trees ahead. The facility had no fence or front gate, and only one road entered from the eastern side, the side we were covering. Three far more significant roads accessed the plant from the western side. Our current position put us at the facility's back door.

Wilkes checked the AR's condition, dropped the mag, and then slapped it back in.

I returned to Willard, removed the laces from his boots, rolled the guy over, and tied his hands and feet. I gestured to Wilkes, and we dragged him to a seating position with his back propped against a tree. The guy was groggy, regaining consciousness, his head lolling lazily from side to side. I slapped him around a little, then splashed some of the Gatorade from his drink bottle on his face, took a swig myself, handed it to Anna, and then picked up the Ka-Bar. I held it in front of Willard's eyes as he regained his senses. His sudden awareness filled him with shock. From his perspective, it was as if he'd been teleported. One moment, he was having a quiet smoke, and the next, he was naked against a tree with the edge of a very large knife way too close to his face for comfort.

"How many of you, Willard? How many men?" I asked him.

"Wha...?" he replied.

"In the water treatment plant. Do you understand?"

The bewilderment continued. I glanced at my watch: 11:50. I brought the blade under his nose and sliced his septum. Not much, just enough to get some focus. He tried to rear back, banged his head on the tree behind him, then stammered, "Four...fourteen!"

"You're sure? Fourteen, including you?"

"Yeah...yes."

"So, thirteen."

His head made the right kind of movements.

"Where are they — their location?"

"Covering the roads and, I...I don't know what you call it," he blubbered, blood and mucous leaking down onto his upper lip and into his mouth. "The...the control room, and the b...building that houses the pumps."

"Is that where the sarin is?"

He hesitated, so I gave him a closer inspection of his knife.

"Yeah...yeah...the stuff is there!"

"Where is that? Where in the facility?" I held up the printout.

"In the middle."

"Show me." I pointed to an area that had a nest of exposed pipes snaking from the ground and a bunker beside them, roughly in the center of the facility. "Here?"

He nodded. "Yeah."

"How many of you guarding the sarin?"

"Four, maybe five."

The walkie-talkie in my breast pocket crackled. "Yo, Willard. You good? Over"

"Be convincing," I warned him, rested the blade across his legs, inches from his girlfriend's disappointment, held the comms in front of his mouth, and pressed the transmit button.

"All good," said Willard. "How are you?"

"You're supposed to say 'over,' dumbass, when you're finished talkin' so as I know when to talk. Remember? Over."

"Over."

"There ya go. Fuckin' walk in the park here, dude. How about you? Over."

Willard froze.

"Willard, you good? Over."

I poked Willard with the knife.

"Fuckin' A," Willard blurted. "Over."

"Ask him about hostages. How many, where are they holding them."

He fumbled the switch.

"Yeah, what?" said the voice. "Over."

"How many hostages you got? Over."

"Twenty, maybe. Over."

"Where you got 'em? Over."

"Get off the fucking comms, Willard."

"That it?"

"What."

"You didn't say over."

"Neither did you. I got shit to do, and you're lucky, otherwise I'd come down there and stomp on your fuckin' ass. OVER."

I patted Willard on the shoulder and pocketed the toy. "Meh, you tried. How many you got guarding the hostages?"

"Two. Maybe three."

Basically, the Brothers were scattered all over the facility. "You people killed anyone in there yet, Willard?"

"No."

"But you're going to, aren't you?" He knew it, and we knew it.

"It's LeFranc. It's his plan. I'm not killing anyone," he insisted.

"No, you're innocent. I can see that. Is LeFranc in there with the rest of you?"

"No. He's at Disney World. Wanted to see it, y' know, go down."

Anna muttered, "Jesus, Mary, and fucking Joseph..."

"I'm going to gag you now, Willard, and then we're gonna go say hi to your friends." I took the shirt sleeve I'd cut, stuffed some of it in his mouth, and tied the rest tight around his head so that it bit into his open mouth. "You move," I continued, "the explosive charge I've placed under your nutsack when you were out cold will go off. You understand?" Willard froze, horror on his face. "I'm advising you not to move a muscle. Any muscle. Understand?"

He nodded with lots of understanding. I considered covering him up but decided the embarrassment of being found by one of his buddies hog-tied naked might be every bit as effective at keeping him quiet and stationary as the threat of having his balls blown into low Earth orbit. I stood — time to move.

Wilkes was kneeling on the ground over the plastic bag.

"What are you doing?" I asked him.

He finished pressing something into a broken glass bottle with a stick and held it up to show me. On the garbage bag were three other similar bottles and an aluminum soda can with its top peeled off. "Repurposed those Claymores," he said. "C4 — versatile stuff. Throw the bottle, pull this string when it lands, and boom, a shower of the prettiest glass and silver balls you'll ever see will sweep the area clean. Make sure that when you pull the string, you're behind something solid. Someone like fatso there." He gestured at Willard. "Though a tree would be better." He handed me two of the makeshift grenades and gave two to Anna.

"We've still got this one." Anna gestured at the recovered Claymore on the ground.

"I'll take that," Wiles offered with a grin.

"Let's go," I told them. My Seiko said eleven fifty-three. I hoped it was running fast.

"What's the plan, Vin?" Anna asked as we began to step through the trees toward the cleared area around the storage tanks.

"You and I will focus on the control room and pumphouse. The Brothers with the hostages and the men covering the roads will be preoccupied." I passed her the printout. "Tom, the hostage situation is yours."

"Got it," he said as Anna passed him the map.

"There's a grassy area with trees just on the other side of the tanks, between two buildings. We'll cut through there."

I went into the crouch position and moved forward, past the tanks and up to the edge of the main service road. Ahead and to our right was the grassy area between two buildings, vehicles parked outside both. To guarantee control of the facility, all these buildings would have been cleared of hostages.

Wilkes peeled away and started reconnoitering the buildings.

Anna and I were both exposed as we ran across the service road, but our movement attracted no response. A small bunkhouse, another service road to cross, and the nest of pipes came into view. The door to the bunker housing the control room was ajar. I ran up to it and gave it a solid thump with my boot. It flew open. Two targets. Both wearing Hazmat suits. Their gloved hands were turning knobs protruding from a wall of dials, gauges, buttons, and a few levers. They pivoted towards me. Two rapid shots. Headshots. Both went down. Two more shots, headshots, to make sure of it.

Gunfire. Close. The bunker behind this one. I turned and saw two more men in hazmat suits tumble down a short staircase. Anna walked up to them, sprawled at the base of the stairs, and fired again, the hoods of their yellow plastic suits filling with a sludge of blood, brain, and smashed bone.

An explosion. A discharged Claymore. Somewhere close, glass panes shattered. The noise came from a long building partly obscured by the control bunker. I raced to a corner of the bunker and poked my head around. Two gunmen went to the building's broken windows, took out the remaining glass shards with the barrels of their rifles, and searched around for targets. One of them saw me and let off a burst that pulverized some of the brickwork providing my cover. Shots rang out from a tree to my right —single shots. One gunman in the window flew backward into the darkness behind, and then his buddy's head dissolved in a plume of red mist. Wilkes had used the Claymore to lure them to the window so that he could get good, clean shots.

Screams were coming from inside that building. If Willard was on the level, it should now be cleared of gunmen.

Wilkes fired into the dark, empty window frames, once, then twice. More screams. Maybe Willard had underestimated numbers. Wilkes then turned to me and gave the signal — building cleared.

Seiko said it was a minute to high noon. Had we arrived in time to stop the pumps from flooding Disney World with sarin?

"Vin!"

Anna needed help. The pearl-handled revolver had jammed. She gave up trying to clear it and instead threw it at someone coming toward her that I couldn't see, my line of sight obscured by yet another bunker. And then I saw her problem. It was the Wagner guy, the South African — Vin Zyl. The last time I saw him, he had an RPG on his shoulder. Niemiec must have embedded him to plan this operation and train the Patriot Brothers.

Anna pulled the grenade from her webbing, threw it, and yanked the string. It exploded in a bursting white and grey cloud that caused veils of dust to rise from surfaces all around. A nearby wall caught gobs of blood and other matter, the blast singing through the snaking jumble of pipes. The larger chunks hung there momentarily and then dropped off. I ran to Anna, who had been knocked clean off her feet and thrown backward some distance. She landed hard. I ran to her and saw a chunk of raw, mangled meat oozing blood on the ground beside her. Whose meat? Hers? Anna groaned. I couldn't see an obvious wound. I toed the torn flesh with my boot, turning it over. It was part of a hand, the skin displaying the partial tattoo of an animal's skull. Anna groaned some more. I checked her over. She'd been shot in the chest, the body armor dimpled by the round over her sternum. I sat her up as she gulped for breath. The South African had managed to get off a shot before Wilkes's homemade surprise had chopped him into hamburger. The range had been point-blank, the energy of the bullet punching Anna backward and off her feet. Memories of Oak Ridge came flooding back. "You're okay. You okay?"

"I'm okay," she said.

Movement. There, in an adjacent tangle of pipes, concrete blocks, and filters. More gunmen and they were close — two of them coming up behind a stack of concrete blocks. I ran from Anna to draw them away and headed for the corner of another bunker. As I reached it, my fingers gripped a bottle with a string bulging from a pocket. I threw the bomblet over those concrete blocks and held onto the string. It jerked tight, and an explosion rocked the area, the shockwave laced with steel balls and glass splinters. Something brushed against my cheek. When the dust cleared, both men were out in the open, smoking and ripped to pieces on the ground.

Anna was moving slowly and painfully. I ran back over to her. She coughed a couple of times and then gasped for breath. "I'm okay... I'm okay," she reassured me, and then rolled to one side and threw up. "Go," she coughed between convulsions, "go..."

My neck felt warm and wet. I wiped it. My fingers came away slicked with bright blood. Shrapnel had sliced up my cheek. The gash was long and deep, blood flowing down my neck and inside my shirt. I felt a little woozy.

I could see Wilkes approaching the landing of the building that had housed the hostages. He hopped up on the stairs, opened the door, and dazed people started to appear in the sunlight. A woman hugged him.

By my estimates, we had accounted for all fourteen Patriot Brothers, Willard included. I left Anna behind to check the control room. On arrival, I found none of the gauges or dials on the panels covering the wall registering, and only one light illuminated, a solitary "Stand by" light. Just maybe we'd arrived in time to prevent the Patriot Brothers from restarting the facility with sarin tapped into the pipes downstream from the filtration system.

Anna was up and making her way to the adjacent pumphouse with some difficulty. Speaking from experience, catching a bullet wearing body armor is like being thumped by a sledgehammer. She opened the door, looked inside, closed the door, and called out, "It's here! The sarin is here!"

Good to know. We could relax maybe just a little. As for my cheek, the blood was flowing a little less freely, starting to coagulate. I stepped down off the landing and took a few steps up toward the main service road. The firefight had been short but intense. The adrenaline in my system was starting to ebb. I yawned, holstered the Sig, and took the remaining grenade out of my pocket. I was thinking Wilkes could keep it as a souvenir when a splash of color and movement caught my eye. It was Goofy, strolling casually down the road with his big dopey grin and oversized shoes. What the fuck was he doing here? It was only then that I saw, cradled in his arm, an AR. Maybe he saw me, maybe he didn't. He reached up, peeled off the Goofy head, and cast it aside. It was LeFranc, a gas mask dangling loose from his neck. How about that — we'd hitched a ride with the chief bad guy.

The unemployed fitness instructor, baseball fan, and would-be mass murderer hadn't spotted me, his focus on Anna standing by the pumphouse where the sarin was located. He stopped and raised the rifle to his shoulder. "Hey, Goofy!" I called out to him. He turned in my direction, surprised. "Here!" I said, and lobbed the soda can at him nice and friendly. "Have a Coke and smile." And, as his hand closed around the can, I pulled the string.

The FBI arrived, followed by the police, the sheriff's department, Park security, the fire department and its hazardous chemicals specialists, the U.S. Army and its WMD specialists, several ambulances, and the news crews, the latter kept well back. Several network helicopters arrived and hovered nearby, only to be chased off by a U.S. Army Apache gunship.

The Army threw up a thick plastic containment tent over the entire bunker housing the WMD, moved everyone to the far perimeter of the facility, and demanded the area be evacuated at the earliest opportunity. I overheard that they recovered one hundred and eighty-two gallons of sarin – ninety-one gallons of undocumented DF mixed in equal parts with easy-to-come-by isopropyl alcohol.

Willard Pritchard was also recovered, wrapped in a space blanket and stuffed into a black suburban with blacked-out windows by four men in suits who looked and moved like robots. Pritchard was the only surviving Patriot Brother and would no doubt be questioned until he no longer knew what the hell he knew.

By sheer good luck — I was due some — I'd managed to avoid further shrapnel damage from the blast that took out LeFranc, although blood oozed from one earhole, and the ringing in my head lasted a good ten minutes. LeFranc wasn't so lucky, reduced to a red ooze that leaked out of his Goofy suit.

The Disney cops and the sheriff's department were concerned about setting up a crime scene and argued about which of them had jurisdiction. Now that responsibility had been assumed by the Feds, that just left the taking of the credit.

The paramedics and the fire department attended to the hostages, many of whom were in shock, and enlisted Park security to assist with the management of that.

Paramedics cleaned up my wound and kept the two halves of my cheek together with temporary butterfly sutures. They offered me some painkillers, but I had that covered and chewed on a couple of berry bursts. I was coming around to the flavor. They told me the cheek would need a good plastic surgeon, but I was only half listening on account of, as I said, fifty percent of my ears were bleeding. Anna's chest was badly bruised but otherwise okay, and she had no other injuries, which was a relief. Those dividing cells would continue to do their thing uninterrupted.

A black helicopter turned up while the three of us were enduring yet another round of the same questions. This helicopter was permitted to land, which it performed on a manicured square of lawn just off the main service lane. A door opened, and the aircraft regurgitated Bradley Chalmers, who then, unfortunately, trotted totally unscathed beyond the reach of the spinning main rotor blades. I watched him pause to ask a deputy sheriff a question before making a beeline toward the knot of vehicles where Anna, Wilkes, and I were being questioned. He showed one of the senior FBI agents his ID, whispered something in his ear, and the agent moved away.

Once we were alone, Chalmers asked, "So, you want to tell me what happened here?"

"Don't you know?" I replied.

"Want to hear it first-hand."

"We won," I said. Granted, this was not the detailed debrief Chalmers was demanding, but it was the only one I was prepared to give, especially after running through it chapter and verse half a dozen times already with FBI investigators.

"Give me the headlines. I have people to answer to," he persisted.

"Your WMD is over there," said Anna, helping him out, gesturing at the Army team moving about in positive-pressure chemical suits beside their tent. "Disney World wasn't affected other than a temporary shutdown. There is one surviving Proud Brother and fourteen more in body bags. No hostages were harmed."

"Good, good. I'm looking forward to reviewing the details in your written report."

"What are you doing here, Chalmers?" I asked him.

"Here to give you a ride back to DC." He motioned at the shiny black helicopter.

"We've made other arrangements," said Anna.

"I've got a jet," Wilkes informed him.

"And who are you?" Chalmers asked.

"Nobody."

Anna grinned. "A rich nobody with a jet."

"Well then, if you'll excuse us?" said Chalmers, moving to present his back to Wilkes.

"Include Tom, or we all go," I said.

"Okay, fine. But his presence will limit what I can say."

I shrugged a little ho-hum at him.

Chalmers cleared his throat. "So...after you gave us the whistleblower, you were ordered to return to Andrews, but as usual, you disobeyed those orders. However, the SecState is prepared, in light of what's happened subsequently and your tireless results-driven work, to give the general disobedience a pass."

Chalmers held out his hand to shake. "Think of my hand as the Secretary of State's."

I wasn't going anywhere near that clammy paw, and he endured several uncomfortable seconds while it hung in mid-air, unloved.

Clearing the embarrassment from his throat, he said, "The ride back to DC is an order. This case is now officially closed. You identified the whistleblower, Niemiec is no longer with us, and the WMD is now in safe hands. That's a perfect score, right?"

"Chalmers, the only orders you're qualified to give are at drive-thrus," I said.

"There some are loose ends," Anna said, I guessed to take the sting out of my insult.

"What loose ends?"

"Admin stuff — equipment to return, accommodation bill to settle, that sort of thing. We'll be back in DC tomorrow morning. Tom can give us a ride to Dulles, can't you, Tom?"

"Too easy."

"Say, where's that accent from?"

"South," he said.

Chalmers nodded. "Deep in the heart of Texas, if I'm not mistaken."

"You've got a good ear, mate."

Chalmers eyeballed me. "So, I'll see you in DC tomorrow?"

"Counting the moments."

As he turned to leave, Anna said, "Bradley, wait... Before you go. I've been meaning to give you something."

He smiled. "Really? What for?"

"Gisela."

Then she slapped him so hard across the face that I felt it.

WASHINGTON DC

The Gulfstream pulled to a stop the following evening on the Dulles apron. Anna's phone, she said, was full of voice messages and texts from Chalmers wanting to know where we were and what we were doing. Well, we were mostly asleep, and for the time we weren't, it was none of Chalmers' business.

The authorities couldn't hide the operation at Disney World and the water treatment facility, much as they might have wanted to. The media was already starting to make all kinds of connections between Wikileaks, the WMD, Niemiec, and Disney. Eventually, connections to Foord would be made, along with the murders of Adams and Frederickson. Truth is like a corpse. It always floats to the surface — eventually.

The three of us stood at the aircraft's front door. We'd already said our goodbyes, but we said them again anyway.

Wilkes shook my hand, then hugged Anna. "This was fun. You two ever find yourselves needing another dance partner in the future, you've got my number. And if they fire you, the world is full of shit that needs blowing up. Roadrunner Demolitions can always use people who know which end of the dynamite to stick a match to."

We waved, the door closed, and the jet began to roll.

"We'd better let Chalmers know we're on the ground," Anna said as we walked to the terminal.

"Fuck him."

"I'll send him a text with your regards."

"I've got a few things to clear up at Andrews. Why don't you get takeout? I'll meet you at home. A much better plan."

"What things?" she asked.

"The usual. Check the emails, water the indoor plant. You know..."

"You're the world's worst gardener. It's dead. Let's go home."

"Yeah, I won't be long, I promise. Chinese? I feel like Chinese. You?"

"You're ducking and diving. What's up?"

"Nothing. It's a half-hour detour. What's the big deal? Don't go weird on me."

"Hmm..." Anna was dubious. "Well, Chinese it is," she said as her Uber turned up.

I watched her drive away before ordering my own. Sands Aerospace & Defense was reasonably close as the crow flies, as it backed onto Dulles. My Uber arrived fast, but the going was slow, the peak hour traffic heavy. Those egg rolls would be cold before I got to them. "Hey," I said to the driver, "I don't suppose you know any rat runs that'll get us there quicker?" The driver punched something into his phone maps, and a new route was drawn.

"Sure, I can save you seven minutes."

"Better than nothing," I told him. "Let's do it."

He turned off the main road. The shortcut took us through several unlit semi-industrial back streets and side routes. After a while, the driver, checking the rearview, asked me, "Any chance you would be followed, sir?"

"This is Washington. Isn't everyone?"

He smiled. "I guess we all use the same app to get around."

Maybe I was being followed, but I doubted it. And even if I were, some things couldn't be put on hold. This appointment was one of them. Some questions needed answers. Whether or not I took the job at Sands would depend on the answers. Ni, Zr, and Sd. Niemiec and Zruba. And Sands — Sd, I figured — rounded it out with their hunting buddy, Chase Overton.

The Uber took me to the security station. I swiped my card, and the bar lifted. I was surprised the card worked. If I'd been Sands management, given what had transpired over the past couple of months, I'd have canceled my privileges. The senior executive section of the parking lot was virtually empty. Management — last to arrive, first to leave. The Uber driver dropped me off at the front door. I swiped the card and heard the lock *click*. I pushed on in. I knew the layout of the place well enough and headed for Overton's office. The lights were on. His suit coat was on a hanger, but no one was home.

I wandered down another corridor until I found Ely Sands' office. Again, the lights were on, and the door ajar. I knocked. Silence. "Mr. Sands?" I knocked again with interest. The door opened, not much, but enough for me to see that a lake of bright red blood, the color of blood that squirts from an artery rich in oxygen, was all over the desk and carpet. I had the presence of mind to use the point of my elbow to open the door further. Habit. Now I could see Ely Sands. He was slumped against the side of the desk, eyes open but vacant, a hunting knife embedded up to the hilt in the side of his neck, the blade angled up into the base of his skull.

"Come on in and close the door," Chase Overton called out. He was sitting on the couch down the far end of the office, tie loosened, relaxing with a tumbler of something golden in one hand and a Ruger peashooter in the other. "Are you armed?" he asked.

"No."

"Do I need to frisk you?"

"Rather you didn't. Tends to make me laugh, but your call." I noticed there wasn't any blood on Overton. Arterial blood gushes out like a fire hose. He couldn't have avoided being showered in it if he'd been the one who planted the knife in the CEO.

"Been a long day, Cooper... I'll settle for warning you that this pistol aimed at your gut will get off a shot faster than you could reach for yours if you have one. So why don't you take a seat?"

I took him up on the offer and settled into an armchair.

"What happened? You look like shit," he said, gesturing at his own cheek.

"Cut myself shaving."

"Drink?" he asked.

"Sure. So, the gun in your hand pointed in my direction suggests the job offer has been withdrawn."

Overton poured me a scotch from a decanter on the low table between us.

"Maybe, maybe not. Depends. Rocks?"

"Thanks."

He pulled a couple of ice cubes from a bucket with golden tongs and dropped them in the glass. "You've already cost this company a ton of money."

"Just addressing the elephant in the room," I said, "Isn't it the convention in business to stab your boss in the back? For one thing, it's cleaner." No reaction from the accountant with the pistol. I tried a more frontal approach. "Why did you kill him?"

"I didn't kill him."

"Then your partner did. Is he joining us, by the way?"

Overton seemed mildly surprised that I'd put this together. "He'll be here any moment."

Back to Ely. "So, your boss...why kill him?"

"Ely lost his nerve."

"Which nerve was that?"

"The capture of Niemiec and then the raid on the Patriot Brothers down in Mississippi. One followed the other because Niemiec must have talked before he could be silenced."

"Before you got to him?"

"Niemiec's blood's not on our hands."

"Then whose?"

"You're the detective. You tell me. Ely wanted to make a statement to police, get in early, cut a deal." Overton's eye-line lifted to someone walking in behind me. "Look at you," he said to this new arrival. "Fresh as a daisy."

Aldus Picot, the president's chief of staff, came into view, his hair wet and uncombed, wearing a Sands Defense Tee with navy suit pants. "Cooper," he said by way of greeting in that disturbing stretched cat-gut voice of his.

I failed to repay the pleasantry. "Interesting ensemble you're wearing tonight. Did you burn the blood-stained business shirt?" I asked him.

He grunted as he took the other armchair.

"You might not be aware," I continued, "the destruction of evidence carries a prison term. But maybe they'll just roll it into the murder charge. Did you come here with the intention of murdering him? If so, that would make it first-degree. But if one thing led to another and all of a sudden, a hunting knife found its way into your hand, and the next thing you knew, it was tickling Ely Sands' tonsils, then your attorney, if he's good, might be able to get away with murder in the second degree. As long as you didn't rape the corpse or otherwise disfigure it, the judge might go easy on you. So, in your case, anywhere between 25 and 35 years...?"

"Are you quite finished, Cooper?" said Picot, pouring himself a stiff belt.

"No. Did you use that knife on hunting trips with Overton, Andre Niemiec, and Arcady Zrubarov?"

"I don't know what you're talking about."

Picot and Overton exchanged a worried glance of how-the-fuck-did-he-know-that written all over it.

"When you go on safari with your buddies, Mr. Picot, you're never in the photos because you're behind the camera. Maybe you weren't aware that your pal Zruba liked to keep mementos. We were on his boat, having a general look around, and we came across a photo gallery including a holiday snap of your fellow hunters with a dead giraffe. And there you were, reflected in the Land Cruiser's window. Have to say, not your best side." I pulled the now well-worn photo out of my back pocket and passed it to Overton, who passed it to Picot. "We have copies of that, of course," I said, now the only person in the room with something to smile about.

"Is that the only evidence linking me to Niemiec?" Picot asked.

"I have to admit, it's thin but conclusive. And the prosecutor will know where to dig for more."

"How much do you want, Cooper?" said Overton, reading the tea leaves.

"I don't know. How much you got? Dazzle me."

"A million in straight salary, plus a million in stock options. That enough dazzle for you?"

"It's your opening offer. Let's say two million in salary, the same in stocks and a seat on the board."

"I have a gun," said Overton. "You can see that, right?"

"Did I overstep? Look, I have a kid on the way. So I'm already thinking about the college fund. And I have a partner who knows what I know, so, you know..." I considered buffing my fingernails, but that would definitely be overdoing it.

Overton took time out for another glance at Picot and then returned his attention to me. "Two plus two plus a seat on the board. Do we have a deal?" The Chief Financial Officer put his glass down, leveled the Ruger at me, and held out his hand to shake on it.

"Now I'm feeling pressured into it."

"We're not playing games, Cooper.

"Look, don't get me wrong, I am tempted, but what exactly am I getting into? This whole thing started with Wikileaks, and here I am, having just followed the crumbs, which, in this case, is a trail of dead bodies. What don't I know? What skeletons will be revealed when I take up that seat on the board? I don't want to take on any previous bad behavior." Something Inglis told me popped into my head. "And I hear your — or I should *our* — stock is heading south with a ways to go. Did a Senate sub-committee kill one of your programs? What gives?"

Silence.

"Guys...?"

"Tell him," said Picot. "He's going to find out anyway."

In fact, I'd already pieced together most of it, but there were holes.

"We have a new surveillance product. An entire integrated suite. Industry-leading. Hi-def micro cameras with built-in facial identity algorithms that auto-link to provide on-the-move hands-off tracking are integrated with law enforcement databasing that includes cell takeovers and cloning, and that's just the base package. The big picture? Properly set up, this system can scan, say, a full stadium — a hundred thousand people -— and provide a threat analysis on every single person virtually within minutes; the analysis can be filtered any way the client wants it and up to 1000 threats can then be tracked in real-time, almost simultaneously. The Chinese stole the tech from the North Koreans and improved it. We stole it from the Chinese and improved on it further still. It's a fully integrated system from pickup to lockup."

"Everything the autocrat needs to keep a lid on dissent," I said, summarizing.

"You've got a marketing mind," said Picot.

"Track-All Calibrated Defense WeapoN. T-A-C-D-W-N. We call it TAKEDOWN."

"I like the product. Not sure about the acronym."

"Well, when you're on the board, maybe you can do something about it."

"So, shiny new defense weapon. Dictatorships are a growth market. What's the problem?"

"There's no problem—"

Overton cut across his partner. "We wanted the price maximized."

"We created a domestic need," Picot continued.

"What?"

"Keep up, Cooper." Picot freshened his drink. "The sense in government was that when the threat of Islamic terrorism declines, as it ultimately will, there'll no longer be the same requirement for an internal surveillance system like TAKEDOWN. SA&D staked the farm in the development phases. The Patriot Brothers were employed to prove the narrow-sightedness of that position."

"They had the plan you needed, so you sold it to them cheap," I said.

"Tell him," said Overton.

Picot leaned back, stretched out, and crossed his ankles. "We staked DeFranco the $10 mill so they could buy it. It was the Russians who owned the WMD. They bought it for $100 million. The auction was a ruse. As you say, the Patriot Brothers had the right kind of plan, one that suited the Kremlin's strategic goal, which also suited ours."

Niemiec. No coincidence he'd been paid the same amount — $100 million.

Overton took over. "The goal was to prove to the American people that the government couldn't protect them." He smiled with self-satisfaction. "And that's when TAKEDOWN rides in on a big white horse. With our product, an organization like the Patriot Brothers would have been identified and neutralized before it could cause any damage."

"And when the U.S. buys the suite, what despot isn't going to want a piece of this action?" added Picot.

"So, the WMD dug up in the desert. That just fell into your lap?"

"You move in the right circles," said Picot, "you hear things."

The right circles, in this instance being Niemiec. Overton sat back, put his hand behind his head, and half smiled. "I'll admit I had my doubts, Cooper, but you got it almost all figured out. I'm thinking you really are just the man to head up our security here at Sands Aerospace & Defense." Overton turned to Picot. "Don't you?"

"Yeah."

"Great," I said. "It's just..."

"What."

"I'd like to know, why Foord? You know Dexter Foord, right? He was Adams's inside man at the Pentagon. Do I have to tell you who Adams was?"

Overton managed a shrug that could have meant everything and nothing.

I continued. "Anyway, Foord — he was Adams's inside man at the Pentagon who located the WMD in the desert — Foord was all-in with this enterprise. But then he got cold feet. Why? And why would Niemiec use Syrian Tiger Force operatives to take out Foord when he could just as easily have used Wagner? Why get Syria involved at all? I don't get it. Any ideas? Help me out here."

"We had nothing to do with Foord. Ask Niemiec. Oh, that's right, he'd dead. Bummer." He smiled.

"Neither of us was fully briefed by Niemiec on all the operational details," Picot added.

"Life's a mystery," Overton summarized with a level of smugness whose daylights I wanted to punch out.

"So, where does that leave us?" Picot asked. "Do we have a deal? Because there's the little matter of body disposal."

"What? No. I don't recall that being in my job spec," I said, distracted by Overton, who was himself distracted.

"And you are...?" Overton said, addressing someone coming up behind me.

"Chalmers!?" Picot exclaimed, filling in the gaps for me. "What the hell are you doing here?"

I glanced over my shoulder. Bradley Chalmers. And he was waving a pistol around.

"I had you followed," he said to me with the usual sneer. "And now I'm glad I did. So... what's going on here, aside from murder? That your handiwork, Cooper?" He gestured over his shoulder in the direction of Ely Sands.

"No," I told him.

And that's when Overton shot him, the round skimming past my shoulder. Chalmers pirouetted and went down hard.

"Hey!" I yelled involuntarily and jumped up out of the chair. I went over to him and loosened his collar: a chest wound, right side, mid-pectoral muscle. Chalmers' eyes were wide, mouth opening and closing like a goldfish out of water. I felt around his back — no exit wound, the small caliber slug still inside him. The entry wound began to suck, a disconcerting bubbling, gurgling sound, but he'd live. Maybe.

Seeing Chalmers shot like this gave me no joy. In fact, the opposite. If anyone was going to kill this guy, *I* was fucking going to have the pleasure of doing it. Or maybe Anna. "You're gonna be okay, Chalmers," I reassured him. "Think positive thoughts. Like it's me shot instead of you." He was staring at me, the jugular in his neck pulsing. I doubted he knew what was going on.

"You heard him. He doesn't know anything," I heard Overton say by way of justification. "This just keeps it that way."

I had everything I was going to get out of Overton and Picot — a motive, an admission, and most of their plan's mechanics. Chalmers' Glock was at my feet. I took it out of his open hand.

"Vin...?" Anna's voice.

Oh, shit...

"Jesus! What the hell is this...?" Overton snapped.

Sounded like she was outside the office, in the reception area. And she was coming in. Overton was too trigger-happy for my liking. I glanced at Picot. He now had a pistol in his hand, too. Nothing I could say would keep Anna from stepping through that doorway, but I said it anyway. "Don't come in!"

"What? Vin, are you okay? I heard a gunshot."

"I'm fine. Just don't come in."

"I'm coming in."

Picot and Overton had angles on me and potentially also on Anna when she came through the door. And then I recalled the interview I had with Ely Sands, meeting him in this office. I got up and ran as Anna entered the room. Shots were fired. She dropped to one knee, pure reaction to the sound of gunfire, then scuttled for cover behind Sand's big-ass desk.

More shots. A window in front of me suddenly displayed four holes. Picot and Overton were banging away at my back and missing. So much for the college fund.

I dived into the seat of the Quadmount and punched the green button on the fire control panel as nine-millimeter rounds *clanged* off the quad's armor plating. Something beneath the seat whined as gears turned and the beast stirred from its slumber. The whole assembly rotated left a few degrees and then swung back to the right as if resetting itself. I pulled the lever cocking the four guns, the action well-oiled, and brought the guns to bear. I crossed my fingers and hoped that Ely wasn't exaggerating, pulled the trigger, and four .50 caliber Brownings burst into life, filling the world with a roar of hellfire and damnation. Unfettered violence filled the room, and, in a few brief seconds, the far wall opposite those fire-belching barrels simply dissolved. After maybe five seconds of insanity, I released the trigger, silencing the demons. Clouds of cordite and dust ballooned around me, the sudden silence dull and woolly in my head. Why Sands wanted a monster like this locked and loaded in his office was beyond me, but I wasn't complaining. The dust began to thin beneath the ceiling AC vents, revealing both Overton and Picot standing in a corner, a little away from the void in the building created by the river of hot lead. I swung the barrels, putting the two men in the system's sight, and their empty hands shot over their heads. A gratifying stain spread over the crotch area of Overton's gray suit pants.

The smoke alarms went off, their screeching and warbling harmonizing with the ringing in my ears. Part of the demolished wall was on fire, ignited by tracer. I coughed out some of the concrete dust, which brought back memories of being buried alive in Idlib, and peeled myself out of the driver's seat. An explosion boomed from another part of the building as Anna came out from behind the desk, bewildered and shaken. But her Sig was up, pointed at Overton and Picot as she moved in to cover them and check on Chalmers. She raised her badge and shouted something at them that I couldn't hear, the ear-splitting cacophony of four unleashed Brownings, each firing off around ten rounds per second in a confined space having overwhelmed my senses.

Anna kicked their pistols in my direction, then turned Overton and Picot around, hands up against the plaster, and patted them down. Satisfied, she put them on their knees with their hands behind their heads, fingers interlocked. With zipcuffs unavailable, the threat of being shot if they moved would have to do.

The building's fire alarm was next to pierce my awareness, distant but also present. And then the sprinkler system in the ceiling suddenly came to life, the water pressure welcoming cold needles against my skin.

The parking lot adjacent to the offices of Sands Aerospace & Defense was filled with the countless flashing red, white, and blue emergency lights of various emergency vehicles engaged in a strobe-off. Fire-fighting crews from multiple precincts had been summonsed along with police, state troopers, ATF, and the FBI.

The 200 or so rounds of .50 caliber jacketed steel and tracer I'd let loose in those brief seconds had ruptured gas lines and electric conduits in the staff kitchen half a building away and ultimately embedded themselves in an earthen retaining wall. The spot theory was that sparks had ignited a build-up of gas, producing that explosion I mentioned, and the resulting fireball had blown out walls, ignited partitioning, paper, carpet, underlay, desks, picture frames, wood paneling, and all the flammable and combustible items in a typical management office. The sprinkler system had been reasonably effective in limiting the damage to around half of the multi-story executive block. The insurance claim would raise an eyebrow or two down at the local Geico office.

Picot and Overton were bundled into an FBI Suburban and driven off at speed as Arlen pulled up. "This has you written all over it, Vin," he said, getting out of the car and looking around at all the emergency vehicles.

"Who called you?" I asked him.

"I did," said Anna. "Something tells me we're going to need people we know watching our backs."

Arlen took in the smoking devastation. "Seriously, you two. What the fuck...!"

I said, "I was playing with matches, and the next thing you know..."

"I believe it." Arlen hugged Anna. "What's it been like working with him? Fun?"

I cleared my throat. "'Him' is standing right here."

Anna smiled. "You can imagine, right? I spend all day giggling."

"I'm sure. So, was that Aldus Picot I just saw cuffed and bundled into an SUV?"

"It was," Anna replied.

"Who was that with him?"

"Chase Overton."

"And he is?"

"My almost-boss at Sands," I said. "The offer of employment was rescinded sometime over the last half hour or so."

"What's the charge?"

"Charges — plural," I continued. "Murder, conspiracy, terrorism, bribery, and impersonating Dr Phil."

Anna added for clarity, "Together with Ely Sands, the murder victim, the three of them were behind the mechanics of the purchase and transfer of the WMD to the Patriot Brothers. Niemiec was their point man."

"Don't forget the Russians," I said.

"Together with the Russians," she agreed. "They bankrolled the operation."

"And Picot, the president's chief of staff...?" Arlen whistled quietly to aid in the processing of that bombshell.

"Yeah, a deeply concerned shareholder," I told him. "Meanwhile, your sister-in-law and I have an appointment with a hot shower. You mind if we borrow your car?"

Arlen tossed me the keys. "Go. Before I forget, you've got an appointment with Secretary Muirhead at oh-nine hundred tomorrow. Both of you."

"Where?" I asked.

"The St Regis."

The following morning, while we sat in a hotel room waiting to be summonsed, Anna said in a low voice, "This place... She wants to be able to say, if it ever comes to it — what meeting?

Before I could agree, a door opened, and an aide popped her head around the corner. "The Secretary of State will see you now."

Anna and I stood and followed her into the SecState's presence. Muirhead sat at the head of a polished wood dining table flanked on either side by a coterie of eager young aides. On the wall behind the gathering was an impressive oil painting of George Washington in uniform, looking serene in victory. "Give us the room," Muirhead said, and the aides focused their eagerness on getting up and out quickly.

"I want to make this brief," Muirhead began once the door was closed. "What we have here is a particularly sensitive case with far-reaching implications for our national security."

National security. Right. Private smirk.

She continued, "The Assistant Director of the CIA has already provided me with a top-line report, and I must tell you that I'm stunned by Picot's duplicity. We don't know how all this will be handled, but I want to remind you that you have both signed secrecy agreements." Muirhead smiled. "Neither of you has a tell-all book in the pipeline?"

Anna returned the smile and said, "No, Madam Secretary."

Hmm...a book. Not a bad idea, perhaps masked as fiction.

"You've done our country a great service. I'm considering recommending both of you for the Legion of Merit. As I'm sure you know, a LoM is virtually unheard of for an officer below the rank of colonel, which neither of you holds. But I think I can probably swing it despite the inevitable fallout once this story, or a version of it, hits the media.

No doubt that "version" would make for an interesting read.

Muirhead continued, "You can't dismiss the president's chief of staff and charge him with murder, among other things, and expect it to be business as usual. There's already a media storm, and it's going to get worse." She shuffled some papers and said, "So, I believe Rita Inglis comes in for special mention? She's a fine analyst."

"Yes, Madam Secretary," Anna said. "And your advisor, Madam Secretary, Bradley Chalmers? How's his recovery going?"

"I don't know what he was doing at Sands, to be honest with you. You saved his life, Vin."

Don't remind me.

Muirhead frowned at me. "You're not very talkative?"

Because a fortune cookie once told me that if you can't say something nice, shut the fuck up. "Anna's got it."

Muirhead continued, "Well, you'll no doubt be pleased to hear Chambers is stable and in recovery. The surgeon says he'll be sore for a while, and there'll be rehab, but he'll eventually recover fully. I'll send him your regards."

No, thanks.

"So now the case is closed, is it not?" Muirhead asked.

Anna and I didn't have to check with each other on this one, as we'd discussed it already. "Yes, Madam Secretary," she said. "Case closed."

"Now you're sure, both of you?"

The question was directed at me. I nodded.

Muirhead seemed to breathe a sigh of relief — the end of a never-ending stream of damaging revelations was finally in sight. "I ask because I've put this to you before, and I've been told one thing, only to have to deal with more embarrassing exposés."

"It's closed, ma'am," Anna assured her.

"Good. Once you've written your reports, you are both on leave. I'm giving you two weeks of paid vacation on top of the standard entitlements. You've certainly earned it. Anna, I believe you're pregnant."

"That's correct, Madam Secretary."

"And Vin, you're the father, am I right?"

I'd better be. "Yes, ma'am."

"Then, for god's sake, look after each other and stop putting yourselves in harm's way. How are your injuries, Vin? I'm told you've been living on painkillers these last couple of weeks."

"I'm fine, ma'am."

"Well, I'm sure there are times you've felt better than you do. If there's nothing more," she said, "on your return to duty, I'll see you both for a proper verbal debrief."

Anna and I stood and headed for the door. I could easily have broken into a run. I wanted out of her presence. Muirhead had a lot to answer for but would never be held accountable.

"Oh, and before you go," Muirhead asked, "would you mind asking Merle Ridge to come in?"

Anna and I walked out into the waiting room where Ridge and Sidney Davidson were seated.

"We heard about Sands," ventured Ridge, his beard trimmed and his old coat dry-cleaned. "Sounds like some hectic shit."

"Congratulations," said Sidney, rising to shake Anna's hand and then reaching for mine.

"How is she?" Ridge asked, motioning at the conference room.

"A pussycat," Anna replied.

"Mister Ridge," boomed the SecState through the walls. "Are you going to keep me waiting all morning?"

Ridge stood, buttoned his jacket, and went off to get his lumps. The door closed behind him.

Through the wall, I heard Muirhead's muffled voice: "Sit down and don't utter a goddamn word till I've had my say..."

Sidney frowned, confused. "What's that about?"

"Performance review," I said.

ST BARTS, FRENCH WEST INDIES

It took us a week to write and rewrite our reports until Arlen was happy with them. Yes, there was still the glaring hole regarding the involvement of the Syrians in the murder of Foord and his family, and knowing for sure who killed Niemiec would probably be useful. Still, the trick with these things is to minimize what you don't know against what you do so that, when they balance out, the scales don't fall over and crush you.

We then did as we were told and caught a plane to St Barts, where Anna's sister Marley has connections, and spent a few days in a hotel resort's pool bar getting wrinkly, drunk, and horny. At least I was.

On the fourth day and the dregs of the third Margarita, at around two in the afternoon, beneath a clear blue sky and a temperature hovering somewhere in the 80s, I asked Anna one of the two questions that had been on my mind. "So, first question. Why Cuba? "

"Oh, we're back to that, are we?"

"You owe me."

Anna motioned to the waiter on the dry side of the bar for another.

"Go on, give me a hint."

"You won't give up, will you?"

"I'm relentless."

"No, you're annoying."

"No one goes to Cuba in an undercover capacity these days unless it's to meet someone, am I right?"

"You're not even tepid." Her eyes sparkled with mischief. *"Igeos-i dangsin-i eodneun hinteuui jeonbu-ibnida."*

"What? What language was that?"

"C'mon, you know."

"Give it to me again."

She sighed. *"Igeos-i dangsin-i eodneun hinteuui jeonbu-ibnida."*

I sobered up quick. "You speak Korean now, too?"

"What I just said was, 'This is all the hint you get.'"

All kinds of dark thoughts were suddenly breast-stroking around in my brain. "Let's swim away from the bar for a minute. We need to, you know, shoot the breeze in private."

"Hang on," she said as the refresher was placed on the bar.

After a moment's consideration, I ordered a triple scotch, and we retired to a quiet section of the pool, put our drinks on the weir edge, and looked out over the beachside umbrellas, across to the iridescent-blue lagoon and the deeper blue of the sea beyond the reef.

"Well, Sherlock," she mocked, "you know I can't say, but I can't stop you from putting it together. Let's see how good you are."

"Okay... Well, Cuban Spanish is kinda different," I began. "Has a vocabulary that's a hangover from the days when Fidel cozied up to the USSR. Also has a little Creole and a little Haitian. I thought Cuba might have had something to do with GITMO."

"You asking, or telling?"

"I'm eliminating. You spent ten months in Cuba, you told me, so knowing you, your command of the language by the end of your stay was pretty good, especially if that's what you were there to learn. I've been toying with maybe someone cooking up a Bay of Pigs mark two with Raoul the target. But, these days, no one gives a flying fig newton about Cuba."

Anna sipped her Margarita and took in the view.

I continued. "On top of that, you officially didn't exist at the time."

"The temperature is beginning to rise just a little," she said.

"But the Korean thing, that changes the game. Cuba is one of the few countries with an Embassy in North Korea."

Anna nodded and added a hint of a smile.

I continued, "Cuban nationals are welcomed by Kim Jong Un's regime, recognized by that distinctive Cuban patois."

"Getting warmer.

"So, you're in North Korea traveling under a Cuban passport. But why? What are you doing there?" I took a mouthful of scotch to get some lubrication going. "You could pass for a Cuban with your command of the language and your coloring. That's going to give you some freedom of movement. I'm guessing you're not alone. I'd say that you're with your team, the same off-the-books six-feet-under status as you. Am I close? Does the frog want to jump out of the steaming pot?"

"No comment."

"So, swinging for the bleachers... I'm gonna say that someone in Kim Jong Un's retinue passed his travel itinerary to someone who passed it to someone, and CIA Special Activities heard about it. The Dear Leader only travels overland if he travels at all. And by train. His own personal train. Maybe he was on his way to Beijing. Maybe there was a stop along the way that would present an opportunity. Maybe you were going to assassinate the guy. You're a trained marksman, a skill you took with you to Syria, but you wouldn't do it with a bullet. Needs to look like an accident. So... maybe an unfortunate train derailment? Maybe there's a West-friendly general or relative, a low-profile aunt or uncle, waiting in the wings to take over. But something went wrong. Maybe the coup was leaked, and the relative got himself or herself whacked. And suddenly, you have no mission. On top of which, you're disavowed. You don't exist, so there's no possibility of a connection to the U.S., let alone to CIA Special Activities, unless they torture you, which they will do plenty of if they catch you. But the assholes who cooked the whole thing up — colleagues of Chalmers — maybe even Chalmers himself — trust that no matter what, you'll take the cyanide pill they'd given you if capture is imminent."

Anna's smile was gone.

"It was a close-run thing, but you got out. Maybe you lost some members of your team who took the pill. And to top it off, because you're still technically dead, your ass owned by Special Activities, even if you wanted to, you were forbidden to reach out and tell the man you loved that you didn't die in his arms that day on the floor at Oak Ridge..."

Anna clinked my glass with hers, unsettled. "Nice story. Like I said, I can neither confirm nor deny."

I threw back the scotch. "That time you slugged Chalmers, it wasn't about Gisela, was it?"

"Excuse me, sir, ma'am," said a waiter, his buffed boat shoes beside my elbow.

I glanced up.

"You were not answering your phones, so the caller contacted reception. Please forgive the intrusion, but the caller was insistent."

"Okay," I said, motioning for the handset.

"Sir, it's for Ms. Masters."

"Who is it?" she asked.

"A police officer in France. Her name is...." He paused to read it off a card, "Brigadier Babette Faurot."

AIX-EN-PROVENCE, FRANCE

Babette was almost relaxed this time around, dealing with a murder that was a little more mundane — an old guy who killed his ancient mother, dropping a pitchfork on her head from a loft when she happened to pass by directly below him. He claimed it was an accident, but then her will turned up with changes in the son's handwriting that left everything to him. Comedy, South-of-France-homicide-style. Anyway, this time around, Babette had some extra bounce in that superb tush of hers.

Anna had called the inspector back while poolside at the resort, and what she said had us on the first available, with connections to Aix-en-Provence. We chose not to inform anyone back in DC about the trip because the case was officially closed, and we'd given our word. I hoped this unsanctioned excursion would prove worth it.

The standard three kisses on cheeks exchanged and some banter about the murderous folly of her latest crop of local dropkicks dispensed with, Babette took us into a meeting room, a laptop under her arm, and closed the door.

"The imposter George that you met. He gave you something. I knew it. I did not know what he gave you, but now everything is clear. He gave you something like this, but something was changed or perhaps missing." Detective Faurot placed a thumb drive on the desk. Anna and I shared a look.

"I understand why you kept this from me; this information is very sensitive to your government. I would have done the same if I were you. So... I cannot tell you what was in Monsieur Foord's mind, but he was nervous that his confession would be lost," the inspector said as she inserted the thumb drive into the laptop. "Forensics has checked the drive. No prints."

"Does the DGSE know about this?" Anna asked.

"*Non.*"

"Then why us?"

"Because I believe whoever murdered Foord also attempted to kill you. Does that not make us on the same team?"

"How did it come into your possession?" Anna asked as Babette searched for the drive on screen. "How'd you get it?"

"After the DGSE left Foord's home, we went back to complete our review of the crime scene. This was found by accident. The day was hot, and a few of our people filled their water bottles in the kitchen. The cupboard under the sink, it flooded a little. I don't know what you call it, but the *sipon de lavabo* was not secure."

"The P-trap," Anna translated.

"*Oui*, okay, the P-trap. We removed it, and this USB key in a tight plastic bag was there, in the bend of the pipe, a blockage. *Monsieur* Foord, he must have had time to put it there but not enough time to secure the joins. Or, I think, he left them loose for this reason."

Foord was far from stupid. The moment Wikileaks went public, he knew his days were numbered. Within the month, he was dead.

The computer screen became a video recording, the bearded Foord freeze-framed.

"I do not know which parts were missing for you, but there are no cuts in this recording." Babette pressed play. *"If you're watching this, it means I'm dead. Tell my wife I'm sorry. Tell her I love her. And the kids. They're too young to understand, but tell them anyway. I'm giving this to you. Do that much for me."*

I heard Anna breathe deeply, reminded that his family paid the ultimate price for Foord's decisions. Maybe he thought the killers would spare his family. He thought wrong. We listened to the rest of the recording. There was no cut this time, as Faurot had said. The passage that had been edited from the version provided to us by George the imposter came and went. It was short, but it was a hand grenade set to blow up in some very important and powerful faces. It was left to Anna and me to pull the pin.

WASHINGTON DC

"Excuse me! Who the hell do you think you are just walking into my office?"

Muirhead wasn't pleased to see us, but I was thrilled to see her. This was one of those days that just made you want to spring out of bed. Muirhead's anger became confusion and concern when two FBI agents, accompanied by Lieutenant Colonel Arlen Wayne, entered the room and covered the door behind Anna and me.

"What the fuck is the meaning of this?"

"I'm sure you recall this," Anna said and placed the laptop on the desk before her, opened it, and pressed play. Foord, on screen, spoke:

"My conscience wouldn't give me a break. I couldn't eat, couldn't sleep, I lost weight... The reports of Bashar al-Assad's sarin attacks against his own people made it worse. Was this the DF that I'd let loose on the world made into the sarin now killing people? If Adams had already sold it, who was the buyer? There are only wrong hands you can put a weapon like that into. And now, the sarin attacks in Berlin."

I paused the video. "If you remember, Madam Secretary, there was a break in Foord's confession. We wondered if the break was an edit. Turns out we were right. Here's the original, unedited."

Anna pressed play.

"So, I went to Adams and asked him straight out. He told me that a deal was done. When the president threatened Syria publicly that the further use of chemical weapons was a red line Damascus had better not cross, through back channels involving the Russians, al-Assad informed the White House that the chemical agents being used against the terrorists attempting to usurp the rightful government of Syria were the chemicals from Saddam Hussein's stockpile that the United States allowed to be smuggled out of Iraq during Iraqi Freedom. And that if the U.S. made good on its threat of a so-called red line, then Syria would release this information to the world.

I hit the stop button. "You knew about this 'red line' deal and the danger it posed to America's relationships with our allies if it leaked. When we raised the possibility that Foord was the leaker, you made sure Anna and I were kept in a Monaco prison while you reached out to the Syrians."

The FBI agents moved in, presented their badges, demanded Muirhead's phone, disconnected her server, and carried them away.

"What are you doing? Stop!"

Two more FBI agents entered the room but stood back, waiting. Muirhead eyed them nervously, then shouted to her PA stationed in the nook outside to call security but received no answer.

"So, this is what's going to happen," I informed her. "The president will ask for your resignation. You don't have to provide it, but that could get embarrassing. More embarrassing than it already is."

You are so finished, Cooper," Muirhead hissed. She glared at Anna. "You, too."

I informed her, "There'll be charges for conspiracy to murder — Foord, his wife and children."

"I don't know what you're talking about."

"Special Agent Masters and I are confident that evidence on your electronic devices will prove that you engaged with the Syrians in a quid pro quo, that if they prevented Foord from leaking the news of deals done during the previous Administration — the deal over the former president's "red line" — the United States would do something for al-Assad. Like maybe a promise to pull back on our assistance to various elements of the Free Syria militia fighting to bring about regime change in Damascus."

"This is ridiculous!" Muirhead shouted.

"Niemiec brokered the deal on your behalf with the Syrians to kill Foord," I told her. "You reached out to him, again via the State Department's back-door contacts with Russia. And the Kremlin, with its relationships in Syria, organized for a retired assassin from the *Qawat Al-Nimr* Tiger Force to take care of Foord. His family was unfortunate collateral. That left Niemic. But he was easy to dispatch. All you had to do was bribe elements within the prison to do it. And you had an obedient go-between in place to set it up — Merle Ridge."

"You're crazy!"

"That doesn't make us wrong," I said and motioned at the FBI agents who moved in, stood the SecState up, cuffed her, and informed her of her rights.

"Cooper...!" she yelled as the FBI escorted her through a gauntlet of stunned State Department personnel.

"And that's how we do it at the Department of Agriculture," I said.

It was a grim day on the other side of the window, a vicious wind and horizontal rain lashing the trees beyond. I couldn't help but think the weather was a metaphor for the media storm raging over the circumstances behind the arrest and subsequent release of the Secretary of State, which followed barely days after the revelations swirling around Chief of Staff Picot. Facts and assumptions were being delivered to the public on a conveyor belt with each fresh news cycle picking over them minutely.

Picot and Overton were remanded in custody, bail not an option for crimes involving murder. The cases against them were considered slam dunks by the Office of the Federal Prosecutor.

The president has accepted Muirhead's resignation. The rest of her future, though, was more uncertain with the charges against her sealed. She was loudly protesting her innocence, however. Not much was known about what Muirhead's seized computer and phone might have revealed, and there was an additional home laptop impounded. Obviously, though, the prosecutor wouldn't have had her charged if he didn't think there was enough evidence to convict. But as far as anyone without access to Muirhead's digital communications could tell, the evidence against her was circumstantial. The Syrians weren't talking, Niemiec was telling no tales, and Muirhead's defense was nothing unusual for a Washington scandal — that she could not recall.

Neither Anna nor I were surprised, given that our briefings were held at the St Regis, away from her official office and diary at Foggy Bottom. It did seem, though, that Muirhead had no involvement in any conspiracy with Picot. What she did, or didn't do, or didn't recall doing, was in defense of the Office of the President.

Meanwhile, the press was treating Dexter Foord's murder as his just deserts. The outcomes for his wife and two kids had been completely forgotten, at least by the U.S. media. The French press, however, was scathing.

Merle Ridge and his jacket were suspended from the CIA, pending an internal investigation. Meanwhile, two inmates and a warden from the Mokotow Prison in Warsaw, where Niemiec was remanded, had recently turned up dead in suspicious circumstances. I figured, therefore, that any case against Ridge over his involvement in the murder of Niemiec would probably collapse through lack of evidence. The way these things usually roll, Ridge will end up with a promotion.

The share price of Sands Aerospace & Defense has tanked, with contracts being canceled left and right, the company reportedly looking for a merger. Or perhaps going back to making fridges.

There were half-hearted calls in Congress to impeach the president. The big question? How much did she know, and when did she know it? There was also speculation that if Muirhead, a loyal servant, were found guilty of any crimes, there would be a presidential pardon coming her way. Whichever way that went, her career in politics was over.

All that was happening out there in the rain and wind-swept capital. But inside, here in this room at least, the atmosphere was calm and happy.

"Vin," said Anna. I turned away from the window as the nurse walked back in.

"Might be a little cold," she said. "We have a heater for this, but it's given up the ghost. Sorry."

"That's okay," Anna reassured her. The nurse squeezed the gel from the bottle onto Anna's bare belly. She sucked in a breath. "Cold."

"Yes, I know. Sorry," the nurse repeated and handed the bottle to me. "Why don't you tuck this under your arm and take the edge off it?"

The monitor's screen came to life as a shifting fan of black and silver snow, which changed shape as the nurse manipulated the ultrasound sensor across Anna's skin. Suddenly, the image of a tiny human coalesced on the screen.

"Vin!" Anna squeezed my hand.

The nurse said, "There's its head and shoulders and little hands. Do you want to know what it is?"

"We've talked about this, haven't we, Vin?"

"Yes, we have. A successful tennis pro."

The nurse grinned.

"No, don't tell us," said Anna, getting us back on track. "It would be like opening your Christmas presents in October. We love surprises, don't we?"

Did we? Yes, of course we did.

The nurse reassured us, "Okay, well, everything looks completely normal for a potential successful tennis pro."

Our future child moved a little on screen.

"Look at that... Amazing, isn't it?" Anna looked up at me, her blue-green eyes awash with emotion.

It most definitely was. I nodded, a lump in my throat.

"Well, I'm just going to bang off a few photos..." The nurse moved the sensor across Anna's belly in several directions, hit the keystrokes on the machine now and then, and we were done. She then handed Anna a towel to wipe away the goop, envied her tan, and left the room.

Anna buttoned her shirt and swung her legs off the table as the nurse reappeared and handed her an envelope. "I've given you a couple of copies for the grandparents and the fridge."

Anna beamed at her. "Thanks. Can I take a look?"

"Sure."

My fellow conspirator gave me the slightest of nods and departed.

Anna lifted the envelope flap, took out an image, examined it, and, just for a moment, frowned. "Did you do this?"

"Well, I hope so," I said. "Otherwise, it wasn't Cheetos you ate for breakfast this morning."

Anna placed the envelope and the ultrasound image of a tiny human holding a large engagement ring in its little hands on the bed and wrapped her arms around me. "The answer's yes, by the way."

The second question on my mind finally resolved, we kissed long and hard, the way I like it.

ALSO BY DAVID ROLLINS

Follow David Rollins on Instagram[1] and Facebook[2]. And for regular contact, including news and essays on a variety of topics, including the sequel to FIELD OF MARS, sign up to my Newsletter[3].

---

1. https://www.instagram.com/

2. https://www.facebook.com/DavidRollins99/

3. https://davidrollins.substack.com/

About the author

David Rollins is a former journalist and advertising creative director/ copywriter. His first book, ROGUE ELEMENT, was an instant sensation. The main protagonist in later works, Special Agent Vin Cooper, has proved especially popular for his dark humor.

David is also a screenwriter and documentarian and lives in Sydney, Australia.